A History of the Egyptian Revolution

Vol. II

SALZWASSER
VERLAG

A.A. Paton

A History of the Egyptian Revolution

Vol. II

Reprint of the original, first published in 1863.

1st Edition 2022 | ISBN: 978-3-37500-062-2

Verlag (Publisher): Salzwasser Verlag GmbH, Zeilweg 44, 60439 Frankfurt, Deutschland
Vertretungsberechtigt (Authorized to represent): E. Roepke, Zeilweg 44, 60439 Frankfurt, Deutschland
Druck (Print): Books on Demand GmbH, In de Tarpen 42, 22848 Norderstedt, Deutschland

A

HISTORY

OF THE

EGYPTIAN REVOLUTION.

A

HISTORY

OF THE

EGYPTIAN REVOLUTION,

FROM THE PERIOD OF THE MAMELUKES TO THE DEATH OF MOHAMMED ALI;

FROM ARAB AND EUROPEAN MEMOIRS, ORAL TRADITION, AND LOCAL RESEARCH.

BY

A. A. PATON, F.R.G.S.

VOL. II.

LONDON:

1863.

CONTENTS.

CHAPTER I.

CHAPTER II.

CHAPTER III.

CHAPTER IV.

CHAPTER V.

CHAPTER VI.

CHAPTER VII.

CHAPTER VIII.

CHAPTER IX.

CHAPTER X.

CHAPTER XI.

CHAPTER XII.

CHAPTER XIII.

CHAPTER XIV.

CHAPTER XV.

CHAPTER XVI.

CHAPTER XVII.

CHAPTER XVIII.

CHAPTER XIX.

CHAPTER XX.

CHAPTER XXI.

CHAPTER XXII.

CHAPTER XXIII.

CHAPTER XXIV.

CHAPTER XXV.

CHAPTER XXVI.

CHAPTER XXVII.

CHAPTER XXVIII.

A HISTORY

OF THE

EGYPTIAN REVOLUTION.

CHAPTER I.

EVENTS IN EGYPT AFTER THE DEPARTURE OF THE FRENCH ARMY.—ASSASSINATION OF MAMELUKES BY THE CAPITAN PASHA.—KHOUSREFF PASHA, GOVERNOR OF EGYPT.—HE IS DRIVEN FROM CAIRO BY THE REBELLIOUS TROOPS.—RISE OF MOHAMMED ALI.—ANARCHY IN EGYPT.—RETURN OF ELFY BEY FROM ENGLAND TO EGYPT.—FAILURE OF ELFY BEY'S PROJECTS.—MOHAMMED ALI BECOMES DICTATOR OF EGYPT AND PASHA OF DJIDDAH.—HIS CHARACTER.

WE now pass from the grand and elevated parts of modern Egyptian history to the dead flat of the petty intrigues and guerilla warfare of little men. From Bonaparte and Nelson—from Kleber and Abercrombie—to Elfy and Bardissy, is indeed a descent; and, if we linger and leisurely survey the more picturesque parts of our historical journey, we shall pass with all convenient speed over the uninteresting level which presents only one object worthy of attention, and that is the elevation of Mohammed Ali from an obscure station to be governor of Egypt, and possessed of the power which served—as will be seen in the sequel—utterly to annihilate the last remains of the Mameluke dominion. The importance of events, and not the mere lapse of years, will now direct us in the apportionment of the space at our disposal.

Like nearly all the celebrated men who have cast their lot in Egypt, Mohammed Ali came from a colder and more bracing region; for Egypt has been from time immemorial the India of the adventurous northerns, civilian and military, of the Ottoman empire. Born at Cavula, in Roumelia, Mohammed Ali shewed in early life both a hankering after trade and personal courage as a soldier. In Roumelia he traded in tobacco, and during the British expedition into Egypt he embarked at Marmarice under the Capitan Pasha; and, as aga at the head of three hundred Albanians and Roumeliotes, distinguished himself in the march on Cairo, after the battle in which Abercrombie fell,—having been the first to enter Rahmanieh on the evacuation of that place by the troops of General Lagrange.

No sooner were the French expelled from Egypt and the English about to leave, than the Mamelukes began again to raise their heads out of the slough into which they had sunk; and, supposing that they had henceforth only to deal with the decadence and disorganization of the old Turkish government, they somewhat too confidently anticipated a resumption of the power that placed at their feet all the sensual luxuries of this favoured land. On the other hand, the great object of the Porte was to retain the power, and prevent it from again falling into the hands of the Mamelukes. Out of this complicated game Mohammed Ali rose the winner of the valley of the Nile.

The first act of the Porte towards a resumption of full sovereignty took place before the English quitted Egypt, and was one of those strokes of policy which were formerly unhappily too common in Turkish history, but which, it is only justice to say, have fallen into desuetude in modern Turkish politics. The principal beys of the party of Murad were invited by the Capitan Pasha to enjoy his hospitalities at the encampment of Aboukir, and confer with him on the future government of Egypt. Several of the beys were averse to trusting their persons in the power of the Ottoman Admiral; but others, regarding the immediate vicinity of the English force and the high character of General Hutchinson as a guarantee for fair treatment, resolved to accept the invitation; more especially as by declining it they might leave an opening for the Capitan Pasha and General Hutchinson to make some arrangement for the future government of Egypt which should exclude them.

The Capitan Pasha received them with sumptuous hospitality; and, under pretext of a visit to General Hutchinson, he induced them to embark in his barge, as if about to confer with the English commander. At a short distance from the shore a boat approached which bore dispatches for the Capitan Pasha, who, in order to peruse them more at his ease, stepped into the other boat and was borne away from the beys, who, upon their barge being rowed round a bluff point, discovered the trap into which they had been allured. Armed boats rapidly bore down upon them, and they ordered their own rowers to put back; but, being overtaken, a struggle took place in which Osman Bey Tambourgi and three others were killed, and Osman Bey el Bardissy and two others were wounded.

General Hutchinson was transported with just indignation at a procedure which associated the English name with an act of treachery so foreign to our principles and usages. He ordered his troops under arms, and reclaimed the wounded for surgical care and attendance,—the dead for honourable sepulture. Nor would he admit the validity of the Capitan Pasha's excuse, that the Beys had drawn their swords on a groundless suspicion,—a statement inconsistent with the other and truer part of the Capitan Pasha's excuse, that it was the wish of the Porte to get quit of the Mamelukes, and that the regulation of the internal affairs of Egypt was within the sole competence of the Divan.

While this was proceeding on the coast, the same bloody drama was enacted at Cairo under the eyes of the Anglo-Indian force. The Mamelukes, who had received pelisses and flatteries from Yousouff Pasha, were one night attacked without pity at Gizeh, the flash of the firing being visible from the windows of the English officers' quarters in Old Cairo. Later on the same night, at eleven o'clock, a detachment of Mamelukes presented themselves at the English quarters and claimed protection, which they received from General Ramsay in spite of the pressing and reiterated messages of the Grand Vizier to deliver them up; General Ramsay very properly judging that it was by open force and vigorous measures that the power of the Porte must be re-established.

That a struggle should recommence between the Porte and the Mamelukes was scarcely avoidable. These inexcusable acts precipitated it. The sympathies of the British troops were estranged, and the Mamelukes, without being much injured, were stung with resentment; so that throughout all the subsequent transactions we are reminded of the old adage, that "honesty is the best policy."

The new Grand Vizier, Yousouff Pasha, who had made his triumphal entry into Cairo as the representative of the resumption of the conquest of Selim, agreed very badly with the younger and more active Capitan Pasha; and the latter, by his influence at Constantinople, procured the nomination of governor of Egypt for Khousreff Pasha, a personage well known in the modern annals of the Ottoman empire; who filled the highest places in the gift of the Sultan; who was for nearly half a century the rival and opponent of Mohammed Ali; who was Pasha of Egypt, when Mohammed Ali was still an aga of Arnauts; and who, long after Mohammed Ali was in his grave, was called to the extraordinary consultative assemblies of the Porte in the most momentous emergency of her modern history. The youth who governed Egypt on the expulsion of the legions of the elder Bonaparte, was still able, in spite of the caducity of age, to sit in council on the measures that accompanied the Menschikoff crisis and immediately preceded the disembarkation of the forces of another Bonaparte on the shores of the Crimea.

Khousreff Pasha, when he arrived in Egypt, was a newly emancipated Georgian slave of the Capitan Pasha. His manners were polished, and his person was handsome; but the presumption of a parvenu was visible to those whom he had passed in the social scale: and it was at this early stage of his career, in the service of Khousreff Pasha, and against the Mamelukes, that Mohammed Ali first made himself talked of in Egypt.

At this period every political circumstance in the country revealed a double action in operation—the rivalry of the agents of the Porte, and their efforts sometimes jointly, and sometimes apart from one another, against the common enemy, the Mamelukes. It was not easy to uproot a power that had so long been nourished on the choice saps of Egypt; and it cannot be overlooked that the Mamelukes, in returning to their contest with the Porte, had considerable advantages. They had been longer in the school of collision with the French than the soldiers of the Porte. Their system of warfare, unequal to a contest with European armies, was yet formidable to the feeble beginnings of the Porte in European discipline. By long habit they knew Egypt better than the freshly arrived agents and troops of the

Porte; and their name carried more prestige with the inhabitants than that of the half consolidated Turkish power. It is true that they were no longer led by the skill and bravery of Murad Bey, and that Ibrahim Bey was now old and rapidly declining in vigour; but Osman Bey el Bardissy and Mohammed Bey el Elfy still remained.

Osman Bey el Bardissy was a Circassian slave of Murad Bey, possessed of amazing corporeal strength and activity; skilful as a horseman, and intrepid in battle. Being also of a generous disposition, the eyes of the Mamelukes were fixed on him as their leader in the absence of Elfy. Nor was expectation disappointed; for even before Alexandria was finally evacuated by the English on the 14th March, 1803, the greater part of both Upper and Lower Egypt was again in the Mameluke power. The important places of Cairo, Alexandria, and some others of less note, remained indeed to the Porte; but even the capital was soon destined to pass away from the hands of Khousreff Pasha, its representative in Egypt. Deprived of a considerable portion of the revenues of the country, he could not pay the troops, and on the 2nd of May, 1803, a violent revolt broke out. The soldiery surrounded the house of the treasurer, whom they kept prisoner. Khousreff Pasha, incensed at this, ordered the artillery to fire on the troops, and the battle became general in the capital. Tahir Pasha, who commanded the troops as Lieutenant-General of the Pasha, now presented himself to Khousreff as a mediator between the insurgents and the governor of Egypt. Khousreff, however, declined a negociation which hurt his self-love, and awakened suspicions of the faithfulness of Tahir, which subsequent events justified; for on the following day he declared openly against Khousreff, his benefactor, and even directed the soldiers to escalade the walls. So much was the governor taken by surprise, that he never knew his position until he saw his palace in course of being battered down. Nothing was therefore left for him but a precipitate flight, with his household, his harem, and those officers who remained faithful to him. By the eastern branch of the Nile he made his way to Mansourah—so renowned in history for the greater disasters of the valiant and pious St. Louis; and no sooner was he gone than Tahir, having matured his plans, assembled at his house in Cairo the principal officers of the law, and was invested by the cadi with a pelisse, as caimakæm or deputy, until the will of the Porte should be known as to the appointment of a successor to Khousreff Pasha, thus virtually deposed.

But Tahir himself soon met with the just reward of his perfidy, in the violent termination of his brief tenure of power. On the 25th May, just twenty-two days after his provisional investiture, two Binbashis, or chiefs of a thousand, named Moussa and Ismael, presented themselves to him with the old complaint that the pay of the troops was in arrear. Tahir Pasha attempted to intimidate them, but in this he failed, and the complaining chiefs abruptly ended the dispute by drawing their swords and cutting off his head, which they threw out of the window. A general fight ensued, and the affair ended with the house being burnt down.

By the flight of the Pasha, and the death of the commander of the troops, Mohammed Ali, whose courage and conciliatory qualities had been equally conspicuous during the troubles—and who had won the applause of the military and the civilians by overawing the turbulent, and protecting the citizens—became the virtual ruler of Cairo. Unable, however, to keep his ground against both the Mamelukes and Khousreff Pasha, he allied himself with the former, and moved against the nominal governor of Egypt, who had now ensconced himself at Damietta; Osman Bey el Bardissy leading the Mameluke and Arab cavalry by land, while the force under Mohammed Ali descended the Nile in the numerous barges of transport.

When the troops of Mohammed Ali arrived at Damietta, they found that Khousreff had planted his artillery along a canal leading from the Nile. A Turkish soldier belonging to Osman Bey el Bardissy, who spoke Arabic, put on the costume of a fellah, and, pretending to be a seller of melons, entered Damietta. Favoured by his disguise, he found no difficulty in sounding the canal. Seeking out the currents, he discovered near the bridge a place where there were not more than three feet of water; and during the night Osman Bey and Mohammed Ali, leading their troops, passed the canal at this point, the water being up to their middles. This sudden and unexpected manœuvre disconcerted the troops of Khousreff. The artillery was seized, and at daybreak the troops, bursting into Damietta, carried it in spite of an active fire of musketry. Khousreff retired to the fort of Lesbeh, at the mouth of the Nile; but being unable to hold out, was obliged to capitulate, and was conducted to Cairo with the honours due to his nominal rank.

Thus ended in disaster the brief government of Khousreff Pasha. But Egypt was not yet regained by the Mamelukes. Mohammed Ali, with a long train of Arnaut and Roumeliote followers, held the balance, which he could incline with decisive effect for the Porte or the beys. Egypt was torn to pieces with faction and revolt; but, nominally, all were the most humble and obedient servants of the Sultan.

Alexandria and Rosetta still remained to the Porte; and the news from Egypt having filled the Divan with disquietude, Ali Pasha Gezairli was sent to govern Egypt.

This officer, having been expelled from Barbary, had lived for some years enjoying the protection and hospitality of Murad Bey in Egypt, and had aided in the resistance to the French after their landing. Gezairli was more of an intriguer than a soldier, and remained within the walls of Alexandria while Osman Bey el Bardissy and Mohammed Ali besieged and took Rosetta and Fort Jullien, which commands the mouth of the Nile. Gezairli, finding he could not get a footing by force, tried fraud, and was overreached by those whom he sought to deceive.

On the 27th of January, 1804, Gezairli went to the camp of Osman Bey el Bardissy as guest; but while there he entered into a secret understanding with Sheikh Sadat of Cairo, to raise the native Egyptians against the Mamelukes. The bearer of the letter being, however, caught and confronted with Gezairli, who could not deny his own communication, he preserved a dead silence. Bardissy and his confederates thereupon adopted prompt measures to get rid of a pasha who sought to extinguish the Mameluke rule. The deputy of Osman Bey el Bardissy proceeded to the tent of Gezairli, and informed him that his horses awaited him. "Horses for where?" said Gezairli. "For Syria," said the Arnaut of Osman Bey. "Your conduct has rendered you unworthy of remaining in Egypt." A number of mamelukes attended him for a couple of days, when, in consequence of secret orders which had been received from the confederates, Gezairli and his suite were put to death. This ephemeral governor of Egypt carried his winding sheet always with him, and met his fate with the resignation of an oriental, his last wish being that he should not be deprived of the honours of sepulture.

These little circumstances show an habitual anarchy unknown to Europe, except during the period that elapsed between the fall of the Roman Empire and the settlement of the feudal system. How miserable the state of society, when perfidy, murder, and rapine, extinguish hope and even *fear*, which is replaced by a hardened indifference—for fear is the exception to the normal security of society, and the sign that a violent end is not the general rule.

An event now occurred which excited general attention in Egypt—the return of Elfy Bey, after a sojourn in England. On the 12th of February, 1804, an English frigate dropped anchor in Aboukir Bay, and disembarked this Mameluke leader. Selim Aga Tamerlane, the former master of the youthful Elfy, had made a present of him to Murad Bey, who returned the compliment by a gift of a "*thousand*" (Arabicé Elf) measures of corn; and hence his surname. Elfy Bey was a brave and intelligent man; but lawless rapine and a disorderly profusion alternately filled and exhausted his coffers. He was occasionally violent in his temper, but habitually effeminate in his manner and person, using the various cosmetics known to the Orientals to hide the approaches of age.

Uncertain how he might be received, or as to the best mode of forming a nucleus of political and military power, Elfy Bey advanced cautiously towards Rosetta, while his partisans and adherents in the capital proceeded to Gizeh, in order to prepare for his reception, and to join him with such forces as might have weight in the immediate vicinity of Cairo, so that the union of material force with the intelligence and audacity of the returned chief, might at once be decisive. But these plans and movements coming to the ears of his rival, Bardissy, and of Mohammed Ali, commander of the Turkish troops, a closer intelligence was established between them, and after two days' conference it was determined to take prompt and vigorous measures to pluck up Elfy by the roots, before he should have time to extend and consolidate his influence.

At Rosetta, Elfy Bey had been received by the authorities with a respect which gradually grew coolcr as the time of his embarkation for Cairo drew near. He ascended the western branch of the Nile without accident; and having passed the canal of Menouf, near the capital, he met some boats filled with Albanians; who, not daring to attack him, contented themselves with pillaging the baggage boats containing all the rich presents he had received in England. Jewellery, trinkets, clothes, and instruments, were in a few days seen for sale in the bazaars of Cairo. Meanwhile the partisans who awaited him at Gizeh, being vigorously attacked by troops under Mohammed Ali, were killed or dispersed. Elfy Bey himself was hunted by the men of Bardissy, and only escaped by preserving his incognito when the cavass bashi of Bardissy passed in his boat. Thus tracked on all hands, and aware of the fate of his partisans, Elfy quitted his boat; and, passing to the Arabs of Hawaytat, was mounted on a horse, and with a couple of dromedary guides sought safety in flight. Being pursued, he saved his life by throwing down his rich dresses and ornaments to occupy attention, while he escaped to an Arab chief in the desert between Suez and the Mediterranean.

But the difficulties of Osman Bey el Bardissy were not ended with the defeat of Elfy. It was not written in the book of fate that he or any other Mameluke should continue the line of the Murads and Ibrahims. Mohammed Ali and his Arnauts could not be put aside by a section or remnant of the Mamelukes struggling for power. On the 24th of February, Mohammed Ali and his Arnauts went to Bardissy and told him that if he did not pay them their arrears they would immediately act against him. Bardissy, whose chief reliance had hitherto been on Mohammed Ali, alarmed at such a demonstration, calmed them with a promise of payment; but the fulfilment of his promise carried with it measures which proved fatal to Bardissy. Heavy contributions were forthwith levied, not only on the native, but on the European merchants, in order to raise the necessary sum. All Cairo was disgusted with these exactions, and the very measures adopted by Bardissy to prolong his rule drew him towards the abyss, and procured for Mohammed Ali the opportunity of finally driving him into the insignificance to which Elfy Bey had fallen. The wily chief, far from identifying himself with these exorbitant exactions, consolidated his popularity with the sheikhs of Cairo by emphatically condemning the measure.

Public opinion being now mature, Mohammed Ali proceeded, in utter disregard of his professions of alliance with Bardissy, to strike the blow which was to make straight the way for the direct government of the Porte. On the 12th of March, 1804, suddenly assembling all his troops by preconcerted signal, he surrounded the house of Bardissy; and the first intelligence that the Mamelukes had of this attack, was the sound of the musketry of the Arnauts as they forced their way into the passages. A battery of field-pieces protected the house of Bardissy, but the chief of his artillery had been gained over by Mohammed Ali, who was a consummate master of the oriental science of intrigue and stratagem; and this was on a small scale the prototype of the greater defections which subsequently made Mohammed Ali so formidable for a brief period. The recreant artilleryman, wheeling round his cannon, began to batter down the palace he was employed to protect; and the unfortunate Bardissy saw that there was no chance of safety but in flight. Suddenly loading his valuables on dromedaries, he issued from his great gate, the Mamelukes hewing a way for him in front. Encouraging his own men with drawn sabre, Bardissy broke through the hostile ranks of the Arnauts; and, though wounded, gained first the fort of the Institute, and then the open country. The aged Ibrahim Bey, of whom the Albanians took less heed, held his own until daybreak next morning, when he also quitted Cairo amidst a shower of bullets, and escaped by the desert. The Pasha, who was prisoner in the citadel of Cairo, was summarily dismissed to Constantinople; and Khurschid Pasha, then at Alexandria, was called to Cairo amid the general applause of an eastern public, always ready to throw off the tyrant of the day.

The government of Khurschid Pasha was only a prolonged anarchy. He was pressed on the one hand by the Turkish and Albanian troops, demanding pay; and, on the other, he found it impossible to collect the land-tax regularly since the Mamelukes, no longer able to maintain an existence in Cairo, scoured the provinces, particularly of Upper Egypt, and carried on a petty warfare with the Turkish troops, agents, and collectors. Khurschid Pasha was thus driven to retrace the vicious circle of his predecessors; and, in his difficulties, acted the tyrant and oppressor of the mercantile and monied interests of the large towns. Sitt Nefeeseh, the inoffensive widow of Murad Bey, was arrested without cause, for the purpose of extorting money from her, and only liberated upon her cause being taken up by the heads of the legal and religious corporations. Khurschid Pasha, without the power to enforce obedience, or to carry on the functions of government, and, consequently unable to act with justice, incurred the same odium as his predecessors, and shared their fate. His government presents a tantalizing monotony of convulsions unworthy of record. Indeed, all the pashas that intervened between the French rule and that of Mohammed Ali, are a will-o'-the-wisp to the historian. A pasha of some sort flits before the eyes, but when we attempt to grasp him he is gone. A daring adventurer is always in pursuit of the possession of power; but no sooner is the game hunted down than the huntsman himself is worried to death in turn. Thus successively rose and fell Mohammed Khousreff Pasha, Tahir Pasha, Ali Pasha Gezairli, and Khurschid Pasha. Mohammed Ali alone stands out the distinct historical figure in the foreground.

During all this time Mohammed Ali increased his popularity with the native Egyptians, by acting as moderator between the sheikhs and the oppressive government. At length, in May, 1805, he was made titular Pasha of Djiddah, in Arabia, having by this time become well known to the Porte for his civil and military capacity. As Khurschid Pasha became more odious by his exactions, the popularity of Mohammed Ali increased; so that, although named Pasha of Djiddah, the avenue to the Pashalic of Egypt gradually opened itself to him, and his first accession to the government of this most wealthy and important province of the Ottoman empire was actually founded upon and favoured by public opinion.

At length, on the 14th of May, Cairo being filled with malcontent deputations from the provinces, the town rose in revolt. The first rush was made to the Mehkmeh, or Court of Justice, the seat of the cadi, who, in a panic, caused the gates to be shut. A deputation of sheikhs then waited on Mohammed Ali, declaring that they wished no longer to be governed by Khurschid Pasha, who had rendered himself odious by his persecutions, and that it was their desire that Mohammed Ali should be his successor. This bold captain, who was no stranger to the preparations made for the purpose of deposing Khurschid, appeared to decline the perilous honour; but, being pressed by the sheikhs, he at length accepted it, and was invested by the ulema with the pelisse in token of his new dignity.

The not unwilling defection of Mohammed Ali was to Khurschid Pasha a fatal event. The commander of his best troops being virtually put in his place by the most influential civilians in Egypt, it was only the possession of the citadel that retained for him the semblance of power; and the adherence of the Porte to his elevation could not be counted on when he was no longer in a position to preserve their authority from contempt. He, however, stood on his dignity and the letter of the law. When a deputation went in order to inform him of his deposition, he replied that he held his commission from the Sultan, and would not resign it at the dictation of his inferiors. At the same time he provisioned the citadel, and proposed to defend his authority by force of arms.

Mohammed Ali, now bound by his interests to side with the sheikhs, blockaded the citadel, the great mosque of Sultan Hassan and its lofty minaret serving both as a post of offence and a tower of observation; and, on the 29th, two mortars were carried up the steep acclivity of mount Mokattam, which overlooks the citadel, in order to bombard it. Khurschid Pasha, on his side, attempted to move the commanders of the Turkish troops in the provinces to come to his aid and vindicate the authority of the Sultan; but the star of Khurschid was on the decline, and they sent his letter to Mohammed Ali, and came to Cairo in order to receive pelisses from him, as well as his orders to keep in check the Mamelukes, who since the disruption of the Turkish government had again began to approach Cairo.

The selikdar of Khurschid Pasha occupied old Cairo, and made every exertion to supply the citadel with provisions; but a spy having informed the besiegers that a convoy of fifty camels was directed toward the citadel by by-paths, escorted by soldiers and armed servants, an attack on the convoy was organised before it could enter the walls. This was successful, and the survivors of the escort, being conducted to Mohammed Ali, were put to death. Khurschid was so indignant at this proceeding, that, on the next day, he bombarded the town severely; while the mortars on mount Mokattam launched their shells into the citadel, under the direction of Mohammed Ali's gunners. At the same time a heavy piece of ordnance battered the great gate of the citadel.

From the outset of these proceedings the ulema had sent their version of the differences to Constantinople. The agents of Mohammed Ali had been equally active; and, the siege having continued to the 9th of July, a capudji bashi, sent by the Porte from Constantinople, arrived at Cairo, accompanied by an officer of the Grand Vizier, who was deputed to examine and report upon the state of affairs. His dispatches were publicly opened, and, being read in the presence of the ulema, it was seen that the government of Egypt was at length conferred on Mohammed Ali, and that Khurschid Pasha was ordered to Alexandria to wait the orders of the Porte. This was followed up by the arrival of a Turkish squadron, having 2,500 troops on board, with a view to act decisively; for Khurschid, finding himself abandoned by his Turkish troops, was, in his desperation, renewing correspondence with the Mamelukes. The arrival of the Ottoman squadron with the fresh troops, and the vigilance with which Mohammed Ali intercepted all correspondence, however, determined Khurschid Pasha to surrender; and on the 3rd of August Mohammed Ali received the citadel, the tenure of which has been—from the days of Saladin, its builder—the recognised proof of the actual possession of the government of Egypt.

Thus did Mohammed Ali arrive at the first stage of his extraordinary career; and it certainly was by a rare union of social, intellectual, and physical powers, that he emerged from utter obscurity to high rank, and subsequently to a power that made itself felt through all the Ottoman empire. Nor can I here resist the temptation of giving a summary of his qualities, although somewhat anticipatory of the period when their development fixed on him the attention of Europe. His personal courage was indubitable: amidst shot falling like hail he preserved consummate coolness and self-possession. His sagacity was extraordinary, whether in relation to things or men. Profound dissembler himself until his hour came, he was at the same time a master in the penetration of the motives of those with whom he had to deal. Nor was any sordid avarice, that worst foe of popularity, one of his defects. In treasure, as in blood, he was *alieni appetens, sui profusus*. An overflowing liberality was in accordance both with his temperament and his political plans. His largesses gained him friends; while the native Egyptians, whom he squeezed to supply his demands, were impotent in their enmity.

But there is much to be said in abatement of his merits. Although superior to a thirst for blood, from mere vengeance and resentment, and an easy pardoner of those who were no longer able to injure him, no compunction ever deterred him from removing the obstacles to his lawless ambition, by fraud or force—most frequently by a compound of both. Nor was he able, with all his perseverance, to conquer his aboriginal want of education. Anxious to introduce European civilization into Egypt, he remained to the end of his life in utter ignorance of the economical principles on which the prosperity of a State reposes. Greedy of the praise of Europeans, and, in the latter part of his career, anxious to count for something in the balance of military power, his illusions on this head shewed to himself and to others the wide interval that separates the scientific organization of European military and political establishments from the Egyptian imitations which cost him efforts so lengthened and persevering. But although unable to resist the dictation of any European power, he was—within Egypt—all-potent in establishing an order that had never existed before, so as to afford those facilities that have proved so valuable to the Indian transit. He found Egypt in anarchy; and long before he had terminated his career, the journey from the Mediterranean to Nubia was as secure as that from London to Liverpool. He learned to read, and attempted to write, after he had attained his fortieth year; and, when we add that the practical result of his efforts was to leave his family in the hereditary government of Egypt, Mohammed Ali must be admitted to have been, without exception, the most remarkable character in the modern history of the Ottoman empire.

CHAPTER II.

Mohammed Ali Circumvents the Mamelukes.—His Power causes Uneasiness to the Porte.—He becomes Pasha of Egypt.—British Expedition to Egypt under General Fraser.

During all this time, as we have seen, the Mamelukes were by no means extinct. A considerable part of rural Egypt was in their power. Mohammed Bey el Elfy and Osman Bey el Bardissy, two able men, possessing a considerable prestige, and having followers well mounted, maintained more close relations with the nomad Arabs than the Pashas of Cairo did; but the period was rapidly approaching when they were to be totally swept away from the political stage of Egypt, by two massacres which were revoltingly characteristic of the oriental school of politics and warfare.

Mohammed Ali, well knowing that with his Albanian troopers he could make no impression on well-mounted cavalry, caused his partisans to open communications with the Mamelukes, proposing, in consideration of a considerable sum of money, to admit them into Cairo on the day of the festivity of the cutting the sluices of the Nile, when Mohammed Ali with all his officers would be outside the walls above Cairo. The stratagem was successful, and the Mamelukes fell completely into the trap.

A long line of bazaars and narrow streets leads from the gates on the north side of Cairo to the citadel, one portion of which—between the gates of Succour and Victory, on the north, and the so-called Bab Zueileh in the centre of the town—is the principal thoroughfare of the Egyptian metropolis; while somewhat to the east of this line, and nearer mount Mokattam, is the venerated mosque of the Azhar, the seat of learning and religion. On the 18th of August, 1805, a corps of mamelukes burst into the suburb of Hoseyneey, principally inhabited by the turbulent butchers of the metropolis, and then proceeded to the Gate of Victory, which was left guarded only by a few fellaheen, who had opened it to some peasants with camels loaded with straw. These were speedily overpowered, and the mamelukes advanced boldly into the town. Mohammed Ali had fully calculated that they would proceed up the main thoroughfare of the bazaars; and therefore, at an advanced part of their progress, near the Bab Zueileh, a considerable number of Arnauts, ambuscaded in the houses, fired upon the mounted mamelukes through the apertures of the carved wooden lattices, and immediately compelled them to retreat backwards towards the mosque and bazaar of El Ghoury. In the narrow streets and crowded thoroughfares cavalry was of no avail against invisible assailants, while every bullet from a window, or from behind the numerous angles, brought down a horse or a man; and, however little we may approve of the way in which the mamelukes were led into the trap, there can be no doubt that it was the most effectual way of putting a cavalry force in the worst case, and securing for Albanian rifles the most advantageous opportunity of action.

If a passage could not be found in front, it was equally impossible for the mamelukes to make good their retreat through the defile of houses and bazaars in the rear; for no sooner were they engaged in the centre of the town, than, by Mohammed Ali's direction, a binbashi, with a sufficient force, blocked up the bazaar of the braziers—the cavern-like shops of which gave ample cover to the oblique fire of the Albanian rifles, which told with deadly effect in this narrow passage. Despair seized the mamelukes. Springing from their horses, they sought to escape in all directions, entering houses and scrambling over walls.

Not far from the great hospital which the munificence of Sultan Kalaoun raised for suffering humanity, is the superb mosque of Sultan Barkouk, the first of the Circassian Mameluke Sultans, upon the desk of which stand to this day large and splendidly illuminated Korans—the admiration of all Egypt. Here the remnant of the mamelukes took refuge, and here the binbashi agreed to spare their lives on the delivery of their arms. Upon acceding to this demand, they were deprived of their dresses and money, and, being bound, were taken before Mohammed Ali.

One of the prisoners was Achmet Bey, formerly governor of Damietta, whom the Pasha addressed with the words—"Well! and you too have fallen into the trap." To this he returned no answer, but only asked leave to drink, on which the guards untied his hands and gave him a porous vase of water. With rapidity he seized the poniard of an aga standing near him, and attempted to plunge it into the body of Mohammed Ali, who ran up a staircase out of his way, while the soldiers threw themselves on Achmet Bey, and he fell pierced with their swords. During the night the mameluke prisoners were kept in the lower part of Mohammed Ali's house, and on the following morning all were mercilessly massacred, excepting those who paid a heavy ransom for the recovery of their liberty.

The power of Mohammed Ali now seemed firmly established in Egypt, and he appeared himself to confide so much in the permanence of his prosperity, that his sons Toussoon and Ibrahim were sent for from Turkey proper, and the former was made commandant of the citadel. But scarcely had Mohammed Ali reached this elevation, when the Porte, faithful to its traditionary policy of never allowing any Pasha to take deep root in a particular locality, and of always keeping the supreme government in function, began to devise means of getting him removed from a command so isolated as to confer a virtual independence. Accordingly, the Capitan Pasha was sent to Egypt with four ships of the line, two frigates, a corvette, and a brig, having on board Moussa Pasha, of Saloniki, appointed to the government of Egypt, the purpose of the Porte being to transfer Mohammed Ali to the Pashalic of Saloniki. This personage was to be supported by the feeble remains of the Mamelukes, who were now no longer formidable to the Porte, and most willing at this juncture to become the instruments of its policy.

But Mohammed Ali managed by skill and dexterity to maintain his ground. All his faithful Albanians swore on a sabre held by the seniors to support his views; and the ulema of Cairo, with whom at this time he maintained close relations, were also set in motion with memorials to the Porte setting forth the advantages of Mohammed Ali's rule. But, in the meantime, the countenance of the Capitan Pasha again enabled the Mamelukes to raise their heads in Lower Egypt; and at Negyleh a sudden and successful attack of Elfy Bey's cavalry on the troops of Mohammed Ali, under the command of his nephew Tahir, augured well for Moussa and Elfy, who were henceforth to rule conjointly in Egypt.

But the next operation of Elfy, which was the siege of Damanhour, a town situated between Alexandria and Rahmanieh, completely failed. The inhabitants defended themselves, as much to avoid pillage as to second the views of Mohammed Ali; while Elfy, instead of receiving the undivided support of the other mamelukes, was the object of the jealousy of Osman Bey el Bardissy and his partisans. This caused the failure of the projects to oust Mohammed Ali from his government; and, while the Mamelukes were divided, the Capitan Pasha was bribed in accordance with the deplorable manners and usages of oriental officials. At length, war being about to break out between Russia and the Porte, the Capitan Pasha sailed for the Dardanelles loaded with presents from Mohammed Ali; and on the 2nd of November, 1806, a capudji bashi of the Porte arrived, bearing firmans formally constituting him Pasha of Egypt.

Neither Osman Bey el Bardissy, nor Mohammed Bey el Elfy, long survived the failure of their schemes. The former, devoured by disappointment, was struck down by bilious fever; and a remedy, administered to him by a charlatan, proving worse than the disease, terminated his troubled existence. Elfy, disappointed at the failure of the siege of Damanhour, was near Cairo preparing to retreat into Upper Egypt, watched at Embabeh by Mohammed Ali — who, as his troops consisted mostly of infantry, could undertake nothing decisive against the well-appointed mameluke cavalry. An attack of cholera, in which his body became quite livid, however, carried off Elfy, who was buried with all the honours customary on such occasions. Mohammed Ali was sleeping in his tent near Gizeh when an Arab brought him the news of the death of his enemy, and immediately received a largesse for the intelligence.

At this period took place the second and minor British expedition to Egypt of 1807, which—futile in object, inadequate in means, disgraceful rather than disastrous in its results, and altogether uninteresting in its details—

need not detain us long. A division under General Fraser landed in the environs of Alexandria, and took possession of that city without firing a shot. Britain, having broken with the Porte, designed to revive the rule of the Mamelukes, being evidently not fully aware of the irreparable blows which this oligarchy had received, and of the vigour with which the affairs of the Porte were managed at this period by the Vizier who was subsequently destined to employ his talents with dire effect against his imperial constituent; and while General Fraser was awaiting a demonstration of the Mamelukes on the coast, Mohammed Ali was in Upper Egypt, chastising and pursuing them up the Nile, in the vicinity of Siout.

No sooner was the Pasha informed of the disembarkation, than he returned to Cairo with that promptitude and energy which afford such a contrast to the dilatory and lethargic methods of the orientals. Well knowing what chord to touch, he appealed with effect to the religious feelings of the sheikhs and the ulema; and suddenly exactions and irregularities were forgotten, in sympathy for, and confidence in, a champion of Islamism, who, when the danger was past, shewed them to their astonishment how latitudinarian he could be. Provisions and funds were liberally given; and Mohammed Ali descended with celerity to the environs of Rosetta, where a first attempt at settlement by the British had met with some resistance. Unable, with a feeble and insignificant force, to maintain their ground against a man of energy with the resources of Egypt at his back, and cut off by impassable distance from Mameluke aid, a retreat upon Aboukir and Alexandria became imperative, after several combats, which did not prove very deadly to either party. Mohammed Ali and his troops blockaded rather than besieged Alexandria; and the British government, at length convinced of the futility of an expedition which, in dimensions and results, afforded such a contrast to that which we have previously described, withdrew the troops to Sicily, to the great satisfaction of Mohammed Ali, who restored the British prisoners with acts of courtesy.

CHAPTER III.

General Appropriation of Landed Property by the Pasha—The Wahaby War—Decline of the Mameluke Power—General Massacre of the Mamelukes—Massacres of Mamelukes in the Provinces.

Being now free from the English, Mohammed Ali began to develop his plans for taking firm root in Egypt. He saw that, by extracting large revenues, he could maintain his influence by rich presents to Constantinople. His military position in Egypt was improved, and the increasing and advancing power of the Wahabys rendered him more than ever necessary to the Porte. With the interior of the country tranquil, and freed from civil war, one might expect the task of the historian at this period to be the record of a lucid interval of prosperity, however brief, after foreign and domestic wars of a character so devastating. Such, however, is not the case; and we have now to relate an act of spoliation—unaccompanied, to be sure, by bloodshed—but of a grasp more comprehensive and ruinous than anything that had been done by the predecessors of Mohammed Ali.

It was in the years 1808-10 that Mohammed Ali effected a revolutionary transfer of landed property in Egypt. Not content with greatly increasing the taxes on the soil, he ordered an inspection to be made of all title deeds; and, on one pretext or another, his agents objected to their validity,—contesting the legitimacy of the successions, imposing additions to the land-tax, and in a great multitude of instances retaining the title-deeds, which were burned. A few influential sheikhs were spared; but, wherever the government chose, the land, for want of titles, gradually lapsed to the miri; so that in a few years the Pasha became landlord of nearly the whole of the soil of Egypt, some insignificant annuities being granted in compensation. Mohammed Ali's elevation to power was, as already said, founded on public opinion; but his first acts, after the consolidation of his rule, were the most flagrant defiance of public opinion, and of the sacred rights of private property in the modern annals of Egypt. The Mamelukes, the French, and the intervening pashas, had overwhelmed the people with exactions; but no attempt had been made to tear up by the very roots the pacific and legal possession of property.

The commotion which these proceedings caused was violent in the extreme, and society was agitated to its inmost depths. Even the women and the children crowded the mosques, and made the Azhar resound with their wailings. Classes and individuals, utter strangers to politics and political discussion, stood aghast at an event which rendered reasoning superfluous, and precipitated all the rights of property into a common abyss. The sheikhs met in assembly, and used every resource, both of representation and petition to the Pasha and the Porte; but Mohammed Ali was firm in his purpose. The vehement representations of the sheikhs against the additional land taxes, and even the persevering refusals of Said Omar Mekrum, the nackeeb of the shereefs, to go near the divan of the Pasha, were declared by him to savour of a stiff-necked and rebellious spirit, which must be repressed. And, throughout this curious struggle, the firm defence of the indefeasible rights of property was conveniently characterised by a lawless governor as an aggression, and an invasion of the supreme authority. Said Omar Mekrum was exiled to Damietta. The military governors of provinces arbitrarily collected contributions without the intervention of the Coptic clerks; and thenceforth began that direct grinding of the peasantry, which, before the death of Mohammed Ali, greatly reduced them in number, and impoverished them almost to the minimum of possible human existence.

If we cast our eyes abroad at this period (1809), we find that events in Arabia were preparing a triumph for Mohammed Ali, and an extension of his political power. This vast country—the cradle of Islamism—was now overrun by the Wahaby reformers, who, from small beginnings, had mastered both Mecca and Medina; and, although without the science of European warfare, made up for their deficiencies by an enthusiastic and undaunted bravery in action, as well as by great powers of endurance in the arduous campaigns of this torrid region. Their peculiar doctrines were based on the self-denial of the early Moslems, which made them avoid both those stimulants which expend the nervous and muscular energies, and those lethargic habits which are alternately the effect and the cause of inaction.

The barren shores of the Red Sea being in a great measure devoid of ports and of navigation, and the trade of Suez having sunk into insignificance, it was not easy to transport an army from Egypt to Arabia. By a series of most painful efforts, wood, cordage, and other materials for shipbuilding, were carried from the ports of Turkey to Egypt, and across the desert, on the backs of camels to Suez. Numbers of men and of those useful beasts of burden perished in the attempt; but at length, after incredible efforts, eighteen vessels were launched in the space of less than a year, and fitted up for the conveyance of troops and provisions. But a baptism of blood accompanied their launch, for the solemnity of the departure from Cairo of the troops destined for the Arabian expedition was chosen for the final massacre of the Mamelukes. The infirmities of Ibrahim Bey had shewn the Mamelukes that they could no longer hope for any revival of their supremacy; the remaining heads of them were therefore disposed towards a passive and luxurious existence, giving no further umbrage to the Porte or to Mohammed Ali, and contenting themselves with as large a share as they could grasp of the produce of Egypt. Mohammed Ali, on his side, was not displeased to patch up an accommodation with those turbulent barons of Eastern feudalism, so as to have more elbow-room to carry out his designs of a virtual sovereignty under the mask of zeal for the service of the Porte, and at the same time to have them more securely in his power when the convenient moment came for getting entirely rid of them.

Shahin Bey, the elected successor of Elfy Bey, had made his submission to Mohammed Ali, and signed an arrangement, the conditions of which were advantageous to him. From the Pyramids up the left bank of the Nile to beyond Beni Souef, and including the Faioum, was assigned to him as an appanage; and, on his presenting himself for investiture to Mohammed Ali at Cairo, he was loaded with rich gifts of shawls, pelisses, and diamond-mounted daggers. The other Mamelukes, even although jealous of Shahin Bey, were also gradually obliged to yield. The beys at Siout on the Upper Nile wished at first to refuse tribute. But the Mamelukes being no longer a corps united under an Ali Bey, or a Murad, as in former times, were fain to yield on finding that Mohammed Ali himself had come to Siout with an army of several thousand men to collect the tribute.

After this there was not even the shadow of a rising. Many of the Mamelukes came to Cairo and sank completely into sloth and sensuality, passing from the wild to the tame state like beasts fatted for slaughter.

In February, 1811, the chiefs destined by Mohammed Ali to extirpate the Wahaby reformers, and restore Arabia to the Caliph of Constantinople, went to encamp at Kubbet el Azab, on the desert near Cairo. Here 4000 men were united under the orders of Toussoun Pasha, the son of Mohammed Ali, who was destined to command the expedition. On the following Friday the youthful general was to receive the pelisse of investiture, and thereafter to proceed to the camp by the gate of Victory—the astrologers having fixed on this day as propitious to the success of the enterprise. All the civil and military authorities, and the principal people of the country, were informed of the approach of the ceremony; and, on the night before, the Mameluke chiefs were invited to take part in full costume. A simple invitation to the Mamelukes in a mass, on any other occasion, would have been answered by the habitual oriental mistrust of such hospitality; but, with a skill in the ways of evil worthy of a better cause, Mohammed Ali so managed that the obvious motive of the departure of an army, and the association of the Mamelukes with all the other authorities of the country, not only lulled their suspicions, but even flattered their self-love.

On the 1st of March, 1811, all the principal men of Cairo flocked to the citadel. Shahin Bey appeared there at the head of his household, having come with the other beys to pay his respects to Mohammed Ali, who received them in the great hall. Coffee was then served, and a conversation took place. When all those who were to take part in the procession were assembled, the signal for departure was given, each person taking the place that was assigned him by the master of the ceremonies. A corps of delis, commanded by Oozoon Ali, opened the march; then came the waly or municipal governor of Cairo, the aga of the janissaries, with Turkish troops; then came the Albanians, especially devoted to Mohammed Ali, under the immediate command of Saleh Khosh. The regular troops came last, and the mamelukes had their place assigned between the infantry and cavalry at the rear, and the Albanians, who marched in front of them. The plateau of the citadel on which are situated the chief buildings is elevated high above the level of the city. Down on the lower level, and close to the public place of the Roumeyleh, is the gate of Azab—a picturesque object flanked with round towers, painted in stripes of red and white. Between the high courtyard and this gate is the old access to the plateau—not the modern macadamized slope, but a steep winding passage with sharp angles, and cut in the rock.

Down this road came the procession, and no sooner were the delis and agas out, than Saleh Khosh ordered the gates to be shut, and communicated the order he had received to exterminate the mamelukes to his Albanians, who immediately turned about, and, jumping aside, or leaping up the rock, began to fire on the horsemen. To charge down the steep rock was useless or impossible, for the gates were shut and exit barred; and on the sloping or angular rocks the heavily mounted mamelukes, powerful on the plains of Egypt, had no chance with Albanians whose home is only the mountain side. Behind the mamelukes were the infantry troops closing the procession, whose advantage was still more decided; for they poured volleys of musketry down on these devoted men from the parapets above.

The mamelukes now wished to return by another road into the citadel; but not being able to manage their horses on account of the unfavorable ground, and seeing that many of their people were killed and wounded, they alighted, and abandoning their horses and upper clothes, remounted the road, sabre in hand, but were fired on from the windows of the citadel above. Shahin Bey fell pierced with balls before the gates of the palace of Saladin. Suleyman Bey, another mameluke, ran half naked, and frightened, to implore the protection of the Harem of the Viceroy, according to oriental usage, but in vain. He was conducted to the palace, where he was decapitated. Others went to beg for mercy from Toussoun Pasha, who took no part in the events of the day.

The troops had orders to arrest the Mamelukes whereever they might be found. Those taken were conducted to the Kiahia Bey, and instantaneously decapitated. Many persons not Mamelukes were also killed. The citadel flowed with blood, and the dead filled up the passages. The dead body of Shahin Bey was, with barbarous stupidity, dragged about with a cord round the neck. On every side were seen horses, expensively caparisoned, stretched by the side of their masters, and the richest dresses saturated with blood—for gold embroidery and the most costly cloth stuffs, with elaborately finished and decorated arms and caparisons, were what the Mamelukes mostly delighted in; and all these became the booty of the blood-thirsty soldiery. Of four hundred and sixty Mamelukes who had mounted that morning to the citadel, not one escaped. A few French Mamelukes, in the service of Mohammed Ali, who had remained behind after the departure of Menou, and had been locked up by the Kiahia Bey in a room adjoining his own, were saved. A bey of the house of Elfy had three French Mamelukes in his service, but they did not mount on horseback on that day.

Amyn Bey, another Mameluke, was saved by accident.

Being prevented by pressing business from arriving in time, he found himself outside the gate just as the head of the procession was issuing from under the arch. He waited a little until they were gone out, but seeing that the gate was suddenly closed, and then hearing the musketry, he put spurs to his horse, and never stopped until he found his way across the desert into Syria.

Scarcely had the procession begun to move when Mohammed Ali showed signs of agitation, which increased when he heard the first discharge of musketry. He grew pale, fearing lest his orders might not have been properly executed, and that some struggle might ensue fatal to himself and his party. When he saw the prisoners and the trunkless heads he grew calm. Soon after, his physician, a Genoese, entered, and said with the sickening gaiety of sycophancy, "The affair is over; this is a fête for your Highness." To this Mohammed Ali gave no answer, and only asked for a draught to quench his thirst.

Meanwhile the crowds of citizens in the town were waiting to see the procession, and expectation was succeeded by surprise when only the Delis forming its head were seen to pass, followed by grooms hurrying away in silence. This sudden movement caused an agitation among the spectators, and then the cry having arisen, "Shahin Bey is killed," all the shops were shut, which was invariably the case when turbulence, bloodshed, and their concomitant, rapine, were apprehended. The streets became deserted, and only bands of lawless soldiery were seen, who rushed to pillage the houses of the Mamelukes, violating their women, and committing every atrocity.

The Turks, who could only marry women of an inferior class, saw with displeasure that those of a higher rank, disdaining their alliance, displayed eagerness to marry

Mamelukes, and therefore took care to avenge themselves. The houses of the beys were full of valuables. Several of these cavaliers were making preparations for marriage, decorating their apartments, and purchasing rich clothes, cashmeres, and jewels. Not only the houses of these persons were pillaged, but others besides. Cairo appeared like a place taken by assault, the inhabitants not shewing themselves in the streets, but awaiting indoors what destiny had in store for them.

The murder and pillage continuing on the following day, Mohammed Ali descended from the citadel to re-establish order and stop bloodshed. He was in full dress, and accompanied by a large armed force. At each police post he reprimanded the officer in charge for having permitted such disorders. Mohammed Ali himself had only taken the lives of the Mamelukes—he had only massacred a political party addicted to cashmeres, diamond-mounted pipes, and enamelled pistols, as well as to sharing the political power with the agents of the Porte. He himself had laid the axe to the very root of Mameluke appropriation, and therefore all mangling of the branches excited his just reprobation as a superfluous expenditure of labour. Near Bab Zueileh the Pasha met a Mogrebbin, who complained of the pillage of his house, protesting that he was neither soldier nor Mameluke, on which Mohammed Ali stopped his horse, and sent an armed force, who arrested a Turk and a fellah, whose head they cut off. Advancing towards the quarter of Kakeen, he was informed that the sheikhs were assembled with the intention of complimenting him; but the Pasha answered that he would himself go to receive their felicitations, on which he proceeded to the house of Sheikh Abdullah el Sherkawy, and after having passed an hour with him he returned to the citadel.

The following day Toussoun Pasha went through the

town, followed by a numerous guard, causing those who were found pillaging to be decapitated; for more than five hundred houses had been sacked on this occasion. Meanwhile the Mamelukes were diligently sought after. Even the old ones, who in all the troubles had never quitted Cairo, were unmercifully killed. Many made their escape by changing their costume for that of Delis; others escaped to Upper Egypt dressed as women.

In the citadel, the dead bodies were thrown pell-mell into pits dug for them, the relations of the murdered being so overwhelmed as not to be able to bury them decently. The mother of the Emir Merzouk, son of Ibrahim Bey, was however allowed his dead body, which was found after two days' search. Protection was also given to the widows of the Mamelukes by Mohammed Ali, who allowed his own men to marry them. The secret of this sanguinary affair had been confided to only four persons, on whom the Pasha could rely; but he had at the same time written, through his secretary, to the commanders of the different provinces ordering them to arrest and put to death all the Mamelukes they could lay their hands upon. This order was mercilessly executed, and their heads were sent to Cairo, and exposed there. Thus altogether more than a thousand persons perished, including twenty-three beys.

CHAPTER IV.

History of the Wahabys.—Wahaby Doctrines.—Kermelah, the Wahaby Leader, Defeats the Shereef of Mecca.—The Wahabys become masters of Mecca.

Such was the bloody spectacle with which the still more sanguinary Wahaby war was inaugurated. But before we proceed to give an account of this protracted struggle, it is requisite to say something of the origin of a movement which from small beginnings grew to dimensions which endangered the traditional Islamism of Arabia, until stopped by the vigorous arm of Mohammed Ali.

Mohammed Ezbor Abd-el-Wahab, the author of the reform of the Wahabys, was born in the year 1696; and, destined by his father to the calling of an alim, was learned in the theology and jurisprudence of the Moslems. Having pursued his studies at Bussorah, he made a pilgrimage to Mecca and Medina; and returned to his native village, where he became remarkable for such austere asceticism as obliged him to quit it for Derayeh, which was destined to become the capital of the sect of this fierce reformer, and in which place he had formed relations with influential persons who concurred with him in his extreme and rigid system of social and religious reform.

It is not to be denied that the Moslems of later centuries had fallen from the primitive virtues of those who had spread the doctrines of Islam over half the old world.

Inheriting the rich countries which their ancestors had wrested from the Greek Empire, and no longer stimulated to sacrifice or exertion by the contests with the Crusaders of Europe, the hardy virtues had become the exclusive appanage of those northern Moslem populations who, settled on the banks of the Danube and on the heights overlooking the Adriatic, had to bear the brunt of resistance to the land forces of the Emperors of Germany, and the maritime strength of the Republic of Venice. All the Arab countries of the south were sunk in sloth and luxury. Arabia proper, from its torrid climate, its scanty endowment with the good things of this earth, and its nomad population inured to privation, was the only exception.

But even the scanty luxury of the settled parts of Arabia was in the eyes of the austere Abd-el-Wahab an offence in the sight of God, and a departure from the primitive ways of his people. In some respects he was the Protestant of Islamism. He stripped away the whole body of tradition that obscured and encumbered the simple original doctrines taught by Mohammed. But while doing this, he at the same time reprobated that homage to the memory of Mohammed which turned the Prophet into a demi-god, and idolatrously invested him with characteristics proper to the Supreme Being.

The doctrine of the Wahabys had therefore nothing of novelty in it, but was simply a return to the primitive usage of Islamism, the duties enforced being fasting, prayer, almsgiving, and the pilgrimage to Mecca. At the same time, there was the strict prohibition of stimulating liquors, excesses in carnal lusts, games of hazard, usury, false witness, the use of tobacco and other narcotics, the wearing of silk dresses by men, and the elevation of pompous domes and mausoleums to dead men, which, becoming shrines, tended to idolatry.

Such were the doctrines taught by Mohammed-Abd-el-Wahab with considerable eloquence and powers of persuasion, and enforced by the severe example of the preceptor. The ascendancy which this remarkable man thus acquired over those in his sphere was also enhanced by a circumstance of a temporary nature, without which the Wahabys could never have risen to the dominion of Arabia. Souhoud, the Sheikh of Derayeh, who protected Abd-el-Wahab, was a man of military prowess and considerable ambition, who availed himself of the eloquence of the teacher, and the rapid progress of his doctrines, to extend his own temporal dominion; and his son Abd-el-Aziz also being a daring and successful commander, the result was that, between the years 1746 and 1791—the period comprised in British history between the Scottish rebellion and the French revolution—the whole of that large district called the Nejd was conquered by the Wahabys, village after village; sometimes by stratagem and sometimes by direct attack, in the course of which they developed an art of warfare perfectly suited to the country, the climate, and the semi-barbarous organization of their opponents. Abd-el-Wahab himself lived to see the expanded power of his adherents; having survived to the 14th of June, 1791, when he died at the advanced age of ninety-five, leaving eighteen children, the result of his twenty marriages.

It may well be believed that the progress of these enthusiasts, on whom firm faith had conferred energy and success, was viewed with the utmost alarm at Mecca, that Vatican of Moslem tradition. The Shereef of that city, considered so holy by the Moslems, easily comprehended that the conquests of the Wahabys were not likely to be confined to the Nejd; and that that district being entirely subdued, Yemen and Hedjaz were not likely to escape. The Shereef Ghaleb therefore, in 1798, the year of the French expedition to Egypt, sent an army against the Wahabys, which at first had some show of success; but Kermelah, the Wahaby leader, although commanding a very inferior number of troops, knew how to deal with those of the Shereef. Before the decisive action he told his men not to give way nor retreat, whatever might happen. The Shereef of Mecca, assuming from the confidence of the attack made by Kermelah, that his force must be much larger than it really was, lost courage and made a disorderly retreat, which being followed up by the chastisement of some wavering tribes of Arabs, the Wahabys had nothing more to fear on the side of Mecca. It was therefore towards the head of the Persian Gulf that they now turned their arms; but the Pasha of Bagdad, having assembled a large army and shown a bold front, peace was rapidly concluded. The governor of this important pashalic having, as usual, enough to do in assuring his own position at Bagdad, evinced no disposition to enter upon a campaign in the heart of Arabia.

Far from this, without seeking any direct attack upon Bagdad, the younger Souhoud, with an army of twenty thousand men, moved upon Kerbelah, not far from the Euphrates, and near which is the tomb of Husseyn, the son of the Caliph Ali, regarded by all the Shiite Moslems as a place of uncommon veneration. In fact it is a sort of Loretto of the Persians, and at this period was the depository of prodigious wealth, the offerings of the numerous pilgrims who annually flocked to this far-famed shrine. Here the Wahabys spared neither man, woman, nor children; the mausoleum was broken down, and the soldiery penetrated into the sanctuary. "Spare my life," said the warder, "and I will show you the hidden treasures;" but an Arab, eager for carnage, pierced his side with a lance, and nothing of what was concealed was discovered. Nevertheless, great riches fell to the Wahaby commander—sabres mounted with precious stones, a pearl the size of a pigeon's egg, vases and lamps of gold and silver, as well as other ornaments of precious stones and metals. In addition to this, Kerbelah was a place of great trade with Persia, and the plunder of the warehouses and private dwellings was immense, including four thousand Cashmere shawls, and a great deal of hard cash, mostly Dutch and Venetian ducats.

In the following year (1802) the Wahabys at length marched upon Mecca, and entered it without firing a shot. The Shereef Ghaleb, not judging it prudent to await his fate within its walls, had retired to Djeddah, whither Souhoud followed him; but an epidemic having broken out in the army of the Wahabys, they were compelled to retire, and Ghaleb re-entered Mecca. Nor did this reverse of the Wahabys come single. The pillage of Kerbelah and the desecration of the tombs of Fatimeh, the daughter of Mohammed, and of her grandson Husseyn, had created loudly expressed indignation through all Persia; and this feeling found, as is usual in the East, an interpreter who gave effect to his fanatical feelings by assassination. Abd-el-Aziz, the son of the elder Souhoud, being occupied with his prayers in the mosque, the assassin entered, and, standing behind him, seemed engaged in prayer: but just as Abd-el-Aziz prostrated himself with his forehead to the ground, the assassin, watching the opportunity, plunged into the loin of the praying prince a dagger which he had hidden for the purpose; and before many hours Abd-el-Aziz, who had so often led the Wahabys to victory, was a corpse. The Persian assassin was massacred on the spot, his body burnt in the market place, and in his turban was found a note which ran thus: "Thy God and thy religion make it a duty to kill Abd-el-Aziz; if thou escapest, great rewards will be thine; but if thou fallest, paradise is open to thee."

The younger Souhoud, the son of Abd-el-Aziz, and grandson of the elder Souhoud, now succeeded his father; and, in the year 1809, the Shereef Ghaleb, no longer able to maintain a struggle with the Wahabys, made his submission, and asked for the protection of Souhoud, who ordered him to send away the force of Turkish soldiers in his service. The Wahaby chief then proceeded with a large army to Mecca, and had a distinguished reception from the Shereef and his family, who even complimented him on the sacred mount of Arafat. At a subsequent visit the tomb of Mohammed at Medina was opened and despoiled of the treasures of ages accumulated there. In addition to this, the pilgrimage to the holy cities by the caravans of Syria and Africa was interrupted during several years. The Imams of Sanaa and Muscat submitted themselves to the son of Abd-el-Aziz; and, at the period of the massacre of the Mamelukes, Souhoud was the virtual sovereign of the vast country stretching from the Red Sea to the Persian Gulf, and from the Indian Ocean to the desert of Syria. To subdue this real potentate was the enterprise upon which Mohammed Ali now entered,—a task arduous in the extreme, and the successful issue of which, if less prominently before the European public than the conquest of Syria, was inferior to nothing accomplished in other spheres of operations by Mohammed Ali and Ibrahim Pasha, in earning for them the reputation of military ability pre-eminent above that of all their native compeers in the warfare of the East.

CHAPTER V.

THE SHEREEF OF MECCA AND MOHAMMED ALI CONCERT MEASURES TO ATTACK THE WAHABYS.—CAPTURE OF MEDINA BY TOUSSOUN PASHA, SON OF MOHAMMED ALI.—THE WAHABYS REGAIN GROUND.—MOHAMMED ALI DISEMBARKS IN ARABIA.—FINAL CONQUEST OF THE WAHABYS.

THE submission of Ghaleb, Shereef of Mecca, to the fierce reformers of Derayeh had been feigned, not real. The inhabitants of Mecca subsisted almost exclusively on the profits derived from the vast annual concourse of pilgrims to a city which, to the Moslem world, was associated with a sentiment of veneration, but the pilgrimage to which was to the people of Mecca themselves the daily bread of the carnal body. Mohammed Ali therefore, before thus embarking his army, sent first an agent to communicate privily with Ghaleb, to sound his views, secure his assistance, and to pave the way generally for the success of the expedition, by the acquisition of such other information on the dispositions of the Arab tribes hostile to the Wahabys as would enable the force from Egypt to act with decisive effect.

The military and political fame of Mohammed Ali had already extended to Arabia; and the Shereef Ghaleb, anxious for the re-establishment of the regular pilgrimage which had filled his coffers, gave a cordial reception to all the plans and proposals of Mohammed Ali, and sent back his own confidential man to Cairo with the agent of the Pasha, to assure him of his support, as well as to aid him with his intelligence and local experience. Active preparations were therefore made, both in men and in money, to carry through the expedition; and there can be no doubt that, although the Shereef Ghaleb was not himself a successful general, the information which he furnished was of great value in assuring the success of the intended operations.

On the other hand, Souhoud was not idle. Spies which he kept in Cairo informed him of the preparations of the Pasha; and an army of fifteen thousand men was collected without delay to combat the enemy. Eight thousand men disembarked from Suez at Janbo on the sea, situated to the north-west of Mecca, which serves as the port of Medina. Ghaleb had promised to Souhoud to defend Janbo with his own troops; but, breaking his promise, both Janbo on the sea and Janbo inland fell at once into the power of the invading force. Flushed with this easy success, Toussoun Pasha, who commanded the expedition, advanced with the ardour of youth to the defiles of Safra. The Wahabys posted here advantageously, on rocks overlooking a narrow winding road, did not deter Toussoun from the attack. The first rush of the Turks drove the Wahabys before them, but advance only increased their difficulties. Every step was marked with blood; and, the steep defiles aiding the defenders, the Turks halted, and, losing heart at the prospect of the insurmountable difficulties before them, suddenly gave way. The Arab blood now got up, and a pursuit utterly disastrous to the Turks took place. Prisoners, wounded horses, camels, and baggage were all abandoned in the disorderly flight; and Toussoun Pasha ignominiously regained Janbo inland, having lost nearly the half of his troops.

Mohammed Ali, on the receipt of this intelligence, acted with exemplary severity and redoubled activity.

Orders were transmitted to put to death the kiahya of Toussoun Pasha, who, losing heart, had been the first to retreat in the defiles of Safra. At the same time, extraordinary measures were resorted to in order to raise funds to equip the necessary reinforcements, and the property entailed for the benefit of mosques and other institutions was unceremoniously laid hands on, in spite of the complaints of the ulema, who, however, were not in a position to resist. The whole of the career of Mohammed Ali shows that Islamism sat very loosely on this bold captain; and very little attention was paid to these complaints during his long career. But there were other parties in Cairo more difficult to deal with. The Albanian chiefs, Saleh Khosh and others, through whom he had risen to power, who were his instruments in the death-blow dealt to the Mamelukes, and who had returned to Cairo after the disastrous expedition to Arabia, were dissatisfied with the privations of an arduous campaign, and envious of the wealth and power which their former companion wielded in pomp and security within the walls of the luxurious capital of Egypt. Arrested in their houses, and surrounded with troops, they were completely in the power of the now autocratic Pasha; who, however, spared their lives, and even allowed them their property and arrears of pay, on condition of their leaving the country.

The new campaign in Arabia was attended with more success. Toussoun Pasha, having received reinforcements, renewed his artillery; and, obeying orders, decapitated the kiahya, as a formidable example to the captains under his orders. He advanced boldly to Medina, having previously secured the friendship of the Arabs on his way; and, the artillery being put on the breaching batteries, the fire commenced. The inhabitants of Medina were favourable to his enterprise, their interests being associated with those of the Shereef and the renewal of the pilgrimage, and opposed to those of the Wahaby garrison, those fanatical roundheads of Moslem puritanism. Toussoun Pasha, having laid his mines, communicated with the inhabitants, so that in the ensuing assault they might be distinguished and spared by his soldiers. On the following day, the mine having blown up, a part of the wall fell, and the Turks rushed in, massacring a portion of the garrison, upon which the rest shut themselves up in the citadel, but were allowed to capitulate.

This was the first decisive blow that had been struck against the great Wahaby power that had extended so far and so wide. The value of the success did not so much consist in the capture of a town, as in the liberation of the last resting-place of the Prophet from sacrilegious hands, with all its moral influence upon a nation in whose minds the formalism of Islam, as contrasted with its primary spirit, had taken the deepest root. The effects of this stroke were forthwith felt throughout the rest of the Hedjaz. Ghaleb, who awaited at Jeddah with trembling anxiety the result of the expedition, received Toussoun with joy and gratitude as a God-sent deliverer. Mecca was abandoned by the Wahabys, mistrustful of its population, and now compelled to concentrate their forces, so that this chief sanctuary of the Moslem nations was entered by Toussoun without firing a shot.

The pride and joy of Mohammed Ali at the intelligence of these successes may easily be imagined. If his paternal affection was gratified, his ambition was also inflamed by an accession of power, and his self-love tickled by additional claims on the favour of the Porte, of which the keys of Medina, transmitted to Constantinople, were a striking external symbol. Nor was the palace of the Sultan without the usual trunkless heads of dusky tinted

Wahabys, to enforce the oft-repeated lesson of what awaited those who were disobedient to the temporal and spiritual power of the Sultan and Caliph. The fate of one of those Wahaby chiefs reminds us forcibly of the cat playing with the mouse within its fangs. Madayfy, carried prisoner into Egypt, had his fetters taken off before he entered Cairo; he was then conducted in a sort of pomp to the citadel, a spectacle to the citizens who lined the streets, after which the kiahya invited him to dinner and lodged him well for four days. He was then embarked in chains for Constantinople, and beheaded on his arrival there.

It was now high time for Souhoud to act with vigour. In midsummer 1813 the heats were oppressive, and therefore the season was arrived when the acclimated Arab had a great advantage over the Turk, to whom the climate of even Egypt was sufficiently severe, and that of Arabia positively oppressive. But Toussoun, gay and flushed with victory, was eager to follow up his advantage. He therefore directed his lieutenant, Mustapha Bey, to advance with a force upon Tarabay, a considerable place to the eastward of Mecca, surrounded with date plantations in a plain intersected with ditches. Here the leader of the Wahabys was a woman of amazonian courage and authority—Ghalyeh, the wife of the Sheikh of Sobeih. The result of a hot engagement was a complete victory on the part of the Wahabys, and the disastrous retreat of Mustapha Bey upon Tayf, aggravated by the horrors of thirst and privation under a broiling sun, which destroyed a great many men and beasts of burthen. At the same time, the Wahabys, again taking courage, menaced Medina, while the communications could be kept up only with great difficulty.

On the receipt of this intelligence, Mohammed Ali promptly determined to repair the evil by his personal presence in Arabia; for, with the Mamelukes destroyed and the Albanians dismissed from Egypt, his presence could now be spared from the seat of government. Nor had he anything to fear from the Porte, to which he was not yet an object of suspicious apprehension, but the lever of its hopes for the re-elevation of the power of the Ottoman Caliphate in the original seat of Islamism.

On the 28th of August, 1813, Mohammed Ali disembarked at Jeddah, the port of Hedjaz, where he was received with great honours by his son and the Shereef Ghaleb. He then proceeded to Mecca, where he performed all the acts of pilgrimage, and conversed frequently with the learned men established there. Mecca is not only a place of religion, but, in pacific times, a fair for commerce, and a place for the intercommunication of knowledge from the remotest parts inhabited by Moslems, —the negro of Central Africa, the Chinese from the Yellow Sea, the Agha from the highlands of Croatia, and the Tartar from the steppes of the Ural or the Caspian. Here at Mecca, as well as at Jeddah, Mohammed Ali received every honour from the Shereef Ghaleb; but, notwithstanding these reciprocal civilities, Mohammed Ali, digesting the information he received on all hands, came to the conclusion that Ghaleb had neither sufficient zeal nor ability to prosecute the war. He therefore resolved to depose him, which change was accomplished without bloodshed, but still in a manner truly oriental, and foreign to the usages of the European nations.

The arrival of Toussoun Pasha in Mecca was the occasion selected for this stroke of policy. Mohammed Ali, knowing that the Shereef would go and pay his respects to Toussoun, gave his son directions how to proceed with the deposition. After pipes and coffee, during which the Shereef conversed with Toussoun in presence of their numerous suites, that of Toussoun retired, on a signal, as if to leave the two grandees in confidential communication; and, observing this, the attendants of the Shereef also quitted the apartment. But the Pasha and his guest did not remain long alone; for a door was opened from another apartment in which soldiers had been concealed, and out stepped Abdeen Bey, who politely asked the thunderstruck Shereef for his dagger, which he at once yielded up. To gild the pill, Toussoun informed him that the act did not originate with Mohammed Ali, but was the execution of an imperial mandate, and that the advocacy of the Pasha of Egypt might be counted on in his favour. Mohammed Ali himself sent immediately afterwards to confirm this view of the arrest, and enjoining him to write to his family and kindred not to hazard a rising in his favour, with which recommendation Ghaleb unhesitatingly complied. The sons of the Shereef, on their way to offer their submission to the Pasha, were also seized and imprisoned, but treated with the greatest civility. Meanwhile, the house of the Shereef was taken possession of, and his treasures, amounting to nearly fifty thousand pounds sterling, appropriated. The Porte subsequently ordered some restitution of his wealth to be made to him. He and his family were then removed, first to Cairo, and then to Salonika, where he lived only four years; disappointment, and a climate so different from that of his native land, having brought him to a premature end. Nor was the Wahaby camp without a change: shortly after the arrest and fall of Ghaleb, Souhoud, now an old man of sixty-eight, died at Derayeh, on the 17th of April, 1814; and with him lapsed the power and vigour of Wahaby warfare into the less able and efficacious hands of his son.

To this change of commanders must be attributed the speedy change of fortune on the part of the rivals for the possession of Arabia. The courage, the perseverance, and the momentum of authority, which had hitherto been on the side of the Wahabys, were now to be found in the counsels and actions of the Turkish commander. The place of Souhoud was occupied by his son Abdallah; but his warlike qualities and influence were not inherited by this the last tenant of the virtual sovereignty of which Derayeh was the capital. In the first serious engagement, which took place on the 10th of January, 1815, Mohammed Ali defeated a force of twenty thousand Wahabys under the immediate command of Faycal, another son of Souhoud; after which Toussoun Pasha pushed his advances into the Nejd, but wanting provisions and stores, was fain to come to an accommodation, without venturing to follow up his successes to Derayeh.

Events in Europe now determined Mohammed Ali to return to Egypt; for, if the Wahabys were not annihilated, the holy cities had been freed from their presence, the pilgrimage to Mecca was re-established, and the power of the reformers was confined to the Hedjaz. In addition to this, the return of Bonaparte from Elba to France threw for a time a dark cloud on the prospects of Europe, and consequently of the Ottoman Empire, with which the politics of Europe had become more and more closely interwoven. It was after his arrival at Cairo, which took place on the 18th of June, 1815, the very day of the final extinction of the power of Bonaparte, that Mohammed Ali, now convinced of the vast superiority of the European system of warfare over that of the Orientals, resolved to introduce into Egypt the modern tactics. Long after feudalism had ceased in Europe it continued in the Ottoman Empire, and it is scarcely yet entirely extirpated from this vast agglomeration of nations and provinces. Up to the 17th century the kings of Europe called together their mailed barons when war was projected. Then began the great revolutions, which ended by establishing large standing armies directly officered by the nominees of the king; and the lapse into desuetude of military service in return for land, either freehold or copyhold. It was more especially during the age of Louis XIV., under the Turennes, Vaubans, Cohorns, Eugenes, and Marlboroughs, that the modern system of warfare was developed. But no analogous change took place in the armies of the Ottoman Empire. The Khan of the Crimea and the hereditary Beys of Bosnia and Asia Minor continued, as of old, to lead their men to do battle for the sovereign on the banks of the Danube; but as brave vassals, not as commanders trained by science to the system of modern warfare. Now and then a French or German renegade was to be found in the corps of artillery or engineers; but this was the rare exception, not the rule. Sultan Selim had in the beginning of this present century made some feeble attempts to impart a European organization to several regiments; but turbulence and barbarous fanaticism was an invincible obstacle to the introduction of a scheme of exercise associated with infidel Frankdom.

The intelligent and observant Mohammed Ali was fully impressed with the vast superiority of the European art of war. An eager auditor of the translations of the European newspapers, which for years had been filled with the story of the marvellous successes and reverses of Napoleon Bonaparte, there can be little doubt that he looked forward to the scientific organization of the troops of Egypt as a means,—if not of securing independence at that early stage, at least of prolonging the tenure of a power which was a virtual sovereignty; while that very abasement of the power of the Mamelukes by which the authority of the Porte had been reestablished, gave him elbow-room for carrying out schemes of armament, which at no distant day were to produce at Constantinople sentiments of apprehension and exasperation which had been unknown even in the palmiest days of Mameluke rule.

But however favoured by such circumstances, the old spirit of the military corporations of Turkey was averse from the innovation, and unprepared for the introduction, of Frank tactics, by the mere fiat of a man in advance of his contemporaries, even although wielding the power of Pasha of Egypt. On the 2nd of August Mohammed Ali went to Boulak to exercise the soldiers of his son Samad; and, having put them through several exercises, he declared that he intended henceforth to adopt European tactics, and that whoever opposed or resisted should be severely punished.

Murmurs of dissatisfaction and expressions of indignant surprise were manifested by the malcontents, who immediately resolved to get quit of the Pasha; but, through a fortunate circumstance, the conspiracy failed. A certain Abdeen Bey, having given a dinner or festival, was made a confidant of the intention to surprise the Pasha before day-break in his palace; and he, without attempting to dissuade them, and even promising to join them, went out privately, and, mounting an ass, proceeded straight to Mohammed Ali, whom he informed of what was intended, after which he returned home and rejoined the conspirators. The Pasha, on receipt of this intelligence, went from his palace on the Ezbekieh to the citadel, which he entered on the side of mount Mokattam; and, being supported by a considerable force on which he could depend, he caused the gates to be shut.

The chief conspirators, baulked of their object, did not dare avow themselves; but their disorderly mob of adherents broke loose upon the town, plundering many houses, and the Humzawy cloth bazaar kept by Levantine rayahs. The damage done was made good by

Mohammed Ali, and the revolt having spent its fury without its object being attained, the authority of the Pasha was again felt. Abdeen Bey received a large sum in recompense of his invaluable service, while the heads of the conspiracy, whom Mohammed Ali might have visited with exemplary severity, were left unmolested—a proof of that rare command of temper which Mohammed Ali frequently exhibited on the most trying occasions throughout his career.

The news of these events being spread with vague exaggeration through the Hedjaz, filled the mind of Toussoun with apprehension; and he resolved to return immediately to Cairo, having previously caused salutes of artillery to be fired, expressive of the falseness of the report that had been spread, and of the satisfaction he experienced at the prosperous aspect of his father's affairs. Toussoun, who was received with great honours on his arrival at Cairo after his second and more successful campaign in Arabia, proceeded from thence to Alexandria, where his father was residing, and where he saw for the first time his infant son, Abbas, born during his absence, and destined to be the Pasha of Egypt in the middle of the nineteenth century. Having furnished an heir to the fortunes of his house, Toussoun himself was not destined to be a witness of the later and more chequered career of his remarkable father, or to form a link between the sway of Mohammed Ali, and that of his grandson.

Toussoun Pasha, on his return, led a life totally opposite to that which he had been compelled to live in Arabia. There—owing to the exercise, the occupation of mind and body, during an arduous campaign, and in a climate where all nature forbids indulgence to the rational being as peremptorily as the written injunctions of Mohammed—the health of Toussoun was excellent; but, on his return to the banks of the Nile, he substituted the excitements of the voluptuary for those of the warrior. On the day after the arrival from Constantinople of a Georgian slave of exquisite beauty, his nervous system being unstrung, he was seized with severe headaches, followed by cold perspiration, which carried him off in a few hours.

Mohammed Ali was on the western bank of the Nile, at the foot of the Pyramids, when his officers first received the intelligence of the death of his favourite son, a disaster that seems to have made a deeper impression upon his mind than any other domestic affliction; for Toussoun, voluptuary as he was, had far more of that spontaneous kindness which begets affection than the iron-natured Ibrahim. His officers, all of whom were sincerely attached to the Pasha (for no man ever requited more cordially the service rendered him), did not dare to inform him at once of an event which was sure to affect him profoundly. Such is the prejudice of Eastern usage, that the repugnance to be the bearer of painful intelligence, or the eagerness to announce a happy event, is carried far beyond those limits which are usual in the political society of Europe. On this occasion, Mohammed Ali was informed that Toussoun had arrived ill, and immediately prepared to go and see him; but the body had already been removed, and his kiahya had no resource but to break to him the sorrowful intelligence.

"Say no more," said Mohammed Ali, with a wave of his hand: his countenance fell, and, as if conscious that all efforts to compose himself were utterly useless, he threw himself on the ground, surrendered himself to a paroxysm of grief, and for three days maintained an almost dead silence.

To the south of Cairo, between the palm-clad banks of the Nile and the sterile precipitous heights of Mount

Mokattam, is a region of suburbs and tombs, where, here and there, the fretted cupola of Saracenic architecture is seen crumbling to its kindred desert. Here is the last resting-place of the Imam Shafei, that great doctor of Islamism whose interpretation of the Koran is adopted throughout all Egypt and Syria.* To this spot the body of Toussoun was followed by his sorrowing father on foot, and there, in a receptacle prepared for the purpose, the bones of the rest of the family of Mohammed Ali are also preserved.

Although Toussoun Pasha, in leaving Arabia, had come to a compromise, which left the Wahabys in possession of their capital Derayeh, and of a considerable part of the north-east of Arabia, yet it was no part of the intention of Mohammed Ali to relax his efforts until they were entirely subdued. He therefore peremptorily ordered Abdallah, the son of Souhoud, to proceed to Constantinople, and at the same time to restore the treasures which his father had found in the tomb of the Prophet at Medina and elsewhere. On this the Wahaby chief answered that those treasures had been dissipated in his father's time, and implored Mohammed Ali not to insist upon the journey to Constantinople, offering to pay any reasonable tribute, and to submit to the authority of the Porte. This letter was accompanied by presents, which Mohammed Ali sent back, with the expression of his serious displeasure at the disobedience of his orders; for it was not tribute or a declaration of submission that Mohammed Ali aimed at, but the extinction of the once formidable political and military power of the Wahabys. Their chief was at no loss to comprehend this, and hot war now recommenced between him and the Pasha.

Toussoun being now no more, it was to Ibrahim Pasha

* Except in the town of Nablouse, where, as at Bagdad, the rite of Hambaleh is adopted.

that the command of the expedition was entrusted; and in the course of it he first showed that eminent natural capacity as an Oriental general, which at a subsequent period attracted the attention of Europe. This prince, endowed with a robust frame which was not until long afterwards weakened by excesses, was a daring and fearless soldier, even far beyond the average of a nation naturally brave. Utterly wanting in knowledge of European strategy, he nevertheless possessed a strong masculine judgment and an intelligence in military matters that placed him far above his compeers, who were ignorant of mathematical science and of the tactics of Europe. He had neither the political acuteness of Mohammed Ali, nor that suavity of manner which his father possessed in so eminent a degree as sometimes to enchant his friends and adherents, while it often served to neutralize the hostile and attract the indifferent. His temper was irritable and even ferocious, so that he would be for days, to his own people, as unapproachable as a tiger in his lair. On the other hand, his nature was more truthful than that of Mohammed Ali. He was not addicted to finesse, and, in fact, despised it: he indulged in no far-stretching schemes for the future, but exercised a vigorous and masculine judgment on what was laid before him. Although stern, severe, and sometimes even cruel, he was perfectly methodical in business; and consequently possessed to a considerable extent the virtue of justice, which is a most essential element of dispatch, and the quickest closer of complicated transactions. If the generosity of Mohammed Ali created and sustained the attachment of adherents, his disorderly prodigality brought him into frequent difficulties. But it was not so with Ibrahim Pasha. His lever was fear—not attachment: he was accumulative for the public treasury and the privy purse, and a stranger to munificence; and it is not to be disputed that one of the principal causes of the trouble which the affairs of Syria gave to the Porte, and to the powers of Europe, was the strict economy and vigilant supervision which Ibrahim Pasha practised in the State and in the army.

In September, 1816, Ibrahim Pasha left Cairo for Arabia; but, instead of proceeding to Suez with his force, he ascended the Nile in boats to Kench, near Thebes; and then, taking with him his artillery and baggage, which were transported on the backs of six thousand camels collected for the purpose, he proceeded across the desert to Cosseir on the Red Sea, and from thence in a fleet of boats and barks that had been provided, crossed over to Sanbo, the port of Medina, from thence immediately proceeding to the Holy City itself. But he did not at once enter into action, the plan of Mohammed Ali, which Ibrahim was instructed to carry out, being to await the union and concentration of the means of attack, and then suddenly to act with decisive vigour.

This plan was successful. The wavering chiefs of the Arab tribes, scattered over the eastern parts of the Hedjaz and the west of the Nejd, at once saw that they had to deal with a man of resolution and energy, who not only had with him large military resources, but who in his first forays had brought in large numbers of camels and cattle. The immediate result of the vigour of Ibrahim Pasha was the defection of several important tribes hitherto entirely in the interest of the Wahabys. But the smallest towns were defended with vigour, and at Derayeh the Wahabys made a final stand with all the resources that remained to them in men and *materiel.* The reduction of this place was the most arduous undertaking of the campaign.

This capital of a warlike and primitive race of Arabs was such a town as might be seen in various parts of the

Peninsula at the period when Mohammed gave forth those doctrines to the simplicity of which the Wahabys wished to return. The pompous fanes of Cairo and Granada found no counterpart in the homely Arab Nejd. Several straggling little towns on the slopes of hills, each surrounded by its wall and bastion, with a few of the simplest mosques, composed the capital of the Wahabys. With a force of less than six thousand men, and a dozen pieces of artillery, Ibrahim Pasha sat down before the place on the 6th of April. Assuredly it was not the masses of combatants that constituted the interest of the final struggle of the puritans of Islamism.

But it was soon seen that the contact of the Turks with the European art of war gave them a preponderating advantage over their opponents behind walls. Although the bastion was a Turkish invention, and had first been constructed at Otranto when there were hopes and fears of Italy sharing the fate of the Greek empire, yet there had been in the Turkish art of war, all through the eighteenth century, a notable absence of the rapid progress in artillery and engineering which had taken place in the armies of Europe ; and it was the quick and unscrupulous appropriation of those European advances in projectiles and drill that really furnished the family of Mohammed Ali with the means of first putting down the resistance of the Oriental forces in their immediate vicinity, and subsequently of creating that power which was turned against the Porte itself.

The Wahabys saw with astonishment the solid curtain and bastion of the detached fort crumble to the dust under the well-directed fire of Ibrahim Pasha's artillery. A panic seized them, and they evacuated the place, leaving behind them their wounded, their ammunition, and their provisions. While the Turks posted to intercept their retreat pursued them into the gardens of the central town, many prisoners were taken, whose heads were cut off, the treasurer of Ibrahim Pasha paying for every pair of ears brought in to him, in accordance with the old Turkish practice. The Turks, following up this advantage, took possession of another height on which were posted two pieces of artillery that gave them much trouble. Ibrahim Pasha thus infused into his troops that confidence of final victory which is half the battle. No sooner was this advantage gained, than fortune still further favoured the besiegers by the arrival of caravans with gun carriages, ammunition, medicines, and an abundance of provisions of various descriptions to sustain both the moral and physical energy of the soldiers.

On the other hand, the besieged were fortified with the courage of despair. They declared to each other, and believed, that surrender would not be followed by quarter—that the male inhabitants would be put to the sword, and the women and valuables would become the property of the ruthless victor. New entrenchments, not directed by science but executed with prodigious activity, were carried out by the defenders, and vigorous sorties kept the besiegers on the alert, while the large extent of ground covered by the scattered capital rendered the strict blockade of the place impossible, so that provisions and supplies from without were from time to time furnished. Nor was the diminution of Turkish life, by the unceasing Wahaby musketry, steadily aimed from the walls at every head that appeared above the trenches, an inconsiderable offset to the decided advantage that Ibrahim Pasha had in artillery served by European officers, and hospitals tended by European medical science. The climate also came in for its share as an active force in the struggle. The heat, dysentery, and ophthalmia, which had but a very slight effect on the besieged, carried its ravages into the Turkish camp. Ibrahim

Pasha himself had an attack of opthalmia, which blinded him for several days; and two months of suffering were spent before this last stronghold of the Wahabys, without any prospect of success being obtained. Another bastion was successfully breached by the European artillery officers; and Ibrahim Pasha, impatient of delay, and eager to make a decided impression on the scattered scheme of Wahaby defence, ordered his men to mount the breach. To his surprise and disappointment, murmurs, succeeded by a mutinous refusal to march, showed the stubborn commander how suffering and despair had torn loose all the bonds of discipline; and, as misfortunes never come single, a frightful accident seemed to interpose a final obstacle to perseverance in the siege.

On the 21st of June, one of those whirlwinds that suddenly rise in Arabia blew some sparks from a camp kitchen fire to a large tent which was the powder and ammunition magazine. In a moment several hundred packages of powder and cartridges flew into the air, with a prodigious explosion that shook the very hills, and scattered burnt and blackened human limbs around. It was at this juncture that Ibrahim Pasha showed an indomitable firmness and courage that rose to heroism. "All is lost," said Ibrahim to the messenger of Ouzoun Ali, his lieutenant, "except our courage and our sabres: tell your master to be on the alert to repel attack, and I will do the same." Without a day's delay, Ibrahim sent off messengers to all the posts in his rear for supplies of powder and ammunition, to make up the losses incurred; and, foreseeing that this crisis would infallibly embolden the Wahabys to attempt sorties, he addressed his troops and stimulated them to fresh efforts. His harangues had all the more effect as coming from a commander who was reserved, rather than given to an expansive loquacity.

These presumptions were fully confirmed by the conduct of the Wahaby chief. Although not endowed with much military talent, the opportunity of striking a successful blow on the besieged was too obvious not to be seized by Abdallah Ebn Souhoud, who, although—from his avarice and lack of genius—enjoying little of the popularity of his father and grandfather, yet was not devoid of personal courage. Accordingly, a party of fifteen hundred Wahabys broke out upon Ibrahim, who gave orders to his people steadily to retire in the direction of an eminence, where three pieces still stood with a sufficiency of ammunition. Incautiously following up what appeared to be an advantage, the Wahabys suddenly found themselves in the midst of showers of grapeshot, which laid low numbers; and, seized with panic, they retreated as suddenly as they had advanced. Abdallah, learning that Ibrahim Pasha was absent from the camp to chastise some villages that supplied the Wahabys with provisions, made another desperate sortie in the intense heat of an Arabian midsummer,—the women braving the balls that whistled about their ears, in order to carry jars of water to cool the lips of their husbands and brothers in the ardour of combat. But the Turks, living in the midst of death, repelled the attack with collected resolution.

Again the tide turned, and while the Wahabys were astonished rather than dismayed at the failure of their efforts, supplies of men, ammunition, and provisions, began gradually to revive the courage of the Turks; and the resources left scattered in his rear, to occupy various parts, being now united at Derayeh, Ibrahim, without waiting for the succours sent by Mohammed Ali, resolved to make a final assault with all his strength. Ordering the artillery to batter uninterruptedly, he at the same time directed the riflemen in the advanced trenches to aim at the embrasures, and pick off the people within the walls. After dark, leaving in the trenches only the men necessary for their defence, he ordered his troops forward, posting cavalry in ambuscade to repel a sortie. At several points, the Wahabys, being prepared for an assault, resisted manfully; but a body of eight hundred infantry penetrating into gardens where they were not expected, the Wahabys were overpowered, and a redoubt defended by artillery was captured. The successful repulse of the Wahabys by the cavalry, and the discouragement produced by the loss of one of their leaders—the brother-in-law of Abdallah, whose right foot was carried away—now effectually turned the scale in favour of Ibrahim.

A fort commanded by Saad, the son of the Wahaby chief, was held by one hundred and fifty men; and, although they had a large store of ammunition and artillery, they had provisions for only two days, under the supposition that they were so far within the circle of defence as not to be exposed to the Turks. These men, being compelled to capitulate, Ibrahim Pasha was able to attack the inner towns of Sahal and Gharybeh, which were not citadels with garrisons, but inhabited by families. The horrors of the siege, which had hitherto been at a distance from the women and children of the besieged Wahabys, were now felt in all their fulness. Showers of shells crumbled to pieces the dwellings of the families of these brave men; and it was amidst the cries of terror-stricken women and children that these two towns capitulated. Tourfieh followed; and, inclosed on all sides in his residence at Toureyf with his family and four hundred black slaves, Abdallah was at length, on the 9th of September, after a bloody five months' siege, compelled to ask for a suspension of arms.

The Wahaby chief, accompanied by two hundred of

his people, went to the tent of Ibrahim, and was well received by him. Abdallah, according to Oriental usage, wished to kiss the hand of the Pasha, who, however, withdrew it; during five months of dogged resolution he had sought victory, not the humiliation of a chief respectable for his valour.

"The war has ended," said Abdallah; "such are the decrees of fate."

"If you wish to hold out, I will supply you with powder and ammunition," said Ibrahim, with a politeness in which the courtesy of chivalry was too largely alloyed with contempt.

"No," said Abdallah, scarcely restraining his tears, "God has willed my humiliation."

Abdallah asked for peace; but Ibrahim informed him that he was not allowed to leave him at Derayeh, his orders being peremptory on that point. On this Abdallah asked for twenty-four hours to consult, and took his leave. Ibrahim, however, ordered patrols of cavalry to be on the outlook lest he should attempt to escape. There can be no doubt that Abdallah, if mounted on a swift dromedary, had a great chance of getting clear off: but his numerous family, his friends, and his capital, were all hostages to Ibrahim; and, fearing lest they might suffer by his flight, he again returned to the Turkish camp, recommending his family to the protection of Ibrahim, and imploring him to do no damage to Derayeh. Promises to this effect were made, and Abdallah, guarded by four hundred horsemen, commenced his journey for Cairo, where he arrived on the 17th of November, 1818.

He was admitted to kiss the hand of Mohammed Ali, who, admiring the courage of the Wahabys, received him with honour, and asked him what he thought of his son Ibrahim. "He has done his duty," said Abdallah, "and we have done ours. Thus has God willed." On the 19th he started for Constantinople, where, notwithstanding his surrender at Derayeh, and the intercession made by Mohammed Ali for his life, he was during three days shewn through the town, and then decapitated with his companions.

The gloom and terror that the news of the death of Abdallah spread over the unhappy Derayeh was but too soon succeeded by the desolation of this devoted city. The valour of its defenders, the natural and artificial strength of its position, the climate fatal to the invader, and its remoteness from the accessible Turkish resources, all conspired to make the Ottoman commander leave behind no such fastness that might endanger a commencement of any future revolt of the puritans of Islamism. In a few brief weeks the melancholy cry of the jackal was heard amid the scenes that lately echoed the hum of a patriarchal Arab capital. Voluntarily the people of Derayeh levelled their walls with the ground to appease the victor. But the root as well as the branch of Derayeh was doomed. The date trees, those many-gifted providers of the nourishment, necessaries, and luxuries of the Arabs, were cut down. Without a metaphor, the axe was laid to the root of the subsistence of Derayeh; while, within the towns, house after house was burnt down, with the express intention of utterly annihilating the place as a residence, and compelling all the inhabitants to seek other abodes.

CHAPTER VI.

THE UPPER NILE, ITS CLIMATE AND TRADE.—CONQUEST OF SENNAAR, DONGOLAH, AND CORDOFAN RESOLVED ON.—THE EGYPTIANS ENTER NUBIA.—THE UPPER NILE OCCUPIED.—ITS MATERIAL ASPECT.—SENAAR AND ITS TRACES OF ARAB CIVILIZATION.—THE COUNTRIES OF THE UPPER NILE ANNEXED.

IF we survey the globe, there is no part of it so thoroughly unknown as that vast Alpine region of eastern central Africa, in which both the White Nile and the Niger take their origin. From the vast volumes of water poured into the Atlantic and the Mediterranean, and from the elevation of the nearer mountains and plateaux already ascertained, it may fairly be presumed that the central peaks rise to heights which rival the great chains of other continents; but the Humboldts of the African Andes have still to appear. The blue river supposed by Bruce to be the great Nile, turns out to be only a brief tributary of this lengthened stream. The true source of the Nile, its situation, its physical region, and human inhabitants are still the great mystery of African geography. Abyssinia, forming the easterly termination of this mountain region before its rapid descent to the Red Sea, is inhabited by a Caucasian race, and has much of the temperature of an European climate: but further to the north, and remoter from the equator, latitude is more than compensated by the cessation of the highlands; for from the entrance of the Nile into the more level country we find the torrid heat and vegetable productions of the tropics, while, instead of the tawny high-featured Ethiopian and Caraite Jew of

Abyssinia, we have the pitch black negro of Senaar and Cordofan.

It was to these regions of the Upper Nile that the Pasha, Mohammed Ali, turned his attention after the fall of Derayeh. If the conquest of the Wahabys added to his renown, it exhausted the resources of Egypt. Arabia, if difficult to obtain from the valour of its inhabitants, was equally disadvantageous to retain, owing to its scanty and dispersed material advantages, as well as the constant liability to rebellion. In the countries beyond Nubia the inhabitants were unskilled in war. Its resources were abundant, valuable, and approximated to the great and accessible highway of the Nile. The climate alone was the worst enemy of the white man. In the time of the Mameluke Sultans, and before the development of the passage by the Cape, Cairo was, through Venetian instrumentality, one of the great magazines of the Indian trade. This, however, had passed away, and it was on the gums, the gold-dust, the ostrich feathers, and other productions of the upper country that those merchants subsisted who tenanted the gorgeous Saracenic khans of the seven saloons of Cairo. But military ambition and mercantile greed had never approached the land confines of Abyssinia, and the extension of the power of the Pasha of Egypt from the Nejd to the Senaar reminds us rather of the Turks in the days of a Selim and a Solyman than of the Ottomans of the nineteenth century of the Christian era.

Nor was it alone by force of arms that Mohammed Ali looked forward to complete the conquest of the semi-barbarous tribes of the upper country. Three ulema learned in the laws and rites of Islamism accompanied the expedition. Their mission was not only to preach the doctrines of the Koran, but at the same time to enforce upon those savage clans the political precept that temporal obedience was strictly due to the heir of the Caliphate.

In June, 1820, three thousand boats were assembled at Cairo for the purpose of easily transporting to the upper country the men, ammunition, and stores requisite for the expedition. Between three and four thousand infantry, with several hundred of the gigantic Ababdeh Arabs, the whole being under the command of Ismael Pasha, one of Mohammed Ali's sons, departed for Assouan; the north-west winds, prevalent at this period, swelling their sails and moderating the intense heat of the summer solstice. At the same time, a force of cavalry ascended the valley of the Nile by land.

The general rendezvous was at Assouan, from whence the little army passed into Nubia. No opposition had hitherto showed itself. This region, beyond the first cataract, where every shred of cultivable territory between the river and the mountain is carefully husbanded, is inhabited by a Berber race, a relic of that vast Numidian nationality which once occupied the greater part of northern Africa; but, driven remote from the coast of the Mediterranean by the Arabs, still straggled in considerable numbers from the Red Sea almost to the Atlantic, and has given to this portion of the world the name of the coast of Barbary. Unwarlike at home, they fulfil servile employments in Cairo, and the forced frugality of the scanty soil of Nubia becomes penuriousness amid the greater plenty of the Egyptian capital. Early to quit the sterile region between the cataracts; laboriously to accumulate pittance on pittance in the domestic servitude of Cairo, and then to return to a semi-independent indolence in Nubia, is the height of the ambition of the modern Berber. A grudging assistance, rather than an opposition, was what Ismael Pasha met with in the date-growing lands of Ibreem and the horse-rearing Dongolah. It was not until five days' march beyond the latter place that opposition first showed itself. The Sheikhieh Arabs attempted to draw the force of Ismael some distance from the Nile, and then attacked it with several thousand men mounted on horses and dromedaries. But the steady and well-directed fire of the Turkish force, now partially drilled and manœuvred to some extent on European principles, sufficed to check this numerous horde with the loss of only a few men. Then, passing the Nile on the backs of their horses, the Turkish cavalry completed the rout, and the army could continue its course.

But the Nile no longer furnished that depth of water which permitted the navigation of large barks; so the troops marched in its vicinity—the infantry in detachments, and the artillery carried on scaffolds supported by two camels abreast. In this way they reached successively Berber and Shendy. These places, where Turks found still some traces of Arab civilization, were governed by "Maleks." This word, which in the large sense is "king," may with reference to these subordinates of the sovereignty of Senaar be accurately entitled "Reeves," as applying to persons seized or possessed of the lieutenancy of power.*

At Shendy, Malek Nimr, unable to resist the force that entered the territory, made a studious display of submission; and the chief of the Sheikhieh, who had retired here on receiving the promise of Ismael that no harm would befal him, expressed himself equally ready to forward this easy conquest, of which he gave substantial proof on the march to Senaar, by pointing out pits in which Indian corn was concealed.

* The original and literal meanings of the titles of the "powers that be" are not uninteresting,—Sultan signifying "power;" Malek, "possession"—hence, "Mameluke" possessed; "Reeve," seizure, seisin. The office in Germanic and Frank is Graf, Greffier: gripe, griffin, and *grab* are derived from it.

All the aspects of nature were now changing to the little army of Ismael Pasha. The great Nile, which only acquires its full volume after the junction of the Abbara which drains Eastern Abyssinia, was above that confluence, and, particularly in the low season, no longer the river of the imposing magnitude they had been accustomed to: further up, above the confluence of the Blue and White Niles, the former—by which they held on their way to Senaar—was still smaller. The alluvial soil of Egypt is a foreign deposit of perennial floods on the Lybian desert; but here they had arrived at a part of the rich aboriginal territorial reservoir itself, where, instead of the scattered artificial groves of palm and crops produced by inundation and irrigation, wide-spread full-growing natural woods reciprocate a heated humidity with those clouds and rains of heaven which are so rare in Upper Egypt. Man, too, is different from the "bonny tawny Moor" of the north coast of Africa; for the tint has gradually sunk through the dusky brown of Nubia to the glossy black of Senaar and the neighbouring Cordofan. The climate is deadly to the European. The true features of Africa, hitherto masked by the cool climate of the environs of the Mediterranean, here reveal themselves. In the Nile, the hippopotamus, which is rare in Egypt, is present in numbers, while the plains are traversed by the winged step of the ostrich and the giraffe; the elephant and the rhinoceros drag their huge bulk through the open glade; the tiger and the panther have their lair in the jungle, and myriads of monkies swarm in lofty trees.

But even in this distant region the blessings of Arab civilization are felt to a certain extent; and, if we are ready to sneer at the decadence of the East, let us remember that this remarkable nation, which transmitted to Europe the civilization of the Romans and Greeks, has scattered far into the heart of Africa scintillations of its own laws, ethics, arts, and manufactures. The Koran has for ages attuned the souls of these low races to a poetry and a morality far above the grovelling level of the aboriginal mind; and in this world of material want the town of Senaar presented to the eyes of the Egyptians smiths, jewellers, carpenters, masons, tailors, weavers, and tanners, who rudely resembled those of Cairo. But in this land of the vigorous generation and production of the animal and vegetable kingdoms agriculture was still further behind. The plough was unknown. A pike, pressed with the foot so as to make an aperture in the ground, was the native substitute for an instrument familiar to the Egyptians from the days of the Pharaohs. Here all was primeval; the land was measured by stone-casts, and the waters of the Nile were crossed by the Senaarry, with his wife and children, on the back of an ox, or swimming alone assisted by a log-float. It was only considerably down the Nile that navigation was available for the slaves, the gums, and the ostrich feathers which Senaar exchanged for the coffee of Arabia, and the products of the looms of Cairo and Manchester.

Circumstances favoured the advance of the son of Mohammed Ali; and those regions in which he was soon after to perish by the hand of a patriot assassin were, in the first instance, annexed to the Pashalic of Egypt without any attempt at resistance. Disunion was in the councils of the two brothers who held the power at Senaar: one, who wished to give in to Ismael, was treacherously murdered by his brother; but the other, unable to raise a party, or organise a force competent to resist the invader, was compelled to fly. Mohammed, a deposed king of Senaar who had some years been languishing in a prison, resumed the shadowy sceptre; and, acknowledging himself to be the faithful vassal of Sultan

Mahmoud, the invader became his liberator from bondage—the constituent of his renewed lease of power, and the captor of his rival, who narrowly escaped death at the hands of Ismael, and was only saved at the intercession of the sheikhs. Thus fell the Upper Nile into the power of the family of Mohammed Ali, a fief which his grandson still holds of his sovereign. But it was long before this acquisition was consolidated. Years of massacre, revolt, pillage, and conflagration, accompanied and followed the death of Ismael, which so soon clouded the satisfaction with which Mohammed Ali viewed the lustre of his family, and the extension of his dominion to the confines of Abyssinia.

The exactions, insults, and haughty demeanour of Ismael had so exasperated Malek Nimr at Shendy, that this barbarian collected large quantities of straw, under pretext of forage, feigned a dancing festival, and, after nightfall, surrounded the dwelling of the son of Mohammed Ali with his men, and drove the attendants of Ismael into the house. Then, lighting the straw, the house took fire, and those who escaped the sword perished in the conflagration. Such was the end of Ismael Pasha.

CHAPTER VII.

Revolution of Manners in Egypt.—New Organization of the Army and its Administrative Departments.—Improvement of Alexandria.—The Canal of Alexandria.—Egyptian Manufactures not successful.—The Pasha fosters Education.—Civil Administration.—The Overland Passage to India revived.—Palaces and Gardens of Mohammed Ali.—His extensive and intelligent Intercourse with Europeans.

It was at the close of the European struggle of the first fifteen years of this century that Mohammed Ali began that great revolution of manners which so utterly changed the social, political, and mercantile aspect of Egypt. The vast superiority of Europe in arts and arms was too evident to all men of intelligence to be longer resisted. But the association of the reforms with a religion which is odious and even contemptible to the Moslems was the great obstacle to an attempt at a general change. Sultan Selim had lost life and throne in the attempt; and it was by a miracle that Mahmoud and Mohammed Ali died in their beds. These two extraordinary men, subsequently sworn foes of each other, moved in parallel lines to the combat of the most obstinate prejudices of the modern Turk and Arab.

But it was no easy matter in these earlier stages. Mohammed Ali had no sooner, in August, 1815, announced his intention to discipline his troops in the European manner, than a revolt broke out among them; the bazaars were plundered, and Mohammed Ali himself was obliged to retire behind the towers and solid walls of the castle of Saladin, in order to save himself from a planned assassination. But this momentary burst of discontent had to give way to the settled unalterable resolves and persevering plans of the Pasha, now secure in his stronghold. Some of the leaders of the troops were gained by largesse, and the rest intimidated into submission. The first step was a costly one; and in course of time the discipline of Europe became habitual not only to the Egyptian, Turk, and Arab, but even to the negroes from the upper country, who were formed into corps and trained to the manual and platoon exercise under the care of Monsieur Seves, an officer of the army of Bonaparte, who, being thrown out of a career in France by the events of 1815, sought his fortunes in Egypt, and, having embraced Islamism, had since risen to the highest military rank under the name of Soliman Pasha.

This new organization of the army subsequently developed itself in large proportions. A school of infantry officers was formed at El Khankah, where languages and military exercises were taught. On the other side of the Nile the palace of Murad Bey, so repeatedly mentioned during the campaign of the Pyramids, became a cavalry school where another soldier of the imperial armies, Monsieur Varin, instructed a corps in the equitation and drill of Europe on those very sands where, since the days of Saladin, the Mameluke youth had been taught to use the mace and sabre against Tartar and Crusader.

Nor was artillery neglected. This arm, often so decisive and important, had to be created in a country where pieces cast in the seventeenth century still garnished the walls of forts, and were directed by men who had not the rudest elements of those mathematical and technical acquirements which knit the art of the artilleryman so closely to the science of the engineer. It was the artillery well pointed against the impetuous Mameluke cavalry that had decided the fate of Egypt at

Embabeh, and Mohammed Ali was not the man to neglect the lesson. A Spanish colonel, Seguera, organised the artillery school of Mohammed Ali, so much to his satisfaction that the rank of bey was conferred, with many expressions of content; for the Greek war and the other embarrassments of the Ottoman empire left Mohammed Ali virtual master of Egypt, and dispensing honours within the attributes of the sovereign. The Divan, anxious to profit by his talents and resources, swallowed these affronts, biding the time when some conjuncture in the vortex of affairs might enable them to make Mohammed Ali share the fate of other powerful individuals, who, keeping their heads for a time above water, had been ultimately swallowed up in the *system* of the Porte.

Master of a large revenue—in the prime of his talents and activity—and virtually independent of the Porte, Mohammed Ali neglected none of the auxiliary roads to the consolidation of his power. A large part of the citadel was turned into an arsenal where the skilled workmen of England and Europe directed the industry of hundreds of native Egyptians in the casting of cannon, and accoutering of the soldiers from head to foot. The tide was at the flood, and Mohammed Ali took it with matchless confidence and precision.

At the period of the French invasion Alexandria was at its lowest ebb of decadence. It was no longer the prosperous emporium of the Venetian trade: within and without its precincts, the ruins of warehouses, mosques and tombs, chiefly met the eye. But at the conclusion of the Anglo-French war its commerce began rapidly to increase; and Mohammed Ali, not content with having an army on the European model, conceived the idea of having also a navy, of which Alexandria should be the arsenal. He had already got frigates constructed at Venice and Marseilles; and conscious of the multiplied power which a naval predominance gives even to small armies, he, in the year 1829, commissioned Monsieur Cerisy, of Marseilles, to construct a naval arsenal in Alexandria, an institution which subsequently assumed large proportions. French naval instructors were also drawn to Egypt, and Turco-Egyptian pupils received a practical training in the dockyards and on board the ships of war of England. Various other French and English engineers rendered signal service to Mohammed Ali, among whom we may mention Galloway Bey, a man of signal ability.

With a view of getting a large revenue out of Egypt, of the resources of which he was now so to speak exclusive master, Mohammed Ali readily opened his ears to all projects which might bring back to this favoured land its former productiveness; and none seemed so suitable as the cultivation of cotton, for which both the soil and the climate are eminently favourable, while the large demand for this raw material in the manufacturing centres of Europe left no doubt as to a market being found for it. An inferior cotton plant was indigenous to the soil of Egypt; but it was the introduction of the American sea island cotton plant that formed so great an epoch in the modern history of Egypt: and its extension produced a large proportion of that considerable revenue which gave such a financial lever to the Pasha in his subsequent struggles with the Porte. The indigo culture went in companionship with that of cotton. The West had furnished the former, while from the East Indies were brought cultivators of indigo, who introduced into the valley of the Nile those improved processes through which the products of Hindostan had for generations excluded the indigo of Egypt from the markets of Europe. From Asia Minor were brought rayahs skilled in the culture of opium, and thus another important and lucrative branch was added to the agricultural productions of Egypt. The plantation of forest trees has, at the same time, gradually diminished the extreme dryness of the climate of Egypt, and showers of rain are now less rare and extraordinary than they were at the beginning of the century. Nor was the ornamental neglected. In the delicious island of Raoudah, between Cairo and the Pyramids, and in which the Mamelukes used to enjoy the shade of the sycamore and the orange, Ibrahim Pasha, through the instrumentality of a Scotch horticulturist, planted a garden which the hot sun and abundant water of the basin of the Nile rapidly developed into a most luxuriant growth of whatever could delight the eye, the taste, or the sense of perfume. Here were the bamboo of India, with its heat and shade; the fruits of the Antilles; the spices of the Asiatic Islands; and the fauna and flora of the Amazons, with their magnifoliage, their brilliancy, and endless variety. Here was the science of the horticulturist, and here the taste of the landscape gardener, who agreeably surprised the Briton with a park, showing the variety of natural scenery, but the details of tropical vegetation as a substitute for the arboriculture of the grove, and the glades of our northern demesnes.

The Nile is the great artery of Egyptian commerce; but neither its Rosetta nor its Damietta mouths are favourable ports for those large vessels of long course through which an extensive foreign trade can be kept up. The contest between the sands of the sea, and an impetuous river holding so large an amount of alluvium in solution during its course, and depositing it so largely at its mouths, has created bars which render Rosetta and Damietta fit only for the reception of those numerous coasting barks which carry the rice and corn of Egypt to the rocky and less alluvial coasts of Syria. The port of

Alexandria—defective in some respects, not only from exposure to the north-west winds, but also from want of depth at the entrance—is still the only one in Egypt fit to be a naval arsenal and a great emporium of commerce. But it is situated at some distance from the Rosetta branch of the Nile. The restoration of the canal connecting Alexandria with the river, was therefore one of the most useful and important works of Mohammed Ali. It bore the name of Sultan Mahmoud, and commemorates the verbal homage to the Sovereign, with which this crafty chief honeyed over the bitterest potions he administered. The canal itself, however, has proved of much benefit in connecting the only considerable port of Egypt with the artery of the Nile, the populous capital, and the productive Delta; and until the opening of the railway between Alexandria and Cairo it was largely used for the overland transit to India.

Under the influence of this commercial development the aspect of Alexandria rapidly changed. Houses in the European fashion covered the Frank quarter, and the merchants, no longer confined in khans, peopled the streets and squares that rose up in the vicinity of the new port, and spread their villas and gardens along the banks of the canal. Several large English, French, and Greek houses carried on a most extensive and lucrative commerce. Messrs. Briggs and Thurburn, a great British firm, in one year purchased the whole of the cotton crop of Egypt. It is impossible not to condemn the methods by which the Pasha came into possession of so much private landed property; but the improvement, in the adaptation of the culture of this rich region to the commercial wants of Europe, showed an energy and an intelligence beyond his age and nation.

It is impossible to assign the same praise to the manufacturing efforts of the Pasha. Under the impression that, as Egypt possessed materials such as cotton and indigo, the land of their raw production might also be the seat of their manufacture, he forgot that a government trenching on the sphere of private speculation in a country where all nations shun labour, and to which nature has denied coal, could never compete with manufacturing countries abounding with individual enterprise and capital, as well as in the coal, the iron, and the schools of mechanical ingenuity which designate by broad and unmistakeable lines the spheres in which agricultural or manufacturing industry can develope themselves with success. In short, the manufacturing schemes of Mohammed Ali were an utter failure, with some few exceptions, such as the red woollen Tunis cap-making, carried on at Fouah under economical conditions similar to those of Barbary; and which—forming an indispensable part of oriental costume, even as modernised—found a ready market in Egypt itself.

The medical and educational institutions introduced by Mohammed Ali into Egypt deserve every praise. At the period of the French invasion the science of medicine, once so esteemed and studied by the Arabs, had declined into ignorance and imposture. Simples, juggles, and talismans were all jumbled up together in the practice of the native Egyptian; who, not content with the symptoms of a disease as a key to the remedy to be applied, would superadd fanciful calculations suggested by the names of the relatives of the patient. To Dr. Clot, a native of Marseilles, afterwards raised to the rank of bey, Egypt owes the establishment of medical institutions, comprising civil hospitals, in Cairo and the provinces; the organization of the medical service of the army; and last, not least, the establishment of a medical school which turns out young surgeons both for the military and the civil service.

The insane, who used to be kept chained in barred dens, like wild beasts, were taken away from the hospital of Kalaon, where many an Indian overland traveller has seen this afflicting and degrading spectacle, and tended in accordance with the humane usages of modern Europe. In the great plague of 1835, which carried off one hundred and fifty thousand souls—of whom thirty-five thousand were in Cairo alone—Clot Bey distinguished himself by his zeal and courage. "You have come out of a battle that has lasted six months," said Mohammed Ali to him, in acknowledging his services.

A council of public instruction was organized by Mohammed Ali, chiefly with a view to the military and civil service of the government; not confined to Turks and ignoring the native Arab Egyptians, as had been hitherto the case in Egypt, but reviving the system of Sultan Hassan in developing the native Arab element. In this respect Mohammed Ali went far beyond the renowned Mameluke Sultan. Not only were numerous European scientific works translated into Arabic, and made text-books in the medical and polytechnic schools, but French was taught as the most convenient opening to the knowledge of Europe, and pupils were sent to England and France in order to complete the studies begun in Egypt.

A complete revolution took place in the internal government of Egypt. All oligarchy was merged in one common vortex, with a majority of the titles to landed property. The Pasha became almost the one great landlord of this magnificent and productive domain, while a new and uniform bureaucratic system was applied to Egypt, which was divided into great provinces ruled over by mudirs, who maintained the canals, apportioned the cultivation of the land, and collected the harvest and revenue. These provinces were subdivided into districts under mamours, who immediately supervised the details of agriculture and revenue, and who possessed summary police powers. Thus Egypt became nearly one great farm, held at a nominal rental of the Sultan. From this Mohammed Ali derived the usufruct: his bureaucracy were the overseers, and the population of Egypt the servants. Under this system the state grew to compactness, symmetry, and power; but the opulence, the ease, and the liberty of private individuals was extinguished. The landed gentry and the wealthy ulema gradually declined. The upper servants of the State, enjoying large salaries, took the place in society formerly occupied by the Mameluke beys and sheikhs, holders of landed property. The oppression of individuals grew excessive. It was no longer the sudden exaction of the Mameluke bey, followed by an interval of exemption; but a terroristic and inhuman systematic pressure on the labour and resources of every individual. Nor was the heavy new taxation confined to agricultural provinces. A classified capitation tax, entitled "ferdeh" (individual or personal) was collected from the towns with extreme rigour, and the bastinado applied in all cases where the tax was in arrear, and often with little regard to the ability to pay.

The most favourable side of the new system introduced into Egypt was the improved police, the protection of the Franks residing in towns from native insolence and fanaticism, the security of roads and of the great highway of the Nile to both the native and the foreign traveller, and the transformation of the Bedouin tribes on the borders of the cultivated land—from men whose hands were against every man into auxiliaries of civilization, into breeders of camels, and carriers of merchandize; so that, from being one of the most insecure countries for a European traveller, Egypt became a land in which the stranger might peregrinate without fear of molestation.

The salient circumstance in this revolution of manners was the resumption of the overland transit to India by way of Egypt ; the development of the steam navigation, and the police order produced in Egypt by Mohammed Ali, concurring simultaneously to this end. In the latter part of the eighteenth century, the great extension of the British empire in India had caused attention to be drawn to the necessity of a more direct communication between the dependency and the dominant country than by the long and circuitous route which Portuguese enterprise had opened by the Cape of Good Hope. Two ships—the Endeavour and the Enterprise—were fitted out for the purpose of keeping up the communication between Bombay and Suez ; but the dangerous and uncertain navigation, and the unsettled condition of Egypt under Mameluke rule, proved obstacles to any decided preponderance of advantage over the longer route, with its trade winds and ample sea room. The orderly Egyptian police, and the rising steam school of Britain in the nineteenth century, however, created facilities which were not to be thrown away; and, without entering into details with which every newspaper reader of this age is familiar, it may be stated that passengers and letters are now conveyed overland to India with as much safety and regularity as the most fastidious can desire, and with that celerity which characterizes the railway communications of the most civilized countries of Europe.

But long continued and painful efforts were requisite at the outset in order to establish the communication. It was with a single carpet-bag of letters that Waghorn—a naval officer of extraordinary shrewdness and corporeal activity—first crossed the desert as the more immediate harbinger of the revived overland transit. Steamers on the Nile were slowly organised, while, from England to Alexandria, the communication was kept up by Admiralty steam vessels; and, at length, in 1840, a wealthy mercantile company, under contract to the British Government, placed on both the Mediterranean and Indian Red Sea lines steamships of power, dimension, and accommodation, commensurate with British science and British capital.

Nor were the other maritime powers of Europe idle. If France, and still more Austria, are unequal to Britain in maritime resources, they possess, in the vicinity of the ports of Marseilles and Trieste to the African continent, and the scales of the Levant, a manifest advantage over any country of the north of Europe, of which they have not failed to avail themselves by the establishment of extensive schemes of steam navigation to those Eastern parts. These facilities the natives of Britain have taken the fullest advantage of, because regarding them—in accordance with the enlarged maxims of modern economical science—with feelings of honourable rivalry rather than of a timid and ungenerous jealousy.

Passing from the public institutions of Egypt to the private establishments of the Pasha, we find him constructing or embellishing luxurious habitations in Alexandria, and in Cairo and its environs. The season was usually passed in the latter capital after the heats of summer had ceased, the apartments of the Pasha looking out on a garden perched on the summit of the citadel. Below was the wide-stretched city—not an unbroken expanse of roofs, but varied more than any other city, either of the East or West, with the numerous and beautiful domes and minarets of the various phases of Saracenic architecture—from the melon-crowned fanes of the lieutenants of the Caliphs of Bagdad to the lightest, airiest, and most elegant minarets of the Circassian Sultans, under whom the Moslem architecture of Egypt arrived at perfection in fantastic grace and unimitative local quaintness, before its decline into the unartificial baldness of the common Turkish type.

Winter in this delicious climate implies the cessation of the overpowering heats that prostrate the energies of the natives of northern countries, but not the privation of bright exhilarating sunshine, or of the luxuriant vegetation of the tropics. At Shoubrah—a short distance from Cairo down the Nile, and connected with it by a continuous avenue of acacias and sycamores—was a garden and pavilion, the reverse of the rich wildness of Roda. Here, thick groves of the luxuriant orange were disposed in symmetrical mazes, alleys, and terraces in the style of Italy; while the numerous jets of a fountain cooled the midday atmosphere of the pavilion.

Whatever Mohammed Ali may have been as a political character, no man showed more consummate tact and courtesy in the reception of strangers. Whether it were the diplomatic or commercial agent of an European Power, or the passing traveller attracted by the wonders of the valley of the Nile, this Pasha, untutored in universities and unlearned in the European boundaries and subdivisions of human knowledge, could yet read at a glance the nature of man; and by the intuition of genius was marvellously successful in saying the right thing at the right time. His demeanour was perfectly free from pomp and hauteur; and all his most important political and commercial business was carried on with an easy garrulity which, in politics, like playful humour in literature, is often one of the most unmistakeable characteristics of power.

Knowing well that he was in his own person one of

the curiosities of Egypt, and anxious to stand well with Europe, he was by no means unwilling, when occasion offered, to make himself the topic of conversation. The learned and ingenious Sir John Bowring has preserved a specimen of this vein.

"'Do not judge me by the standard of your knowledge. Compare me with the ignorance that is around me. We cannot apply the same rules to Egypt as to England: centuries have been required to bring you to your present state; I have had only a few years. You have numbers of intelligent persons who comprehend their rulers and carry on their work. I can find very few to understand me and do my bidding. I am often deceived, and I know I am deceived; whereas many are deceived and do not know it. I seek everybody who can give me information.'

"'I have been almost alone for the greater part of my life, finding nobody except Boghos Bey to second me. It was only for the last fifteen years that I can say I have lived; and now I can accomplish more in four years than in the fifteen that are past. I doubted the aptitude even of my own children—even of Ibrahim Pasha; but I have now learned that he is to be relied upon and fully trusted. We cannot go on as fast as we wish, nor do everything we desire to do. If I were to put on Colonel Campbell's trousers (looking at the Consul-General who is six feet high), would that make me as tall as Colonel Campbell?'

"'Europeans who come to Egypt often think that they can do with Arabs just what they can do with their own people. They are wanting what they cannot get; and fancy the Arabs will work as Europeans work, and this cannot be. When I went to Upper Egypt, an officer was recommended to me as a very distinguished man, and I was told that at all events I must secure his services, and I did so. So he came to me, and I asked what I was to do to have things settled according to his notions; and he answered, "You must have this, and this, and this." To which I said, "But this, and this, and this are not to be had." So I sent him about his business.'

"'Your country, England, has reached its present eminence by the labours of many generations; and no country can be made suddenly great and flourishing. Now I have done something for Egypt. I have begun to improve her; and she may be compared, in some respects, not only with Eastern, but with European countries. I have much to learn, and so have my people; and I am now sending Edhem Bey with fifteen young men to learn what your country can teach. They must see with their own eyes; they must learn to work with their own hands; they must examine your manufactures; they must try to discover how and why you are superior to us; and when they have been among your people a sufficient time, they must come home and instruct my people.'

"'The English have made many great discoveries, but the best of their discoveries is that of steam navigation.' I told him that the inventor of steam navigation was an American, and he replied, 'Had they not had fathers like you, they would not have been such clever children.'

"'I had not the benefits of early education. I was forty-seven years old when I learned to read and write. I have never seen countries more civilized than my own; so I do not expect to do what you are able to do, and to reach the height at which you have arrived.'

"'The difficulty is to begin. I had to begin by scratching the soil of Egypt with a pin; I have now got to cultivate it with a spade; but I mean to have all the benefit of a plough.'

"He frequently spoke of the difference between European and Oriental modes of government. Once he said to me, 'In your country you must have a great many hands to move the machine of state; I move it with my own. I do not always exactly see what is best to be done; but when I do see it, I compel prompt obedience to my wishes, and what is seemingly best *is* done.'"

Thus the reader may see that Mohammed Ali had not only the masculine intelligence and will to govern Orientals; but also some amount of wit, with its expansive and illustrating power, to recommend him with plausibility to intelligent Europeans who visited Egypt. Strong and general predispositions were thus engendered in his favour, both in European society and in the European press, which even his subsequent unjustifiable proceedings to the Porte only partially removed.

CHAPTER VIII.

Retrospect of Turkish History.—The Greek Revolution.—Causes of the Maintenance of the Turkish Power in Europe.—Conduct of Mohammed Ali during the Greek War.—Energy of Sultan Mahmoud.—Mohammed Ali purposes to Invade Syria.—Ibrahim Pasha Besieges Acre.—Acre Surrenders to Ibrahim.—The Turks Defeated at Homs.—The Battle of Konieh Gained by the Egyptians over the Turks.—Arrangement at Kiutahia.

While Mohammed Ali was consolidating his power, that of the Sultan was threatened with imminent dissolution.

It was in the middle of the 17th century that Turkey found herself at the maximum of her dominion. The Empire of the East being completely absorbed, the Greeks had not even a glimmering of hope that their emancipation would take place. The Armenians of Asiatic Turkey had been so thoroughly absorbed, that, although Christians, they had even adopted Turkish as their vernacular language. The Servian state of Stephan Dushan had been entirely incorporated with Turkey. Hungary, since 1526, had shared the same fate, with the exception of a few countries on the Austrian frontier, which were the debateable lands between the Turk and the Emperor.

Three great states stood firm against the almost overwhelming tide of Ottoman invasion—the Empire of Germany, the Kingdom of Poland, and the maritime Republic of Venice; and all three contributed in a remarkable manner to the turning back of this terrible inundation. The raising of the siege of Vienna by the aid of Poland was followed by the conquest of Hungary by the armies, generals, and resources of the House of Hapsburg; and, accompanied by a vigorous flank movement of the Venetians in Dalmatia, brought about those treaties of Carlovitz and Passarovitz, which restored the central basin of the Danube to Christendom. From this period dates the German civilization of Hungary; and from this period Turkey ceased to be imminently dangerous to Europe. But the decline of the Ottoman Empire arose not only from the loss of territory, but from her remaining relatively so far in arrear of the science and military organization of Europe, which arose from the strictly binding spirit of the Moslem religion, as well as from that indisposition to the persevering processes of science which characterises all the Ugrian races from Hungary to Tartary. Great strength of will, considerable finesse in discovering and defeating the schemes of their seditious and rebellious rayahs, and great bravery to combat the open foe in the field of battle, have in all ages been the distinguishing characteristics of the Ottoman Turks. But after the art of war had in modern times been subjected to extraordinary improvements by a Turenne, a Vauban, an Eugene, a Marlborough, and a Frederick—not to advance in proportion was for the Turks to retrograde. Indisposed themselves to adopt the new science of Europe, their national and religious pride revolted at being commanded by men they counted infidels; and being in the latter part of the eighteenth century pitted against the rising power of Russia—a nation essentially imitative, and greedily adoptive of the talent of Western Europe—the result was a further loss of all the rich territories on the north of the Black Sea and Caspian from the Pruth to the mouths of the Volga.

It was with no complacent eye that Austria, in the beginning of the nineteenth century—now no longer hostile to Turkey—saw that, where she had sown, Russia reaped so largely; and though she was more deeply engaged than Russia in the struggle that sprung out of the French Revolution of 1792, the latter had comparatively free play in her pressure on Turkey. Domestic revolt, too, came in aid of foreign invasion, and the Servian rising of 1804–6 and the succeeding years, headed by the heroic Karu George, was only too deplorably justified by the tyranny and oppression exercised by the old unreformed Turkish Government on this brave and meritorious population. The remains of the Empire were consumed by a feudal system that had taken the place of that administrative unity and compact power which had been wielded with such tremendous effect by the Selims and the Solymans. Bosnia, the seat of a heroic population which occupied the great bastion of mountain territory forming the north-west angle of Turkey in Europe, was divided into numerous districts, each ruled over by a bey—generally a descendant of those Croat nobles who, in the fifteenth century, had embraced Islamism; and who now, from fear of Christian emancipation, gave the Porte partial succours in the suppression of the Servian revolt, but steadily resisted an administrative fusion with the rest of the empire. The state of Albania was even worse. In the pashalic of Yanina, Ali Pasha Tepelene had raised up an *imperium in imperio*, in which the power and authority of the Porte was openly and successfully defied, as if this part of the Adriatic had been utterly foreign to the Ottoman dominions. Even in Asia Minor, which is the heart's core of the empire, and the especial seat of the Turkish population, the Dereh Beyliks, or beyships of the valleys, constituted a group of turbulent feudal baronies, holden of the Porte by slight and unwilling tenures, and in which the welfare of the feeble

State was subordinate to the interests of the potent vassal.

But the hardest blow was yet to come. The Greek population of the southern part of Turkey in Europe and the islands, maintaining more intimate relations with Christendom than any other Rayah nations, conceived the idea of a resurrection on the ruins of the superincumbent Ottoman element. With a few rare exceptions, the Greeks of the eighteenth and preceding centuries were sunk in illiterateness; but, in the nineteenth, by their inborn intelligence, they quickly imitated the civilization of Europe. Wealth was gained by merchandize and navigation; the youth frequenting the medical schools of Christendom assimilated readily to the habits of the European capitals, and heard on all sides expressions of sympathy with Greece and of hatred and contempt for Turkey. The writings of Chateaubriand, and other honest and eloquent but vain and superficial men, became known to the few, while the great bulk of the nation was conscious of the grandeur of its antecedents—conscious that no epic poet had surpassed its own Homer, and that no human intelligence had ever approached—much less equalled—that of Aristotle in variety and profundity. The capital bore the name of the first and, in some respects, the greatest of the Eastern Cæsars; and even those beyond the pale of the church that they styled orthodox conceded to them a preference in the vain pretensions of an apostolic succession over the younger church of Rome. This recollection of the genius of Attica, and the colossal proportions of the political and legal fabric of empire, combined with the visible presence of the still standing Eastern church, was more than enough to inflame the pride of any nation, while Europe was auxiliary and sympathising.

But the power of Turkey in Europe, although seriously menaced, was not overthrown; for in the great moral qualities of sincerity and bravery, the intelligent and mercantile modern Greek is (particularly as regards the former virtue) inferior to the Osmanli Turk. Moreover, the great bulk of Turkey in Europe, from the Gulf of Thessalonica to the mouths of the Danube, and from Adrianople to the borders of Albania, is inhabited not by Greeks, but by Bulgarians, who have formed a sort of dead weight which neither their Greek, Servian, nor Russian co-religionists have been able to utilise against the Porte. The Greek, with his intelligence and the assistance of Europe, has proved a formidable enemy to the Porte. The Servian, by his dogged energy, bravery, and patriotism, has made an unseemly gap in the administrative unity of Turkey in Europe; while Russia, with her vast resources, pressed so frequently, so long, and so heavily on the Ottoman Empire, as to alarm and stir up the first powers of Europe to place limits to her aggressions. But the Bulgarian, orthodox Greek by religion, and far outnumbering either Greek or Servian, has, from peculiarities of national character, proved far from hostile to the Ottoman Power in Europe.

As this peculiar political *vis inertiæ* of the Bulgarians is at the root of the apparently unaccountable tenure of Turkey in Europe by so small a proportion of Moslems; as, to every thinker of large views, there is a direct and immediate relation between the extreme regions of every heterogeneous empire in questions of general cohesion and continued supremacy of the dominant race or dynasty; and as, in this particular Ottoman Empire, the disturbance of that supremacy by the Greeks gave a freer scope to Mohammed Ali, while the Russian war of 1828–9 contributed still farther to the rise of this remarkable man,—it has been impossible, in our survey of the condition of Turkey immediately preceding the open revolt of Mohammed Ali, to leave out of view this peculiarity of the Turkish rule in Europe. It is also impossible to write the history of Egypt and ignore Turkey in Europe; and the pressure of Russia on Turkey cannot be elucidated without taking into account the events of which Egypt, Syria, and Asia Minor were the theatre.

To the existence of this laborious, obedient, and we may even say submissive Bulgarian race, may be fairly attributed the hindrances which the Greeks experienced in attempting anything like the revival of a Byzantine kingdom, or empire, on the fertile plains of Thrace and Macedonia; and the restriction of Greek emancipation to the Morea and a small part of the neighbouring country, with a few islands in the Ægean Sea.

It is not however our intention to describe in detail the successive phases of the Greek Revolution, which belong rather to the history of Europe than of the Arab races. But, although the excessive exhaustion which resulted therefrom to the Ottoman Empire favoured the internal consolidation of the power of Mohammed Ali, it is at the same time impossible to deny that he performed his duty vigorously to his sovereign, the Sultan, during these vicissitudes. No sooner had the Greek Revolution shown its formidable character, than Mohammed Ali, in 1821, sent a squadron of sixteen vessels, large and small, well provisioned, and carrying eight hundred land troops, to join the Ottoman squadron in the Dardanelles; and, on its being seen that the revolt in the Morea could not be suppressed by the ordinary forces of Roumelia, an army of twelve thousand men, disciplined in the European manner, was despatched to the Morea under Ibrahim Pasha in August, 1825.

No reasonable person can doubt that the suppression of the Greek rising would have been ultimately accomplished; but the battle of Navarino, on the 20th of October, 1827, being terminated by the destruction of the Turkish and Egyptian squadron, and followed by the active military and diplomatic intervention of France, Britain, and Russia, Greece was henceforth lost to the Porte. In this concurrence of domestic revolt and foreign war, at a period of the decline of her political institutions, Turkey was like a ship in a storm, whose crew were in a mutiny, and whose tackle was worthless and worn out. But, in the midst of this tremendous crisis, the gigantic political figure of Sultan Mahmoud appeared at the post of the pilot, weathering the storm with a genius and an energy that challenges the admiration and sympathy of the world. From north, south, east, and west, the elements seemed to gather themselves together for a final effort which should engulf the Ottoman vessel of State; but it was not written in the book of fate that the hour of the break-up was arrived. At the darkest crisis of the tempest, the soul of this great semi-barbarian never quailed. Bursts of passionate rage occasionally made his mind the too faithful mirror of the wild uproar of the political elements around him; but his spirit rose with the buffets he had to contend with, and he died at the helm just before the dawn of a new era for Turkey, and its entrance into the calmness and security of a general pacification, which guaranteed the integrity and independence of the State by the five great Powers of Europe.

Mohammed Ali had certainly a genius of greater range than that of Mahmoud; but he had fewer difficulties to contend with, in destroying a perverse and selfish oligarchy: for the breaking of the Mameluke power was already done to his hands by Bonaparte, and there was no grievous pressure from without on the capital stock of the resources which he wielded in Egypt. In fact, from the isolation and productiveness of the country, the gaps made by the Greek war were soon filled up. It was otherwise with the empire at large, governed by Sultan Mahmoud; for, after the janissary power was broken, and before his civil and military reforms were completed, the Russian wars of 1828-9 brought Turkey into the most grievous difficulties; while the disastrous invasion of Roumelia, which ended with the treaty of Adrianople, was like an assault on one of Turkey's own fortresses, when the old crenellated towers had been knocked down, but before the new fortifications were completed.

We have hitherto freely eulogised the conduct of Mohammed Ali—his personal courage and political skill, the generosity and nobility of his nature, and that superiority to the prejudices of his nation and religion which made Egypt a secure asylum, and even an agreeable residence for persons of all creeds. But we now come to the second part of his career, which the most sympathising must utterly condemn; in which a reckless ambition prompted him to trample underfoot the most solemn obligations, and allured him by the prospect of independent power to strike his sovereign and august benefactor in that moment of aggravated exhaustion and prostration when, by all the laws of humanity, he had a right to claim undeviating obedience and eager assistance. Mohammed Ali maintained a traitorous correspondence with those chiefs of Roumelia who were opposed to the unfeudalising tendencies of Sultan Mahmoud; but the severe example that had been made in the person of Ali Pasha of Yanina, a few years before, rendered the Pasha of Scodra apprehensive of engaging in the intrigue, and he at once placed the communications in the hands of the Porte.

Mohammed Ali, not daring publicly to declare war

against the Sultan, of whom he held his investiture, accused his neighbour, Abdullah Pasha of Acre, of favouring the export of the products of Upper Egypt viâ the Syrian desert, instead of by Alexandria—an act of self-condemnation on the part of the ruler of Egypt; for trade will never leave its natural and legitimate channels and issues, unless it be diverted by a monopoly, or by some interruption repugnant to sound administration. To blame Abdullah Pasha for the results of his own unsound economical theory and practice, recals the fable of the wolf and the lamb. The Porte vindicated its dignity by pointing out that the governor of one province could not make himself the censor and disciplinarian of a neighbouring governor, without trenching on the prerogatives of sovereignty. But these reasonings had no effect on Mohammed Ali, who was bent on the conquest of Syria, for which the acts of Abdullah were merely the pretext.

The number of men with which Ibrahim Pasha, who was named General-in-chief, undertook the conquest of Syria, was far larger than that which Bonaparte led across the desert to Acre; and equalled, if it did not surpass, those with which the whole French expedition to Egypt was attempted—amounting to six regiments of infantry, four of cavalry, and a proportionate force of artillery—in all between thirty and forty thousand men. Nor is this surprising. Having unlimited authority in Egypt, the whole population was at the disposal of Mohammed Ali; and his large revenue enabled him to complete the scientific armament of this army, by European aid; while Egypt, having been from time immemorial the granary of Syria, the advantages of commissariat, so important in military operations, were entirely on the side of the invading force.

A large squadron effected a passage by sea, carrying

the heavy artillery, ammunition, and supplies, and having on board Ibrahim Pasha and his staff, including Solyman Bey (the French officer of the empire, named Selves, already mentioned); while the cavalry and the bulk of the infantry, having started for El Arish in the first days of November, 1831, crossed the desert, and having taken Gaza and Jaffa without meeting with resistance, the squadron and the army effected a rally at the latter port. Ibrahim Pasha, disembarking with his staff, took the command in person, and marched northward to Acre, where Abdullah had concentrated his strength in the hope of turning back Ibrahim, as Djezzar had turned back a greater commander. But the command of the sea was not in the hands of Abdullah. No Sydney Smith, cruising on the coast, intercepted the heavy siege material, or repelled assault; and Ibrahim, copying the plan of Bonaparte, deliberately landed his artillery and stores at Caiffa, the port that had proved so fatal to the plans for disembarking the heavy battering cannon destined by Bonaparte to reduce the fortress.

While the army skirted the bay and advanced to Acre by land, the squadron, disburthened of its battering train, attacked the place by sea, and enabled the besiegers to sit down before it under great advantages. The squadron, instead of disturbing, aided the attacking party; and, instead of the light field pieces which played on the strongholds of Djezzar, it was with a regular siege train that Ibrahim Pasha assailed this historic city. Having described in the earlier part of this work the former and much more important siege, it is unnecessary to prolong the notice of the second leaguer of Acre. But it must be admitted that the defence of Abdullah was a gallant one. His batteries replied to those of Ibrahim from the 26th of November, when the place was first invested, until February, 1832, when, a breach having been effected, two vigorous assaults were made, but without success. At the same time, the troops of Ibrahim, accustomed to the mild winters of Egypt, with dry air and bright sunshine, were decimated with fever and discouraged by the terrible moral pressure of nostalgia.

In addition to this, the forces of the Porte in the north of Syria were not idle. Although having neither the discipline nor the resources of Ibrahim, and ill-calculated to withstand the shock of a regular engagement, yet, if skilfully used, they could do much to harass and distract a besieging force. In order to clear his rear, Ibrahim Pasha advanced suddenly to the northward; and Osman Pasha, of Aleppo, having imprudently risked a close engagement in the plain of Zeran, suffered a total rout. This circumstance leaving Ibrahim free to pursue the siege without interruption, his plans were further advanced by the return of spring, so congenial to the Egyptian troops, while the besieged were hard pressed for want of provisions and stores. The last terrible assault was made on the 27th of May, after daybreak. The battle continued through the whole heat of the day, and it was not until the afternoon, when many hundred men had been killed in the breach, that the place was surrendered.

From Acre Ibrahim marched to Damascus, which—situated in a luxuriant valley, without any considerable fortifications, and entirely commanded from the heights of Salahieh—was abandoned to him without firing a shot, the authorities having taken to flight. This city might have proved a new Capua to the general of the Egyptian troops; but Ibrahim, halting merely to replenish his commissariat stores, pushed on to Homs, where the Pasha of Tripoli had under his orders thirty thousand men, forming the vanguard of the Ottoman armies. Instead of waiting in Damascus until this army was increased by reinforcements from Aleppo, Asia Minor, and Mesopotamia, Ibrahim's decisive march to the north brought him into collision with a force, not only inferior in number, but inferior in that unity and organization which more than made up for the difference in personal valour between the private Egyptian Arab, and the more stubborn tenacity of the Osmanli Turk.

It was at Homs, the first city on the road from Damascus to Aleppo, that the two armies met on the 8th of July, 1832. Ibrahim did not make the first attack; but, placing his infantry in solid masses in the centre, with the cavalry and artillery at the wings, he awaited the assault of Mohammed Pasha of Tripoli, who advanced in three columns. A well directed deadly fire of musketry and grape was opened on the Turks as soon as they were fairly within range; and, four battalions of the Egyptian guard vigorously charging the centre with the bayonet before the Turks had recovered from their confusion, while at the same time the cavalry acted on the wings, the Turkish army was put to utter rout, by the simplest and most inartificial application of the rules of European warfare to a contest with commanders who had not the most distant idea of its rudiments.

The victory was complete. The camp, the commissariat stores, the baggage, and the ammunition of the Turks, along with about two thousand prisoners and thirty-six guns, fell into the hands of the Egyptians, and the army of the Sublime Porte thus becoming an utter wreck, all Syria was placed at the feet of Ibrahim. A large proportion of the tribes of those curious countries, attached to the Porte neither by the ties of nationality nor religion, gave their voice at once to the strongest; and Ibrahim Pasha received letters of congratulation and verbal assurances of support, which would have been addressed to the Pasha of Tripoli had he been the victor on this decisive day. Even the remnant of the Turkish army was harassed and plundered by the Anazeh Arabs, a great tribe extending from the borders of Syria to Tadmor and the Euphrates. Aleppo, to which Hussein Pasha, commander-in-chief of the Ottoman armies, advanced from Asia Minor, shut its gates and refused him supplies, which compelled him to retire to the defiles of the Taurus, while the Aleppines made no difficulty of receiving the victorious Ibrahim.

Meanwhile, Hussein Pasha, the Turkish seraskier, encamped at the defiles of Beylan, near Alexandretta, and fortified this passage from Syria into Asia Minor by several strong batteries. Ordinary skill and courage, joined to the strong position, might have given Ibrahim Pasha a severe check; but the artillery of the Egyptians being better served, and the tried and confident troops carrying the heights at the point of the bayonet, the Turks again took to an ignominious flight. Henceforth, the opposition which the Turks made to Ibrahim was insignificant. They nowhere seriously held their ground; and the Egyptian army, taking the high road to Constantinople, left the Taurus behind and advanced to Konieh, the chief city in the southern interior of Asia Minor. In the eyes of the Ottomans this place is invested with a semi-sacred character, from its having been—before Broussa, Adrianople, and Constantinople—the capital of Turkish power, and still containing the remains of the revered Mollah Hunkiar, with a university and mosques, associated with a religion considered orthodox, and such learning as the Ottomans possess and delight to honour.

Reschid Pasha, who had successfully pacified Roumelia, and who is not to be confounded with his greater namesake, the vizier of Turkish reform, was placed by the Porte at the head of its beaten and renewed—its re-beaten and rawly-renovated—armies, and opposed to Ibrahim Pasha, to whom prudence and courage had given victory, and to whom victory had added that confidence and experience which are the sure earnests of ulterior success. Under these circumstances, Konieh was the easiest of all the conquests of Ibrahim—a victory without a battle, in which thirty thousand Egyptians drove nearly double that number of Turks before them, and menaced the Sultan in his capital. It was on a thick foggy morning, in the month of December, 1832, that the two armies met. Reschid bravely led his men into the thick of the fight; while the Egyptians were enabled by the Turkish cannonade to find out the position of their adversaries, their own guns remaining silent; but he soon perceived that, in the fog, his Arnauts had failed to follow him. Bedouins near at hand, hearing a language they did not understand, took him prisoner. This event carried consternation into the Turkish ranks. The whole army of sixty thousand men took to flight, after a trifling loss on both sides. Ibrahim Pasha was thus master not only of Syria but of Asia Minor, which was the centre of the Turkish power and resources. So low had now sunk the sun of the great house of Orcan; so potent had the vassal become in an empire suffering from oppressive foreign war, effete domestic institutions, and the fatal suicidal policy of France and England, who, on the disastrous day of Navarino, abandoned their natural ally to further the schemes of their natural rival.

It is impossible to describe the consternation which was produced in Constantinople by the battle of Konieh, and the subsequent advance of the Egyptians. The Greek and Servian revolts, and the wars with Russia, were all on the borders and outlying provinces of

Turkey; but, if any part of the empire could be considered a citadel of the loyalty and nationality of the Ottomans, it was Asia Minor. Yet the sacred Konieh had seen the military disasters of the Sultan; and Kiutahieh, a great stage nearer to the Bosphorus, was immediately after the head-quarters of Ibrahim, from which he menaced the capital. Nor was it either the power or the legitimate rights of the Sultan which stopped the advance of the Egyptians. The language of Mohammed Ali was haughty in the extreme; and he informed the Porte that if the government of Syria as well as of Adana, which forms the south-eastern maritime province of Asia Minor, were not given him he would cause Ibrahim to march to Constantinople and enforce his demands.

The fear of a collision with the European powers prevented Ibrahim from showing himself in the immediate vicinity of the capital. Russia, which had been chiefly instrumental in reducing Turkey to this state of weakness, was not prepared to see a total collapse of the Ottoman empire, which might have brought about some new and unforeseen arrangement subversive of her preponderating influence. She therefore sent Prince Mouravieff to Alexandria, politely insisting on orders being sent to stop the march of Ibrahim. Russia moreover contributed a military force, which landed in Turkey and encamped on the Bosphorus in order to ward off the contingency of an Egyptian attack on the capital. The other powers, without sending troops, held the same language; and, after some correspondence, an arrangement was at length made by which Mohammed Ali was confirmed in the government of Syria, and Ibrahim Pasha, in addition to being governor of the holy cities, was made, on the 3rd of May, 1833, mohassil, or collector of the revenues of

Adana. This final arrangement was made on the 14th of May, 1833, by the so-called Convention of Kiutahieh; and on the 15th of May the names of Mohammed Ali and of Ibrahim Pasha appeared in the official calendar of the Porte as the incumbents of those high charges, with which was included the governorship of the island of Candia. Thus a great part of the empire was virtually severed from its trunk, and a power aggrandized that might at any time be turned against the remainder.

The result of all this was the treaty of Unkiar Skelesi, concluded between Russia and the Porte on the 26th June, 1833, which engaged the latter to shut the straits against the ships of war of all nations, by an article of a secret and segregarious character, which was justly considered, by the great powers of Europe, as inconsistent with that comitial action on the most important questions of the European family by which the balance of power can be alone secured. The reversal of this isolated policy at a later period carried the European influence of the Emperor Nicholas to its culmination; but, unhappily for that monarch, its readoption precipitated him into an untimely grave, after the most galling humiliations.

CHAPTER IX.

A Survey of Syria at the period of the Egyptian Conquest.—Mount Lebanon.—The Druses.—The Pashalic of Aleppo.—Jerusalem.—The Seat of Government Established at Damascus.—Factions of Aleppo.—Beginning of Discontents among the Natives of Syria.—Sack of Safet.—Insurrection of the Mountaineers of Nablouse and Mount Cassius.—Disarming of the Inhabitants of Mount Lebanon.—Exasperation of the Population of Syria.

The geographical configuration of Egypt has necessarily had much influence on its history. While Egypt is a plain, Syria consists chiefly of a couple of ranges of mountains, running parallel to the sea; and while Egypt has always bent under the conqueror, Syria—at first, on account of its intestine divisions, the easy prey of conquest, has always proved a troublesome acquisition in the sequel. Those infinite varieties of religion and nationality which facilitate the invasion of the country are monuments of the incompleteness of former subjugations; while the prominence of the feudal principle in the political divisions of Syria sprang from the same accidents of political geography. In vain did Turkey trace on the map boundaries of Pashaliks; they remained pale and indistinct beside the bolder lines of feudal authority; and it was not until all the transactions recorded in this history were terminated, that the provincial campaigns of Omer Pasha in Syria, in Koordistan, in Bosnia, and Albania, produced a more vigorous centralization of the administration of the Ottoman Empire.

Mount Lebanon is the political key of Syria; and as

the possession of the citadel of Cairo was during many centuries held to be the visible sign of the command of Egypt, so the possession of Mount Lebanon is considered indispensible to a firm grasp of Syria, commanding as it does the access between Damascus, the luxurious chief city, and Acre, Sidon, Beyrout, and Tripoli on the coast.

The external aspect of Lebanon is delightful to the sight of man. The base of the mountain is bathed by the waters of the Mediterranean, which for nine months of the year present a surface of unruffled azure ; and in this latitude even the storms of winter are few and far between. The palm and the orange grow luxuriantly on the low narrow strips of land, between the mountain and the sea ; further up, where the ground rises rapidly, we have as yet none of the savagery of mountain scenery : the vegetation of the fig, the vine, and the mulberry, is traced symmetrically terrace above terrace, like giant staircases ascending from earth to heaven. Numerous villages, hung on airy rocks, denote ages of insecurity, that have compelled the industrious inhabitants to leave the bounteous plains for the picturesque but more niggard region of the hills and fortresses. Further up—where the climate is too cold for the temperate plants already mentioned, and more subject to the mist, the thunder-cloud, and the beneficent rain,—the cedar and the Italian pine present a growth far beyond that of the scanty fir of our own " land of brown heath and shaggy wood ! " Highest of all—the home of the eagle and her brood—are the peaks of a Makmel or a Sanin, robed half the year in snow, and recalling the accurate felicity of a Volney, or the music of a Moore—winter crowning the heights, and summer sleeping at its feet.

Such are the mountains of the Druses and Maronites ; but their nooks are not more sequestered from the dwellings of man than the faith of the former people is segregated from that of the Christian or Moslem. The Druses have a philosophy derived from that of the Karmates, those rude opponents of the present form of Islamism, who sought to allegorise its precepts, to establish a doctrine of internal sense, and to substitute metaphysical theories for stringent external formalities. The manners of the Druses, patent and occult, were during several years one of the subjects studied by the author of this history, and have a prominent place in his work on the Modern Syrians. Their religion, long obscure, has been brought to light by the late erudite Baron Sylvestre de Saçy.

The Deity, or rather the last and greatest impersonation of the divinity on earth, was a caliph of the Fatimite dynasty of Egypt, who was born at Cairo in the beginning of the eleventh century. Hakem b'emr Allah, as we have seen, was a fierce persecutor of the Christians and Jews, upwards of thirty thousand monasteries in Egypt and Syria having been destroyed by his orders; the synagogues of the Jews sharing the same fate. This monster was whimsical almost to madness, and cruel beyond anything recorded of ancient tyrants; for upwards of eighteen thousand persons perished during his reign. A profuse generosity seems to have been almost his only virtue.

The Druses to this day believe that Hakem was the last and most perfect of the manifestations of the Divinity; and that next to the Deity is the Divine Idea, or Spirit of Universal Intelligence—a sort of spurious "Holy Ghost"—the first of all the creatures of God and His instrument in the creation of men and things, and of which Hamza was an incarnation. It is a prophet—Hamza, not Hakem, who gives his name to the Druse era—which is 408 of the Hegira, or A.D. 1033. The deluge was considered not to have been material, but an allegory having reference to the inundation of Islamism. Many doctrines have also been added in the course of ages since the death of Hamza.

The modern Druses are divided into two classes, the Akkals and the Djahils—the former initiated into the mysteries of the religion, and the latter uninitiated. The former live in great purity and simplicity, enjoy profound respect, and take precedence in all assemblies; and the lives of the whole tribe are spent in politics, in agriculture, and, until latterly, in petty mountain warfare. They are strangers to art, science, or commerce; but the Druse women are all taught reading and writing. A most remarkable feature in their system is the profound mystery in which they seek to veil everything political and religious, and with considerable success; for the greatest crime that a Druse can commit is to reveal a national secret. There is perhaps no nation in the world which carries the principle of mutual assistance and co-operation so completely into practice.

Every one of the seven nobles who governed the corresponding number of districts in the mountains of the Druses might be compared to what the chiefs of a highland clan were at the beginning of the last century: with a loose allegiance to the Sovereign, and arbitrary power over the vassals, but with this difference, that the respect paid to the Akkals considerably tempered the exercise of arbitrary authority. Each chief generally lived in a castle perched on a cliff, enclosed within massive walls, but not calculated to resist artillery. They led a rude life, surrounded by devoted retainers, in the practice of a simple hospitality, with falconry and jousting for recreation; but agriculture and war were their serious occupations. The attachment of the Druses to their hereditary chiefs was enthusiastic, and did not extend to the Sultan until the advent of the Egyptians.

On the contrary, they had no sympathy with the dignity, unity, and power of the Ottoman Empire, their chief object being to baffle the efforts of the Pasha of Sidon, always resident at Acre.

The other populations of Mount Lebanon were chiefly Maronite—a sect of Syrian Christians, united to Rome, although preserving their own primitive discipline. Their settlements are northward of the Druse country, in the direction of Tripoli and the cedars. Here, as in the middle ages, the power of the petty nobles was entirely subordinate to that of the clergy; and like the Druses they had no attachment to the central government of the Sultan.

The Prince of Mount Lebanon occupied a middle station between these chiefs and the Turkish Government. This dignity was occupied successively by the now extinct houses of Tanooh and Maan; and about a century and a half ago came into the hands of the Beni Shehab—a Moslem family from Mecca, which had been settled in Anti-Lebanon for several centuries.

In days of yore, when the preponderance of the Druse over the Christian population was absolute, the immigration of the Christians for the cultivation of the land was much encouraged. The Christians took to the plough and pruning hook; the Druses stuck to the sword. While the Christians were fruitful and multiplying their numbers, the increase of the ranks of the Druses was prevented by their deadly feuds; and hence we see that now, in all the Druse districts except Shouf, the Christians form the majority. This, in itself, was an immense revolution, which was completed by the old Emir Beshir Cassim. This crafty man forsook Islamism, turned Maronite, persuaded the Emirs of Meten (the house of Belemma), with whom the Shehabs intermarry, also to embrace Christianity, and by his talents and position formed a party which completely overturned the Druse power.

To the north of Mount Lebanon is another range of mountains, skirting the coast—not so lofty, but more productive, particularly in that superior description of tobacco collected at the neighbouring port of Lattakia. This district—remarkable for its natural beauty, and terminating in mount Cassius, at the mouth of the Orontes—is inhabited by another of those anomalous sects, which, although historically related to Islamism and Christianity, are yet in doctrine and practice so widely different from both. Large masses of the Magians, in the origin of Islamism, accepted it only through fear and *pro formâ*, but secretly kept up among themselves the rites and precepts of the older religions of Asia. Of these, the Nosairies and Ismaelis (the assassins or Hashasheen of the middle ages) regard Ali, the son-in-law of Mahomet, as an incarnation of the Divinity, and Mahomet only as a prophet. Abel and St. Peter are also supposed to have been previous incarnations of the Divinity, while Adam and Jesus were supposed to have been contemporary prophets. This people speak the Arabic language; but yet, by faith, by manners, and by marriage, they remain quite distinct from the other races of Syria: and, as the tree is known by its fruits, their grovelling superstitions place them below every other tribe of this heterogeneous land in manners and civilization.

These mountaineers were nominally under the Pasha of Tripoli; but, crossing the Orontes, we come to Aleppo, the second city of Syria, and capital of the most northerly pashalik. Built with solidity, it had been for centuries the seat of a great overland commerce between India and Europe; and in the reign of Charles II. upwards of fifty British houses were established in

Aleppo. There were also Venetian, Dutch, and French factories, which altogether formed a large European community in the midst of the fanatic Moslem population. The total number of the inhabitants of the city had not been less than two hundred thousand souls. But in the eighteenth century the trade gradually declined: the British factory became extinct during the French revolutionary war; and in the beginning of the nineteenth century we find the population reduced to considerably less than half of what it once had been.

At this period the Moslem population of Aleppo was divided into two fierce factions—the shereefs, or green-turbaned descendants of the Prophet, and the janissaries or military faction: the former, eminent for birth and wealth, being in a state of humiliation; and the latter, at this period, enjoying full power. Just as with the Mamelukes before the French invasion, the Sultan's authority was represented by a pasha, who lent his seal to all public acts, while the real power was in the hands of the beys and agas,—each of whom counted amongst his protegés, not only his immediate tail and some wealthy rayahs, but even the consuls of the European Powers; for without some such intermediary no business could be transacted, nor redress for grievances obtained. Sometimes there was no pasha at all, but merely a muhassil, or collector, to receive and transmit the tribute. At length, in the eventful year 1815, Chapan Oglon was sent as Pasha to Aleppo. He resided at the villa of Sheikh Abu Bekr, outside the town; and for some months after his arrival, no governor could be more popular, as he did not aim at the shadow of authority. At length, a rich caravan which had started for Constantinople was robbed, and two of the principal janissaries of Aleppo were known to be implicated in the affair. Chapan Oglan, in this instance, insisted on the necessity of the property being restored, or compensation being made; otherwise the merchants would represent their case to the Porte, and might probably procure his recal. The majority of the other janissary chiefs desired to retain a pasha who interfered so little with their oligarchy; and, as this business offered a fair excuse for assembling a meeting of the beys and agas, they repaired to the suburban palace of Abou Bekr. Suspecting nothing, they were accompanied by but few attendants. They were well received by the Pasha, who, after some discussion, went out of the room; and, sending in the soldiers whom he had concealed in the adjoining apartments, the assembled chiefs, to the number of thirty, were murdered in cool blood. Thus did the Porte get rid of the most formidable members of the old Janissary party.

The great event in the history of Aleppo, immediately preceding the Egyptian occupation, was the earthquake of 1822, which, throwing down whole streets of houses, buried six thousand persons in their ruins—a blow from which this solidly constructed city has not recovered.

The largest and most important of all the pashaliks of Syria was that of Damascus, which then extended southward and eastward to the great desert, and included at that time Jerusalem, with the massive cyclopean relics of the great temple of the Hebrew Solomon, where the children of Israel still weep their dispersion; with its Mount of Olives recalling the life and death of Christ, and its Byzantine architecture—monuments of the great middle age fabric of the church, and of its arduous but unsuccessful enterprise, the crusades; those pilgrimages of Latinity in buff and steel, with lance and mace, which the muse of a Tasso has reproduced in the most complete and harmonious of epics. Here Moslem pride still held its political supremacy; and, in the light egg-dome and perfect lines of the mosque of Omer, Arab art continued boldly to challenge a comparison with the more stupendous but not more beautiful proportions of the most celebrated fanes of Christendom.

Damascus, one of the four holy cities of the Moslems, was fixed upon by the Egyptians as the seat of the government of all Syria; a locality well suited for this purpose, being nearly equidistant from the north and the south. Provisions were moderate in price, from the vicinity of the fertile grain-producing Hauran, the Auranitis of the ancients. Water, a first necessity in a hot country, is in overflowing abundance. The climate is mild, for the dense vegetation cools the air, and the construction of the houses (an uninterrupted tradition of the antique) aids in reducing the temperature, while the fevers of autumn, although prevalent, are not deadly. Damascus was the seat of an ancient aristocracy of birth, deriving their incomes from the renowned Ager Damascenus, with its wide-spreading orange and apricot groves, watered by the seven arms of the Pharpar and Abana. This small society, in life and conversation, offered a complete contrast to the rude mountain chiefs of Lebanon, occupied with semi-barbarous warfare and the sports of the field. The courtyards of these men, resplendent with mosaic, and cooled by the umbrageous orange, or spouting marble fountain, were frequented by the learned and pious doctors of Islamism. A numerous clientage seemed to confirm the Greek doctrine that it was better to be wealthy than to be wise, the latter being always found at the doors of the former. Many mosques of quaint native elegance still attest the liberality of this class, as well as capacious and lofty khans for the convenience of the stranger, the merchant, and the indigenous traveller.

But the bulk of the inhabitants of Damascus were

notorious for their turbulence and fanaticism, particularly those of a suburb called the Meidan—the Faubourg St. Antoine of Damascus; and when troubles arose, this populous suburb poured out its thousands of fanatical and sanguinary men into the town, who were as ready to overawe authority as to plunder their more peaceably disposed fellow citizens within the gates. In fact, up to the period of the Egyptian invasion, the inhabitants thought themselves entitled to control an exorbitant Pasha; and an occasional revolt and massacre was the little tacit saving clause in the compact that engaged them to respect the right divine of the Sultan to govern wrong. Indeed, one of the governors, named Selim Mohammed Pasha, on attempting an exaction, had been murdered by the mob, and his body dragged through the streets, shortly before the campaign of Ibrahim Pasha, which we described in the previous chapter. But no sooner did the Egyptians settle themselves in this proud city, than it felt like the wild horse which first makes the acquaintance of rider and bridle. The conquest of Syria, and the advance of Ibrahim into the centre of Asia Minor, filled the Damascenes with astonishment. The Egyptian government used a reasonable courtesy towards the comparatively speaking wealthy aristocracy of this ancient city; but to the general population their attitude was that of masters. The Egyptians were, nevertheless, hated and feared by the local influential families; though the intelligent Christian population to a man gave their sympathies to a government that promised to give them protection against the ignominy and exactions that had pressed them down since the days of Mohammed.

To organize the government of Syria, after the Egyptian conquest, was indeed no easy task; the majority of the population, not only indifferent to the

Porte, but always ready to throw off the government of the day, were equally indisposed to submit tacitly to that pressure of taxation and conscription, and to that defenceless disarmament which would place a free and energetic people at the mercy of an unscrupulous ruler, bent on erecting a State quasi-independent of the Porte, and utterly indifferent as to the inconvenience and suffering it might occasion to the Syrians. But to proceed at once with violent measures would have been to play the game of the Divan at Constantinople. The greater part of the first two years was therefore devoted to the acquisition of information; to the discovery of the secret enemies of the Egyptians; to a consolidation of those alliances that might prove most convenient and serviceable; and to an organization of the military defences, in the event either of local revolt, or of a capacity or disposition on the part of the Sultan to resume his own. In short, it was the superfluous wealth of Egypt that furnished the capital stock of resources at the outset of this adventurous Syrian speculation.

Shereef Pasha, the near relation of Mohammed Ali—possessed of considerable political capacity, distinguished by courteous and dignified manners, and in whom a kindly disposition in many things was mingled with occasionally deliberate and revolting cruelty—was the Governor-general, with a large salary and emoluments. In the financial administration he was assisted by Hannah Bahri, a Syrian Christian, of singular energy and ability, whom the sagacity of Mohammed Ali had picked out of comparative obscurity, and who enjoyed the rare distinction of being elevated to the rank of a bey. The entire abnegation of the old spirit of Moslem fanaticism, with which Mohammed Ali and his son Ibrahim not only elevated but vigorously sustained such men, at once mark their superiority, and extract the tribute of the admiration of the historian. Bahri Bey being a Christian, the other members of the Council never rose at his entrance. This was the subject of a complaint to Ibrahim Pasha; but, like a skilful courtier, saying nothing of the disrespect shown to his person, he laid all the stress on the disregard of the decoration on his breast, which was indicative of the rank given him by Mohammed Ali. Ibrahim Pasha a few days afterwards went to the divan. All the members rose; and, before they were seated, Ibrahim said, "Bey, come here." Hafiz Bey, a Moslem, stepped forward, on which Ibrahim Pasha said, "No, Bahri Bey." Hafiz retired confounded; and on Bahri Bey approaching, he said, "Buyuroon"—be pleased to sit: to the rest of the council he added, "Otoor," which means simply "sit." Ever after this scene, the council rose to Bahri Bey.

The Christians—by their local knowledge, by the ramifications of their intelligence and correspondence with all parts of Syria, as well as by their aptitude for accounts and the details of the administration—proved of invaluable service to the Egyptians. Nor was the government behindhand in substantial proofs of favour. The prohibition to wear light coloured turbans and garments, and to mount on horseback, was removed; and the Frank costume, which no traveller ever dared to wear without considerable risk to his life, became his best protection. Disloyal and rebellious as Mohammed Ali was to his sovereign and benefactor, and oppressive as he was to the Syrians, it is impossible not to admit his tolerance. Colonel Campbell, our agent and consul-general in Egypt at this time, in a report on Syria, writes on this subject as follows:—

"The Syrian Mussulmans, whatever may be said of the diminution of their fanaticism, deeply deplore the loss of that sort of superiority which they all and individually exercised over and against the other sects. Pride, selfishness, and ignorance may be said to be the characteristics of a Mussulman; and from the bottom of his heart he believes and maintains that a Christian, and still more a Jew, is an inferior being to himself. With such principles it is no matter of astonishment to remark that the political equality to which the other sects have been raised by the present government of Syria creates a sort of religious disaffection towards their rulers, which I am inclined to believe has more deep roots than all the other just motives of complaint which they possess. The Christians, as well as the other sects who have been benefitted by such changes, are necessarily attached to the present system, and dread any change that would tend to restore to the Mussulmans that supremacy of which they would certainly make them feel the return into their hands. The condition of the Jews forms perhaps an exception, and cannot be said to have improved comparatively with that of other sects: this is owing to a personal feeling, both of Mohammed Ali and Ibrahim Pasha, as also of all the Christians and other sects in Syria, against them."

Aleppo and its district was the object of the serious study of the military Ibrahim and the civilian Shereef. Its population had given the Porte a great deal of trouble, even after the massacre we have described in the earlier part of this chapter; for although the heads of the janissary faction had been long taken off, the body itself remained, as well as the sons of those unfortunate individuals and the older chiefs of inferior note. The most influential man among them was an individual called Abdallah Babolsi, of low extraction, rough exterior, and destitute of education, but possessed of unbending energy, inflexible attachment to his own people, and generosity in pecuniary matters—qualities which he used by turns to serve his friends and intimidate his enemies.

Able as Ibrahim Pasha was to crush any rising in the town, he was too politic not to avert the danger which would arise from the existence of a focus of disorder in the northern capital, situated but a few days from the Taurus. He therefore made Abdallah the Mutsellim; and appointed, at the same time, the Bey-el-Adlieh as head of the shereefs. On condition of Abdallah's keeping the *canaille* of the janissary faction in order, the Egyptians shut their eyes upon his system of protecting his own men; and the Bey-el-Adlieh, a man of ancient family, but dilapidated fortune (literally dilapidated, for before the earthquake he possessed whole streets of good houses), although not a shereef, was very popular, from his high character, with all the parties. Superior to the Turks in military force, the Egyptians matched them in the policy which rules by division of factious opponents.

It was in the north of Syria that the bulk of the Egyptian troops were generally quartered. Antioch, from its salubrious climate, its abundant forage for cavalry, and its beautiful situation, was a favourite residence of Ibrahim Pasha, who built here a palace and large barracks. The civil governor of the district of Aleppo was Ismael Bey; but the military and civil operations of the government were so mixed up that nothing was done without the approbation of the Seraskier, Ibrahim. Contiguous to the Pashalic of Aleppo, but forming part of Asia Minor, was the fertile but insalubrious district of Adana, with its capital of the same name, and its Tarsus, commemorated by St. Paul. Achmed Menikli Pasha, one of the bravest and most skilful lieutenants of Ibrahim, was the governor of this district, which, being near the frontier, was treated with more mildness than those of Syria, the inhabitants having been allowed to retain their arms after they had been taken from all the other districts.

To be brief, the two cities of Damascus and Aleppo, with their contiguous regions, presented no great difficulties to the Egyptian government, but this was not the case with the Pashaliks of Tripoli and Acre, including the turbulent mountain populations of Lebanon, to which we may add Nablouse, which latter belonged to Damascus. Up to the middle of 1834 none of the acts of the Egyptians tended to disclose the project of raising the taxes, or of conscription and disarmament. The only complaints made by the natives arose from vexatious acts committed by the Egyptian soldiery, and instances of sordid venality in the lower classes of the administration. It was on such pretexts that a rebellion, which soon became dangerous to the Egyptians, broke out at Salt and Karak, and, extending towards Jerusalem, compelled Ibrahim Pasha to shelter himself in this latter city. The son of Mohammed Ali was here secure; for Jerusalem is encompassed with strong walls and contains a mixed population, most of whom are unconcerned spectators of the military struggles and political intrigues that from time to time distract the rest of Syria. This revolt soon gained ground in Samaria; for, although amongst a remnant of the singular people, rivals to the Jews, and cognate in language, nationality and religion still linger within the precincts of the Sichem of the Samaritans, yet the mountainous district of the modern Nablouse is inhabited by the bold and energetic Moslem population who harassed the armies of Bonaparte in their march to and from Acre, and who rose vigorously to throw off the Egyptian yoke.

In this anarchical crisis the severest sufferers were the Jews resident in Safet, the Medina of the Hebrews;

who, attributing to that place a sanctity exceeded only by Jerusalem, had settled here in numbers, and were in easy circumstances. Attacked on the 16th of June by armed Moslems, their homes were violated, their property plundered, their women dishonored, and those who resisted murdered. For thirty-three days this wretched town was in the possession of these barbarians; and the property lost or destroyed on the occasion by the Jews was estimated at not less than seventy thousand pounds sterling. The Christians of Syria, being more numerous, offered an effective resistance to the Moslems, who attempted to make them share the fate of the Jews of Safet; and at Nazareth, Bethlehem, and Jerusalem, the attempts of the Moslems were unsuccessful.

Mohammed Ali, who, with his known activity and presence of mind, had embarked at Alexandria with all the troops he could collect, and a large supply of money, landed at Jaffa, and soon gained over to his cause seven of the most influential chiefs. This union of craft with an imposing display of strength disunited the Syrians. The fierce mountaineers of Nablouse were prepared to resist, but the men of Hebron came to an accommodation. At Zutah the brave Nablousans attempted to make a stand; but the steady Egyptian columns and the well-pointed artillery put them at once to flight, and Mohammed Ali on the 15th of July made a triumphal entry into Nablouse, where all the arms were without difficulty surrendered. At the same time Salt and Karak, which attempted to resist, were carried by assault and partially destroyed.

In the meanwhile other revolutionary movements had occurred in the Nosairi mountains. A regiment of regular cavalry was attacked by four thousand Nosairies while marching from Lattakia to Aleppo, and forced to retreat, after losing about half of its men. The Nosairies' rebellious—quoad the rebellious Egyptian government—forced the port of Lattakia (whence the delicious tobacco of the neighbourhood is exported to all parts of the East), and immediately began to plunder the property of the government and of the Christians. The latter, however, had repaired on board their vessels, waiting the result of these events. The Egyptians sent a division of seven thousand regulars under the orders of General Selim Bey, who, with the assistance of eight thousand Druses and Maronites, commanded by the Emir Halil—the brave son of the Emir Beshir, the Prince of mount Lebanon—marched upon the stronghold of the Nosairies. Beaten and everywhere disarmed by the superior forces opposed to them, the Nosairies offered to capitulate through the medium of the Emir Halil; but Selim Bey having presented such conditions as appeared of great hardship to the Emir Halil, this chief left the mountains of the Nosairies with his followers, and returned to Lebanon. While continuing to treat with Selim Bey, a large corps of Nosairies, anxious to revenge themselves upon the Druses for the part they had taken in favor of the Egyptians against them, followed Emir Halil rapidly in his retreat, overtook him in a defile, and killed many of his men. They then voluntarily submitted to Selim Bey; and, giving up their arms, sent four thousand of their men to enter the ranks of the Egyptian army. Ibrahim Pasha distributed these among his guards, leaving a garrison of two thousand eight hundred men in the mountains, as a proof of his solicitude for their tranquillity, as he expressed himself to them in his address.

The rising in the northern and southern districts of the great mountain chain of Syria that runs parallel to the coast was then taken up as a pretext for disarming the internal towns of Damascus and Aleppo, as well as all the flat country, on the ground of their having had secret intelligence with the insurgents. This was accomplished without difficulty; and thus all Syria was subdued and rendered powerless, except the important district of Lebanon—the highest and central mountain-chain, which is the key of the whole land—inhabited by a more warlike and energetic race than either the Moslems of Nablouse or the Nosairies of mount Cassius; and abounding in positions so difficult of access, that but for the circumstance of a large Christian population sharing the tenancy of this Syrian Switzerland, and the complication arising out of internal contests of authority between the Druse and the Christian element, it is much to be doubted if even Ibrahim Pasha, with all his vigour, could have succeeded.

After the occupation of Syria, Ibrahim Pasha and the Emir Beshir had found out each other to be natural allies. The Egyptians were delighted to have for a confederate the powerful and crafty prince of Mount Lebanon, and made sure that so long as he held by them, they had nothing seriously to fear in the interior of Syria. The Emir Beshir, who had long since secretly adopted Christianity, and leaned on the Christian element for abasing the Druse chiefs, was only too happy to close with any general authority in Syria that might leave him in possession of a decided supremacy. Thus the government of Syria and the Prince of Lebanon were united against their common enemy—the Porte and its Druse partisans. We may also mention a circumstance of a personal nature which, if it did not create this alliance, certainly tended to lubricate the intercourse of the Emir Beshir with the government of Mohammed Ali. On the Emir Beshir, a few years previously, visiting Egypt, he had been received with most flattering courtesy and gratifying splendour by this Pasha, who, whether as friend or foe, did nothing by halves; and to whom we may reasonably attribute the foresight of contingencies in which the Emir Beshir might prove of signal utility.

The decree of the Emir Beshir, for the disarmament of Mount Lebanon, was dated the 25th of September, and ran as follows:—"His Highness Ibrahim Pasha, the Seraskier, having observed that many of the inhabitants of the mountains used their arms for criminal purposes, and as it is difficult to detect the malefactors, he has demanded the arms of the whole population; wherefore the Emirs will use all their exertions to get them and send them to our palace." The decree concludes with enjoining a favourable reception of the troops of Ibrahim.

Ibrahim Pasha having concerted with the Emir Beshir the means to be adopted for the disarmament, left Homs unexpectedly, and reached Baalbek on the 3rd October, 1836; and, on the following night, surrounded with three regiments the district of Shouf, the chief seat of the Druses, while a fourth under Suleyman Pasha, moved from Beyrout upon Beteddim and arrived at the same time with Ibrahim Pasha. The Druses, taken by surprise and menaced with having their villages burnt, delivered up their arms. The Meten rose in revolt, but the heights being occupied by Ibrahim Pasha and Emir Halil, a surrender took place. On the ninth of October the disarmament of the Druses was completely achieved. The Christian population had been led to believe that they would be exempted from the decree, and therefore looked gleefully on whilst the Druse teeth were drawn; but their own turn followed, and while they were at church on a Sunday morning, the officers of the Emir Beshir (mostly Christians) surrounded the villages, and the houses were ransacked for arms, many acts of atrocity being committed.

It was thus that, in less than sixteen months the

whole of the population of Syria was disarmed. More than eighty thousand muskets, and a large number of pistols, swords, and cutlasses were carried to the arsenal of Acre to be converted into horse shoes; and in order effectually to extract the means of resistance from an unwilling people, each district was assessed in the number of muskets to be given up, even although they had them to purchase for the occasion.

No sooner was Syria disarmed and thus deprived of the power of revolt, than Mohammed Ali, not content with so negative a success, resolved to render Syria an active element in his career against the Ottoman Empire, which a hollow peace masked for the moment. But how miserable did the means employed defeat his ultimate objects! The conscription set on foot by him supplied him with a class of soldiers far superior in moral and physical vigour to those of Egypt; but their sympathies were not with him, and the mode of the conscription created feelings of exasperation far more intense than those of the disarmament. The rusty rifle that hung on the wall was often readily given up; but the rending of family ties was intolerable from its mode of operation. The sorrows of the European father, even in the case of wounds and death, are assuaged by the consciousness of a service rendered to the lawful sovereign; but this was not so in the case of the conscription among the Syrian Moslems, whose hearts were with the Sultan and with Islamism.

The mode in which the conscription was carried on added greatly to the horror that was felt against it. Thus, if ten or twenty soldiers were wanted from a given place, a hundred or a hundred and fifty persons, who appeared of age for the service, were indiscriminately seized in the streets, and indeed anywhere, by the agents of the government, and carried to a public building.

There those that had money soon found the means of liberation, by bribing the inferior agents; and families of the poorer classes would sell their last rags in hope of obtaining the same benefit in favour of their relations. After some days' detention, during which the subaltern officers would resort to every subterfuge in their power to extort from the prisoners or their relations the last para, the number wanted for the army was marched off to the depôt and the rest set at large, deprived of nearly all they possessed. Thus the ultimate benefit received by the government was small in comparison with the injury inflicted on the people. The tax of blood was the least evil. Impoverishment, with vague apprehensions of the next levy, weighed down the spirits of the people; and later, in the hour of conflict, Syria was lost to Mohammed Ali, not more by the arms of the Sultan and his allies, than by a revolt which made the whole land rise as a huge wave throwing off an incubus.

Another of the evils unavoidable in a state of war was the seizure of animals for transport. The army which Mohammed Ali was obliged to keep up in order to sustain his false position, being far beyond what the Syrians had been accustomed to, and beyond the scanty resources, of a depopulated country, the most serious disturbance of the ordinary commerce took place. No merchant could count with certainty upon carrying his goods to a port. In the midst of a journey, a whole caravan would be seized, and the goods left on the ground at the mercy of the elements; while even the rumour of an approaching seizure would scare from a seaport and retain in the mountains the animals wanted for the transport of commodities. These proceedings constituted in themselves a heavy tax on the produce of Syria, a country which was particularly deficient in the abundance and excellence of those raw products by which the manufactured goods imported could be paid for.

In order to counteract the deficiency of produce, and render Syria independent of other countries for supplies of grain as well as other growths suited to the climate, a forced cultivation was resorted to by Ibrahim Pasha, who embarked money in the enterprise, and made his officers take shares in it. But that natural and spontaneous development which follows zealous and skilful private enterprise did not result from the efforts of the Pasha. Agricultural prosperity, like the individual ear of corn, grows better by care and industry, but must—after all—*grow*, and cannot be fabricated by the mere force of governmental will.

Sometimes the inversions of economical science by the government partially wrought their own cure, the exactions of labour having led to a sort of protective combination among workmen. The authorities being in the habit of seizing a certain number of hands, to whom they paid wages much beneath the regular rate, this naturally raised the price of all non-governmental labour; and the consequence was that the labourers formed themselves into communities for mutual assurance against the loss accruing from deficient government pay, by an average eked out of the higher private labour; the whole system being substantially a tax on the general employer, and an additional drain on the general resources, for objects foreign to the general interests.

The immediate result of this irregular and violent appropriation of labour and personal liberty was an extensive emigration into Asia Minor and Mesopotamia, which was in some measure made up by a corresponding emigration from Turkey proper, when the conscription was instituted by the Sultan. But this severe and oppressive government managed to establish a much more regular system of police than had previously existed; and the tribes of the desert, who used to press on the cultivated land and commit depredations were, by a combined system of hire for military purposes and of terror of vengeance, kept in good order. The conqueror of the armies of the Sultan certainly made himself feared by the tribes of Syria; and the result of the salutary terror which he inspired was—that in only a few cases was it found necessary to resort to capital punishment in the later years of the rule of Mohammed Ali; and, except when tribes were in open revolt, Syria became as safe for the traveller as the countries of Europe.

Nevertheless the conscription, the disarmament, and the supercession of the influence of the wealthy Moslems, were fatal to all real stability of the Egyptian rule in Syria. The government was treading on a smothered volcano. It was not that the Syrians could either understand or enjoy the liberty of some European countries; but the pressure of the functionaries being unrestricted, the exasperation made the country ready to rise. The Egyptian bent under the yoke; but the Syrian was by character recalcitrant and rebellious. Egypt produced a large revenue; but Syria, with its scantier population and means, ingulphed the surplus from the wealthier valley of the Nile, and those very Syrian populations that offered no obstacle to the expulsion of the authorities of the Sultan, were generally ready to rise and cast off the heavier pressure of the Pasha's rule.

CHAPTER X.

Syrian Discontents revive the Hopes of the Turks.—Armaments of the Sultan.—Viscount Ponsonby dissuades Mahmoud from Precipitate Measures.—The Sultan resolves on War.

The principal Syrians, too wary to commit themselves in collision with the authority of the stern and relentless Ibrahim, were yet far from having accepted the Egyptian rule as an accomplished and indefeasible fact, or from doubting that in the long run the permanent system of the Porte would efface the accident of a revolt by a Pasha, howsoever gifted with military and political genius. The probable future was divined by the light of all the past history of Turkey. Accounts of these feelings of the Syrians were constantly sent to the Sultan, and kept alive in the breast of this vigorous-willed, but ill-fated, sovereign the determination to try once more his imperial strength with his haughty subject.

Prominent among those who instigated the Sultan to war was Hafiz Pasha, a Circassian of handsome person and polished manners, who, in those days of decadence and treachery, united honesty and fidelity with great personal bravery and activity; but certainly was deficient in the strategic genius and experience in directing large masses of troops, which was needed to enable him to cope with the Egyptian commander and his able French Adjutant-General. Mohammed Ali was absent from Egypt during the winter of 1838-9, having undertaken, notwithstanding his advanced years, a journey to the distant regions of Sennaar, in order to satisfy himself of the gold production of that district; and this was considered a favourable opportunity for making the preliminary preparations, with a view to striking a blow either before or soon after his return.

Accordingly, in January, 1839, councils of war were held at the Porte, a levy of 80,000 men was ordered, and much movement was visible at the Seraskierate. On this, the diplomatists at Constantinople most favourable to the Porte took the alarm; and, sharing in neither the sanguine illusions of Hafiz, nor the impatient unappeasable exasperation of Mahmoud, foresaw that events were approaching which might shake the empire to its centre; for up to this date no concert had been established among the great Powers in order to avert those fatal contingencies. A wide gulf still separated the policy of France, of Britain, and of Austria, from that of Russia, with its exclusive pretensions and its isolated pressure on the Ottoman empire. It was, therefore, feared, not without reason, that the impatience of the Sultan might precipitate that finally destructive crisis in the affairs of Turkey which it was the anxious desire of the great majority of the Powers of Europe to avert.

The representative of Great Britain at the Porte at this period was Viscount Ponsonby, one of the most remarkable diplomatists of his age. His personal appearance at once created a predisposition in his favour, being both venerable and aristocratic. To the courtesy of the perfect man of the world he united great firmness and high integrity. He had been a spectator of all the remarkable European events since the first French revolution; and although, in youth, a member of Parliament, and by habit and connection a supporter of Mr. Fox, he—in mature age—had none of those superficial views on foreign affairs which have beset many of the well-meaning and philanthropic members of the Liberal party in England. With the sound sense of a Briton, he preferred a bird in the hand to two in the bush; and conceived that amicable relations with Turkey and Austria were better securities against the ambition of Russia than any revolutionary combinations arising out of the disruption of the integrity of those two empires. He justly conceived that the attitude of Mohammed Ali in Syria was pro-Russian, because it was anti-Turkish; but he judiciously opposed the indiscreet zeal of those who, by inadequate efforts, would expose the Porte to still further defeats and humiliations.

A great council was held at the Porte on the 22nd of January, 1839, in order to discuss the question of peace or war with the Egyptians; and thereafter measures were taken on a large scale for arraying an imposing force to be employed against Mohammed Ali. Eighty thousand men were ordered to be levied, in addition to the force already under arms. Unfortunately, the means at the disposal of the Sultan were by no means commensurate with his fierce aspirations to a vindication of his sovereign rights against his wily and powerful satrap; and the emptiness of the treasury compelled the government to continue monopolies which had been condemned not only by the maxims of a sound commercial policy, but by positive compacts ratified by Britain and the Porte. In an interview which Sultan Mahmoud had with Viscount Ponsonby, the latter strongly recommended the greatest prudence in his conduct, and said that "his Highness could not at this moment have sufficient grounds on which to form a sound judgment of his position." The Sultan thanked the ambassador for his communication, and without altering his policy, renewed the assurances previously given that he would do nothing precipitately.

The other diplomatic ministers held the same language, but the great office-bearers in the intimate counsels of the Sultan, although far from fully sharing in either his deep-seated resentment or buoyant confidence in success, yet, with true oriental sycophancy, explored the current of their master's wishes, and did not dare to risk his displeasure by an uncourtly frankness on the doubtful chances of the coming conflict.

Mahmoud at length resolved on war, and a message was sent to the Great Council to the following purport:— "Hafiz Pasha informs me that my army is able to defeat the Egyptian army in Syria. The Capudan Pasha tells me that my fleet is strong enough to defeat and destroy the Egyptian fleet. It remains for you to be courageous and do your duty." To this Hati-Sherif the Great Council returned for answer, 'that his Highness's ministers would do everything in their power to act in conformity with the pleasure of their master." The brave, courteous, and sanguine Hafiz had perseveringly inflamed the ardent imagination of the Sultan by representations that there would never be again so favourable an opportunity for driving the Egyptians out of Syria. These, concurring with an opinion expressed by Reschid Pasha, then on a mission to Paris and London, that active hostilities for the Sultan against Mohammed Ali were not to be expected from France and Britain, decided the final resolutions of the Sultan.

The period has not yet arrived for a thorough penetration of the views of the British government at that period; but there appears to be little doubt that the apprehension of a renewal of the direct interference of Russia on the northern frontiers of Turkey prevented at this time active assistance being given to the Porte, however fully sensible the British government may have been of the danger and evil of Mohammed Ali's position in Syria. There was, between Viscount Palmerston and Reschid Pasha, some question of a treaty securing the eventual interests of the Porte in such a way as to induce the Sultan to abstain from immediate, hasty, and adventurous action; and Viscount Ponsonby entered therefore into communication with Nouri Effendi, the Turkish Minister for Foreign Affairs, who, however, expressed himself convinced that no treaty would be of any use to the Porte which had not for its object the destruction of Mohammed Ali. The Sultan at the same time declared to the Austrian internuncio that the terms on which he would arrange the matter could be nothing less than the evacuation of Syria by Mohammed Ali, and the reduction of his forces to such a number as would be compatible with his condition as a subject.

Mohammed Ali himself, on his return from Sennaar in March, was equally indisposed towards an accommodation. Abbas Pasha, his grandson, who was intrusted with the government of Egypt during the absence of Mohammed Ali, had been alarmed by the reports received from Constantinople of the warlike preparations of the Sultan, and wrote to press the return of the Viceroy to Cairo. Shortly afterwards a circular was sent to the consuls-general and agents in Egypt, throwing the responsibility of these complications entirely on the Sultan, and announcing the determination to oppose force by force. A copy of this communication having reached the Sultan, he was highly exasperated, and issued orders to hasten the equipment of the fleet and press the despatch of troops and military stores to the army. Mahmoud said that he would rather die than not endeavour to destroy his rebel subject; while the language of those about the Sultan was, "We hope for success, because all the Syrians are enemies of the Pasha." Viscount Ponsonby wrote home on the 20th May, "Nobody here doubts of war, and the general opinion is that the army of the Sultan will be defeated."

CHAPTER XI.

CAMPAIGNS OF NEZIB.—EGYPTIANS CONCENTRATED IN ALEPPO.—TURKISH CONCENTRATION AT NEZIB.—NIGHT BOMBARDMENT.—BATTLE OF NEZIB.—DEATH OF MAHMOUD.

IN Syria, Ibrahim Pasha displayed his well-known activity in preparing for the storm. Conscripts, *nolentes volentes*, were seen manacled, in motion towards the army, upon the high road between Damascus and Aleppo; great quantities of biscuit and other commissariat stores were collected in Aleppo for the use of the troops; and, in the end of April, rumours having reached him that the Sultan's troops had crossed the Euphrates, Ibrahim immediately held a council of war in Aleppo, which was his headquarters at this period in consequence of its large resources and its vicinity to the northern frontier.

At the council it was determined to concentrate the troops, and couriers were sent in all directions in order to bring them together. On the Sultan's side the troops crossed the river very slowly, the Euphrates being very high on account of the April floods, and only seven barges having been found in the neighbourhood of Bir, to which place the troops had been drawn from Orfa, Diarbekir, Malatia, and other places in Asia Minor, Kurdistan, and Mesopotamia.

In the first days of May, every mosque, khan, and public building in Aleppo was crammed full of Egyptian troops; and at the same time, in order to overawe the disaffected Moslem population in Damascus and Tripoli, the Emir Beshir received instructions to have large Christian forces in the environs of those cities, prepared to nip in the bud any appearance of outbreak in the interests of the Sultan. Thus Ibrahim Pasha, compelled to cast an eye to the rear as well as to the front, had need of all his craft and of all his physical force; for even the Arabs to the east of the Jordan were in motion, not daring to enter into overt or forward hostilities, but fully on the alert to join the winning party and make their harvest out of the fallen. The Druses of the Hauran were still more certain to rise. Close to its fertile plains, which are the granary of Damascus—and in which extensive ruined cities, with countless still-standing columns, attest the wealth and population of the Auranitis of the ancients—is the Ledgea, less favoured by nature, but from accidents of surface an easier harbour for the troublesome. The Druse population of this district, under the well-known leader Shibly, "the naked," had opposed a most obstinate resistance to the Egyptian projects of taxation and conscription; but although this chief, yielding to superior force, had made his peace with Egypt, and gave them an unwilling support, the people were to a man ready to rise.

Those under the immediate hoof of Ibrahim were more wary in committing themselves for the Sultan. Ismael Pasha, of the Ottoman army, having written to the musselim of Aintab that the Turkish troops were advancing, and "that he was to get everything ready for them, as he made no doubt of his fidelity to the Sultan,"—this municipal officer mounted his horse, and, going to Aleppo, placed the letter in Ibrahim Pasha's hands, who having read it, desired the musselim to return to his post and let them write what they liked, for he was his musselim and had nothing to fear.

The accumulation of so many troops in Aleppo produced much temporary inconvenience, the requisition of provisions for the army being so great that even bread could not be obtained in the bazaar. One day Ibrahim Pasha called Abdallah Babolsi, the musselim, or mayor, of Aleppo, and required of him a guarantee for the security and tranquillity of the town of Aleppo during his absence. The musselim replied, "If your Highness will leave me four or five thousand troops, I remain responsible that during the time you are in the camp everything remains in the greatest quietness here." The public report among the Christians of the town was that the population was very disaffected, and that, in the event of Ibrahim Pasha meeting with a repulse, a rising would ensue.

The amount of the Sultan's forces was about 80,000 men, of whom 25,000 were Bashi-Bazouks, or irregular horse militia—a force at one time constituting a formidable part of the Ottoman armies, the men being well mounted, and possessing the impetuous qualities of the Turk and of the Kurd. Since, however, the introduction of the European art of war into the military organization of Turkey, it is doubtful whether the presence of the Bashi-Bazouks is not more pernicious than useful—their disorderly and marauding habits neutralising the services they render in the forage, the skirmish, and the *reconnoissance*. Supported by a numerous artillery, this force was numerically more than a match for the forces at the disposal of Ibrahim; but the experience of the Egyptian commander, aided by the advice and assistance of the French Suleyman Pasha, more than made up for the difference in the number of troops.

The Egyptian Seraskier, learning that Hafiz Pasha had taken up a position close to Nezib, and that a considerable skirmish had taken place between the Bashi-Bazouks of the Sultan and the Bedouin cavalry of the Egyptians at Telbashir, ordered the advance of his troops from Aleppo, which was carried into effect on the 31st May, 1839.

The Ottoman position situated at Mezar, south-west of Nezib, being too strong, from its heights, to be stormed in front, was turned by a flank movement so as to come on the camp of the Turks, which was in three lines—the two first of infantry and the third of cavalry. The artillery consisted of 140 pieces, and the troops on each side amounted to about 40,000 men; so that, notwithstanding the larger force under the command of Hafiz Pasha, the superior organisation of the Egyptians enabled them to make proportionally a more effective concentration at the decisive point. The ground of the Turkish camp was not badly chosen, that to the left of the Ottoman camp being very uneven, which rendered the battle in that direction very disadvantageous to the Egyptian army.

Hafiz Pasha having been informed that several regiments of Syrians intended to pass over from the Egyptian to the Turkish ranks, opened a fire of shells on the Egyptian camp at eleven o'clock on the night of the 23rd of June. Four batteries of howitzers were carried forward in the silence of the night to within a short distance of the Egyptian camp, which soon became a scene of disorder and confusion. But Ibrahim and Suleyman Pashas lost no time in mounting their horses; and although several hundred Syrians passed into the Turkish lines, yet the activity which Suleyman Pasha displayed prevented a greater number of fugitives from leaving the camp. These indications of the hollowness of his own position, however, showed to Ibrahim Pasha the necessity of striking a decisive blow by a general engagement.

In consequence of this resolution, the Egyptian army was under arms at daybreak, and a division in six columns was directed against the rear of the Ottoman camp. The first column consisted of sixty guns, followed by twenty-four battalions of infantry, while nine regiments of cavalry—forming the fifth and sixth columns—brought up the rear. The intention of Suleyman Pasha, to whom is due the conception and manipulation of the manœuvre, was to form an oblique line on the left of the Turks; and, to prevent his troops being broken in their traverse movement, he had filled up the intervals of his columns—next the Turks—with extra infantry, in order to form an unbroken line if taken in flank. Approaching the village of Nezib, which poured a well-directed fire of artillery on the Egyptians, Suleyman Pasha made his troops turn left-face in order to take the Ottomans in flank. At this moment a sharp cannonade took place between the two armies; but the Egyptian artillery, which fired very rapidly, having exhausted its ammunition was obliged to slacken its fire. At this critical moment the right of the Egyptians had already given way, and a European staff officer of Hafiz Pasha advised him to march with the bayonet against the Egyptians; but, whilst Hafiz Pasha hesitated, Suleyman Pasha, assisted by his aides-de-camp, sword in hand forced the fugitives to reform in line under the deadly fire of the Turkish artillery.

The cartridges for the cannon of Ibrahim Pasha having arrived, the Egyptian grape-shot again began to play' and the Bashi-Bazouks of Hafiz fled in the greatest disorder. The Turkish commander and his staff-officers fell upon the fugitives sword in hand, to compel them to return; but the terrible fire of Egyptian grape made a rally impossible, and the Turkish troops, who had begun the contest without confidence, gave it up in despair. The army of the unfortunate Hafiz began now rapidly to melt away. A large body of infantry, which, during the action, had shown coolness and courage, left the field of battle, throwing away a great number of muskets; and the Turkish cavalry, which, by the bad generalship of Hafiz, had remained useless and unaiding spectators of the fray, were swept backwards, and carried along by the ebbing tide of Bashi-Bazouks.

Such was the disastrous battle of Nezib. The Turkish army left on the field more than a hundred pieces of artillery, besides its camp, baggage, and ammunition, only the military chest being saved. The number of killed and wounded Turks was estimated at four thousand, and the number of Egyptians at three thousand, in round numbers; but the actual loss of the Turkish commander was incalculable, and the army of the Sultan may be said to have ceased to exist—a demoralised and disorganised rabble, destitute of artillery, commissariat, and baggage, having preceded and accompanied Hafiz Pasha in his retreat to Marash.

Sultan Mahmoud did not live to learn the issue of his great venture against the most formidable of his vassals. Five days after the battle of Nezib, and several days before the intelligence of the disaster reached Constantinople, he breathed his last. "It is evident," writes Viscount Ponsonby on the occurrence of this event, "that the disease had existed many months. He was not aware himself of his situation, so that he continued to do everything calculated to hasten a catastrophe. He went off at last rapidly. It is astonishing how much and how generally he is lamented. It is not when a man is dead, and no longer the dispenser of rewards and punishments, that the voice of flattery is raised. It, therefore, is reasonable to believe that a man so lamented was really esteemed when alive. It is certainly the greatest loss the rayahs could suffer. He always protected them, and even at the expense of offending his own people. He had great qualities derived from nature. He had great views for the country he governed; but he stood alone, and could not find instruments to do the work well he desired to have performed."

Such was the most remarkable of the later sons of Orchan, who sunk into the tomb utterly exhausted by fierce resentments, corroding disappointments, and excesses of dissipation which prematurely undermined a physical constitution originally vigorous.

In contemplating the career of such a man, a tinge of melancholy passes over the mind; for Mahmoud was a truly remarkable man, and in his efforts to make the empire renew its youthful vigour, he underwent the toil of spring, the heat and burden of summer, but did not receive the rewards of autumn.

CHAPTER XII.

Defection of the Admiral of the Turkish Fleet to Mohammed Ali.—The Fleet at Rhodes.—Arrival of the Fleet at Alexandria.—Surrender of the Fleet to Mohammed Ali.

Equally fatal to the Sultan were the events of which the Mediterranean was the theatre. The Ottoman fleet, which had been fitted out at a great expense, was intrusted to the command of a man whose character was disfigured by defects of a more serious kind than those of the unskilful but faithful Hafiz. The stigma of the darkest perfidy can never be effaced from the name of Achmed Fevzi, Capitan Pasha, or High-Admiral of the Turkish fleet. The sombre veil that still covers the secret relations of this disreputable officer with the agents of Mohammed Ali has not yet been rent; but acts and facts compel us to infer that the naval officer to whom Mahmoud intrusted his fleet must have been tampered with by the Pasha of Egypt.

On the 9th of June the fleet left the Golden Horn for the Dardanelles, where it remained at anchor. On the morning of the 4th of July the Capitan Pasha received the official notification of the death of Sultan Mahmoud. The accession of his son, the Sultan Abdul Medjid, mingled the signs of rejoicing with those of mourning. All the ships of the fleet were dressed with flags, and fired a royal salute; and in the afternoon of that day they weighed anchor and stood out of the Dardanelles—the fleet comprising eight ships of the line, twelve frigates, one corvette, four brigs, two schooners, three fire-ships, and one steam-vessel.

As the fleet had been for a long time under orders for the coast of Syria, all the officers supposed that to be their destination. But, on arriving in Besika Bay, the Capitan Pasha informed Captain Walker, a most able British naval officer then attached to the Ottoman fleet, that the Sultan had been poisoned, and four of the principal officers of his household beheaded; that this had been done by the Russian party, who had assumed the government; and that, to prevent the fleet from falling into the hands of Russia, he intended to cruise outside the Dardanelles, so as to be ready to act with England and France. When off Tenedos, the fleet fell in with the French Admiral Lalande, whose force consisted of two ships of the line and a brig. After the usual salutes had been exchanged, the French Admiral, accompanied by the Prince de Joinville, came on board to visit the Capitan Pasha.

The Turkish Admiral, evidently uneasy in conscience, had sent a message to the French Admiral, through one of his officers, with the same story of the Sultan having been murdered by the Russian party, to which he added the statement that he proposed to go to Candia. Admiral Lalande pointed out that Candia was in the hands of Mohammed Ali, and that to take the Ottoman fleet there would be to deliver it up to that Pasha. He, however, said that he had no orders to interfere by force with the movements of the Ottoman fleet. In continuance of his system of duplicity, the Capitan Pasha afterwards informed Captain Walker that he had communicated all to the French Admiral, who highly approved of his plans; and that he (the Capitan Pasha) intended to proceed to Rhodes. Captain Walker then requested that he might be allowed to send letters on board of the Vanguard, a British ship of the line then in sight, so that the British ambassador and admiral might be made acquainted with his intentions; but the Capitan Pasha replied that the French Admiral had promised to communicate all particulars to them.

Nothing of consequence occurred during the run down to Rhodes, except the departure of the Kiahya Bey on the 6th July, who separated from the fleet ostensibly to communicate with Hafiz Pasha by Tarsus or Scanderoon, but in reality to concoct the betrayal of the fleet with Mohammed Ali. Accordingly, on the morning of the 12th, the Egyptian steamer-of-war, the Nile, joined the fleet, having on board the Kiahya Bey on his return from Alexandria. He communicated with the Capitan Pasha, and in the afternoon the fleet made sail to the southward, accompanied by the Egyptian steamer. On the morning of the 13th, the Vanguard parted company; and so anxious was the Capitan Pasha to get to the southward, that he carried such a press of sail as obliged him to leave behind a line-of-battle ship and frigate which were bad sailers. The approach of the Nile steamer to those ships, with orders to rendezvous off Alexandria, was the first intimation Captain Walker received as to the Capitan Pasha's intention of proceeding there. When the British officer spoke to him on the subject, he told him that he had received by the Kiahya Bey a letter from Mohammed Ali, who offered to put the Egyptian fleet under his command; but, before doing so, he wished to consult with him as to the best steps to be taken for the good of the Turkish empire, and that he meant to proceed off Alexandria for that purpose. On the following day, the 14th of July, they fell in with the Egyptian fleet, consisting of eleven ships of the line, three frigates, and two brigs, which were cruising about ten miles off Alexandria; and so ignorant were the Turkish admirals and captains of the change in the Capitan Pasha's plans, that many of the ships cleared for action.

It was at four o'clock in the afternoon that the Turkish fleet became distinctly visible to the astonished people of Alexandria; and, on the following morning, Mohammed Ali was looking at the fleet, separated by a short distance from his own, while the Nile steamer was seen nearer the shore standing for the port, with the Capitan Pasha's flag at the main, and his barge towed astern by the steamer. At nine o'clock the Nile entered the western harbour, and immediately Hussein Pasha, Mohammed Ali's first secretary, was sent from the palace in the Pasha's own boat to meet him and bring him on shore. After anchoring, a salute of nineteen guns, fired by the Nile, was returned by the forts the moment he landed. He was then received by the Pasha's high officers, and, mounting the Pasha's own horse, rode to the palace situated on the rocky peninsula that embraces the harbour, preceded by janissaries, with files of troops posted on each side all the way.

As soon as he entered the palace gate, Mohammed Ali went out of his room to meet him; and the admiral, seeing him, unbuckled his sword, gave it to one of the officers behind him, and, walking respectfully towards the Pasha of Egypt, bowed to the ground, as if meaning to kiss his dress, while Mohammed Ali embraced and kissed him, saying, "Welcome, brother!" After this, they walked arm-in-arm into the Pasha's room, all the officers following them. They sat near each other on the middle of the sofa, the Capitan Pasha telling Mohammed Ali that for a long time past it had been his wish to have the honour of seeing him.

After coffee and pipes, the bystanders were dismissed, and the two Pashas remained by themselves for an hour.

A little later, at half-past ten, the Turkish Admiral walked out of the room barefooted, his own servant not being there to give him his shoes. After walking about twenty paces without his shoes, his servant brought them as well as his sword, upon which he went to the "Palace for Guests" with the same pomp as on his arrival. On entering this palace, Hussein Pasha and the other officers of Mohammed Ali kissed his foot. He asked them to take seats, and gave them coffee, telling them, with the effrontery of a Judas, that he thanked God that his desire to meet the Pasha of Egypt was gratified, and that he had obtained Mohammed Ali's permission for the landing of the vice and rear-admirals.

On the 16th the Turkish fleet anchored off the western entrance of Alexandria, about six miles from the town, when all the admirals and captains went on shore to wait upon Mohammed Ali. Captain Walker also landed, and did not again return to the fleet; for, on the 17th, when the Capitan Pasha proposed to him to cruise with the united fleets, he declined, stating as the reason that he was not authorised by the British Government to serve under Mohammed Ali. To this the Capitan Pasha replied, with a flimsy show of rectitude, that it was still the Sultan's fleet, but united with the Egyptian for the good of the Turkish empire. Captain Walker having informed the Capitan Pasha of his intention of proceeding to Constantinople, the latter asked him if it were not possible to remain; and, on being answered negatively, the Pasha gave himself the air of being much hurt.

The political agents of the five European Powers in Alexandria were utterly astounded by this event. All of them were personally well inclined towards Mohammed Ali, so far as their duty permitted; and, excepting the Austrian consul-general, who was usually in a state of feud with the Egyptian government, all of them were more or less under that sort of spell with which Mohammed Ali by his fascinating manner used to bind to his interests even those who landed in Egypt with prejudices in his disfavour. But such an event as this took them completely aback, and they in a body represented to the Pasha how groundless were the accusations which the Capitan Pasha had brought about the poisoning of Sultan Mahmoud, which was so little in conformity with the depositions of the European doctors who had attended that sovereign during the course of his illness. Mohammed Ali replied that he did not pretend to exculpate the Capitan Pasha, but as long as Husreff Pasha was at the head of affairs he could not reckon upon a sincere reconciliation. He must therefore aim at something positive. The consuls maintained that the best method would be to restore the fleet to his Highness, and to send to Constantinople without delay some person charged to make in his name his submission to the Grand Seignior. They urged that the Capitan Pasha, having quitted the Dardanelles, after having received the order to proceed with the fleet to Constantinople, had committed an act of high treason, and that the representatives of the great courts were unwilling to believe that he was ready to make himself an accomplice of the Capitan Pasha, by accepting the fleet at his hands. Mohammed Ali loudly protested against such an argument as this, alleging that "in time of war it was permitted to receive deserters."

The officers of the Turkish fleet continued to come on shore for presentation to Mohammed Ali, and at one levée he said, with that cool and deliberate inversion of the truth which almost savours of comedy, "My sons, henceforward all differences between Constantinople and Egypt must be removed, and we must consider ourselves as one entire body. Our sovereign is young, and a pure jewel, and we must support him with fidelity, and aid the nation with all our hearts." On this the officers expressed much satisfaction, and requested permission to adopt the uniform worn by the Egyptian navy, which had that amplitude of hose characteristic of the eastern costume, instead of their own Frank uniform which was said to resemble that of Russia. To this the Pasha replied that they might do in this as appeared best to themselves. This colloquy bears every appearance of having been pre-arranged in accordance with the Pasha's views, which were directed towards an amalgamation of the two fleets.

After this the Turkish fleet anchored within the capacious port of Alexandria; and so desperate did the fortunes of the Sultan at this period appear, that Husreff Pasha, the prime minister of the Sultan, actually wrote to the Capitan Pasha to say that if he would return with his fleet to Constantinople, no notice would be taken of his late defection, and that a full pardon and oblivion of the past would be accorded. To this the Capitan Pasha replied, with a renewal of his duplicity, that he had not been, and did not intend to be, disloyal to his sovereign; that what he had done had been for the interest of the Sultan and of the Turkish empire, and to remove the fleet out of the power of the intrigues of Husreff Pasha; and that he would not return so long as the latter remained in power.

CHAPTER XIII.

Action of European Diplomacy on Turkish Affairs.—Survey of Britain.—Survey of France.—Survey of Austria, Russia, and Prussia.—The Secondary States.—Jealous Apprehensions of Russia by Europe.—Prince Metternich.—Viscount Palmerston.—M. Thiers.

Hitherto we have chiefly followed purely oriental currents of history; but we are now arrived at their confluence with the great streams of European events—at a period when we are impressed with the decisive action of the diplomacy of Europe in the affairs of the East, and when Turkey takes rank definitively as a member of the European family. It was no longer a struggle between a Sultan and a Pasha; but a complicated game in which the primary, secondary, and tertiary moves were studied and prepared from motives not immediately relating to Egypt and Syria.

It is therefore now requisite to take a survey of the states of Europe, especially those which by the extent of their territory and by their military power had the management of the grand police of Europe.

We begin with Britain, which, by its maritime power, was destined to take a chief part in the events which were preparing in the east of the Mediterranean. The character of the Briton is substantially Saxon, with laborious habits, and of a phlegmatic temperament, but coloured by Gaelic sensibility and Norman strength of will. With Saxon municipal institutions at an early period of her history, the constitutional liberty of modern times has been a natural sequence; and thus public liberty is not only congenial to the British character, but essential to it. When rulers have forgotten this in modern times, punishments of stringent severity have inevitably followed. When Charles I., deceived by the congeniality of absolute government to the Roman, Gaulish, and Slavic races of France, Italy, Spain, and Austria, sought to infringe the liberties of the British Saxons, his head was the forfeit of his inability to perceive this necessary distinction. A century later, when George III. thought to treat the British colonies of America, as if their inhabitants were not of our own flesh and blood, the disruption of this exhaustless region of territorial wealth from the rest of the empire was the result.

Phlegmatic moderatism has preserved Britain from wild democracy, and from those express and determinate wars of ambition which have kept France within comparatively narrow limits. As in the lives of her merchant princes, the political fortunes of Britain have been made up of parts taken as opportunities offered, with avoidance of hazardous speculations, and seizures inopportunely attempted in defiance of the world. The liberty she has enjoyed, combined with a felicitous insular situation, have carried her wealth and power to a height unparalleled in the history of the world. Requiring neither political centralization nor large standing armies to infuse terror into domestic factions, and, in short, being able to preserve order at home chiefly by moral force, and a semi-religious veneration for the law, she is embarrassed, encumbered, and unwieldy at the commencement of every general war, like one of her great ships on quitting a port or clearing an estuary; but when the sea-room is large, the emprise high and arduous,—when opposed by tempest, or impelled by favouring gales,—her firmly knit strength, her long endurance, her easy pliability, and her airy buoyancy, extort the tribute of admiration from the most reluctant nations.

Totally dissimilar from the so-called constitutional States of the continent, which are in reality military monarchies with elective consultative councils, the government of Britain is an aristocratic republic of birth, prudently studious of the opinions entertained by the aristocracies of wealth and intelligence, with an august and popular dynasty taking the supreme place in the political hierarchy. The Whig and Tory factions, into which this aristocracy is divided, have the function of preserving the principles of liberty and authority in harmonizing contrast; and, for the first time in the history of the human race, a great and complicated government is seen to realize that model which Aristotle, the greatest master of political science, considered the most perfect.

But two blots still remained on our reputation for justice; one, an artificial enhancement of the price of bread, from which no class of society derived any pecuniary benefit; the other, the sabbatarian shackle on the rational liberty of the Lord's-day Christian;—a violation of the principles and practice of the earliest and most illustrious of the leaders of the Reformation, and of the letter and spirit of Christianity, which, to the astonishment of Protestant Europe, had survived the removal of all the other obstacles to civil and religious liberty.

During the greater part of modern history, the rival of Britain has been France. More highly favoured than herself in climate and extent of soil, and with a great extent of coast on the Atlantic, the Channel, and the North Sea, she possesses the additional advantage of excellent ports in the Mediterranean.

The nationality of France is more Gaulish than Frank, being distinguished by a greater amount of sensibility, a greater plasticity of impression, and an intelligence more rapid than that of the other Northern nations. If Britain and Germany be the chief seats of Reason, France is essentially the country of "*Esprit*," which is the dress or decoration of Reason. The French sense of external beauty is far higher than the British; and our ingenious neighbours, in ornamental art, as contrasted with the utilitarian character of British manufactures, have an eminence of taste analogous to that which in the world of ideas renders their exposition of thought more felicitous than our own.

The government most congenial to the French nation is that of a centralised military absolutism: hence the radical contrast in principle between the British and French Revolutions of the seventeenth and eighteenth centuries. The errors of Louis XVI. were the converse of those of Charles I. The French monarch, instead of taking time by the forelock, by an economical and equitable despotic government, at the twelfth hour enthroned anarchy. The greatest error that the Briton can commit is to curb the rational liberties of the people; nor can France make a greater aberration than to seek a Saxon liberty which is repugnant to the Celtic genius.

The most composite of the greater European States is Austria, the mortar of which, if one may so express it, is Germanic—its very heterogeneousness being a proof of the extraordinary power of the cement. However differing from the British empire in materials, position, and form, that of Austria has the same vital principle, in being the domination of a Germanic race over non-Germanic races. The speculative sciences have had few pioneers in Austria, resulting from the large proportion of Slavic population—the Slavic genius tending rather to develope the State than the individual man. But in the German provinces of the empire instruction is generally diffused. Poverty and crime are more rare than in

France or in Britain; the technical sciences are pursued with ardour; and in music—whether as the colourist of passion, and the handmaid of poetry, or in its highest and most independent functions as the creator of those elevated moods of the soul which cannot be described by a language that takes its imagery from the phenomena of external nature—Austria has produced or cherished men of the highest genius. Her union with Britain in resisting the ambition of France on two great occasions—the absence of all maritime rivalry, and the vicinity of her large military resources to the Russian Empire—pointed her out as the natural counterpoise to that Power, and created close and intimate relations between her and Great Britain.

The Russian Empire is mostly Slavic or Slavicised Ugrian, but availing itself largely of Germanic science and perseverance in every sphere of military, political, and industrial activity. The Germanic race in Russia being much scantier than even in Austria, the number of thinkers, of great artists, or of pioneers of science is considerably smaller, but great aptitude is shewn for the lighter accomplishments. Her boundless territorial wealth, and the solid qualities of her Germanic civil and military servants, and industrial technicians, have created that power which, previous to the collapse during the Crimean war, was not inaptly termed a "Colossus minus the lantern."

Prussia—although neither a great maritime power like France and England, nor, like Russia and Austria, having a frontier to Turkey—was nevertheless an important power of the European Pentarchy, having, at various periods of modern history, developed military strength and resources far beyond her proportions of territory and population; and although possessed of a large Saxon population in her Rhenish provinces, the constitution of Prussia is, even since 1848, although not nominally, yet essentially autocratic, from various causes, —the chief of which are the large Slavic population in her eastern provinces, and the circumstance that the whole of her political arrangements are subordinate to objects of military defence. Several neighbouring countries in the north of Europe, more exclusively Saxon or Scandinavian, were distinguished by constitutional liberty, commercial wealth, and intellectual culture; but were not populous enough to weigh in the balance of power, and act with high executive police powers by the delegation of Europe in common with the five powers who constitute what is called the European Pentarchy.

The south of Europe, although a maritime region adjoining Turkey, took no part in the negotiations respecting the fate of the Ottoman Empire. Napoleon Bonaparte had extinguished the once brilliant Venetian republic, and Italy had in modern times fallen into political decadence. We Britons are told that Romanism is the cause of this,—an unsatisfactory statement: it appears to us that the ultimate cause is much deeper, and that Romanism is only the symptom of a national character for which the analytical spirit of the north in religion is unsuitable. Had free enquiry been better suited to the imaginative and impassioned Italian race, than the mystery, the illusion, the symbols, the associations, the vague ecstatic raptures, and the pompous artistic splendour of Rome, it is clear that, on the revival of letters and the restoration of the equilibrium between reason and sentiment, the Italians, in common with the northern nations, would have ceased to be Romanists. This has not been the case. The Roman Catholic religion, acting by association upon the imagination, and by its accessories appealing to the artistic taste, is evidently as suitable to the southern and western Romans and Celts, as Protestantism to the northern races.

But the Italians excel all the other Europeans in the sense of the beautiful—covering that fascinating land with the most sublime structures, and rising to ideal beauty on canvass, with the ease, confidence, and power of the Greeks in sculpture; producing poets that surpass those of all other countries, with the solitary exception of the British Shakespeare; and musicians whose works strike from the first, by their grace, spirit, and invention; and to which, if inferior to those of Germany in depth and earnestness, as well as in the mechanical and scholastic qualities, the most cultivated taste nevertheless turns with pleasure, attracted by that deep master-craft of creative genius which shews itself in an easy natural development and consistent unity of mould.

Spain had also been in decadence. She had made the ends of the earth feel her power, and at home the 17th century was a period of splendour in literature and art. But her valiant race had too easily gained and dissipated the treasures of the new world; and Spain, no longer a preponderating state, was slowly recovering from arduous intestine struggles, which renovated her energies and laid the foundations of an economical prosperity which is not yet fully evolved.

Such was Europe, the history of which has been so admirably traced by Guizot, although one must regret that a better comprehension of national character has not accompanied his illustration of national laws. Towns had made the Roman Empire: it fell, and the towns remained. New agglomerations took place: the Slavic and Celtic races developed military monarchy; the Italian races revived individual taste and intellectual culture; the Germanic-Saxon races cultivated free enquiry in religion and liberty in politics. The wars of religion, on the revival of letters, and the expulsion of the Moslems from the greater part of Europe, were followed by wars of dynastic ambition. France, twice dangerous under Louis XIV. and Napoleon, had been twice checked; and Russia was in the eyes of Europe the troublesome and the formidable power. The diplomarchical constitution of Europe was far from being complete, so as to meet every emergency; but the destruction of every monarch or minister who dared to substitute his individual will for the comitial action of the European Pentarchy had been erected into a principle.

While Russia had grown by Germanic genius, utilising the resources of a vast fertile territory and a large Slavic population, the Asiatic races on her eastern and southern borders declined and receded,—not from want of physical courage, but of that science which makes it effective. At the head of this bulky state was the Emperor Nicholas, who is certainly destined to fill a large space in the history of the nineteenth century. Of a handsome and commanding person, with a refined courtesy when he chose to exercise it, great capacity for labour, and knowledge of the details of military administration, Nicholas inverted the order usually found in active-minded and powerful sovereigns—to develope unmeasured ambition in the prime of life, and in age to bequeath prudent counsels to their successors. Louis XIV., who, with mediocre political, military, and artistic intelligence, was, nevertheless, a great master of kingcraft, recommended those who followed him to avoid war and palace-building; and the truly great Frederick, in spite of ultimate success, said, in the tranquillity of age, "Ich mache den spass, nicht wieder." Nicholas, in his old age, had not the courage to bear with power and prosperity, and to respect the integrity of the Ottoman Empire; but, in the prime of life, his conduct on the Egyptian question was admirable, for the same reasons that furnish the condemnation of his later policy.

By her pressure on Turkey in the latter part of the eighteenth and early part of the nineteenth centuries, Russia had reaped the fruit of the previous Austrian wars, when Turkey was really formidable to Europe, and it was with no friendly eye that Austria saw province after province of Turkey and Persia added to the already gigantic Muscovite Empire. The direction of the political affairs of Austria was in the hands of Clement Wencelaus, Prince Metternich, a statesman of large philosophic views, high personal integrity, and consummate court training. By his energy he had been chiefly instrumental in bringing the wars of the French Empire to a conclusion satisfactory to Europe. The two cardinal principles of his political career were the cultivation of amicable relations with Great Britain, and the preservation of the integrity of the Ottoman Empire; for he clearly comprehended that little fruit of his policy would remain to Europe if Russia were to be freely permitted to exercise that dangerous and preponderating power of which the France of the Empire had been so lately deprived. Hence an important treaty concluded in 1838 with Great Britain, the foreign affairs of which were at that time administered by Henry Temple, Viscount Palmerston.

The time has not yet come for a complete analysis of the long varied career and exceptional character of Viscount Palmerston; and we shall therefore confine ourselves to what is sufficient to elucidate the events that preceded the important treaty of 1841, which secured the integrity of the Ottoman empire. Viscount Palmerston was certainly one of the most remarkable men of the nineteenth century. Having stepped from the university immediately into public life, he had in middle age acquired the experience of those whose career is ended; and he retains, even in advanced age, much of the buoyant and sportive activity of the prime of life. This inversion of the order of normal nature, which rarely preserves vigour to the experience of age, renders him an intellectual phenomenon. Strong and healthy in body, and strong and healthy in mind, with matchless experience and capacity for labour, he was a living encyclopædia of political, commercial, and geographical knowledge. He possessed in an eminent degree the rare faculty of the true statesman, who, out of a bewildering mass of details, discerns, evolves, and utilises the essence of truth. As an orator he was distinguished by concision, and the skill of the consummate tactician who brings his full power to bear on the weakest part of his opponent's argument. Enjoying constitutionally, as well as by a potent self-imposed discipline, the most admirable good humour, he has enjoyed great social influence, even in periods when his policy has been loudly condemned by eager opponents. An estimate of his political acts as Minister for Foreign Affairs, and leader in the combinations of domestic party, must be left to another generation; but we may safely predict that future historians will not deny the strength of his British feelings, the brilliancy of his powers, and the gigantic magnitude of his labours. Yet he has been accused of having been the paid agent of Russia; and, incredible as it may appear, the walls that echoed this charge were not those of a lunatic asylum.

The dispatch of powerful squadrons to the Mediterranean, with the vigour and intelligence displayed by Viscount Ponsonby and Sir John McNeil, our representatives at the courts of Constantinople and Teheran; the courageous and unflinching support which Viscount

Palmerston gave to the British agents in the East; and the bold and decisive measures of the Anglo-Indian Government on its western frontier, without actual declaration of war against Russia, kept in check this formidable power. The actual invasion of Afghanistan by an Anglo-Indian force, which infused respect into Persia; and the treaty of 1838 between Britain and Austria, which, although nominally only securing reciprocal advantages of a commercial character, was, from its mention of the Danube, in reality an intimation to Russia that the concessions of Turkey in her favour in that quarter had arrived at their utmost limit, were finally decisive circumstances that impressed on Russia the conviction that prudence was the better part of valour.

Unprepared at this time to enter into conflict with public opinion, Russia adroitly evaded the storm; and, acting with Europe in this great oriental crisis, left France again isolated from Europe on a question in which this latter Power had not the smallest national interest, apart from the other Powers. The incarnation of this erroneous policy of isolation was M. Adolph Thiers, an intelligent writer, and a fluent speaker; possessing great good nature in personal intercourse,—making no useless and unremunerative expenditure of resentment in the struggles of party, evincing great dexterity in influencing the press, and the coteries, dispatching the business of an office, and dealing with the ordinary passions and foibles of ordinary men; but deficient in a knowledge of the true principles of national economy, and in the political morality which adjusts the policy and interests of the individual state to the recognized principles of European law, and the requirements of international harmony: wanting in short, in the manifestations of that higher intelligence which wafts to distant ages and foreign nations the reputation of a true statesman. Monsieur Thiers, the brilliant historian of the French Consulate and the Empire, was unconscious of the moral of his own tale, and himself succumbed, as a too venturous gambling politician, in the contest with the comitial action of the European Powers.

His political morality in action reproduces itself in his voluminous historical work. Ever and anon his sense of reason and justice revolts against the passions and prejudices of the dominant national pamphleteer and partizan military chronicler; but this revolt is in the long run always unsuccessful. He condemns the reckless ventures of Napoleon in general, but is elaborately apologetic in his details. On the other hand, the artist deserves our warmest eulogy, and M. Thiers is one of the greatest masters of historical narration. We read Guizot, as we take a salutiferous and not very palatable medicine. We are satiated and bewildered with the delicious intoxication and Circean fumes of Lamartine. But the style of Thiers, strong, clear, and agreeable, is equally remote from either extreme.

CHAPTER XIV.

Count Nesselrode announces Overtures of Russia to England.—First Mission of Baron Brunnow.—His Negociations with Viscount Palmerston.—Exception to the Acceptance of the Proposals of Russia.—Second Mission of Baron Brunnow to London.

The immediate direction of the Chancery of State of the Russian empire had been for many years in the hands of Count Nesselrode, a statesman of diminutive physical stature, but of remarkable intelligence, which is shown in all his gestures, conversation, and public dispatches; and no greater proofs can be adduced of his tact and practical ability than the extraordinary lengthened tenure of his high and envied office in such a country as Russia, where unscrupulous intrigue and unprincipled combination drive the most potent into sudden disfavour.

In August 1839 Count Nesselrode informed the Marquess of Clanricarde, British ambassador at the court of St. Petersburg, that the Emperor Nicholas, having reason to believe that the British Government was better disposed towards Russia, and entertained a more favourable and just opinion of his views and policy than heretofore, was desirous of improving this disposition to the utmost, and of strengthening the good understanding which so happily existed; and that therefore he had directed Baron Brunnow to proceed to London and offer the most unreserved explanations of the views and policy of Russia. Count Nesselrode added that, unless he were himself to proceed to London, it would not be possible for the Emperor to send thither any person more thoroughly acquainted with the foreign affairs and policy of Russia.

Baron Brunnow arrived in London on the 15th of September, and left England on the 12th of October, having in the interval had several long interviews with Viscount Palmerston, and with other members of Her Britannic Majesty's Government. He was frank and unreserved in his conversations, and said that the Russian government had witnessed with great satisfaction what they conceived to be evidences of greater confidence on the part of the British government in the sincerity and good faith of Russia with regard to the affairs of Turkey; that the Emperor felt that he deserved that confidence, and was anxious to draw closer the ties between Great Britain and Russia; that he looked upon the Sultan as a Sovereign who was his ally, and entitled to his support, and that he considered Mohammed Ali as a revolted subject; that he concurred with Britain in thinking that the best arrangement would be to confer upon Mohammed Ali the hereditary Pashalik of Egypt, and restore the rest of the territory in the occupation of the Pasha to the Sultan.

Russia therefore approved of the British proposal to blockade the ports of Egypt and Syria, if Mohammed Ali declined the proposed arrangement; but, with reference to the Egyptian threat of marching on Constantinople, some of the allies must come to the aid of the Sultan, and the Emperor thought that on account of its local position, Russia was the power which could most easily afford assistance; and that it should be given, not by virtue of the treaty of Unkiar Skelessi (which was a particular pact between Russia and Turkey, the articles of which constituted a *quasi-protectorate* of Turkey by

Russia, offensive to the rest of Europe), but that the aid should be given in virtue of the engagements about to be entered into between the Powers of Europe and the Sultan. Baron Brunnow then proposed a division of labour, so that the operations which might become necessary in Egypt and Syria should be undertaken by England, Austria, and France; and that whatever might be requisite within the Straits, and in Asia Minor, should be executed by Russia. Baron Brunnow added that if a convention to this effect were signed, the Emperor would not renew the treaty of Unkiar Skelessi, and that although the co-operation of France would undoubtedly render the execution more easy, Russia would be perfectly ready to act without France, if she could not be persuaded to concur.

On the communication of proposals so satisfactory and important, and contrasting so strongly with that spirit of occult hostility which for several years had marked the relations of the two governments, a cabinet council was held; and Viscount Palmerston thereafter stated to Baron Brunnow what were the sentiments of Her Britannic Majesty's confidential servants on the overtures of Russia. The government declared itself ready to adopt the whole arrangement, with the exception of one single point. Every State is considered as having territorial jurisdiction over the sea which washes its shores as far as three miles from low water mark, and consequently any strait which is bounded on both sides by the territory of the same sovereign, and which is not more than six miles wide, lies within the territorial jurisdiction of that sovereign. But the Bosphorus and Dardanelles are bounded on both sides by the territory of the Sultan, and are in most parts less than six miles wide, and consequently the territorial jurisdiction of the Sultan extends over both of these straits; and the Sultan has a right to exclude all foreign ships of war from these straits, if he should think proper to do so. Now, by the treaty of 1809, Great Britain acknowledged this right on the part of the Sultan, and promised to acquiesce in the enforcement of it ; and it was but just that Russia should make the same engagement. But Her Majesty's Government were of opinion that if, for a particular emergency, one of those straits should be opened for one party, the other ought at the same time to be opened also for other parties ; and that if it should become necessary for a Russian force to enter the Bosphorus, a British force should at the same time enter the Dardanelles: and, as the bulk of the British squadron would probably be required off the coasts of Egypt or Syria, the smallness of the number of ships that could be spared for going up the Dardanelles would of itself shew that their presence was intended to record a principle and to manifest union, and not to proclaim distrust or to exercise control.

Baron Brunnow expressed great regret at this decision of Her Britannic Majesty's Government, because his instructions did not provide for this case, and he should therefore be obliged to refer the question for the decision of his government, so that much valuable time would be lost. He added, that the will of the Emperor being for him the sole rule of his conduct he must stop at this point and, reporting to his court, must wholly reserve to the Emperor to pronounce upon it. Lord Palmerston fully admitted the weight and justice of the motives which hindered Baron Brunnow from going further; and, on the suggestion of the Russian Envoy that something should be immediately done in the way of coercing Mohammed Ali, especially with a view to the immediate surrender of the fleet, Lord Palmerston expressed himself inclined to prefer the arrival at some preliminary concert among the European Powers; so as to merge the question of the fleet in the larger one of a final arrangement.

Baron Brunnow departed from London, and, having brought to the knowledge of his government the details of his communications with the British Secretary of State for Foreign Affairs, Count Nesselrode announced the intention of the Emperor of Russia to accede to the wish of the cabinet of London with reference to the Bosphorus and the Dardanelles, and therefore directed Baron Brunnow to return to London in order to complete the arrangement. In January, 1840, definite measures were suggested by the Russian envoy to Viscount Palmerston, obviating the important exceptions taken to the proposals of his previous mission. We give briefly the shape which the arrangement had taken in the beginning of this not unmemorable year.

The Allied Cabinets, considering that they had formally promised the Porte assistance which the latter accepted, determined to settle among themselves the basis of a pacification affording assistance and securing independence to the Ottoman Empire. This basis was to embrace the grant of the Pashalik of Egypt to Mohammed Ali, with the right of transmitting to his descendants the administration of that province, but with the full recognition of the sovereignty of the Sultan. Mohammed Ali, on his part, was to evacuate Syria and Candia, and to give back the fleet to the Sultan. But, in case this arrangement should be declined by Mohammed Ali, and he should menace Constantinople, Russia would send its Black Sea fleet with a body of troops to be disembarked for the defence of that capital, whilst, on the other hand, the combined fleets of the other Powers should act on the coasts of Egypt and Syria. Moreover, in order to prove the union existing among the Allies, the Russian fleet and troops should be called into the Bosphorus while Austria, Great Britain, and France would cause two or three vessels of war to enter the sea of Marmora and cruise between Gallipoli and the Gulf of Mondania; this measure being exceptional, and not prejudicing the principle of the exclusion of all foreign vessels of war in time of peace.

CHAPTER XV.

Mission of Colonel Hodges to Egypt.—His Instructions.—Colonel Hodges' Presentation to Mohammed Ali.—The Divan of Mohammed Ali described.—Decisive Language of the British Agent to Mohammed Ali.—Mohammed Ali Refuses to Yield, and Prepares an Armed Resistance.

Meanwhile Viscount Palmerston had recalled Colonel Campbell, the British Political Agent and Consul-General, from Egypt. This, in many respects, able—and, in all respects, honourable—officer, had, unfortunately for himself, laid before the British Minister a series of considerations advocating Mohammed Ali's tenure of Syria at a period when the British Cabinet had arrived at the conclusion that decisive measures must be taken, in order not only to get back the fleet, but to restore Syria to its lawful sovereign.

A successor was therefore required, unentangled with any long continued intimacy with Mohammed Ali, and unaccustomed to proffer on behalf of his government menaces which were not subsequently supported by acts and facts. The admonitions to Mohammed Ali having never been accompanied or followed by military and naval demonstrations, or by positive hostilities, ceased to have any effect upon a man naturally self-willed and hitherto almost uniformly successful in his enterprises.

Colonel Hodges had, in the principality of Servia, given proofs of no common sagacity, and was moreover possessed of the moral and physical energy requisite for a mission of menace to an unbending military chief. Many persons have expressed the opinion that had more conciliatory language been used, Mohammed Ali could have been brought to evacuate Syria without the war which in the autumn of this year desolated that fine country; but it is difficult for me to adopt this view, considering that Mohammed Ali had illusions as to the power of his Syrian armies, the material strength of Acre, and the passiveness of the Syrian population; and also the incautious and ill-judged assurances of moral if not of actual military and naval support which he continued to receive from France down to the period of hostilities.

Colonel Hodges, proceeding from Belgrade to Alexandria, viâ Vienna and Trieste, received his instructions from Lord Beauvale (subsequently Viscount Melbourne, on the death of his brother, the then Premier), the British Ambassador at Vienna, which were characterised by remarkable good sense. "It will be well," said Lord Beauvale, "that you should state that the British Government has no feeling of envy or hostility towards him (Mohammed Ali); that the order and security which he has established in Egypt are more valuable to England, by opening a short communication with India, than to any other nation; that the commercial prosperity of Egypt re-acts upon us; and that for these reasons the continuance of the system which Mohammed Ali has created in that country, is of high value and importance to us.

"In Africa we are friendly to his power and to its permanence: if we are less so in Asia, it proceeds not from any hostility to his person, but because in Asia his presence acts as a solvent to the empire of the Sultan—an empire which his conquests in that part of the globe can neither support nor replace; which they can only weaken and destroy; and which we are determined to sustain.

"If the object of Mohammed Ali be really the establishment of his family, it is only in Africa that establishment can be fixed. There he will have Europe friendly to him; and, reconciled to the Porte, he may pursue the consolidation of the structure he has raised, with every facility for success, and with the certainty of transmitting it to his descendants.

"In Asia, on the contrary, there can never exist between him and the Sultan but an armed truce. He must either overthrow or be overthrown. But the chances are not equal: the loss of a battle expels Mohammed Ali from Asia; the gain of one opens at most to him the road to Constantinople, which is too strongly guarded for him to make an impression upon it. Full and final success is therefore impossible to him; the utmost he can gain in Asia is the temporary occupation of some additional districts; the utmost he can lose may be read in the history of all conquerors when checked in their career."

Such were the sound views expressed in simple and manly English by Lord Beauvale, and for the exposition of which Colonel Hodges had been selected by Viscount Palmerston. The author of this history accompanied that officer to Egypt in the latter part of 1839, as private secretary, and henceforth he hopes to be pardoned for interweaving with the texture of his history some of his own personal impressions. The first scene had an effect never to be forgotten. We entered, in a French steam-packet, the old port which then contained the combined fleets of the Sultan and Mohammed Ali, amounting to fifty vessels of war and including nineteen sail of the line. The pace of the steamer slackened, and we slowly moved up a majestic avenue of line-of-battle ships, with here and there an immense three-decker, in all the pride, pomp, and circumstance of naval architecture. There stood the motionless sentry, high perched on the poop, the setting sun glistening on his bayonet, and warming the congenial tints of his red fez and dusky visage into the semblance of a statue of rose-coloured granite. Just as we dropped anchor the sun went down, the drums rolled from ship to ship, the evening guns were fired, and up rose a thin vapour that drew a grey veil over the embers of the glowing horizon, while we heard for the first time the solemn and impressive tones of the call to prayer from the minarets on shore.

The presentation of the British Agent to the Pasha of Egypt took place with considerable pomp and ceremony, according to oriental usage. At an early hour a detachment of infantry, commanded by a field officer, with a military band, and a considerable body of Mohammed Ali's janissaries assembled in the great square of the Frank quarter, and the cortége, accompanied by all the British residents on horseback, proceeded over the sands of the peninsula to the palace of the Pasha, the windows of which opened on the wide azure of the Mediterranean; and in that torrid climate even the sun of December rendered its ample halls, with white marble floors and staircases, refreshing to the sense. As may well be believed, the reception was courteous. Colonel Campbell (brother of the Sir Colin who, as British Commissioner, accompanied Bonaparte to Elba) presented Colonel Hodges, who in turn presented Mr. Charles Alison, now Minister Plenipotentiary in Persia, and the author of these sheets, who, after pursuing some studies in history and international law, was about to commence his apprenticeship as a politician.

Mohammed Ali, at this stage of his career, was a thick-set man, but not so much so as to be pronounced corpulent. His features were remarkable neither for beauty nor the reverse; but if ever man had an eye that denoted genius, Mohammed Ali was that person. Never dead nor quiescent, it was fascinating like that of a gazelle; or, in the hour of storm, fierce as the eagle's. His dress was of a brown colour, embroidered with dark blue silk, and he wore on his head, not the turban of the earlier years of his pashalik, but the simple red Tunis fez.

The old times were not unrepresented. The last of the Mamelukes, who had escaped all the successive massacres, and was now in the hoary caducity of old age, wore on this occasion the ample turban and flowing crimson robes of those haughty slaves who for centuries had been successively elevated to, and precipitated from, an almost regal power. The shades of Murad and Ibrahim, Bonaparte and Kleber, flitted transiently through the mind, as we gazed on this survivor of a wide historical cycle, long since accomplished and vanishing in the distant spheres of doom. Here I saw for the first time Boghos Bey, the faithful minister for foreign affairs and commerce. He, too, wore the old oriental costume without any mixture of modern Frank innovation. His clean white turban and scrupulously neat person, in spite of his age; his diction and his courtesy—both of the best old French school—were all perfectly characteristic of the Levantine civil satellite of a great bashaw. But the climate of Egypt had left its mark on this Armenian from Asia Minor, and a white cataract in the eye reminded us that we were in the native soil of ophthalmia. Timid, supple, and a rayah, Boghos Bey had no confidence in himself; but he was invaluable to Mohammed Ali, from his great intelligence, his experience in mercantile affairs, and the oily suavity of the relations which he established with all the principal members of the European colony, diplomatic and mercantile. He was entirely devoted to the interests of the Pasha, and the poverty in which he died was a convincing proof of his honesty and fidelity. None of the immediate family of Mohammed Ali were present. Ibrahim was heading his legions in Syria; Abbas Pasha —in the sequel the successor of Mohammed Ali—was his deputy at Cairo; and Said Pasha, then a youth of eighteen or nineteen, was pursuing the studies requisite for a naval career in one of the corvettes at anchor in the roads.

After coffee was presented, and a speech delivered to the Pasha along with the credentials, and the interchange of the compliments usual on the occasion, Colonel Hodges alluded to the new edifices and improvements of Alexandria; to which the Pasha replied that he was doing his best to regenerate his country and merit the esteem of Europe. Colonel Hodges then assured Mohammed Ali that his labours in this respect were fully appreciated by Europeans. To this the Pasha replied emphatically, in consequence of conceiving that his power was referred to: "I do not know whether it has been appreciated hitherto, but please God, it shall be so henceforward." A magnificent furred pelisse was then put on the shoulders of the diplomatic agent; and, after taking leave, a grey blood Arab charger—another present from the Pasha—awaited the agent at the foot of the stairs.

These were the mere preliminary courtesies and ceremonies; the real tug of business was yet to come, and the interviews between the Pasha and the British agent in the earlier months of 1840 came like thunder-claps to awaken Mohammed Ali out of the illusions in which he had indulged as to the passive spectatorship of Europe enabling him to realize his airy visions of an Arab empire.

In January, 1840, Colonel Hodges proceeded to acquaint the Pasha, impressively, that it was England's firm determination to maintain the integrity of Turkey under its present dynasty, and that any opposition offered by his Highness could only entail upon him the most ruinous consequences; for that Her Majesty's Government were determined to carry out their policy by measures which could leave no doubt as to the spirit of it, even if they acted alone. The Pasha was evidently much agitated; and Colonel Hodges awaited his reply, when Boghos Bey, who stood by him, requested him to be composed and to allow Colonel Hodges to proceed. Finding that his Highness was not disposed to continue the subject, Colonel Hodges remarked that Prince Metternich, with whom he had a short time before an opportunity of conversing on the Oriental question at Vienna, had authorised him to state to his Highness that the Austrian Government were determined to back the policy of England to its fullest extent; and that he, the Prince, believed the other Powers were equally agreed on the subject,—for the correctness of which statement Colonel Hodges referred his Highness to M. de Laurin, the Austrian Consul-General. Mohammed Ali here burst forth violently, "Much words are useless. I don't deny the power of England, nor can I tie her hands; but if they pretend to confine me within the limits (meaning, as Colonel Hodges presumed, of Egypt) I swear I will do anything before I submit to be thus sacrificed. As for supporting the Turkish dynasty, who can be more zealous than I am? the very people about me would rise against me were I to attempt its overthrow." Colonel Hodges said that the occupation of the Turkish provinces in Asia was incompatible with such an assertion; to which the Vizier replied that, before the battle of Nezib, it was not concealed at Constantinople that unless he had a predominant share in the administration of the empire, it could never be restored to any degree of quiet or order, owing to the obstinacy of Husreff Pasha; as even the affections of that man (the Capitan Pasha, who had retired) were alienated. "I now hold," said he, "firm possession of those provinces, and still they are not submissive. I am an old man, upwards of seventy-one, but I will never consent to the cession of them during my lifetime." The Pasha confirmed this determination with a solemn oath, and evinced a desire to close the conversation. He had much reliance on the justice and humanity of England, and was sure she would hesitate before she caused the effusion of blood which might spring from her present policy. "Write," said he, "and I will answer all."

On a subsequent occasion Colonel Hodges told the Pasha that England had in no way changed her old habit of never coming to a rash decision; but that the decision once made, she would strike boldly, and with such a force as must command success. He entreated Mohammed Ali to be assured that England would only resort to such a measure when he had proved to her that all means of persuasion were unavailing; and recalled to his memory a circumstance of no remote date,—which unhappily might bear a strong analogy to his own case, should he persist in his present course,—which was, that Napoleon Bonaparte refused the offer of the Allied Sovereigns that he should be the ruler of France, with the Alps and the Rhine as a boundary, but that at a later period, having sent Caulincourt to treat with the Allied Powers, his tardy offers of acceptance were rejected.

Mohammed Ali having talked of his "rights," the British Foreign Secretary was not backward in reading him a homily thereon, with the stern canons of legal prescription for his text. "I have to instruct you," said Lord Palmerston to Colonel Hodges, "on the next occasion on which Mohammed Ali shall speak to you of his rights, to say to his Highness that you are instructed by your Government to remind him that he has no rights except such as the Sultan has conferred upon him; that the only legitimate authority which he possesses is the authority which has been delegated to him by the Sultan, over a portion of the Sultan's dominions, and which has been entrusted to him for the sole purpose of being used in the interest, and in obedience to the orders, of the Sultan; that the Sultan is entitled to take away that which he has given; that the Sultan may probably do so, if his own safety should require it; and that if, in such case, the Sultan should not have the means of self-defence, the Sultan has allies who may possibly lend him those means. You should also take an occasion of suggesting to the mind of Mohammed Ali that—to a garrison which capitulates in time, honorable conditions are granted; but that a garrison which insists on being stormed, must take the chance of war."

These stormy interviews and sharp admonitions inflicted profound wounds on the self-love of Mohammed Ali; and partly from miscalculation of the relative forces at his disposal and those of the European Powers that had taken him to task; and partly from an exasperation in which temperament, rather than sober judgment, was at work,—he commenced the vain task of putting himself in such an attitude of military defence as might impose respect on the allies of the Sultan—a futile effort of the Nile frog to expand to the sturdy proportions of the British bull and the Muscovite bear.

From the first entrance of the Turkish fleet into the harbour of Alexandria, great discontent had manifested itself on the part of the crews. It was the admiral, and not the fleet itself that had committed this foul defection. Obedience, discipline, and profound ignorance on the part of the ship's captains and companies had enabled him to consummate his ill-starred designs; but these feelings had given way to surprise, and had been succeeded by indignation. Coupled with the Egyptian fleet, lying under the batteries of Mohammed Ali, and still commanded by a traitor, the crews could undertake nothing expressive of their unflinching loyalty; and even the officers, whose antecedents and consciences absolved them in their own eyes and in those of others from complicity in the defection, were by no means insensible to the unwearied caresses, hospitalities, and attentions of the Pasha and his officers. To make still more sure of his objects, Mohammed Ali, in December and in January 1839–40, had amalgamated the crews of the Turkish and Egyptian squadrons, the former being at the same time clothed in Egyptian uniforms. Count Medem (afterwards minister in Persia) and M. de Laurin, the Russian and Austrian Consuls-General, questioned Mohammed Ali on this measure, to which he answered very coolly that "the sailors themselves were anxious and willing to change the Muscovite costume for the Turkish."

To explain this, it must be remembered that the Turkish costume had become almost European; while the Egyptian, with its wide trousers, retained much of the oriental ease and latitude. In spite of all this, the discontent did not diminish. Deli Mustapha Pasha, vice-admiral, declared that he would never give up alive the ship that was entrusted to him by the Sultan; and Omar, the rear-admiral, refused to accept or wear the new uniform of the Egyptians.

On land, Mohammed Ali displayed his accustomed activity, however unavailing or inadequate to the emergency. The Egyptian troops, which, after the end of the Wahaby war had occupied a great part of the Arabian peninsula, were recalled to Egypt. Kurschid

Pasha was one of the best lieutenants of Mohammed Ali, uniting bravery with prudence. On his arrival at Alexandria he received the command of the division to defend the coast. His address was exceedingly good natured, and the author well recollects his personal appearance, which was corpulent to an extreme rarely seen. A thumb having been carried away from its socket, he was surnamed both by himself and others "*Parmaksiz*" or the thumbless Kurschid.

Regiments of national guards were ordered to be formed from the inhabitants of Alexandria and other places. But this measure, pompous on paper, proved null in execution, from the paucity of volunteers and the total indisposition of the people of Egypt to co-operate with any chief, however able, against their lawful sovereign, whose "caliphate" or "succession" has moreover somewhat of a pontifical character—the civil, military, and religious organism flowing through the Grand Vizier and Sheikh ul Islam from a common centre.

In anticipation of a blow being struck in Egypt, which was the centre of his power, and taking alarm at the curiosity that European officers had shewn as to the defences of Alexandria, Mohammed Ali issued orders to disarm the two squadrons in the port, and form six regiments from the ships' crews and marines to defend the coast from Rosetta to Alexandria, and westward towards the Lybian Desert. He also directed that all the guns should be brought on shore and placed in battery to strengthen the positions of Aboukir, the Catacombs, Marabout, and the entrances of the ports of Alexandria. At the same time Damanhour was selected as a convenient place for a camp of reserve, from which troops could be directed with equal facility on Rosetta or on Alexandria. This magnificent project was only partially carried into effect, strong symptoms of disaffection in Syria having indicated that country to be ripe with immediate danger to the Pasha.

Colonel Hodges, on the last day of March, made a communication to Mohammed Ali which left no doubt that the hour of decisive action was at hand, and that of diplomatic negotiation passed away. He asked the Pasha, "Pray what does your Highness purpose doing with the Turkish fleet?" to which he replied, "I shall keep it as a weapon taken from the hand of my enemies, until my differences are settled with the Porte, and then I shall send it back to the Sultan." To this Colonel Hodges rejoined, "If the officers of the Turkish fleet knew their duty to their religion and to the Sultan, they would return with their ships to Constantinople; and," added he, "I do not conceal from your Highness that I am instructed by my government to advise their adoption of such a course." On this, the Pasha, in a state of the greatest excitement, jumped up from his Divan, and cried, "Now you place me in a state of war. I warn you that the first defection I perceive, I will shoot the offender." Colonel Hodges contented himself with answering:—"Your Highness may rely upon it, that threats will not prevent the performance of my duty. I view with regret the measures you are adopting, which only prove the eagerness with which you are rushing on certain destruction."

From this period no further representations were made to Mohammed Ali. Courteous persuasion had been followed by strong arguments which had produced no effect. Peremptory language and menace had been equally disregarded; nothing remained but the "ultima ratio regum."

CHAPTER XVI.

The Convention of July 15, 1840, is Signed in London.—Its Provisions.—The Convention Notified to Mohammed Ali.—His First Refusal.—His Final Refusal.—Mohammed Ali deposed by the Sultan, and Egypt and Syria Blockaded.

The negotiations between Baron Brunnow and the British Government, the details of which were candidly imparted to the French Government, as well as the ill-timed obstinacy of the Pasha, have no doubt prepared the reader for the concurrence of Austria, Russia, Prussia, Great Britain, and of the Porte, in coercive measures against Mohammed Ali. These took the preliminary form of a convention, or treaty, dated 15th July, 1840, for which extraordinary Powers were granted to the plenipotentiaries of the consenting powers. The Porte was represented at these London conferences by Shekib Effendi, a statesman of robust physical frame and masculine intellect, although not having had the advantage of an European education.

This treaty or convention was an extension or embodiment of the arrangements concluded between the British and Russian Governments, and in accordance with the language and acts of Admiral Roussin, the French Ambassador at the Ottoman Porte. The two Straits of the Bosphorus and the Dardanelles, as well as the capital, were placed in security against all aggression,—the operation of the Allies there to be considered only as a measure of exception adopted at the express demand of the Sultan, and in no way derogating from the normal exclusion of foreign ships of war from these straits.

A separate act prescribed the mode in which Mohammed Ali was to be dealt with. The Sultan promised to grant him not only the hereditary administration of the Pashalik of Egypt, but, moreover, the fortress of St. Jean d'Acre and Southern Syria for his life. But the Sultan, in making these offers, attached to them the Sybilline condition that Mohammed Ali should accept them within the space of ten days after the communication of them should be made to him at Alexandria. If within this term he should not accept the arrangement, the offer of the life-administration of the Pashalik of Acre was to be withdrawn, and after ten days more—or, in all, twenty days—even the offer of Egypt was no longer in force on the part of the Sultan.

Rifaat Bey was the commissioner appointed by the Porte to notify to Mohammed Ali the terms determined upon at the London conferences. This statesman, since elevated to the rank of Pasha, distinguished by polished manners and appearance, was of a conciliatory disposition, and by no means deficient in intelligence. He had been previously, and has been since, in high employments, having been more than once Minister for Foreign Affairs, and ambassador at European courts of the first class. He was not remarkable for any energy or activity, but has rarely shewn deficiency in tact and discrimination.

In the middle of August, a month after the convention had been signed, Rifaat Pasha had his audience of Mohammed Ali; and, after the customary salutations, the Constantinople envoy made known to the Pasha those terms with which the reader is already familiar.

To this Mohammed Ali answered, with professions of astonishment that his real views should have been so mistaken—which aimed at restoring the Ottoman Empire to its ancient force,—"The propositions which are now made to me are evidently absurd, and of a nature to cause my ruin. France is ready to come to my aid, and has more than once offered to me her intervention; but I have always refused it, because my intention is not to allow the troops of the Christian Powers to ravage the Mussulman territory, and I am ready to sacrifice my life and everything that I possess to the love of my nation."

"But," said Rifaat Pasha, "your insisting upon not abandoning any one of the provinces which are now under your sway, only proves too clearly that you really have your own interest and that of your family in view, and not that of the Ottoman Empire, as you wished to make me believe just now. My mission is only for the purpose of notifying to you the arrangement concluded between the four great Powers."

On the Consuls-General of the four Powers proceeding to Mohammed Ali on the following day, in accordance with the instructions they had received, Mohammed Ali said, "Rifaat Bey has in truth informed me of the object of his mission, and of the decisions of the conference of London. The reply which I have made to him is that which you ought to expect from me. I cannot accept the terms which are offered to me; and you know the character of Mohammed Ali too well to suppose that he will allow himself to be buried alive."

On the 5th of September, Rifaat Bey, together with the Consuls-General of the four Powers, waited on Mohammed Ali in order to receive his final reply to the demands of the Sublime Porte. The Pasha, being confined to his room by a painful indisposition, gave his official answer through the medium of his confidential secretary and minister, Sami Bey; the same who governed Widdin during the Russian occupation of the

Principalities, and renowned in the Ottoman Empire for his oriental scholarship, and his diplomatic experience.

After having inspected, along with the four consuls, the credentials of Sami Bey, Rifaat Bey said, "We are come at the expiration of the period of twenty days to ask what is the decision to which his Highness has come with regard to the stipulations of this second alternative of the convention."

Sami Bey replied, "Before the expiration of the second period, the Pasha had accepted the inheritance of Egypt, out of deference to the decisions of the four great Powers, and to the orders of his benefactor the Sultan; and I now confirm to you officially this resolution. With regard to Syria, his non-acceptance not being a refusal, His Highness, considering his numerous services to the Ottoman Empire, is desirous of submitting a request on this subject, as well to his lawful sovereign as to the four great Powers; and he flatters himself that Rifaat Bey, as well as the consuls of the four Powers, will have the goodness to communicate it to their respective courts."

The object of this evasive answer was to enable M. Thiers to gain time, in order to complete the military and naval preparations subservient to a policy which ministered neither to the advantage of France nor to the honour and prudence of this statesman. But it was a definite yea or nay that the agents required on this occasion, and the proposals for delay by Mohammed Ali, having been unaccompanied by the offer of the immediate surrender of the fleet, were regarded as a non-acceptance.

On receiving this intelligence, the Porte notified to all the missions at Constantinople the deposition of Mohammed Ali from his post as Pasha of Egypt, and also the establishment of a blockade of the ports of Egypt and Syria; and the Consuls-General of the four Powers took their departure from Alexandria. The tempest lowering over the head of Mohammed Ali had thus been braved with inconceivable infatuation. The policy of Thiers had appeared to offer a secure harbour of refuge—an illusion that was quickly dispelled, when the storm, at length bursting, aroused the Pasha from his fallacious security.

CHAPTER XVII.

Rigorous Policy of the Egyptian Authorities in Syria.—The British Fleet off the Syrian Coast.—The Austrians and Turks.—Operations near Beyrout.—Ghazir Occupied.—Djebail and Batroun.—Hostility of the Mountaineers to the Egyptians.

A period sometimes arrives in political affairs when all the efforts of soldiers and statesmen to avert a crisis are as futile as attempts to smother an earthquake or erect dams against a rolling flood. Vain were the precautions and proclamations of Suleyman Pasha, major-general of the Egyptian troops, in presence of the irrepressible ferment in the popular mind of Syria. Partial risings had taken place in mount Lebanon in the course of the summer, in consequence of the mountaineers having been obliged to work in the coal mines; but a force of above ten thousand men having been sent to Beyrout with Mohammed Ali's usual promptitude and decision, the mountaineers were, without being conciliated, compelled to adjourn their rising to a more favourable opportunity.

But the identification of the forces of four out of the five great Powers of Europe with the interests of the Sultan, again placed the Egyptian Government in a most critical position, without even the firing of a shot; and in August, not only the mountaineers of Lebanon, but the Nosairis of mount Cassius, the Moslems of Nablouse, and the Druses of the Hauran were again in a state of agitation. Suleyman Pasha, having informed the consuls at Beyrout of Mohammed Ali's refusal of the conditions offered him by the Sultan, the coast of Syria was declared in a state of siege. Every individual, whether native or foreigner, introducing into Syria writings or proclamations fomenting disobedience or revolt, was to be punished by death, while the prospect of penal servitude was held out to all who chose to be guilty of concealment of the Sultan's proclamations. The Egyptian Government in Syria at the same time spread reports of the aid France was about to give Mohammed Ali. The Moslems of Damascus and Aleppo were led to believe that the object of the Allies was to establish Christian supremacy in Syria, which the Egyptian Government was alone in a position to resist; while the Christian population of the mountains were on the contrary led to fear the revival of Druse supremacy and Christian abasement.

A small British naval force had been for some weeks off Beyrout, under the command of Commodore Napier, a man of daring gallantry, whose forward enterprising spirit had led him in a varied career to serve as a soldier as well as a sailor in the troubles of western Europe; and who, in his own peculiar profession, had earned well merited fame by encounters of ship to ship during the latter years of the Anglo-French war, and, finally, by a naval action off Cape St. Vincent, which had discrowned Don Miguel, the sovereign of Portugal. The bulk of the fleet rejoined the squadron of Napier on the 8th of September, off Beyrout, under the command-in-chief of Admiral Sir Robert Stopford, an experienced and honourable officer, but certainly past the age when extraordinary personal activity could be fairly expected. The fleet itself was in the highest state of efficiency, as might be expected in the case of an insular people, whose ships, colonies, and commerce encircle the globe. All the admirals and captains of a certain standing had seen war. Even the juniors required no schooling to the tug of actual combat. A fleet, unlike an army, never rusts; and the sailor is, so to speak, always in campaign. Navigation with its contrasts of climate, its alternations of weather, its constant exertion and occasional danger, disciplines the mind to foresight and the body to arduous enterprise.

Austria was represented in this expedition by a small force of frigates, on board which was an archduke of the Imperial House, who had been brought up to a naval career, and who has since been cut off in the flower of youth. The remains of the Turkish naval forces were commanded by Walker Bey, that British officer who had been surprised into a passive spectatorship of the defection of the most effective part of the fleet, and on board this remnant, hastily fitted out for the occasion, was a small force of four or five thousand Turkish troops.

As Beyrout was surrounded by a slight wall without a ditch, it did not appear to Commodore Napier desirable to make a first attack there; because, had the Allies succeeded in obtaining possession of the town, they would have been penned in by a superior force, and would have had no opportunity of communicating with and arming the mountaineers, without whose assistance it would have been impossible to make any impression on Suleyman Pasha's army. Under these circumstances the commodore suggested to the admiral, who was commander-in-chief of the allied forces by sea and land, that they should put the troops ashore in Djouny Bay, in the province of Kesrouan, and there entrench themselves, and arm the mountaineers who, they had reason to suppose, would flock down and join the Sultan's standard.

The invention of steam as applied to shipping had prodigiously increased the military power of the Allies, who had the command of the coast; and of this full advantage was taken, in the very first operations. After dark on the 9th September the Turkish troops and marines were moved into the steamboats, the operation being accomplished by two in the morning. Soon after eight they proceeded off Beyrout Point, to draw the Egyptian troops in that direction, and there wait until the sea breeze set in. The Egyptians, anticipating a landing, issued out to the westward, prepared to drive the Allies into the sea, before they should have time to form; but a brisk fire of shells being opened upon them from the fleet, their columns were disordered, with some loss of life. Between nine and ten o'clock the azure of the Mediterranean began to be slightly ruffled by the sea-breeze which sprang up; and upon this Napier and Walker, with the troops, weighed anchor and stood across the bay to Djouny where they took up a position on an elevated promontory jutting out from near the base of mount Lebanon. The position was immediately entrenched, and the approaches to it completely swept by the guns of the protecting naval force, while at the same time lighter craft commanded the coast-road from Beyrout. In the immediate vicinity, the Dog river not only intercepted the mountains by a deep ravine, with its towering rocks and gloomy shades, but afforded abundance of cool and delicious water. A Turkish battalion was landed to the north of the river, so as to prevent the advance of the Egyptians from Beyrout, when they discovered the real point of attack. On the heights was a convent, and Commodore Napier took up his quarters in the chapel, which served for dining room, bedroom, and powder magazine. His establishment was landed from the ship which he commanded; and he says in his narrative, "I looked back to the month I passed there as one of the happiest of my life. Provisions were abundant, wine not bad, and archdukes, princes, pashas, and emirs were entertained; and I fear the laws of the prophet were frequently infringed by our Turkish allies."

On the 11th a flag of truce was dispatched to Suleyman Pasha to summon him in the name of the Sultan to surrender the town of Beyrout; but as he returned an evasive answer, the British admiral ordered the destruction of the castles and forts to the right and left of the town. Firing was kept up at intervals for three successive days; the effect of the fire on the town being tremendous. Many soldiers were killed in the streets by shot and shell.

One of the most useful auxiliaries of the Allies was Mr. Richard Wood, one of the interpreters of the British Embassy in Constantinople, who had been invested with extraordinary powers by the Porte for temporary purposes. This gentleman had been educated in Syria, was well acquainted with the language and principal personages of these mountainous regions, and all through the operations gave proofs of intelligence and zealous activity. He caused Arabic versions of the convention of London to be distributed in the mountains, which had an electrical effect on their inhabitants. Intelligent enough to understand that the Egyptian Government could not keep its ground with such odds against it, they thronged the rugged roads, leading like spiral staircases from the fastnesses above to the coast, and eagerly supplied themselves with the muskets provided for them. Eight thousand stand were thus distributed, and more applied for them than could be furnished with them.

The principal place in the neighbourhood is Ghazir, situated far above the sea on the brow of a hill. Besides cool pure air, it enjoys a very romantic situation, being in the middle of an amphitheatre of lofty mountains, partly covered with wood, and watered by brooks in all directions. At the highest part of the hill was the palace of Emir Abdallah Shehab which overlooks the whole coast, with the promontory of Beyrout, its town and shipping, and the Bay of Djouny seawards, while in the opposite direction the landscape is rugged, rocky, and mountainous.

A powerful feudal Christian family had at one time possessed this place, but by divisions of inheritance, and profuse expenditure in horses and retainers, they had been reduced to poverty; and the Emir Abdallah Shehab was, at this period of the war, the wealthy man of the district.

Mr. Wood, availing himself of the impression produced by the bombardment of Beyrout, marched up to Ghazir with two hundred Turks and a hundred marines, to free the inhabitants from the presence of the troops of the Emir Beshir, the great ally and support of the Egyptians. Here the inhabitants received the Anglo-Turks with the greatest enthusiasm, intermingling in their ranks and offering prayers to the Almighty for their success. At the same time the troops of the Emir Beshir, offering no cordial resistance, were speedily dispersed. After this the Emir Abdallah wrote a letter of submission. Mr. Wood conducted him to a tent where he presented him to Sir Robert Stopford and Selim Pasha, who commanded the Turkish troops, and whose confirmation of him as Governor of Kesrouan had an excellent effect on the mountaineers.

Meanwhile Ibrahim Pasha, having correct intelligence of what was going on, endeavoured, along with Emir Halil, to enter the province of Kesrouan, with a view to intimidate the mountaineers who had taken arms, whose villages were menaced with fire if they joined the Allies or refused to give up the muskets distributed. Nor were fair promises neglected, while seeking to intimidate the mountaineers. Remission of the obnoxious capitation tax for three years was held out; but the Allies, not to be outmanœuvred, promised its total abolition.

Acting on the principle of striking sudden and unexpected blows in various directions, the towns of Djebail and Batroun, to the north of Beyrout, were assailed by the light movable shipping of the fleet; but these efforts were not unattended by casualties. At the former place the ships opened their fire upon the castle, which was returned by musket shots. A landing was made—the marines advancing briskly to the assault; but, on reaching within thirty yards of the tower, a destructive fire was opened from a crenellated outwork, having a deep ditch in front, which was completely masked from the fire of the ships. The men falling fast, and the wall of the castle being impracticable, with no gate accessible, and only the muzzles of the muskets visible through the loopholes, the men were judiciously drawn off. But at night a party of armed mountaineers was established in the town, and at daylight it was found that the Albanians had evacuated the castle during the night, leaving their wounded behind them. An attempt was made to bombard the fort and camp at Tripoli, but the distance was found too great to produce the desired effect from the sea.

The public spirit, at first slow, timid, and groping, now shewed a bold front in favour of the Allies, and the Egyptian power, fragile at the best, became irreparably damaged after the first shocks. That knowledge is power is under no circumstances more true than in war. The Allies had excellent information of all the movements of the Egyptians. The armed mountaineers, hovering on their flanks and rear, attacked small parties and convoys, while the Allies could send ammunition and provisions, with escorts of four or five men, two or three hours into the country. The peasantry, who had been forced under pain of death to leave the villages occupied by the Allies, began to return in great numbers, and a regular market was opened in one of them, to which a confluence of the provisions and resources of the country directed itself.

All the efforts of the emissaries of M. Thiers to retain the mountaineers in the Egyptian interest were unsuccessful. The superior of the French Lazarists arrived off the coast in a French steam vessel from Alexandria, with a view to prevent the Catholic inhabitants of Mount Lebanon from embracing the cause of the Sultan, and taking arms against Mohammed Ali; but the Austrian Consul-General in Egypt, having information of the design, apprised the Austrian admiral, Baron Bandiera, of the fact; and before the superior had time to land, the French prefect of the convent of the Lazarists at Antourah—two hours distance from Djouny—visited the emissary. He had first obtained the consent of Admiral Stopford, which was necessary, inasmuch as the convent of Antourah was within the British advanced post; a permission which was readily granted because the admiral was not ignorant that the only advice which could be given to the new comer was to return forthwith, without putting his foot on shore, since the Christian mountaineers of all denominations had pronounced themselves for the Sultan and his allies. The consequence was that the Lazarist superior, seeing his labour in vain, at once returned to Alexandria.

CHAPTER XVIII.

NOMINATION OF SIR C. SMITH.—VIGOUR OF SIR C. NAPIER.—SIDON TAKEN.—THE EMIR BESHIR DEPOSED.—OMAR'S OPERATIONS.—BATTLE OF THE 10TH OF OCTOBER.—DEFEAT OF IBRAHIM.—SURRENDER OF BEYROUT.—BOMBARDMENT OF ACRE.

ON the 30th of September the Sultan nominated Sir Charles Smith, a distinguished British artillery officer, to be virtual commander of the Ottoman troops in Syria, to the great discontent of Izzet Mohammed Pasha, the titular governor of Acre and its dependencies, who was the chief representative of the Porte in these military operations. "Be it known unto you," recites the firman of the imperial will which gave such disgust to the Pasha, who belonged to the old leaven of Turkish pride, ignorance, and corruption, "that Sir Charles Smith, the most illustrious among the noble followers of the Messiah, being a man of the most eminent abilities, it is most necessary and advantageous that you should act under all circumstances according to his opinion and judgment; and you shall not deviate from the path of his instruction, but you shall exert yourself to the utmost, as you will be held responsible for the commission of any action contrary to the advice and opinion of Sir Charles Smith. Conform you therefore scrupulously to all that is above written and give due credence to the imperial cypher."

Izzet Pasha played to the best of his ability the passive part assigned to him, without, however, being entirely able to conceal his disgust, and as little his overbearing and savage character, which brought down upon him the hatred of those who were placed under his orders. One day he ordered five hundred blows to be given to his cook for having put too much salt into the soup. One of Admiral Stopford's interpreters, who, fortunately for the wretch, was present, interceded for him and obtained his pardon.

But Ibrahim Pasha still held, not only the high road from Beyrout to Damascus, but many of the more central and populous points of Lebanon. A revolt had been fomented and extended with signal success, which gave confidence to the troops of the Sultan, and inflicted discouragement on the Egyptians. But no positive encounter had taken place between the respective land troops. Napier and Jochmus, however, felt that this crisis of demoralization must not be thrown away, and that a blow must be struck while it lasted. Accordingly on the 23rd, at night, a strong force was left to cover the camp at Djouny, one of the first rules in war being to obtain the possession of a secure basis. The remaining force of the army, consisting of four battalions of Turkish infantry, a battalion of British marines, and two detachments of Austrian rocketeers, was formed with a view to attack at daybreak the advanced guard of Ibrahim Pasha, consisting of a thousand men under the Emir Massoud, entrenched at Ardali in a very strong mountainous position; but being taken in the rear, after fatiguing marches over precipitous ground, a part of the Egyptians were dispersed, and four hundred, having their retreat cut off, were made prisoners. In this affair the loss on the part of the Allies was small, but the results were important, in consequence of its having been the first success of the Turks over the Egyptians that had taken place for many years.

Commodore Napier was the soul of the expedition;

and, fully comprehending that delays were to be avoided in the face of an army disheartened, disorganised, and partially defeated, his counsels were all for vigorous and decisive action—for striking fresh blows before the enemy could recover himself. The force at the command of the Allies was small; but the elements conspired in their favour. Not only sea and land, but rain and air—not only revolt in the mountains and blockade by sea, but steam itself co-operated in conferring ubiquity of intelligence, of movement, and of action.

A reconnaissance was made of the coast from Beyrout to Sidon, at which place the Egyptians were found busy in fortifying the town and barricading the streets. The admiral then decided upon an attack on Sidon, and on the 26th of October Commodore Napier joined Admiral Stopford with a force of 1400 Turks and marines. The town was duly summoned, and, on the refusal of the authorities to give it up, was bombarded. A landing was then effected. Captain Walker headed the Turks in the assault that took place after a breach was made; Commodore Napier, the English; and the Archduke, the Austrians. The assault was made in three places under the fire of the ships, and to prevent the garrison from running away, the steamers kept sending bombs away beyond the town and so kept them in. The Egyptian troops fought well from the houses, but were turned out and driven back to the barracks, where, at last, they were compelled to lay down their arms about sunset; and the garrison, composed of between 2,000 and 3,000 Egyptians were made prisoners.

On the following day Mr. Wood assembled the Divan of Sidon, and read to them the powers with which he was invested by the Porte, and in the name of Izzet Pasha established the government in the name of the Sultan. Public prayers were offered by the Mufti for the success of his arms, and the greatest enthusiasm was displayed by all classes of the inhabitants, who were as usual ready to throw off the government of the day. This event had a great moral effect upon the mountaineers around Sidon, and several Emirs of the house of Shehab came down to the coast and made their submission. The Sheikh of Dair el Kamar came personally to Sidon, and stated that Ibrahim Pasha was there with about four thousand men, so that it was impossible for the inhabitants to leave their families and come down for arms, as the moment it became known to him he would revenge himself on their families and burn their houses in their absence.

The old and once influential Emir Beshir was in the utmost perplexity. Ibrahim Pasha, anxious to retain a man who had given solid proofs of his power and authority during so many years, neglected no art of persuasion, no display of force, and no precautions of espionage to retain him within his toils. But this hoary chief, not daring to declare openly for the Allies, had nevertheless lost all confidence in the star of the Egyptians. He therefore sent to Commodore Napier a message by a priest, with a request to meet one of his emissaries at the advanced posts of the Allies after dark; proposing as terms—first, the observation of secrecy during the negotiation; secondly, that he should retain his government, and be guaranteed in it by the four Powers; and thirdly, that he should be allowed time to withdraw his sons and grandsons from Ibrahim Pasha before he declared himself. The first and third of these propositions were accepted, but Commodore Napier did not feel justified in hampering himself with any pledge; and Mr. Wood, as the political agent of the Porte as well as of the British ambassador, being impatient of delay, was obliged to grant the Emir a term, so as to preclude further injury to the interests of the Sultan in Syria. On its expiration on the 8th of October, a firman superseding him was delivered to another member of the house of Shehab, the Emir Beshir El Kasim, who had found means to escape with a few horse from the neighbourhood of Beyrout, and had joined the camp of the Allies; and who, at the head of a troop of mountaineers proved a most useful commander of an irregular rifle force, having in a smart skirmish obtained a considerable advantage over Osman Pasha, one of the lieutenants of Ibrahim, at Merouba.

Ibrahim Pasha, having persisted in his system of dividing his forces, in order to cover more ground, the Allies combined to take advantage of his mistakes. On the 8th of October, in the afternoon, General Jochmus occupied the heights of Ardali, where the action of the 24th September had been fought; and Commodore Napier and Selim Pasha, with Colonel Hodges, marching thither on the 9th, resolved to drive the Egyptians from their position at Kalat Maidin, which was of prodigious natural strength, being covered by a deep ravine, and presenting three successive lines of entrenchments. The elevation of the position, from the depth of the ravine to the highest redoubt, was, perhaps, a thousand yards, and in many parts the rocks were nearly perpendicular.

It was in the operation which we are about to detail that the well-known Omar Pasha earned his first horse-tail. The youthful Lattas was of a nation of heroes. Born at Ogulin, on the borders of the Croatian Switzerland, and close to the frontiers of the north-west corner of the Ottoman Empire, he was of that race which the arms of a Selim and a Suleyman could not entirely subdue, even in the zenith of the martial power of the sons of Osman. Strangers to the wealth and luxury of Venice and Ragusa, the profession of arms and the lays of the minstrel have formed the business and charmed the leisure of these heroic mountaineers. When Servia and Hungary had been prostrated by the Porte, Croatia was the link between the haughty republicans of maritime Venice and the successors of Charlemagne. But times were altered; and Turkey, no longer the menace of Europe, had become the cordial ally of those who led the van of European civilization and upheld the balance of power. No longer in the immediate service of Austria, but in that of the Porte, the youthful Lattas, adopting the Turkish language and Moslem religion, pursued one of the most curious and remarkable careers of which modern history affords an instance. In the campaign we record, the ex-Croat officer, now become Omar Bey, shewed, in a subordinate position and in the execution of plans devised by others, those qualities of comprehensive intelligence, of wary caution, and of undaunted audacity at the moment of decisive action, which—exercised in larger fields, and in independent commands—have procured him a solid reputation as a general-in-chief, and have associated his name with the unfeudalization of the Ottoman Empire, the consolidation of its domestic administration, and the skilful defence of its frontiers against the most formidable of its foreign foes.

With the double view of saving a great loss of life, and of obtaining greater results, Omar Bey was directed to march at night with two battalions of Turks on Argentoun; and, descending into the deep gorge of the Dog river, with great caution and secresy, to cross over to Beckfeya in the rear of the Egyptians, and effect a junction with the Emir Beshir. Had Omar Bey been discovered in the bottom of the gorge, his corps would have been destroyed; but this very dangerous manœuvre was executed by him with great skill, and, at about two o'clock next day, a firing in the rear of the Egyptian position announced to Napier and Jochmus that the movement projected had been executed.

Commodore Napier, having ascertained that Ibrahim Pasha commanded the Egyptians in person, had ordered up to the heights of Ardali the three remaining battalions from Djouny, and two Turkish field pieces; so that when the fire of Omar Bey was heard approaching, the Allies had also seven battalions ready to attack in front. One of these battalions, with the mountaineer rifles, were directed to cross the ravine which separated the Turks from the Egyptians, and to arrive on their line of retreat by the road to Brumana; while four battalions were to storm the heights of Kalat Meidan, and two more to remain as reserves on the heights of Ardali. The feelings of Napier at this moment have been described by himself in that racy style of undisguised self-glorification with which, next to his unquestionable merits, his contemporaries are most familiar, and which too frequently recals the dubious literary taste of an equestrian circus address:

"It was rather a new occurrence for a British Commodore to be on the top of mount Lebanon, commanding a Turkish army, and preparing to fight a battle that would decide the fate of Syria; but the very novelty was exciting to a degree. I was in my glory. Standing on an eminence, surrounded by the general officers and my own staff, I fancied myself a great "commander;" and, surveying the enemy, who had not quite so brilliant an appearance as the Scottish host—although I could not exclaim with Marmion:

> "Oh, well Lord Lyon, hast thou said,
> Thy King from warfare to dissuade
> Were but a vain essay.
>
> For, by St. George, were that host mine,
> No power, imperial or divine,
> Should once my soul to rest incline,
> Till I had dimmed their armour's shine
> In glorious battle fray!—"

yet I said to my friend Hodges, "If we can get the Turks and mountaineers to mount that rugged hill, and Omar Bey attacks at the same time their rear, Ibrahim will get such a dressing as he never had before."

After two hours' fighting, and the display of the most daring gallantry on the part of the Turks, the heights were carried, aided by Omar Bey, who struck boldly into the rear of the Egyptians, and at the close of the action was joined by Napier and Jochmus, who had crowned the heights. Thus, taken in front and in rear, Ibrahim Pasha had to throw himself into the gorge, not twenty-five men of any of his corps remaining together at sunset, and he himself escaping with difficulty, accompanied by a few horsemen. Eight hundred prisoners, with all the stores and ammunition, fell into the hands of the Allies on this occasion, as well as a green banner, which was subsequently presented to the Sultan with due solemnity. Night alone put an end to the conflict. In the dark the troops of Omar Bey unwittingly got into collision with a part of the native force under Commodore Napier, and the conflict was ended with difficulty; opponents, reciprocally supposed to be prisoners, and who refused to surrender, turned out to be allies.

As the displacement of the keystone of an arch entails the collapse of everything around it, this defeat of Ibrahim Pasha brought other disasters in its immediate train, which cleared all the hill country of the Egyptians. Suleyman Pasha having been weakened by the detachment of four battalions to support the commander-in-chief, had withdrawn himself altogether from Beyrout in the night of the 9th of October, and concentrated himself in a camp one hour and a half east from the town, having the river between himself and the place. But the news of the entire defeat of Ibrahim Pasha having reached Suleyman Pasha's camp, his troops were seized with a panic; and, abandoned by them, he fled in the direction of Damascus with a few squadrons of horse. At daylight Sir Charles Smith and Captain Henderson, of the Gorgon, landed at Beyrout for the purpose of ascertaining how matters stood, when a colonel of the Egyptian army treated for terms of surrender for two thousand of his officers and men, the town being no longer defended. Another body of infantry of Suleyman Pasha's corps in camp followed their example; and thus not only Beyrout, with its stores, but twenty field pieces, with camp equipage, fell into the hands of the Allies. Tripoli was also evacuated, without firing a shot, upon an Austrian corvette anchoring off the town.

Between Sidon and Acre inwards is the southern portion of the Lebanon chain, inhabited by the Moutalis, who, as the name denotes, adopted the Shea or Ali-ite form of Islamism, in common with the Persians, and in contradistinction to the Sunnite Turks and Arabs, who hold by the rite of Aboubekr. This population begged to be furnished with three thousand stand of arms by the Allies, in order to take possession of the passes; and on the 29th October, when it was finally determined that the siege of Acre should be undertaken, Omar Bey was detached for the purpose of advancing from Sidon with two thousand Turks upon Tyre, from thence to occupy the pass of the White Mountain to the northward of Acre. On the 31st the admiral made sail from Beyrout roads, having previously embarked in a squadron, with three thousand Turks under the immediate command of Selim Pasha, and small detachments of royal artillery and sappers.

Omar Bey reached the position assigned him at the same time that the fleet appeared off Acre, on the 2nd of November, and at two p.m. on the following day the cannonade and bombardment commenced with great spirit. Sir Robert Stopford directed the operations from a steamer, and Commodore Napier, in the Powerful, followed by the Princess Charlotte, Thunderer, Bellerophon, and Pique, having got well round the shoal, now bore up and ran along shore towards the north angle. As the ships neared the fortress, the colours were hoisted from two flagstaffs, one on the citadel, and the other lower down. Commodore Napier desired the bow-guns of the Powerful to be fired to prevent the Egyptians pointing with correctness. At this time, the southern division, led in with great judgment and gallantry by Captain Collier of the Castor, were fast approaching their position; and, when well within range, the Egyptians opened their fire, the shot going considerably too high. In a few minutes they passed the circular redoubt, where only three or four guns were mounted, and then anchored abreast off the sea wall, defended by forty guns, in six and a half fathom water.

The Egyptians had not calculated upon the fleet lying close in under the ramparts of the fortress, which resulted in the British broadsides telling fearfully, while the balls from the fortress flew over the hulls of the British vessels. An accident of a tremendous character, producing the most decisive results, also occurred. During the bombardment, the principal magazine, and the whole of the arsenal blew up, in consequence of a shell supposed to have been projected from the Gorgon. By the explosion, two entire regiments, formed in position on the ramparts, were annihilated, and every living creature within the area of 60,000 square yards ceased to exist. The loss of life was variously computed at from 1200 to 2,000 persons. Masses of solid building were also blown to a great height up in the air, and came down again in a shower of fragments, which greatly damaged the fortifications on the land side.

During the night, the governor with a portion of the garrison, quitted the town, which was taken possession of by the allied troops at daylight on the following morning. The British officers found the devastation indescribable; dead bodies of men, animals, and fragments of wall being scattered in all directions.

There was great difficulty in restoring order, in consequence of the propensity to plunder, and the confusion of languages. Another explosion also took place; for five casemates, filled with fixed ammunition, had been neglected, although near the smouldering crater of the former explosion, and notwithstanding the instructions of Sir Charles Smith for their removal. The ammunition blew up three days after the bombardment, at intervals of five or six seconds between the ignition of each; and in a moment the garrison was enveloped in darkness, accompanied by showers of balls and the explosion of shells of every denomination.

CHAPTER XIX.

Policy of Britain and France.—Dejection of Mohammed Ali.—Napier off Alexandria.—Letter to Mohammed Ali.—Interview with Mohammed Ali, and Convention.—Storm on the Coast.—Napier's Convention Disapproved by Admiral Stopford.—Virtually Accepted by Viscount Palmerston.

The important event which we have just described removed the last remnant of film from the eyes of Mohammed Ali. A bold attack of the united French fleet on the maritime forces of Britain, Austria, and Turkey, then scattered along the coasts of Egypt and Syria, and aided by the Egyptian squadron making a sortie from Alexandria, must have delayed the evacuation of Syria, and prolonged for some time at least the power of Mohammed Ali in Asiatic Turkey. But the prudence of Louis Philippe, aided by the sound sense and experience of M. Guizot, and other statesmen of eminence, withheld from M. Thiers that support of his adventurous policy which was isolating France from Europe, under the erroneous impression that the interests of that highly military nation were to be found in a rivalry with England in Egypt, and in the support of the quasi-independence, and hostility of this part of the Ottoman Empire to the metropolis. All this was founded on the assumption that Great Britain had an eye to the annexation of Egypt—a doctrine professed and entertained by no British party, and by no eminent British statesman, the maintenance of the integrity of the

Ottoman Empire being a broad and secure principle, recognised by all those European statesmen most distinguished for political genius and political morality.

On the 8th of November the consul-general of France had a public audience for the purpose of presenting some officers, when Mohammed Ali—who was at that time in conference with Achmet Pasha, and other officers of the fleet—before them, and in the presence of many Europeans, loudly complained of the treatment he had received from the French Government, telling M. Cochelet that the present disastrous state of his affairs was entirely owing to his having listened to the counsels of France. Then, addressing those around him, he said that he had lost all confidence in the French Government, that he had abandoned the hope of its affording him any effectual aid in the present crisis, and that in future he would be guided by his own views.

The following day he received the intelligence of the fall of Acre, which threw him into the deepest dejection. He however shortly afterwards despatched a courier to Ibrahim Pasha, with instructions to evacuate the whole of Syria; and intimated to those in his confidence that he was now prepared to give up the Turkish fleet, and comply with all the demands of the Sultan, provided he could be insured the quiet possession of Egypt. Up to this point he had gaily kept up his spirits, conversing on the events of the war with the coolness of a spectator; but for three successive days after the intelligence of the fall of Acre, his silence, loss of appetite, and his despondency, were visible to all about him. "Effendumuz keifsiz," "Our lord is healthless," was the expression which I heard for some days from his officers, after the fall of Acre.

Admiral Stopford having thought it necessary to increase the squadron off Alexandria to six sail of the line, Commodore Napier went thither to take the command, in order to make a powerful demonstration, whilst the rest of the squadron, with the exception of a ship of the line, was to be withdrawn from the coast in consequence of the advanced state of the season. On the 21st of November Napier arrived off Alexandria, and before communicating with the squadron, ran in and reconnoitred the defences. The sea face was covered with guns; but, with the exception of the castle, Napier judged that there was nothing which could resist a strong naval force: at the same time an attack without troops could have led to no result.

On joining the squadron, Napier was put in possession of the copy of a letter from Viscount Palmerston to Viscount Ponsonby, stating it to be the opinion of Her Majesty's Government that, if Mohammed Ali should at an early period make his submission to the Sultan, restore the fleet, and evacuate Syria, he should have the hereditary tenure of the Pashalic of Egypt. In addition to this, Ibrahim Pasha, having given up his system of scattering his forces, had concentrated them at Zahle and Damascus, where his chief depôts of provisions had been established; and, with the cavalry at his command, was able to defeat any force that might have been sent against him, either in the plains of Cœlo-Syria or on the comparatively level country in the environs of the capital. Cognizant of the real aspect of affairs, and judging correctly of the impression that the fall of Acre must have made on Mohammed Ali, Commodore Napier determined to take on himself the responsibility of opening a communication with Mohammed Ali through Captain Mansel of the Rodney, who had previously made the acquaintance of the Pasha. This officer, entering Alexandria with a flag of truce, conveyed to Boghos Bey a letter of which the chief purport is not worth detailing, but the appendix to which, like a feminine postscript, was the most important part:

"Will his Highness permit an old sailor to suggest to him an easy means of reconciliation to the Sultan and the other great Powers of Europe?

"Let his Highness frankly, freely, and unconditionally deliver up the Ottoman fleet, and withdraw his troops from Syria: the miseries of war would then cease, and his Highness in his latter years would have ample and satisfactory occupation in cultivating the arts of peace, and probably laying foundation for the restoration of the throne of the Ptolemies.

"He may rely upon it Egypt is not invulnerable; he may rely upon it Alexandria itself may be made to share the fate of Acre; and his Highness, who has now an opportunity of founding a dynasty, may sink into a simple Pasha.

"I am," &c.

The reply of Boghos Bey was conciliatory, and far from insisting on the retention of Syria and the fleet. Mohammed Ali gave it to be understood, by a variety of circumlocutions and excuses, that the war in Syria had been precipitately entered into at a period when his favourable dispositions towards a settlement were misunderstood. In short, both the tone of this letter and the information afforded to the Commodore by Mr. Larking, Her Britannic Majesty's intelligent consul, induced him again to write to Boghos Bey, pressing for a distinct answer, as he had no discretionary power and must act against the Pasha according to the best of his abilities, but that he was nevertheless ready to have an interview with the Pasha.

On the morning of the 25th, Commodore Napier entered the harbour of Alexandria in the Medea steamer, passed through the Turco-Egyptian fleet, and anchored off the palace. He then landed and proceeded to the house of the British consul, Mr. Larking; and on the following day, at noon, he proceeded to the palace, where a battalion of Egyptian troops presented arms in the courtyard, while a band of music was playing martial airs. After several days of discussion and negotiation, a convention was agreed to, dated the 27th of November, 1840, by which Mohammed Ali engaged to evacuate Syria, and to restore the fleet; and at the same time a suspension of hostilities was to take place. Not only was the Egyptian army to have the liberty of retiring from Syria with its artillery and stores of every description, but free passage was to be given to vessels bringing back wounded and invalids by sea. The convention being moreover based on the statement that the Allied Powers had recommended the Sublime Porte to give Mohammed Ali the hereditary government of Egypt, a guarantee to that effect was implied but not established therein.

Among the reasons that induced Commodore Napier to arrive at a prompt conclusion of negotiations was the state of the weather at this advanced season. On the very day after the conclusion of the convention, a storm came on, such as had been seldom seen in the Mediterranean by the oldest persons, and of which the author of this history was a witness, he residing at that time in the marine residence of Mr. Larking, Her Majesty's consul, who had charge of the archives and of the political affairs after the departure of the diplomatic agent. The wind blew from the north-west in violent gusts. Black and murky clouds covered the face of the heavens, sometimes chequered with openings through which the sun shot brief and transitory rays; and the sea, like mountains and valleys in motion, rolled its huge waves, which, breaking on the rocks and islets between the new harbour and the baths of Cleopatra, made the coast a line of white foam. In the old harbour the massive ships of the line and three deckers laboured up and down at anchor, as if influenced by the breezes of the open sea. At night the new Pharos warned those outside of safety and of danger; but the forked lightning rending the clouds was the best lighthouse on that fearful night. For two successive days the storm did not abate; the houses shook with the loud rattle of the thunder, and the harbour—several miles in length—was dotted with merchant ships driven ashore. Napier's squadron successfully rode out the gale: the Powerful was struck by a heavy sea which started her forechannels and endangered the foremast, and the rigging of the Rodney and Cambridge had given out so much that their masts became insecure; but no loss had taken place. The Bellerophon at Beyrout had a narrow escape, having been obliged to cut her cable, and make sail; and after scraping the land as far down the coast as Lattakiah, was saved by a miraculous shift of wind. The Pique, at Caifa, near Acre, was obliged to cut away her masts to prevent her going on shore, and at the same time the Zebra was stranded. Commodore Napier, having weathered the storm, and seeing no further necessity for keeping the squadron at sea, proceeded to Marmarice Bay, where he anchored on the 8th of December, and was much gratified to be received by the fleet with three cheers and the rigging manned.

Admiral Stopford thought proper to withhold his approval and ratification of the convention signed at Alexandria, not only on account of what he characterized as the unauthorised manner and unnecessary haste with which so important a document was executed, while the commander-in-chief was within two days' sail; but on the ground that it would be productive of more evil than good, and occasion much embarrassment. To this Napier answered that his non-communication with the admiral was from no want of respect, but that it was of the utmost importance to seize the opportunity, while the Pasha was highly incensed against M. Thiers, of bringing him without loss of time to terms, without the mediation of France.

Sir Charles Smith also disapproved of the convention in a severe letter, beginning with the words, "Had you fortunately abstained from honouring me with your letter of the 27th instant, I should have been spared the pain of replying to it;" to which Napier answered in a style of blunt nautical parody, "Had I unfortunately abstained from writing to you, and the admiral had quitted the coast, you would have had just cause to have complained of my want of courtesy. I quite disagree with you that the convention was prejudicial to the interests of the Porte, and I am happy to say it has been approved of, with the exception of the guarantee, by Her Majesty's Government, and I am now going to Alexandria to see it carried into execution."

The Porte and the ambassadors at Constantinople also disapproved of the convention. But Viscount Palmerston was, upon the whole, satisfied that a conclusion had been arrived at, and he requested the Lords of the Admiralty to convey to Commodore Napier the approval of Her Majesty's Government. But at the same time it was necessary that Sir Robert Stopford should make known to Mohammed Ali that his demand that the four Powers should guarantee to him the grant of the hereditary government of Egypt could not be complied with; for it would have been inconsistent with the principles which guided the conduct of the British Government to guarantee to a subject a grant of administrative authority made to him by his sovereign: and as one of the main objects of the treaty of the 15th of July was to uphold the independence of the Sultan, such an interference would have been incompatible with it. For these reasons neither Great Britain singly, nor the four Powers jointly, could give the guarantee demanded; but they agreed to counsel the Porte to establish Mohammed Ali in the hereditary tenure of Egypt. With these instructions Sir Robert Stopford complied; Captain Fanshaw, an able officer, having been despatched to Alexandria with the notification.

CHAPTER XX.

Ibrahim Pasha at Damascus.—His Able Dispositions.—His Retreat.—Sufferings of the Egyptians.—Personal Details of Ibrahim Pasha.—His High Spirits.—Evacuation of Syria.—Retreat of Suleyman Pasha by the Gulf of Akaba.

But we must now return to Ibrahim Pasha, who, after his defeats in mount Lebanon, concentrated himself in Damascus, to which point Ahmed Menikli Pasha directed all the scattered corps in the north of Syria, with exemplary coolness, method, and ability. Ibrahim Pasha himself, under the pressure of circumstances enough to unman the boldest, has made his retreat from Syria a memorial of his greatness of mind and military ability, which will bear a comparison with anything that he had previously done in the more palmy days of his Arabian and Syrian conquests. Giving way neither to despair, nor even to dejection, he set about boldly the task of reorganising his shattered divisions, and the providing of food and transport for so numerous a force, including a large colony of civilians and their families of Egyptian origin or connection. The discipline he kept was the admiration of the Damascenes.

Defeated troops are in all ages and countries prone to indemnify themselves by the plunder and maltreatment of the unoffending inhabitants; but the severe examples made by Ibrahim Pasha, and his orderly police, fully answered their purpose on this trying occasion. On the 29th of December he evacuated Damascus. All the bazaars were ordered to be shut; and, having assured himself that nothing was in the illegal possession of his men, he took his station outside the southern gate; and, making the whole army defile before him, he did not pursue his journey until the last man, horse, and camel had quitted the place. Only a small body of Koordish irregular cavalry deserted on the occasion.

At El-Mezereib, Ibrahim Pasha divided his forces into five columns. The artillery, the baggage, and the women, were sent on to Akaba on the Red Sea, to be embarked for Suez; and this corps he entrusted to Suleyman Pasha. The other four divisions made the best of their way to Gaza. When they left Damascus they had only sixteen days' provisions, in addition to which they obtained a small supply of flour at El-Mezereib. The cavalry were sixteen days on the march, the infantry twenty-seven, and Ibrahim's corps thirty-four. Small supplies were occasionally received from the villages, but they avoided the great towns, and made for the Dead Sea, which they kept sight of, and approached as near as the nature of the country would allow.

Gaza was important, for it was still occupied by Mahmoud Bey and some other superior officers of the Egyptians, with three thousand cavalry and nine guns. It is too remote from the sea to be acted upon by naval artillery, and was all-essential to the Egyptians,—Gaza being the key of their line of retreat and the locality of their depôts of provisions; and it is the last town on the cultivable territory of Syria before the desert begins.

General Jochmus, at the head of a body of Turkish cavalry—aided by his intelligent aides-de-camp, Baron Dumont and Count Szechenyi—showed great activity in the earlier part of the retreat, in rousing the hostile populations of the Hauran, the Jordan, and Nablouse, to annoy the Egyptian army. He was desirous of capturing and destroying the stores at Gaza; but these views were not warmly seconded by the British admiral and officers, in consequence of the negotiations then pending with Mohammed Ali. For, although the Napier convention had been disallowed by the admiral, *pro formâ*, the *de facto* evacuation of Syria was in course of rapid accomplishment; and there being no grounds for impugning the good faith of Mohammed Ali as far as this convention was concerned, General Michell, who now commanded the British force, felt that he ought not to be behind the Egyptians in scrupulous punctilio.

The army of Ibrahim Pasha suffered very severely in the retreat through a country deficient in roads, resources, and population; and the inclement weather of the middle of winter told severely on troops from the torrid soil of Egypt. The actual encounters between the Egyptians and the Allies were few and unimportant. At Nedjdel, near Gaza, the cavalry of the two forces got into collision, and in a gallant and successful charge, Colonel, now General, Rose, was severely wounded. It may, however, be said, that the Egyptians accomplished their retreat with a steadiness that does them honour, Ibrahim Pasha being familiar with the military geography of the south of Syria from Dan to Beersheba. The Allies were not without casualties; and Brigadier-General Michell, a most meritorious officer, succumbed to exhaustion and continued exposure to rain in this inclement season, complicated by old wounds received on the fields of the Peninsula.

At length the formal orders to evacuate were given by Mohammed Ali, on the conclusion of the arrangements described in our last chapter. At the same time, the British officers pledged themselves that no further molestation or obstacle should be offered to the complete evacuation; and Colonel Rose, having been sent to communicate with Ibrahim, fell in with him on the

31st January, about four hours from Gaza, which town he entered with him the same afternoon. When he came up with Ibrahim Pasha's column there were two lines of videttes flanking it towards the Syrian side, and mounted and dismounted cavalry, to prevent desertion. He rode for several miles along the column, which was in great disorder, and in fact broken up into groups of men in twos and threes, some armed, others not, and some hardly able to walk. He saw two standards, one without any escort, the other with a guard of two men, who must have belonged to battalions which had been broken up on account of the casualties. Ibrahim Pasha's own horse had had no barley that day; the troops had been three days without water, and had subsisted chiefly on mule and donkey flesh, which sold at a high price. Two hundred determined cavalry might with great ease have swept away all that part of the column which Colonel Rose saw; he entered it at about two-thirds of its length.

Colonel Alderson, who was an eye-witness of their arrival at Gaza, and collected all the information he could, states that Ibrahim left Damascus with 62,499 souls, including women and children; and that on his arrival at Gaza, there were not above 30,000 souls: besides which there were between nine and ten thousand men forming the column of Suleyman Pasha; so that the loss could not have been less than 20,000 souls, or one-third of the whole army. There were many deserters; but several thousands must have perished by hunger, fatigue, disease, and the inclemency of the season; for in such a retreat, without shelter, comforts, or medicines, disease and death are almost synonymous.

The appearance of Ibrahim Pasha himself at this period was that of a man considerably past his prime. He was very fat, with a large full projecting eye, a handsome nose, and a broad forehead projecting over the eyes and then suddenly retiring. He had strongly marked eyebrows and a thin grey moustache. He did not appear pleased when Colonel Rose gave him Mohammed Ali's letter; and it seemed to the Colonel that he was either affecting high spirits, or that he had been drinking too much. He drank frequently from a bottle which hung in front of his saddle, which an Egyptian colonel of artillery said was filled with claret; and though then suffering under a very bad attack of jaundice, his eyes and head being quite yellow, he talked and laughed constantly with his servants. On receiving Mohammed Ali's letter he was agitated, and it took him five minutes to read it, although it only consisted of four lines. Whilst he was thus employed, his camel-rider and chief groom were also endeavouring to read it over his shoulder. Colonel Rose rode with him for about four hours, and accompanied him to Gaza. He spoke with considerable bitterness of the Turks. He said, "Why have you turned out the Seraskier?" Colonel Rose replied that he believed the Turkish Government had recalled him because they were not satisfied with his conduct. He answered, "Oh! they are all alike; they smoke all day, and have people to wash their hands." Colonel Rose said, "The present Seraskier is a very good man and soldier." "Oh yes!" he replied, "as long as he is in the saddle; as soon as he sits down he will rob like the rest;" on which he laughed very much. "I am the only man," he said, "to manage the Arabs and Bedouins, who never had any master before me: I could and did cut off their heads, which the Turks never will do. Lord Palmerston, from London, and Lord Ponsonby, from Constantinople, will have to come here to manage Syria." Colonel Rose said, that certainly they had done so much without coming to the country, that there was no knowing what they might effect were they actually to do so.

The Pasha's reception at Gaza was remarkable: the people flocked from curiosity to see him, but his entry formed a singular contrast to that of the Turkish troops into the different towns and villages which they had occupied for the first time. In the latter case the reception was enthusiastic, the men lining the roads and saluting them with all the varieties of an Eastern welcome, and the women crowding the house-tops, and making with their tongues that extraordinary noise which is meant to denote extreme pleasure. But, on the passage of Ibrahim Pasha, there was a look of deep-rooted dislike on the faces of the people, which even their dread of him could not conceal. He, contrary to the eastern fashion, saluted no one, no one saluted him: certainly, as an inhabitant afterwards said to Colonel Rose, "Not a tongue nor a heart blessed him."

When Colonel Alderson and Captain Loriny went to see Ibrahim Pasha, after having shewn that they did not wish to intrude on his privacy, he received them with loud expressions of joy,—made them sit down, ordered coffee, and, asking if they liked music, sent for an Arab band, consisting of a violin like a tenor,—but with five strings, a dulcimer, a guitar, and two men who sang. The music itself was bearable, but when the men commenced singing at the top of their voices it was anything but harmonious. His Highness had certainly no very refined taste in music.

When they entered, the Pasha was surrounded by his generals, playing vingt-un for handfuls of gazees (gold dollars). He showed his character in this too, being always ready to back his own play, and loud in his expressions of delight when successful. He apologised for being found so employed, but said he had nothing else to do there; but that, when at Cairo, they had their farms to attend to and plenty of business to occupy their time.

He was evidently a man of considerable talent, and of great energy, when needed; and he appeared to have the most unbounded control over those by whom he was surrounded. This influence arose partly from fear of him, and from the known energy of his character and the confidence everyone had in his succeeding in whatever he undertook. His smile was anything but agreeable; and would, as it seemed to his visitors, have sat on his features, whether ordering an execution or welcoming a guest. When amongst his generals, if in a good humour, he showed it by practical jokes, pulling the beard of one, hitting another with his fist, or pushing a third about. They all seemed to bear this as the fondling of a tamed lion or tiger whelp, which his master might declare to be quite safe, but whose sportiveness was felt by those exposed to it might have a disagreeable ending.

The season of the year was very unpropitious for embarking troops on the coast of Syria, and the position of Gaza is most treacherous, being in a *cul de sac* of the Mediterranean, from whence there is no escape should the wind blow on the land; while the surf is generally so high that the embarcation of troops is attended with danger. The Egyptian Admiral, with eight sail of vessels acting as transports, was indefatigable in his exertions, and Ibrahim and his generals were frequently in attendance. There being no quay, the Arabs, whether sick or well, were obliged to strip, take their clothes on their heads, and wade up to their armpits. Thus men women and children were at length set afloat, until the army was conveyed to Damietta. Ibrahim Pasha remained until the last, and embarked on the 18th February; at the same time, the last corps of cavalry took their route by land for El-Arish and Gaza. The last town of Syria was thus put in possession of the troops of the Sultan.

The greatest sufferings of the Egyptian army were those undergone by the division of artillery under Suleyman Pasha, which moved direct south along the road of the Mecca pilgrims to the east of the Dead Sea, and onwards to the Gulf of Akaba. Suleyman marched on the 7th of January out of Mezareib, which may be called the last town of Syria on the land side; and on the 15th, the corps, after much suffering, arrived at Mahaan. This is a place consisting of two walled villages, within a few hundred yards of each other, inhabited by Arabs who make a trade of supplying the Mecca caravan with necessaries, the larger village having above two thousand inhabitants. Here are always large stores of provisions. An attempt had been made by the pursuing Turks to get the inhabitants to sell and destroy their stores; but Suleyman Pasha got a Bedouin Sheikh to represent that if the stores were destroyed the town would be exposed to the vengeance of the Egyptians: and so, on his arrival, 70,000 piastres' worth of provisions were procured for the army. It was only by stern discipline that the famished troops could be restrained from plundering the place; but Suleyman had taken his precautions, and menaced with death those who set foot within the walls. Two men who transgressed the order were actually shot, and this saved both the town and the army.

Suleyman Pasha now turned aside from the Mecca pilgrim road, and took that of Akaba, which is the other horn on the head of the Red Sea, corresponding with that of Suez. Here he arrived, after encountering great difficulties in the transport of the guns through a granitic valley, which was at one place shut in by a ruinous gate. At Akaba the army remained a week, and found an old fort on a rock, where the guns were temporarily stored up in order to be transported by sea to Suez. By far the worst sufferings of the army were on the road from Akaba to Suez, where a great number of horses died, and also many soldiers. The horses were up to their bellies in sand, no water was procurable, and no vegetation was visible, except a few stunted mimosas,—so that even the Bedouins do not encamp here. At Nahlè, there was a little fort garrisoned by a few irregular troops, and inside of it a well of nauseous water. It was a terrible scene, recalling the French retreat from Syria, to see men and animals rush to the well with disease and despair depicted on their countenances. But here again the forethought and firmness of Suleyman had provided disciplinary checks against mutiny. The battalions were watered in successive order, and then marched off again. Unfortunately, the water proved a poison to many exhausted men, who immediately died. Such is the force of habit on the human frame, for the people of many places relish brackish water, and consider it more invigorating than sweet water.

The troops no longer marched together; for the only enemy was hunger and thirst, and the horses were so weak that many mounted men had to pursue the journey on foot as they best could. One night, the moon, which had hitherto shone brightly, was obscured by clouds; and this circumstance excited feelings of superstitious terror in the minds of the soldiers, whose physical systems were already lowered by exhaustion. On a sudden they manifested indescribable joy, on perceiving a long caravan defiling on the horizon, and which proved, as was anticipated, to be the succours sent from Suez by Mohammed Ali's order. But for this timely support the whole division might have perished. At Suez the army found abundance of provisions and water, and rested itself until the detachments were successively drafted across the desert to Cairo, where Suleyman Pasha arrived on the 11th February. Seven thousand men, three thousand horses, and the whole of the artillery of his corps re-entered Egypt, after a retreat conducted by Suleyman, under circumstances of great difficulty, with unquestionable ability.

Meanwhile, the Turkish fleet had been restored in due form to the officers of the Sultan, in the harbour of Alexandria. Admiral Walker hoisted his flag on board the Mahmoudieh, a three-decker of 130 guns; and on the 20th January, 1841, he sailed for Marmarice Bay, that beautiful landlocked anchorage on the coast of Caramana.

Thus terminated all the military operations. With regard to the interior of Egypt, although Mohammed Ali was strong enough not to fear any rising of the peasantry against his oppressive rule, yet he deemed it advisable to issue a proclamation stating his view of his Syrian disasters, a sort of twenty-ninth bulletin of his grand army, couched in the following terms:—

"Everything is new and changeable in this world; so the joys of peace often follow fierce war. When we look at the progress of events, from the Creation to the present time, we see them directed by an Almighty and Unfailing Hand, and that the creature, however he may think or act, cannot alter the decrees of the Creator. No oscillation in the scale of destiny takes place without His permission and command. Hence it has come to pass that Commodore Napier, the commander of the British fleet in these seas, has made known to the Pasha that the hereditary possession of Egypt by his family would be in accordance with the views of the great Powers of Europe. It has, therefore, been found good to spare the blood of the Moslems, and to impart contentment to the subjects, so that everybody may rejoice in peace, and follow his occupations, whether in handicraft, trade, or agriculture. We have ordered our Seraskier to evacuate Syria, and to return with our Egyptian army; therefore, the present writing is made known to all our servants and subjects."

If Mohammed Ali was dissatisfied with the performances of his army, the army was equally dissatisfied with the humour they found him in, after the great difficulties and sufferings they had gone through in support of his Syrian schemes. Sagacious and talented as he was, European flattery and his own complacent vanity had so completely deceived him as to the reality and solidity of his power, that the reactive shock most poignantly offended his self-love. Ibrahim Pasha was also deeply mortified at the result of the Syrian campaign; and for some time Mohammed Ali and Ibrahim Pasha did not see each other. Ahmed Menikli Pasha, the most capable of his Syrian lieutenants, after Suleyman, and who in all circumstances had done his duty with energy and skill, was also disgusted with his reception when he visited Cairo, although the moudirship of Benisouf had been given him.

But we must now close this portion of our narrative with some mention of the diplomatic transactions consequent on the expulsion of the Egyptians from Syria. The first of these was necessarily the submission of Mohammed Ali to the Porte, followed by the grant of the hereditary government of Egypt, and the concluding act of this drama, comprising the cessation of the isolated attitude of France, and the concurrence of the five great Powers in an act guaranteeing the closing of the Dardanelles to the ships of war of all nations,—thereby involving on the part of each of the high contracting Powers an abnegation of isolated pressure on the Ottoman Empire, the observance of which understanding removes the chief danger of contention from among European Powers, and the infraction of which can never take place without imminent peril to the peace of the world.

The principal passages of the submission of Mohammed Ali are drawn up with all the art which acknowledges supremacy to obtain its end; but which, far from betraying contrition, colours even an act of humiliation with the language of self-respect.

"Commodore Napier, of the British fleet, informed me by a dispatch dated from before Alexandria, 22nd November, N.S., that the great Allied Powers have requested the Sublime Porte to grant me the hereditary government of Egypt on the conditions laid down by them; that is, that I shall give up the imperial fleet which is in the port of Alexandria, and that the Egyptian troops shall retire from Syria and re-enter Egypt.

"The Commodore required that diligence should be used in preparing the fleet, in order to its being delivered up, and in withdrawing the troops from Syria.

"After some correspondence, and some discussions with the Commodore on this matter, these conditions were accepted, and an authentic Act, manifesting that it is expected that the favour of him who is the shadow of God should be granted, and serving also as a document to both parties, was concluded and signed.

"Thus, then, when your Excellency shall, if it please God, have taken cognizance of my prompt submission, carried into effect as above, you will be pleased to lay it at the feet of the clemency of my most august and most powerful Sovereign and Master, of whom I am so proud to be the faithful and submissive servant, and to employ your good offices, in order to cause a man advanced in age, and faithful, who has grown old in his service, to experience, without ceasing, the effects of his Sovereign's clemency.

"'He who can ordain—will ordain.'"

Mohammed Ali, in consequence of his submission, coupled with the surrender of the fleet and the evacuation of Syria, Arabia, and Candia, was, on the 4th of February, 1841, gazetted to the hereditary government of Egypt, in the following terms:—

"Moved by that goodness and that paternal solicitude by which he is distinguished, the Sultan, who has always loaded with favours the servants of the Sublime Porte, is pleased to consider the recent events as having never taken place, and has not only consented to pardon Mohammed Ali, his children, relatives, and all his servants; but being desirous also of manifesting his clemency towards Mohammed Ali and towards his children, he has granted to His Highness the government of Egypt hereditarily.

"In consequence, the Sublime Porte has decided upon fixing the conditions necessary for the hereditary succession, and to make certain arrangements, which are the consequence and explanation thereof.

"The Egyptian question, is then, God be praised! ended in the manner which has been seen.

"This matter had caused some uneasiness in the minds of men; but at length it is happily brought to a conclusion, and that is what is communicated to the public."

While the breach was thus closed between the Sultan and his vassal, the termination of the Eastern question created an unseemly difference between France and the other Powers, particularly Great Britain. Exasperation rose so high as almost to lead to war, which, however, was averted by the statesmanlike qualities of Guizot, the largest political figure in France since the first empire—equally eminent as a man of letters, an orator, and a practical statesman.

The works of Guizot betray vast erudition, and the phenomena of history are presented with a masterly scientific classification. The laws of Europe, from the decline of the Roman empire to the full revival of civilization, have been unrolled to explain them. But the various latent forces of nationality, compressed in the iron bonds of a stringent and uniform feudalism, and containing the whole enigma of present and future humanity, have in a great measure escaped this remarkable historian, who is moreover deficient in the colouring of a bright imagination and in those great thoughts, "that," as Pascal says, "come solely from the heart." In oratory, too, he has none of that southerly glow with which a Mirabeau, a Vergniaud, a Foy, and a Lamartine have kindled to enthusiasm the representative assemblies of France. Addressing himself to the business in hand, he is what the English style admiringly a "practical," and the French depreciatingly, "a technical orator."

But great moral dignity cannot be denied to this icy, academic, and somewhat dogmatic nature; the whole of his career having shewn that he was neither to be cajoled nor intimidated by the powerful. In philosophy he is a partisan of those principles of "duty" which a Cousin has so ably contrasted with the "utility" of a Helvetius, a St. Lambert, and a Volney; and in politics, belonging to the British school, he has been as a statesman free from the passion of equality, and the despotism of the majority propounded by a Rousseau and a Louis Blanc,—theories which are utterly incompatible with that constitutional liberty which Guizot has spent his life in the vain and tantalizing effort to acclimate on the uncongenial soil of modern Gaul.

The first care of M. Guizot was to effect the re-entrance of France to the European concert, which he accomplished with leisurely deliberation and dignity, so as to obtain the respect of the other Powers. The immediate fruit of this was the treaty of the 13th July, 1841, concluded in London, by which the Sultan declared himself firmly resolved to maintain the principle invariably established as the ancient rule of his empire—that no foreign ship of war was to be admitted into the Dardanelles and the Bosphorus, with the exception of light vessels for which a firman was to be granted.

CHAPTER XXI.

MOHAMMED ALI'S GOVERNMENT AFTER THE TERMINATION OF THE WAR.—THE ARMY PARTIALLY EMPLOYED IN AGRICULTURE.—MOHAMMED ALI RECEIVES THE DECORATION OF GRAND VIZIER.—DESTRUCTIVE CATTLE MURRAIN.—THE TRANSIT REORGANISED.—THREATENED REVOLT OF AHMED PASHA OF SENAAR.—HIS DEATH.—HIS SLAVE HUNTS.—DEATH OF BOGHOS BEY.—ANGRY SUSPICIONS OF MOHAMMED ALI ON THE DISCOVERY OF THE FINANCIAL EMBARRASSMENT PRODUCED BY HIS ERRONEOUS AND OPPRESSIVE SYSTEM OF TAXATION.—HE PUNISHES THE GOVERNOR OF DAMIETTA FOR CRUELTY AND FANATICISM.

LET us now proceed with the narrative of events in Egypt during the last years of the rule of Mohammed Ali, when his ambitious schemes against the Ottoman empire had broken down, and when Syria, Arabia, and Candia had been restored to the direct rule of the Sultan, though the best of all remained to him—Egypt, with its inexhaustible productive powers and large pecuniary revenue. If the possession of a surplus, after providing for all the civil and military wants of a State, be taken as the test of the value of lands to be governed, Mohammed Ali was in reality better off after 1841 than before, though possessing a smaller extent of territory. His position was no longer precarious. He was not an obstreperous tenant-at-will, but had a diploma securing the richest part of the Ottoman empire to his family. The surplus of the Egyptian revenue was no longer engulphed in the military expenditure of Syria and Arabia, and could be applied to those public works in Egypt which occupied the intelligence and activity of Mohammed Ali, and also excited his imagination and tickled his vanity by the prospect of celebrity which their execution afforded to himself or his successors.

And yet suspicions of treachery haunted Mohammed Ali day and night. He supposed that the Porte would recommence the ancient policy of seeking to upset the refractory ruler of Egypt, by an arrangement with some resolute officer of high rank who could carry out a plot with secrecy and decision. Sending his son, Said Pasha, with rich presents to Constantinople, he endeavoured to regain his former influence, and to free himself from the more inconvenient of the stipulations affecting his new position. The presents had been accepted, but nothing tangible had been obtained; and he therefore philosophically resigned himself to making the best possible use of the sphere that remained to him. Unwilling to disperse his now useless army, he turned their spears into ploughshares and pruning-hooks, and a multitude of civilians were dismissed from their offices in every part of Egypt, in order to make way for military men; the higher officers being thrust into mudirships, and the subordinate ones into lower civil offices,—the flower of the troops being kept in garrison at Cairo and Alexandria.

The common soldiers of the army were not very well pleased with this new condition of soldier-labourer; for the labour deprived them of the leisure they prized as a compensation for the restraint of military discipline, and the discipline appeared an irksome addition to the labour of an ordinary fellah. In the course of time this system was not found to work very well, for the Pasha found out that he had neither a good soldier nor a good labourer, and the army was gradually reduced, and the purely labouring population reinforced.

Having a surplus revenue, and no offensive military projects in view, he turned to defensive schemes. During the war, Colonel Gallice, of the French engineer service, whom he had elevated to the rank of Bey, had raised temporary fortifications to protect Alexandria against a *coup de main;* but a more comprehensive scheme was now adopted, so as to embrace both harbour and arsenal, and to inclose the whole of the *enceinte* of the town, supported by detached forts to the westward of the town, commanding the isthmus by which Bonaparte had first approached Alexandria. But there was a certain difficulty in the application of the European science of fortification to the soil of Egypt. One of the usual processes is to "gazon," or turf over the earthworks, so as to retain them by a vegetable envelope from being blown away as dust. But in Egypt turf does not form easily; and, moreover, the eyes of the artillerymen are unpleasantly affected by the excessive glare of stone and lime, to say nothing of the heat which they evolve. But these were minor obstacles. By dint of the large surplus revenue, and the skill of the French engineers, the fortifications were accomplished in the course of revolving years; but, as they have not yet been put to the test, it would be presumptuous in a civilian to offer an opinion on their efficiency.

Meanwhile, Turkey was far from appearing to consolidate herself, notwithstanding the apparently fair start which she had in 1841. It is true that she got quit of the incubus of a threatened invasion of the heart of the Empire from the slopes of the Taurus. But on the other hand, she got back Syria and its unruly population without getting back Egypt, the large revenue of which would have covered any deficit in Syria. A small number of patriotic men were anxious to consolidate the rule of the Sultan by fair government; but the great majority of the old Pashas desired to maintain the time-honoured system of peculation and plunder, and the various nations of Turkey were violently agitated by their passions, prejudices, or supposed rights. In consequence of the weakness of the government, civil war had broken out between Druses and Maronites in October, 1841; and in the spring of the following year Mohammed Ali sounded the Porte as to whether it would be disposed to accept his assistance. The Pasha even dreamed of having his son, Said Pasha, made governor of the Pashalic of Sidon, which includes a considerable part of Mount Lebanon. But all hints of this description were coldly received at Constantinople.

The liberal gifts of the Pasha were, however, always welcome at a corrupt court; and any distinction that might gratify his vanity, without infringing on the political sphere of the divan, was not to be refused. Consequently, in September, 1842, we find the dignity of Grand Vizier conferred upon him, with a flattering article in the official Ottoman paper, stating "that Mohammed Ali, Waly of Egypt, one of the oldest Viziers of the High Porte, out of gratitude for the numerous marks of favour with which he had been overwhelmed by his sovereign, was devoting all his energy and zeal to the service of the Sultan, who, in recognition of his fidelity to the imperial throne, had conferred upon him a proof of his high satisfaction in the form of a Hattishereef which elevated this Pasha to the rank of Grand Vizier. This favour was solely personal to Mohammed Ali, and the insignia of the honour, as well as a copy of the Hattishereef, were handed over to Sami Pasha as a proof of the confidence of the Sultan."

Such was the language of official courtesy to the rebel of yesterday. Accordingly Sami Pasha proceeded to Alexandria, and the delivery of the rescript and decoration took place with all the pomp appropriate to the occasion, and in the presence of Ibrahim Pasha.

In the summer and autumn of 1842, Egypt was visited with a murrain among the cattle, of extraordinary violence and severity, and which threatened to have the most disastrous effects; for the income of Egypt being chiefly derived from agriculture, and agricultural labour being chiefly performed by oxen, the loss was so enormous that it was necessary to press the horses of the artillery and cavalry into service for the cultivation of the land. I myself saw, sometime afterwards, the tall camel and the diminutive ass yoked together in the primitive Egyptian plough—a spectacle which might have produced hilarity, if it had not been checked by the reflection that the cause of this incongruity was the terrible scourge which Holy Writ informed us was from time immemorial one of the periodical plagues of Egypt. In this crisis Mohammed Ali displayed all his energy, feeling that destiny had laid the axe to the very root of his revenues. Money, ships, and intelligent officers were immediately despatched to Turkey proper, and other countries, in order to supply the deficit. But the animals did not come soon enough and fast enough; and bands of villagers yoked themselves to the plough, with the palm-fibre ropes strapped round their shoulders, in order to get through the indispensable operation of preparing the ground for seed. What increased the evil was, that there was in this year an extraordinary flood of the Nile; and, as the waters receded at a later period than usual, there was the less time to prepare the dried land for the expected crop. At length, in November, the murrain obviously diminished, and the Nile began to fall, after causing unusual damage, much accumulated produce being swept away.

The apprehension of the application of the treaty between Great Britain and Turkey, abolishing monopolies, had for sometime alarmed Mohammed Ali; and he therefore adopted the simple plan of making large grants of land to the members of his family and his favourites. The whole produce of Egypt could thus be controlled to suit his convenience. It sometimes happened that ships from England and other European ports remained for weeks in Alexandria, from inability to obtain produce, although the magazines were full. Mohammed Ali, with all his intelligence in political and military matters, had not an idea of the A. B. C. of political economy; but it is only justice to his successors, to say that they have arranged matters much better, and that European merchants having large capital at stake, and carrying on trade in accordance with the liberal provisions of the capitulations, are no longer subject to the capricious fancies of a single colossal salesman. In other respects, this year was signalized by two measures favourable to European—and particularly to British—interests. A company was formed under the auspices of Mr. Thurburn, of which the Pasha was a large shareholder, for the better management of the transit comprising the steam navigation on the Nile and the car traffic across the desert, which was studded with stations. There was as yet no immediate prospect of the railway being carried out to Suez; but the electric telegraph to this town was in this year resolved on and begun: so that we must do Mohammed Ali the justice to say that in everything relating to the transit he was generally ready to accommodate, and sometimes even to anticipate.

In 1843 the plagues of Egypt showed themselves again. The cattle murrain of the previous year had carried off 200,000 oxen, so that the fine cavalry horses that were put to field labour were in a few months scarcely recognizable, from leanness, rope wounds and grazes. In 1843 the plague was that of locusts which covered the whole land from the cataracts to the seaboard; so that the government, to encourage their destruction, gave the peasantry so much per oke for the dead insects, and men women and children resorted to the usual absurd incantations, and the astrologers and magicians had unusually large gains. Mohammed Ali sent Abbas Pasha to enquire into this fresh source of loss and suffering, but nothing could effectually stop it, and in many spots every ear of corn was soon eaten up. The plague proper, which had begun in that portion of the army employed in field labour, also raged during winter and spring, so that natural accidents of a serious description kept the government and the mercantile houses at Alexandria in much inconvenience.

The position of Ahmed Pasha of Soudan, Mohammed Ali's lieutenant in the countries of the Upper Nile, occasioned him great uneasiness this year. Two of the Pasha of Egypt's most faithful military men died suddenly, and suspicions were entertained that Ahmed Pasha, relying on his distance from Cairo, wished to play Mohammed Ali's former game—upon a smaller scale, it is true. Ahmed Pasha continued to send respectful letters, and presents of ivory, and female slaves for the Pasha's harem; but on various pretexts he refused to come to Cairo. The climate is, however, in itself a rapid consumer of the life of Europeans, and Ahmed Pasha died, conveniently for Mohammed Ali, of the autumnal fever.

Ahmed Pasha, in order to conceal his doings, opened all letters of Europeans, whether going to or coming from Egypt, in the last months of his rule, got them translated and then burnt them; so that some Europeans were half desperate from having no answers to their communications. This Pasha's name was also notoriously associated with those slave hunts in the countries beyond Nubia which at this period excited the attention and the indignation of the philanthropists of Europe. The territory between the White and Blue Nile was the locality of these human battues. According to an active and intelligent traveller, who made himself acquainted with all the details of one of these expeditions, Ahmed Pasha started with nearly 3000 infantry, officered by Turks and Egyptians, 1000 irregular Arab cavalry, four guns and 6000 camels, swelled up by accessions that brought the whole force to 5000 men. When they arrived at Khor-el-Sidr, the cavalry was sent on against the Dinkas Nomade negroes, on the White Nile, while the main corps marched south to Ule, in the Borun country. In five days the cavalry came back with 623 slaves, 1500 oxen, and a few sheep. Next day the booty was divided, one half being apportioned to the government, and the other half to the captors.

The army now went further into the land of Borun, and came in sight of the village at Mount Tombak. The inhabitants, who had taken flight, occupied the tops of the isolated hills, which were surrounded by the cavalry and stormed by the infantry. Here the negroes defended themselves with the courage of despair, but most of the men capable of bearing arms were killed or wounded. Their arms consisted, not of muskets, but of bows and arrows with fine ivory points, so that not a single Egyptian was killed, although many were wounded. At about mid-day the soldiers came back with their human booty. They took from the town all the corn that the troops were still in need of, and the remainder, with the village itself, was burnt down.

On the following day, the slaves, 526 in number, including men, women, and sucking children, were examined by the physicians in order to see how many of the men were fit for military service. The males wore a sheep skin round the shoulder, and the women a frock or shirt. Only seventy-five were found to be fit for arms, most of the prisoners having received gunshot wounds while defending themselves. The Pasha took the unwounded, as well as the handsomest women and boys, as the half belonging to the government, and left the rest to be divided amongst the army. When the families were separated, and men, women, and children were torn asunder, there arose the most melancholy and passionate wails. The soldiers made sure of their slaves in the following way: they stuck the neck of each into the fork of a split pole an arm thick, and bound the two ends behind the head, and the other end of the pole to the saddle, so that they could take them along with them, without giving themselves much trouble. The march lasted usually from six to eight hours, and as the soldiers scarcely took water enough for themselves, the slaves suffered frightfully from thirst, and they received no other nourishment but Indian corn softened with water. Those whose wounds hindered them from marching were shot at once, so that of the whole number captured not the half arrived at Khartoum.

The army now marched to Kerr, a district with ten or fifteen little villages, the inhabitants of which had sought an asylum in two palisaded enclosures. An attempt was made by the Egyptians to bring down this palisade with cannon-balls, but without success. The infantry therefore stormed the palisades, and tried to pull them down with their hands, but were three times beaten back. At length the fire-arms gave the Egyptians the superiority, and the place was taken. Exasperated by the resistance, the soldiers slew all the blacks who, being wounded, could not serve as slaves. Ahmed Pasha saw that in this way he would lose the best slaves, so he sent one of his prisoners into the second palisade, recommending them to surrender immediately. The man went unwillingly, as he said he should not be able to persuade his fellow villagers; and the second palisade was taken in the same manner as the first. The Egyptian loss on this occasion was considerable, several hundred being wounded by the ivory pointed arrows, and several killed by the unskilful use of their own fire-arms. The negroes and cattle were divided in a similar manner. The best slaves were sent under Bedouin escort for the use of the government, and those whom the troops did not choose to take with them were sold at wretchedly low prices to Arab slave dealers. The army then marched to Kormouk, inhabited by brave negroes armed with lances, the chief village being a town containing 1600 huts. The inhabitants having fled to the mountain, the Pasha first burnt the village, and, after waiting for two days, four battalions stormed the mountain, the fifth battalion remaining as a reserve, while the cavalry swept round the foot of the mountain to cut off the retreat of the fugitives. The first battalion attacked a palisade containing 1200 women and children; but the negroes coming down with force from the hill, the Egyptian troops were panic stricken, and, throwing down their loaded muskets, fled. This had an epidemic effect upon the other battalions, which also fled. Six officers and one hundred and eight soldiers fell in this attack. The Pasha took three days to reorganise his troops, at the end of which time a messenger came from the negroes, who appeared to be without water, for the Pasha had encamped at the fountain. The Pasha promised to withdraw on condition that the negroes paid him fifteen ounces of gold. This sum was never paid, and Ahmed Pasha on this occasion had to withdraw, much displeased with the results of the expedition; for he had only made 1875 prisoners, while another Egyptian general at a similar negro hunt, had brought in 5,000 slaves.

The best of these male slaves were enrolled in the ranks of the army, as Mohammed Ali found it cheaper and more convenient to use negroes than Egyptian fellahs, who were withdrawn from the culture of the soil of

Egypt. On their arrival at Khartoum the men were placed in the regiments, and the women and the children divided among the officers. The division took place before the slaves joined the army; and in this expedition, of forty-two that were entrusted to Bedouins, the half died on the road and the Bedouins brought their ears to Khartoum, no doubt to show that they had not sold them for individual profit.

In January, 1844, Boghos Bey died, aged seventy-six years, after a three days' serious illness. All the consuls and leading merchants of every nation attended the funeral of the oldest and most faithful of the servants of Mohammed Ali. The funeral was conducted with pomp, but, from hauteur or fanaticism, none of the superior Moslems showed any sort of respect to the memory of this intelligent and amiable man, who died poor and incorruptible, notwithstanding the rare opportunities he had of gaining large sums by the peculation and bribery so constantly practised in Levantine communities. At the time that I knew him he was distinguished by the neatness and cleanliness of his person and costume, the extreme politeness of his manners, his sagacity in judging of human character, and by the large amount of political information on the European States which he had gradually acquired during the prolonged discussion of many critical questions relating to Egypt that had given occupation to the diplomacy of Europe, as well as by contact with many intelligent travellers of all nations. But although an excellent instrument of Mohammed Ali, he was deficient in moral and physical courage. He would have made a polished courtier and skilful administrator in an absolute monarchy; but he had not the energy and independence requisite for a responsible leadership in a free State, where people will not give confidence to a man who has not unbounded confidence in himself.

Boghos Bey was succeeded by Artim Bey, who had been first interpreter, a complete sycophant of the Pasha, vindictive towards those who thwarted or exposed his schemes, and a complete contrast to his brother Khosreff Bey, who succeeded him as first interpreter, and was a man of conciliatory temper. Boghos Bey, having commenced his career in the British consulate of Smyrna, preserved certain relations of courtesy towards the English, even when his master was on bad terms with the British Government. Artim Bey hated the English, doubtless from an instinctive perception of their unpliant and intractable character in cases of gross corruption; but he was too prudent not to preserve an external show of courtesy towards a nation which he detested. His intelligence was indisputable.

There was considerable distress in the villages this year, as a result of the cattle murrain and of the taxes being exacted in some districts with too little consideration for what had occurred. Some peasants, to escape payment of arrears, fled into the towns; and Mohammed Ali found it expedient to punish with death any townspeople who harboured fugitive peasants. Several executions took place on this ground. Thus Egypt became practically a slave State, so far as the agricultural population was concerned, under the rule of Mohammed Ali. Revolting acts of barbarity were committed under the Mamelukes, but there was not a systematic suppression of personal liberty. The rural state of Egypt this year presents in other respects little to comment upon. The wild boars that had formerly been imported from Cyprus, in order to afford sport to the Mamelukes, were found to do so much damage in the Delta that measures were taken to extirpate them.

I have already pointed out the deplorable condition of the agricultural districts of Egypt. While elegant streets on the European model were rising on the ruins of ancient Alexandria—while a line of telegraph was laid down to Suez, the overland transit improved, and European luxury introduced into the palaces of Cairo—the political and financial affairs of Egypt were in a state of cancer. The great mass of the people were poorer and worse off than they had been at any period of the history previously recorded,—certainly worse than they had been under the Mameluke Sultans; for the precepts of Islamism had still a hold of a large part of the community, and if there were frequently irregular exactions from the wealthy in the towns, the exactions in the country were less systematic. Under the primitive Moslems and the Caliphs, there was a still stronger feeling of religion, and the rulers took a pride in punishing the oppressors of the poor. Under the Greeks and Romans there was a regular system of law. Under the ancient Egyptians there appears to have been involuntary servitude and an abased agricultural population; but they seem to have lived in plenty, except when the ill-famed plagues of Egypt visited the land.

In this year, 1844, partly in consequence of the previous murrain in the cattle, partly from increasing depopulation and flight of the peasantry—in the face of even the punishment of death, a panic seems to have seized the sheikhs in the little towns and villages in all Upper Egypt, on finding that the machine of government would not work. The consequence was, that the council of Cairo made a report, laying bare the real state of affairs. The report showed that when one village had become depopulated, and could not pay its taxes, the burthen was thrown on the neighbouring villages; and the fisc was inexorable in insisting on the maximum. Where there had been formerly a hundred looms, and hand-weaving had fallen off, so that only a third of the looms remained, this remainder had still to pay for the full complement. The report went into minute details proving that the magnificent public works carried on by labour unpaid for by the government was the chief cause of the depopulation; and there can be no doubt that this was one of the principal causes both of the misery and exasperation of the people. All the magnificent works erected by Saladin, Kalaon, Mohammed-el-Nasr, and Sultan Hassan, were magnificently paid for from the treasures of these monarchs: in fact Sultan Hassan beggared himself to carry on the works of the splendid temple that bears his name. But Mohammed Ali, after having ceased to recognise any landed property in Egypt that was not his own, would not even admit that the peasantry had a right to their own labour. "Slaves, instead of freeholders," was in fact the motto of the civil and financial administration of Mohammed Ali, poorly compensated by some showy public works on the models of Europe.

Ibrahim Pasha, who was a shrewd practical man, and had nothing of the theatrical pomposity and vanity of Mohammed Ali, resolved that the truth should be made known to the Pasha, who was in fact in a great measure ignorant of the ruinous state of Egypt, in consequence of the system of oriental favoritism, in which the rule holds good that no communication ought to be made to a superior which is not agreeable. Lest the shock should be too severe for Mohammed Ali's self-esteem, his daughter was commissioned to break the matter cautiously to him; and more than the truth flashed upon the Pasha at this unofficial communication. He suspected that he had been purposely deceived, that it was a pretext to get quit of him, and that Ibrahim Pasha wished to step into his shoes at once. This communication being coincident with a reaction in his nervous system after some harem excesses, he at once imagined that there was a plot on foot, and suddenly proceeded from his palace, on the promontory of Alexandria, to the villa of his brother-in-law, Moharram Bey, situated on the canal. He exclaimed loudly to his immediate attendants, and the household of Moharram Bey, that he was surrounded by traitors, and that he would give up the government and go to Mecca to spend his last days.

Ibrahim Pasha, Said Pasha, and his most intimate friends were refused access to him. Even Sami Pasha, his intimate confidant, was expelled from his room with reproaches, the Pasha maintaining with violence that the sheikhs of the towns and villages would not have made such a report unless they had received a hint to do so from some superior. All this occurred on the 25th and 26th of July, after which Mohammed Ali went to Cairo with a few subordinate officers and his physician. The consuls-general at Alexandria, hearing of these affairs, and of the state of the Pasha's mind, asked Artim Bey, the Minister of Commerce and Foreign Affairs, what the intentions of the Pasha were; but he could give no information. Ibrahim Pasha said distinctly, "that he would not accept the government as long as Mohammed Ali lived."

Mohammed Ali, during the first half of August, went over all the reports, studying the question of the financial collapse which had moved the council to recommend him to remit the debts of villages amounting to nearly £400,000; and, having reproached the council for not letting him know the truth, Ibrahim Pasha offered that the superior officers should mulct themselves, some in six months', others in four months' pay. Thus a reconciliation was brought about. The Pasha received all his officers, paid a visit to Ibrahim Pasha, dined with one of his daughters, and shortly afterwards returned to Alexandria, his reputation somewhat damaged by freaks betraying the passions and caducity of age, rather than the manly stoicism which is associated with true greatness.

At the approach of autumn, and in the beginning of the year 1845, the cattle murrain partially re-appeared, but not with the former violence; and the year 1845, partly in consequence of the financial reforms which had followed the explosion of August and September of the previous year, may be considered a period of revival and prosperity. But in April the Christian community was shocked by one of those outbursts of fanaticism, which had become, comparatively speaking, rare. At the end of March an event occurred at Damietta which attracted the attention of the Pasha. The fanatical population had observed with great dissatisfaction that Christian rayahs had become consular agents. Two Christians—an Armenian and a Copt—had become Moslems. The Copt made his profession of Islamism in the most public manner, and the Moslem mob paraded the whole day through the Christian quarter. On such days the Christians usually remained within doors, as they run the risk of being maltreated. At length, on the day of the festival of the birth of the prophet, a poor old Copt, with a white beard, who worked in a rice threshing-mill, fell into a dispute with a Moslem ass driver; and, after exchanging words, the ass driver went to the governor and complained that the Copt had turned the prophet and his religion into ridicule. Ali Bey caused the man to be brought to the court of justice, and, on this worthless testimony, he was condemned to receive 500 blows of the bastinado. After the man had received several hundred additional blows, a cross was tied on his back, and he was paraded on a buffalo through the town. The procession was then led through the Christian quarter. A shawl placed round the neck of the wretched man, and held on each side, hindered him from falling, for he was now more dead than alive; and at one place near the shore, boiling pitch was thrown on him by a boat caulker, amid the applause of the mob. Mohammed Ali, on hearing of this event, sent to Damietta one of his chief officers, who condemned Ali Bey to five years' imprisonment in the fortress of Aboukir, as well as to pay a heavy fine. The Pasha also pensioned the unhappy wretch who had been the object of this outrage. Whatever defects might exist in the agricultural administration of Mohammed Ali, his punishment of fanatic violence was prompt and salutary.

CHAPTER XXII.

Personal Habits of Mohammed Ali in his Old Age.—Ibrahim Pasha.—Abbas Pasha.—Shereef Pasha.—The Capitation Tax.—Edhem Bey.—New Educational Institutions.—Printing Press at Boulak.—Improvements in Cairo.—Port of Boulak.—Mohammed Ali's Palaces.—Hydraulic Improvements.

Having given the reader a sketch of Cairo and its inhabitants, under the Mamelukes, just previous to the French invasion, with which the great military, political, and social revolution of Egypt commenced, it seems not inappropriate that, before I record the closing scenes of Mohammed Ali's career, I should give some description of the metropolis at the end of the eventful half century which we have so minutely chronicled. Much of the ineffaceable character of a Moslem Arab capital remains, but there are also strong reflexes of the new phase of history evolved by the vigorous will of the individual, and the renewed importance to the commerce of the world which Egypt has assumed through a revolution of communications, independently of the will of any one individual however energetic. But first, I must beg the reader's permission to sketch the person and habits of Mohammed Ali, in his old age, from personal observation.

Mohammed Ali received visitors early in the morning, in a room hung with green Lyons damask, and looking out upon a terrace from which the whole landscape of the valley of the Nile up to the Pyramids was visible, —an orangery in the open air forming a little table-land in the lofty castle. In the midst of this room stood the Pasha in conversation with his physician. He saluted me cordially as I entered, and we proceeded to the window, where he sat down with his back to the garden. His complexion was excellent, the skin of his brow slightly sunburnt, but clear and healthy; his eye still remarkable for lustre and intelligence, but the cheeks and mouth much wrinkled. Coffee was served, and the Pasha began to talk of his wants, which were comprised in "coal! coal! coal!" "That is the one thing needful for me," said the Pasha. He then called an attendant and told him to bring the specimens of this mineral found in the valley between Gheneh and Cosseir. Shortly afterwards the servant reappeared, bringing a little wicker basket with pieces of anthracite. The Pasha then declared his determination to carry out the railway between the two seas, if he should live long enough. Ibrahim Pasha was at that time absent on a visit to Europe, and had written home that the superiority of Frank civilisation was owing to the better condition of the humbler classes. Upon this Mohammed Ali said that he was determined to carry out the improvement of the condition of the fellaheen, or peasantry of Egypt. He even caused a model village to be constructed with improved dwellings; but it is unnecessary to say, that all this was too completely in opposition to the acts, facts, and opinions of all his career in Egypt to make any impression upon me. I, however, never doubted that the railway would be carried out, either by himself or by his successors.

Mohammed Ali usually passed the winter in Cairo, where sunshine rarely fails, and the summer in Alexandria, where his palace on the promontory of fig-trees, caught the cool north-western gale. He rose at the first peep of dawn, when his physician, Gaetano

Bey, presented himself to enquire after his health. He then received his immediate officers and various European merchants, who were in his confidence, and who usually had the titles of consul, or consul-general of the secondary Powers. These favourites were chiefly Greeks, French, and English,—rarely of other nations, although his physician was of Spanish extraction. His chief confidant among the Turks was Sami Pasha, a Moreote, already noticed. In taking his food, at this part of his old age, he attended with tolerable strictness to the prescriptions of his physician, but occasional harem excesses disordered his nervous system. In the afternoon, when in Cairo, he usually drove out in a carriage, to his orange paradise of Shoubrah, and smoked a pipe in his marble kiosk, where Europeans often met him. Notwithstanding the vast resources of Egypt, Mohammed Ali had rarely much superfluous cash. He had always expensive projects in hand, and the knowledge of his liberality drew projectors to his anti-chambers. The business that he had with the mercantile houses was of a peculiar description. They made advances to the verge of their capital, and they got produce in return, which was nominally sold to the highest bidder, but in reality distributed to the favoured houses; not only previous advances, but the skill with which they paid their court to the Pasha entering into the transaction. Mohammed Ali had sagacity enough to distinguish between his friends and flatterers; but he was so fond of eulogy, that those who went to Egypt determined to see everything in a rosy hue, rarely failed to forward their material interests.

Ibrahim Pasha had a mind of a more practical cast in financial matters than Mohammed Ali, and was free from his step-father's eager desire to shine before Europeans; but, greedy and morose, he never obtained popularity. Said Pasha, the younger son of Mohammed Ali, lived mostly at Alexandria, where he was brought up to the naval profession under the direction of intelligent French officers. He spoke French fluently, and, having gone through a course of European reading, he certainly had more enlarged views than Abbas Pasha, his uncle. Abbas was destined one day to succeed Mohammed Ali, having been the son of Toussoun Pasha, Mohammed Ali's eldest son; and it was the wish of the Pasha to bring him forward as much as possible, and initiate him in military and political affairs. Abbas had during the war been sent with a body of troops into Syria, where he stayed a very short time; but he was fonder of field sports, birds, horses, and other animals, as well as of sensual pleasures, than of the details of political business. Consequently, although he was nominal governor of Cairo, the business was transacted mostly by the deputy, Baki Bey, a brother of Sami Pasha. Abbas Pasha, although not much of a politician, was perfectly familiar with Cairo and its inhabitants, and resided not in the castle, but in the centre of the town, close to the great line of bazaars in a quarter called the Kroonfish, where I made his acquaintance, and found him to be perfectly good-natured and entirely free from any sort of ostentation. On higher subjects, his ignorance of science and literature was remarkable, considering the training he had had; but he was by no means deficient in common sense, and knew how to distinguish between such projects as were really beneficial to Egypt, as railways, and those that were of doubtful utility. In person, he was rather inclined to be stout, but not corpulent. He somewhat neglected his dress and personal appearance, allowing days to elapse without being shaved. His great delight was in horses, of which he had a very fine stud, and his challenge to the jockey clubs of Paris and London, in order to test the merits of the old Arab as compared with the British blood horse—which is in reality in great part of Arab origin—was the topic of discussion in sporting circles for a considerable period.

Shereef Pasha, a near relative and formerly intimate friend of Mohammed Ali, who had been governor-general of Syria, was the head of the divan of finances. He was very wealthy and lived in considerable splendour, although his salary had been reduced from £12,000 to £8,000 per annum at the time of the retrenchments which the financial crisis had forced on Mohammed Ali. During the time of his government of Syria his total income with rations and allowances had been equivalent to £14,000 a-year. Partly from family ties and partly from personal qualities he had up to the campaign of 1840, possessed the entire confidence of the Egyptian government. He was a man of most winning and attractive manners and of rare and remarkable intelligence. Many traits are recorded of him which procured the respect and esteem of the European agents exercising consular functions in Syria. On the other hand (a contradiction often visible in semi-barbarous nations) he never recoiled from acts of cold-blooded cruelty in order to fill the treasure chest, or to strike terror into those ill-affected to the Egyptians, or to minister to the prejudices of friends and adherents. Hence the odious maltreatment of several members of the Jewish community supposed (without adequate legal ground) to have been concerned in the murder of a Latin priest named Father Tommaso, will always be a black stain on his memory, five or six of them having died under the lash for refusing to confess participation in a crime of which there was no tangible proof. But unscrupulous agent as he was of Mohammed Ali, he was ready when the last hour of the Egyptians had sounded, to worship the rising sun. Overtures had been made to him by the government of the Porte to remain in Damascus as Pasha, where his experience and the prestige of his personal authority would have proved valuable in the transition from Egyptian to Constantinopolitan rule, and there is every reason to believe that he had either positively or tacitly accepted these propositions. But Ibrahim Pasha, either suspecting this plan, or it having been betrayed to him by some one connected with Shereef Pasha, carried him off prisoner to Cairo; and, it is supposed, would have taken his life, had it not been that Mohammed Ali—mastering his dissatisfaction, and anxious both to preserve so able an administrator and to renew social relations with an old friend to whom he had, during many years, borne a great attachment, and at the same time wishing to preserve a trump card from falling into the hands of the Sultan's government in Syria—patched up a reconciliation between his stepson and quondam friend.

Shereef Pasha understood financial affairs very well; but partly from indolence, and partly to avoid having any disagreeable discussions with his chief, he was deficient in candour relative to his own department, and he could not shake off the oriental indisposition to make communications to a superior that were not agreeable. The great lever of the revenue of the state was of course the land monopoly; but a large contribution was received from the ferdeh. This was the poll-tax which Mohammed Ali screwed out of every Egyptian and Syrian, that he could lay his hands on, and was one of the chief fiscal levers, during the period of his contest with the Sultan, and the complete payment of it was exacted according to a classification. Woe to the peasant or townsman who could not pay his poll-tax, for he was bastinadoed until it was all acquitted. The Divan-el-ferdeh, or the office of the *individual-tax*, was in the Sikket-el-Leboudieh. Passing there I asked my sheikh Ahmed-el-Kotoby what anecdote of a salient description he could give me for my budget suggested by the locality; but he stopped short, and shaking his head and his robe, said, "It is of no use, for you would plunge me into an ocean of narration."

Passing sentries, I found myself in a large hall, along the walls of which were high desks, on which were the books of the ferdeh in ponderous folio, and behind them the Coptic clerks making entries and references. At the extreme right was the clink of gold, and here were the sarafs of the government receiving the gold pieces, weighing and scrutinizing the little gold dollars to see that the obliquely indented rim was unfiled and unclipped, and opposite was the fellah of the environs with his coarse hair cloak or the townsmen in woollen and silk. A curtain veiled from the public the dread sanctuary of the nazir, who seemed to be a Circassian of exceedingly fair complexion. He was surrounded by Coptic clerks, with books in their hands investigating the claims on defaulters. The nazir, or inspector of this department, was like the grand inquisitor of the palmy days of Jesuitism. He was the terror of the rich, who feared lest his wealthometer should reach to those portions of their capital which were concealed from view, and the terror of the poor on account of the bastinado which was applied at his discretion. When a creditor was importunate in dunning, his usual pretext was the inexorable demands of the nazir of the ferdeh; or if the debtor sought an excuse, he alleged the necessity of the discharge of the preferable claim of the government. The address with which the government penetrated to the knowledge of the private means of individuals was fairly matched by the popular ingenuity in evasion.

Edhem Bey continued to be the head of the educational institutions of the Pasha. He occupied, not very far from the Bridge of the Lion, the very locality which had been the Institute of Egypt at the time of the French expedition, and where Monge, Berthollet, Denon, and Cafarelli had discussed science and art with the hero of Embabeh. But the palace had been almost rebuilt. His department was in a satisfactory state, contrasting with the manufactures and some other new institutions of the Pasha, which had proved failures, politically and economically. The printing press of Boulak was in increasing activity, and many of the works translated, such as Montesquieu's "Grandeur et Décadence des Romains," were intended to break down still further the prejudices of the Arabs, and to set them a-thinking. The printing of the Koran has always been resisted by the ulema as unlawful; but, for the first time in the history of Islamism, an edition of the Koran was set up in type, and the Mufti of Cairo, Sheikh-el-Temimy, was asked to set his seal of permission upon it in order to ensure its sale. There was thus a perpetual conflict going on—attack on the part of the free-thinking Turks, and ingenious evasive defence on the part of the ulema.

Edhem Bey pointed out to me the various institutions in his department which might be interesting, one of which was the medical college and hospital of Kasr-el-Ainy, on the banks of the Nile above Cairo. The palace of Kasr-el-Ainy has the appearance of an immense barrack, and forms a quadrangle. Passing into the court-yard I found it planted with trees for the sake of greater coolness, and on ascending the steps entered the galleries of the military hospital. Here the cleanliness and the fresh currents of air denoted the introduction of European pathology, so opposite to the filthy negligence of the native Egyptian. Having looked through the wards, I was shown into a kiosk with divans that overlooked the Nile. This was the visiting room of the physicians after their inspection; and, glancing across the Nile, I saw the luxuriant groves of Rodah and the nilometer in the distance. The blighting desert winds and the heats of summer had not yet commenced, and the birds on the boughs sang in loud chorus, which reached across the waters. I recollected that on this very spot had been held the alarmed councils of the Mameluke Beys on intelligence of the landing of Bonaparte; for the palace of Kasr-el-Ainy and its luxurious gardens had been a villa of Ibrahim Bey.

I then descended to the ground floor, where experiments had been made by a Russian commission for testing the effects of heat on clothes of plague-struck persons; and the conclusion was come to, that with 60° of Reaumer they cease to be pestiferous, the circumambient globules of infecting fluid being dried up. Besides being a hospital, Kasr-el-Ainy is also a medical school; and passing over some mounds of earth, we found ourselves in the botanical garden where there was a pond for aquatic plants. There was also a cabinet of natural history in which I saw a stuffed calf with two heads. This reminded me of the child with two heads, which was born at Damietta in the year 377 A.H., one head being black and the other white, but both from the same neck, the rest of the body as usual. The infant was taken to Cairo, and shown to the Caliph Aziz Billah, who gave the mother a sum of money, but the infant did not survive beyond a few months.

Unquestionably one of the least equivocal benefits which Mohammed Ali conferred on Egypt was the establishment of a printing press on a large scale at Boulak, from which were sent forth those numerous works on modern science and literature, particularly medical works and history, which form an epoch in the history of Egypt. Not being intended as a mercantile speculation, but as a means of spreading a taste for reading among a people that for three centuries had ceased to be literary, the prices of the books were very low. The library for the sale of these books was a large edifice close to the Mehkemeh, with a gallery above all, looking quite new and European. I bought a Life of Napoleon, in closely printed quarto, for little more than three shillings. The Memoirs of the Empress Catherine, of the same size, in Turkish, cost two shillings and sixpence; and the original price of the celebrated Egyptian edition of the Arabian Nights' Entertainments was ninety piastres or about eighteen shillings. During my visit to Cairo the price was much higher, all the copies having been bought up by the five booksellers of Cairo. The mosque libraries of Cairo are mere wrecks owing to the dishonesty of the supervisors and sub-librarians (nazirs and moghairs, the latter expression meaning "changers," and being applied to the person who gives out and receives back books). The library of the Azhar is large, comprising many thousand volumes, but the number I could not learn. The mosque of Mohammed Bey had eleven hundred volumes; the mosque of Yezbek four hundred; and the mosque of Sheikhoun one thousand volumes. The largest library in Egypt was that of Ibrahim Pasha, which consisted of 8,000 volumes. The books of the mosque of the Morea and Greece, brought away by Ibrahim Pasha, and numbering 1,500 volumes, were deposited in the citadel. The largest library of a private individual was that of Habib Effendi, an intelligent Turk, who had been municipal governor of Cairo, and consisted of five thousand volumes. At the time of the flourishing period of Cairo literature, —that is to say under the Mameluke Sultans, comprising the period of Ebn Khalikan and Makrizi—the libraries of the principal mosques were of vast extent, and the multitude of authors quoted in the colossal encyclopedia of biography by the former, show that the literary resources of Cairo at that time must have been extensive, far beyond what the present state of the libraries can give any conception of. Mohammed Ali was perfectly indifferent as to old Arabic literature. He wished to create a new epoch in Egypt, both as a soldier and revolutionist, and it was the modern science of Europe that was more likely to suit his purpose than any amount of the curious theology and literature of the earlier Arabic period.

Constantly needing the services of Europeans, a part of Mohammed Ali's system was to enforce toleration of Franks, Frank science and Frank usages, on the unwilling and recalcitrant Moslems. There began to be greater facility in admission to the mosques, which was sometimes abused in an offensive manner. A broad-brimmed white hatted American was once seen forcing his way into the Azhar and ordering the interpreter to say, "that he believed that there was no God but God." "But you do not believe that Mohammed is the prophet of God," said the man at the gate. "That does not signify," was the rejoinder; "I have just had a tough argument with the Coptic patriarch, and now I wish to have a little discussion with your people." Notwithstanding this appeal, admission was refused. Mohammed Ali was indeed successful in his efforts to compel this greater tolerance. A Christian said to me with pleasant exaggeration, "I believe even if the Christians were to wear green turbans, the Moslems would say nothing; but we do not wear green turbans, for as they are now so tolerant, it would be unfair to come into unnecessary collision with their prejudices."

I sometimes found young Moslems so thoroughly denationalized and dereligionized as to have a jarring unpleasant flippancy. Paris had not only spoiled them for Mecca, but had even rendered them indifferent to the beautiful monuments of the four epochs of Moslem architecture in Cairo; and I recollect one, who pointed to the fact of a certain amount of wine being annually imported at Yeddah and secretly sold as a proof that civilization was extending. But these were the rare exceptions; and in general it was remarked that Moslems were more indisposed to Frank society after their return from a course of education in Europe than before. For this there were several reasons, one of which was, that they did not choose to appear before their fellow Moslems as having been denationalized. The novelty of Frank society had completely worn off during their sojourn in Europe; and at the same time their vanity was often wounded by the consciousness of the fundamental inferiority of the civilization and of the military and political power of the eastern nations when contrasted with those of the west.

The material improvement in the interior of Cairo was in many respects very considerable, and much was contributed to the comfort of the inhabitants. Travellers have justly complained of the filth of the oriental cities, where accumulations of all sorts of offal and rubbish took place with impunity; but in Cairo a system was adopted of fining every person a dollar before whose house a dead dog or cat might be found. With a dishonest population it sometimes happened that people connected with the sheikh of the quarter, who collected the fines, would put a dead dog or cat at the door of a wealthy person for the purpose of extracting the dollar; and this led to Mohammed Ali causing the whole of the cleaning department to be managed by a public board called the Divan-el-cassara, or divan of impurity.

No part of Cairo underwent a greater change than the Ezbekieh. At the time of the French invasion, the Ezbekieh was a large pond like the Birket-el-Fyl, during all the inundation, on which pleasure boats, with coloured lanterns, filled with persons who played upon the guitar, used to move about on certain festivals. Mohammed Ali, by filling it up in a great measure, and planting alleys of trees, has made it a sort of St. James' Park of Cairo. An examination of the architecture of the houses that border it, shew three distinct styles; first, the old usual Arab; secondly, the Greco-Turkish, which was in vogue at the end of the last century and the beginning of this; and thirdly, the pure European, with forms imported from Marseilles or Trieste.

Boulak, the port of Cairo, was greatly improved in the time of Mohammed Ali. A substantial new stone quay was erected for the river-steamers, and as the period of his rule comprised that in which steam navigation became general upon the great rivers of the civilized world, the Nile was not an exception, under a ruler who certainly did not lack intelligence. Here, too, was a villa and farm of Ibrahim Pasha, who was the first to raise water by steam-power for the irrigation of the land; but the enormous expense of fuel, the coal being all from England, and the wood from Asia Minor, or the Black Sea, has prevented the extension of the application of steam to agricultural purposes. The activity witnessed at Boulak is a complete contrast to the scene that meets the eye in the sequestered and ruined quarters of Cairo, with their monuments of the departed grandeur of the Mameluke Sultans. Boulak is typical of the youth of Egypt, renewed by the overland passage and by Frank technical science. The substantial stone quay—the sun on high shining on the broad river, with wooded Rodah in the distance, steamers in the foreground, and in the background, a crowd of boats with sails set moving up and down the river—tall trees, tall masts, and minarets, all rising together; and, oppposite, the verdant islands, beyond which the sharp lines of the pyramids stand boldly out on the horizon—form together a landscape of a most characteristic nature, bringing into juxta-position most striking monuments of the old native, and the newly imported civilization of Egypt.

Further down the Nile, one of the most pleasant creations of Mohammed Ali in the neighbourhood of Cairo, is the orange and lemon-park of Shoubra. The stranger finds himself in a labyrinth of trim parterres and box-wood borders, in triangles, parallelograms, circles, and segments of circles; while all around well-grown lemon and orange trees luxuriate in that texture of foliage which, to other vegetation, is like what satin and velvet are to ordinary stuffs, and the orange itself harmonizes beautifully with the tree from which it grows. There is an aviary, fountain, and kiosk of white marble. Shoubra is the converse of a Damascus house, where marble shines and the orange and lemon relieve; here the orange and lemon luxuriate, and the marble relieves their splendour.

No traces of the magnificent architecture of the Arabs are to be found in the modern palace-building of Egypt. The houses of the wealthier classes which have been recently constructed are mostly in the Greco-Constantinopolitan style, with French furniture inside, Lyons damask hangings, and divans, Aubusson carpets, and pier glasses. But in the divan tissues, the Europeans cannot come up to the Aleppines, whose stuffs, with a mixture of gold thread, silk and wool, have a rich and magnificent effect. A palace of this description had been built for one of the family of Mohammed Ali, on the site of the town house of Elfy Bey, which became the head-quarters of Bonaparte, and subsequently, of Kleber, who was assassinated in the garden attached. One of the best localities for a palace would undoubtedly be the Island of Rodah, with its luxuriant park of tropical vegetation, and its position on the Nile; but unluckily once in every twelve or fifteen years it is under water and the inundation is so high, that the gardeners have to fly for their lives, and the gardens are completely devastated.

If the citadel does not possess the advantage of luxuriant vegetation, it has a healthy airy position. I minutely examined it in 1845-6, when a few columns of granite standing upright were the only remains of the Iwan-el-Kubeer, or great hall, in which had been the throne of Saladin. The ancient magnificence of the castle had disappeared, and I found no trace of the gorgeous gate of bronze, which was so highly ornamented with arabesques; or of the celebrated "Refref," or corniced terrace of Mohammed-el-Nasr, which commanded the view of the whole valley. Nor was I able to make out the locality of the celebrated drummery and musicians' barrack, and the large space of ground opposite it used for playing ball. What most strikes the attention is the new mosque of Mohammed Ali, from its size, its position, its rich material, and the abundance of alabaster columns. It is, however, entirely in the modern taste of Constantinople, and immeasurably inferior to the school of the period of the Mameluke Sultans, which united picturesque outline with the most luxuriant detail, presenting a striking contrast to the heavy Byzantine dome and bald minaret, of modern Turkish mosque building.

Mohammed Ali did much to improve the water-works

of Cairo. The want of water in the upper part of Cairo, behind the Azhar, was supplied by him by means of a water-wheel, at the "Khalidge" or "canal," and by means of machinery it is carried still higher. This was a great boon, for, previously, all the water used in this quarter, so dry and remote from the Nile, had to be purchased from those who made a trade of conveying it in skins on asses' backs. There is a great inequality in the supply of water, some quarters having it all the year, and others only during the inundation. At the Birgouan is a well which during the inundation is of a reddish colour, and hence the prevalence of the idea that there exists in this quarter a well of blood.

Egypt depends for its wealth entirely on the proper irrigation of the land in the agricultural districts. Mohammed Ali well understood this; and hence the canals of the Delta were well kept up, and several new ones added. In old times, besides the cutting of the Khalidge, denoting the rise of the waters to the proper height, there was also a great festivity at the opening of the canal of Abou Monagyeh which was drawn from the Nile in order to water the land to the east of the Delta. This rejoicing was as disorderly as a Venetian Carnival, and used to be celebrated with pomp and licence by all the people east of Delta. Makrizi speaks with horror of the orgies of the opening. Men and unveiled women mixed promiscuously in illuminated boats, moving up and down during the night, while the air resounded with guitars, lyres, and musical instruments. This Abou Monagyeh was a Jew, who enjoyed the stewardship of the province of Sharkieh; and in the year 506 of the Hegira dug the canal, on which he spent enormous sums. He was afterwards imprisoned for peculation, or on account of his enormous wealth; and despairing of release adopted a curious plan to procure his liberty.

He copied a Koran and wrote on it "Copied by Abou Monagyeh, the Jew." The copy was publicly sold and caused much sensation in Cairo. On being asked "Why he copied a Koran?" he answered, "In order to obtain death;" upon which he was let out of prison.

CHAPTER XXIII.

Public Justice—Thieves.—Crimes and Disorders of the Arnauts.—Crimes in Harems.—A Revolt in a Harem.—Swindlers.—Lawsuits.—Criminal Punishments.—Imprisonment for Debt.—Scene in a Debtors' Prison.

Let us now say something of public justice, and of crime, during the rule of Mohammed Ali. The old municipal police was abolished, and all united under the so-called "Zabit Bey," literally the "Fixing or Settling Bey," or in other words the keeper of peace. He had under his immediate orders each of the lieutenants of the eight quarters of Cairo, who again had under them the sheikhs of the Harats, or subdivisions of the large quarters. Formerly, the Daoudeey was the worst part of Cairo, and was originally so called from the name of Daoud, who was Mokaddem-esh-Shürta or head of the detective police, under the Fatimites. We have a curious specimen of this class of men more or less distinctly pourtrayed in the Arabian Nights' Entertainments, in the Ahmed-el-Denf who lived at Bagdad in the time of Haroun-er-Reshid, and who doubtless was not a fancy sketch, but a real character, and who transmitted his reputation for ingenuity in those processes for which the old Bow-street officers were so renowned.

There is, upon the whole, much less domestic theft and larceny in the East than in Europe. No doubt one of the causes of this was the old Draconian code, so that for a petty theft an unprincipled man would not willingly risk his life, or at least, the loss of his hand, which branded him with infamy for life, and at the same time by crippling him hindered him from gaining a livelihood. It may be remarked that thefts of every description are much more frequent in Cairo than in Damascus or Aleppo, on account of the size of the town. Hence the proverb:—

> "Halebi chelebi,
> Shami shoumi,
> Misri harami;"

which means, that the Aleppine is polite, the Damascene deceptively plausible, but the Egyptian a thief. In Egypt the agents of the detective police are called "Bassasseen," and they are generally old skilled robbers, who for the sake of a more secure existence have offered their services to the government. They can tell if a box has been broken open by a professional robber, or by one who is beginning the craft. By examining a broken window shutter, they will know how entrance has been effected into a house, and make the same distinction as to the professional or the unpractised robber; and they know all the thieves in the town. The Daoudeey was also the principal quarter of female prostitution; but Mohammed Ali cleared out the quarter, and banished these women to Upper Egypt.

At the commencement of Mohammed Ali's rule, his own Arnauts maintained a deplorable distinction, as foremost in crimes accompanied by violence; and as it was through the instrumentality of this class of men that the Pasha rose to power, he felt bound, in deference to public opinion, to treat them with summary justice. Instances occurred of Arnaut soldiers getting richly dressed prostitutes, adorned with jewels, into their houses, murdering them for the sake of their ornaments, and then throwing their dead bodies into the Khalidge, during the inundation, or into some of the ponds created during this period by the extraordinary overflow of the Nile. A case of this occurred in the blind alley, called the Alifet Rizq. When it was reported to Mohammed Ali, he ordered an immediate example to be made, and, on the same day, Arnauts in their petticoats were seen hanging at the most conspicuous places and frequented thoroughfares of the town.

Crimes in harems are not infrequent, and sometimes escape detection. The reason of this is, that the harem is a domestic establishment, partaking of the character of the fortress and of the prison. The inmates are not to the same extent under public control and under public protection as those who live in European houses with windows opening on a street. An oriental house is a dead wall, with a wicket door and lantern sort of windows, which are never opened to the street; and not only are the inmates more completely under the control of the master, but the access of the public is also controlled. In Europe if one knocks at the door, whether of a high or humble dwelling, it is opened immediately; but in the East only with precaution, and after a time, during which the visitor has been under examination and probably the subject of discussion. In fact, the oriental house is perfectly suited to the despotic position of the head of the family. Revolts rarely occur, and the "Revolt of the Seraglio," a subject that has been treated by European dramatists, is certainly a rare exception. Such a revolt did, however, occur, in Cairo, during Mohammed Ali's rule, and created a great sensation.

In the Derb-el-Habaleh, or "Ropemakers-road," may be seen a house which has a curious appearance; for the architect, in order to procure for the master a view of the mosque of Sheikhoun, made the rooms of the first floor project in right angled triangles over the basement.

Here lived Ahmed Effendi Abou Shenab, one of those Turks who had been many years in France, but whom Europe had not civilised. He was a man of a cruel disposition, and on his horse once shying he applied his sabre to its buttock in a fit of passion, and this caused the death of the animal. He had ceased to be a Moslem, but had learned only the vices of Europe, and was called by the Arabs, "Formason," or Freemason,—that is to say, a man who had no religion. He had eleven female slaves in his house, whom he treated in a tyrannical manner; for, although intelligent, he was nightly intoxicated. There had long been murmurs in the harem against his tyranny, and an accident brought the discontent to a head. Having thrown a glass of water which had been brought him back into the face of one of his slaves, they consulted together and, during his drunken sleep, cut the rope of the well, and, nine of them being present, he was strangled in the impotence of drunkenness. Two, who had taken no part in the murder, were let off, but the nine were all drowned in the Nile.

The ingenious deceptions of the dangerous classes of Cairo are endless; and one of the classes most addicted to crimes unaccompanied with violence are the gipsies. They are divided into several tribes, and the females sell rings and ornaments in harems, and mark with blue the hands and chins of women. They also circumcise girls. One hears them crying in the bazaars, "Ya binat ashash el areed, Ya binat ashash el rafeia," "Oh women! I have broad and fine sashes to sell." The women of these gipsy tribes do not cover their faces; they have their own laws and secret usages; they all pretend to be Moslems, as in Syria and the other parts of the Ottoman Empire. A curious circumstance once happened, which may be mentioned here. An old woman and a young beauty passed in the street an old Fackih, or Koran-reader, who was known to be uxorious. The younger woman allowed her face to be seen, and, addressing him by name and appealing to his character, requested him to read a document for her. This was a bill of divorce by a husband, which was followed by ejaculations on the part of the beauty and her pretended relative, such as, "Cruel fate! What shall I do! Where shall I go!" In a country where marriages are easily dissolved, they are contracted with equal facility, and so the Fackih asked her if she was disposed again to enter into matrimony? The beauty was not unwilling, so a marriage was prepared, the jewels of his female relations were put in requisition, and on the nuptial night the beauty was resplendent with the borrowed gems. When the guests were all gone, the bride —thanking them for lending the jewels which she promised to restore on the following day—pretended to her husband to go up stairs, but suddenly slipped out, carrying with her all the ornaments. Many asses had been in waiting in the neighbourhood for their mistresses, and the beauty having slipped on her veil, was enabled by the aid of her accomplices to get clear off. I regret that I did not hear whether the culprit had ever been discovered; but it was supposed by the police that she was one of the female gipsies, who are not darker than the Egyptian women of the humbler classes.

I have already stated that women of loose life were sometimes murdered by Arnauts for their jewels. Instances of a different kind occur from time to time, in which the males are victims of female deceit. A woman, handsomely dressed, presented herself in a house where Turkish officers used to live, and requested permission to take up her quarters with them, which they allowed. They were newly come from Constantinople and asked her her name, to which she answered "Khan Halily." When they used to go to the bath, she would say, "Go with little money, for the bath-keepers are robbers." So they used to deposit their money with her, and on returning found it safe. One day all four went to the bath together, and left their purses with her. On their return the purses were not to be found. They shouted, "Khan Halily, where are you?" and then fired off a pistol, and again cried "Khan Halily, where are you?" They afterwards went out, and said to the grocer opposite, "Do you know where Khan Halily is?" "Further on," said he. They asked another, and received the same answer, and even maltreated a peasant who turned them into ridicule. When they found out at last, that the Khan Halily was a bazaar, and the woman was not to be found, their rage knew no bounds; and long afterwards they were joked by other Turkish officers, and asked if they had not yet found the whereabouts of Khan Halily.

As the shawl which is wrapped round the skull-cap is of considerable value, and as even persons in very moderate circumstances go to the expense of a Bussorah or Cashmere wrapper, turban snatching was a most usual form of depredation in dark nights in a large capital so badly lighted as Cairo, where there were no public lamps, and where the wayfarer carried his own lantern. Hence the obligation not to be abroad after an early hour of the evening, without a lantern. In the so called Harat Abdeen there used to be a man who pretended to be a saint, and who had a lantern hanging at one part of the street while he recited verses of the Koran and received contributions. In reality, however, he was an accomplice of the turban-snatching Arnauts, who lived in the quarter. As it was not worth the risk to snatch away any but the best turbans, he saw by the light of his lamp whether the turbans of the people were good or bad; and when a fine turban passed, the signal he gave was by crying out, "Ya Rab!" (O Lord!) Then, when the wearer had passed on to a dark part of the street, the turban was snatched. But this soon came to the ears of the head of the police, who passed himself one night with a fine Cashmere shawl around his tarboosh. "A prize," thought the pretended Wely to himself, as he cried out "Ya Rab!" (O Lord); and when the head of the police reached the darker part of the street, off went his turban, snatched by unseen hands. This officer, however, had a troop of men approaching from both directions; and the Arnauts, seeing the first troop, took to flight in the opposite direction, but had not proceeded many paces, when they found themselves in the midst of the troop approaching from the other direction. The Arnauts were captured and put to death, having first confessed confederacy with the pretended saint, who was beheaded on the spot, and his head put under the mustabah, or stone bench, where he used to sit in the Harat Abdeen, so that for several days all Cairo streamed to see it.

A formidable officer of justice during the earlier part of Mohammed Ali's rule was the mohtisab, or inspector of weights and measures. He was a one-eyed old man of Kurdish extraction, called Mustapha Kashef. He combined the office of aga of the janissaries with that of inspector of weights and measures, and was ill-famed for his extreme cruelty. Once a fat butcher was short of weight in his mutton, and several ounces of flesh were cut off that part of his own body which, in the language of the shambles, may be called the "hind quarter." On another occasion he asked the seller of melons called Ahmed Abou Sitty, who sold fruit at Bab-el-Sharieh, "What is the price of this melon?" Ahmed Abou Sitty (so called Father of Six, because he had married and divorced six wives in one week) took hold of his own ear and said, "Cut off my ear;" "What is the price of this melon?" thundered the Kurd. "Cut off my ear," shouted Father of Six, "I sell cheaper than my neighbours, and no matter what price I ask, you would find me overcharging." The Kurd, being checkmated for once, did not punish him, and Abou Sitty was made sheikh of the fruit-vendors.

One day a respectable looking man was pointed out to me with a red Cashmere turban, riding a sleek fine horse. It was the mokaddem-el-Mezowereen, or chief observer of the swindlers. His vocation was to keep the government informed of everything the swindlers were about; but, when affairs were going badly with one of the fraternity, he occasionally got him out of the scrape for a consideration.

The administration of justice was undoubtedly greatly improved by Mohammed Ali, in civil as well as in criminal cases, and many suitors with well grounded rights, who had failed before the Cadi, succeeded on personal appeal to the Pasha. An instance of this was the celebrated Roduan case, of which we give an outline. On the line of bazaars leading from the castle to the gate of Zueileh is a long shoe-bazaar, called Kassabat Roduan after the original builder and proprietor of that name, who had been one of the Mameluke Beys some time previous to the French invasion, and is frequently mentioned by the historians of the eighteenth century, and known, although emir of the pilgrimage to Mecca, to have been a disorderly and dissipated character. Long after his death his descendant and heir to the property was accosted by a stranger who called himself Roduan, and pretended to be the true heir. A legal investigation took place, and the Cadi ordered witnesses to be produced. The false Roduan procured false witnesses, and gave the cadi a handsome present, but the real Roduan having intelligence of this, promised a larger sum to the witnesses if they would disappoint their employer. "Where are your witnesses?" said the cadi, to the false Roduan. "Here they are," answered he. "Well and what do you testify?" "We testify that in the night this man came to us with money, and paid us for swearing false." As subornation of perjury does not appear to be practicably cognizable by oriental courts of justice, the cadi contented himself with sending away the false Roduan, and said to the true one, "Come to-morrow, and I will confirm your title." When the morrow came, the false Roduan stepped forward, and made out to the pretended satisfaction of the cadi that the affair of yesterday was a trick, his witnesses having been suborned. The cadi, who was no doubt a partner in the speculation of the false Roduan, decreed half to the plaintiff and half to the defendant; but some time afterward, Mohammed Ali took the matter up, and, as the family of the false Roduan died off, their shares reverted to the original family.

Criminal justice was also much reformed by the Pasha. In the midst of this shoe bazaar of Roduan, is a gate where—from the time of Sultan Bibars down to the first years of Mohammed Ali's rule—there was a lamp which burnt all night, and burglars caught in the night were killed at once. A bull's hide was laid out, and their heads cut off. The corners of the hide were then gathered up, and the body, being put on an ass, was conveyed to the washing place at the Roumeyleh. The washers had an office and received altogether about a hundred piastres a month through the so called wekweel-el-haramayn. The ancient law of Islamism in cases of theft was that the offenders should lose their right hand for the first offence, and no doubt, the fear of such a summary punishment kept down larceny; but as this incapacitated the criminal from gaining his bread, Mohammed Ali used to send thieves to work, chained, in the arsenal. This punishment, however, from having been so often applied in the case of trivial political offences, was scarcely held ignominious, and Mohammed Ali therefore determined that thieves should henceforth be marked on the hand with the word haramy (robber,) or at least with the initial of the word. There were, however, other punishments; for, during my residence in Cairo, thieves who had attempted to take off the bronze stanchions of a mosque, were paraded about Cairo with their hands and heads in a wooden frame, reminding me of the designs of Chinese punishments.

The horrible punishments of skinning and impalement were abolished. The former was not uncommon in the time of the Mameluke Beys, as an excruciating ransom of the last penalty of the law. Hence the alliterative expression, "Aslakny la tashnakny," that is to say, "Skin me but do not strangle me," which horrible process was preferred to death. Europeans would probably be of a different opinion, if they had only this abominable alternative.

For debtors, ordinary imprisonment is still the punishment. The debtors' prison is close to the cadi's court; and being desirous of seeing an Egyptian establishment of this kind, I spent a forenoon in it. In this part of Cairo, the new offices built by Mohammed Ali, and the magnificent ancient constructions to the west of them, are altogether divested of the mean but picturesque aspect which Cairo often presents. A suitor might be seen pacing anxiously up and down, with law papers in his hand, long slips of thick paper, almost black with the close writing, and a few seals at the bottom of them, imprinted in bluish ink. At the door of the gaol, was a Kurd, in a short petticoat, who asked, "which of the prisoners we wanted?" but a backschish smoothed all difficulties, and the Kurd started up from the wicker-frame of palm-branches on which he reclined, with easy agility, and, leading me into a dark passage, opened a door with a large wooden bolt, and I found myself among the prisoners. The apartment might be about twenty feet high, the light being admitted by two barred unglazed windows, close to the roof. The walls were perfectly bare, and in the upper corner of the room a spider's web of thick texture fluttered in the slight breeze which ventilated the apartment. On the floor were the mats, carpets, and cushions of the prisoners. Wearing the native costume, and having my brow bronzed by the sun, I was supposed to be a prisoner, and was immediately asked the particulars of the process or "dawa" which had brought me thither. I answered that I had come to see the prison. On enquiry I found the debts for which the people were confined were generally from three pounds to five pounds. One of the prisoners was a Bedouin, who had been entrusted with a camel, which had died in his keeping: he subsisted entirely on charity. They told me their cases very freely. One was a miller, who had not understood his business: he told me that this was the first day of his imprisonment, and added, with evident distress, that "his body was with the cadi, but his mind with his two little children." Another, a very young man, had pawned his wife's ornaments, and spent her dowry; and, being called before the cadi, had been cast into prison. The prisoners occasionally whispered among themselves, and a well-dressed townsman said aloud, "You are here on the part of Effendina, the Pasha, to enquire how we are treated." I explained that this was a mistake, and ordered a pilaff for the poorer prisoners, and coffee to be served all round.

"May God bless you!" said a man with weak eyes, a grey beard, and green turban; and he immediately said in a decided voice, "Elfateha," that is to say, the recitation of the opening passage of the Koran, which is a formula of prayer; on which all the prisoners, in chorus, holding out their hands, and looking upwards, recited this sublime exordium. One of the prisoners was a soldier of fortune, who had not been able to make up his mind to serve with the regular troops. He had been with Kurschid Pasha in Aleppo, at the period of the great revolt and siege in 1819, when, on the occasion of that governor imposing a house-tax, the officers of the Porte were murdered, though after four months' fighting the Pasha put down the revolt by force. This man praised Kurschid Pasha for the number of heads he had cut off as a lesson. He spoke with great contempt of the new Nizam discipline, because, when men march in lines, the coward is never known from the man of iron. I need not multiply these details, further than to say, that imprisonments are not prolonged, since, after ninety days' detention, a debtor, on making oath of insolvency, is liberated.*

* The readers of Melusina will have no difficulty in remembering this sketch as the groundwork of a scene in that romance. It is in the admirable pages of Mr. Lane that the reader may acquire a thorough knowledge of the population of Cairo. Still the mine is so rich, that a dozen writers could not exhaust it; and if the traveller or historian have previously familiarized himself with the colloquial language, the political history, religious institutions, and domestic manners of the Arabs, he will find his materials to accumulate upon him with great rapidity. In these chapters some points of contact with Mr. Lane have been inevitable; but, conscious of his immeasurable inferiority to this great Arab scholar and acute observer, the author of these pages has, as a general rule, selected from his manuscript volumes of notes matter which might not prove uninteresting to persons already familiar with Mr. Lane's delightful works.

CHAPTER XXIV.

The Ulema in the last years of Mohammed Ali's Rule.—State of Arabic Literature.—Party Spirit among the Ulema.—The Wahabys and Arabians proper resident in Cairo.—Popular Superstition, and Imposture of Pretended Enchanters.—Execution of the last Wizard.

Apart from the government is the local Arab aristocracy, or leading families, who are distinguished by ancient birth, and in some instances by considerable property. Their occupations, too, are interwoven with the learning and religion of the Arabs. For the youth are carefully educated in Arab Moslem learning, and in mature life are nazirs, or inspectors of mosques, or fill other offices, such as that of mufti, or chief doctor of the law, or nackeeb-el asraf. They consider themselves greatly superior to all the pashas of Turkey; but, as they have not the political power, or the large government salaries, their position is in reality inferior to that of the leading Turks, although they are treated with a certain amount of deference. In Damascus there really is, or was until lately, a powerful native aristocracy; but in Cairo the Mamelukes having been for so many centuries the leading people, there have been always very few native Arab families of any account. This was remarked by the Venetians, under the Mameluke Sultans, and since then there has been no change, except for the worse, as Mohammed Ali's spoliation of title deeds still further reduced this class.

One of the leading persons of this description was

Sheikh Sadat, who was very fanatical, although he was said to have been originally of Jewish extraction. He was very wealthy and had a magnificent house, and moreover was honorary wekeel of the house of Ali and nazir of the mosque of Hosseyneyn. The acknowledged head of the ancient native families was the Sheikh-el-Bekri, a lineal descendant of Abou Bekr, one of the first of the Caliphs. Sheik-el-Bekri held the office of chief of the Shereefs, or descendants of the prophet, and his income was said to be about twelve pounds per day. He was hospitable, and had a large house of dependants. This was the principal family in Cairo during the French occupation, and by no means fanatical towards Franks. One of the females of the family was even lax in her morals, having been mistress of a French officer, and was put to death on the departure of the French. I was taken by a friend to one of the sheikhs' evening festivals, and he received me very kindly. The house was splendidly illuminated, and the head of the family, a fine old man with a white beard, wore bright crimson robes. The Ananeey family claimed descent from Omar, and Sheikh-el-Ainany, a merchant who belonged to both the corps of merchants and ulema, had an income as small merchant and nazir of a mosque which did not exceed £200 per annum. A family who claimed to be descended from Osman, formerly resided in Cairo, where they still have some property; their wekeel, or legal representative, being the cadi.

Of the ulema, Sheikh Attar was allowed to be the most versed in polite literature, and was transferred to be Imam of the mosque of the Egyptian pupils in Paris. Sheikh-el-Dessouky (Mr. Lane's sheikh) was the best in pure philology, having, as was said, "all the dictionary in his head." As a general scholar, there was none better than Sheikh Mohammed Shehab. I made the acquaintance of the latter, whose conversation Mr. Lane described as "the most delightful banquet which can be offered to his friends." He is of the illustrious Koreishite house of the Hedjaz, one portion of which remains at Mecca, and another branch has turned Christian, after having enjoyed the Emirship of Mount Lebanon for many generations, as I stated in my account of the Emir Beshir.*

The house of Sheikh Mohammed Shehab, was close to the Bab-es-Shareey, or gate of vermicelli sellers, which was one of the gates of Fatimite Cairo, but now, like Temple-bar, is in the midst of the town. His divan opened on a garden, and, it being Bairam, was full of visitors. The house gave signs neither of poverty nor of wealth, and the company included a fair mixture of the better classes of native Caireens, for only one person present besides myself was in the Egyptian-Turkish dress. A few trees, growing on the terrace that overlooked the canal, enlivened the apartment and the house of Burkhardt, and a similar garden overlooking the Khalidge, but without trees, was pointed out to me. The Sheikh had two servants, a male Nubian and a woman, and used to sit on the balcony smoking his pipe, and looking down on the Khalidge. The sheikh asked me after Iakob Effendi (Mr. Burton), who, I perceived, was generally liked in Cairo, but I could give no intelligence of him. He also told me that his property was in Mecca, and that his relations managed it; but that the Syrian branch of the family having been settled there

* I saw this family in exile at Constantinople. The old Emir Beshir, although much broken by age, had that true nobility of look which many years of power, combined with inherent personal dignity, confer. His son, the Emir Ameen, was enormously fat, and had returned to Islamism (in appearance, for he was a thorough Christian at heart—I mean in his political sympathies), no doubt in the hope that the government would restore to him the principality of Mount Lebanon, an expectation which was not realised.

for seven hundred years, all connexion between them had been broken off. The circumstance of one of the oldest families of Mecca, belonging to the tribe of Mohammed himself, adopting Christianity was considered perfectly marvellous, and viewed by several of the company with a species of horror, the expression of which was accompanied by sundry quotations from the Koran, in reference to those who disbelieve its doctrines. It is a curious circumstance that, although Hakem was one of the most remarkable of the Fatimite Caliphs, and although his mosque stands in gloom and desolation to this day, as a huge and conspicuous ruin, this company—composed of Caireens of more than average intelligence—had the most obscure and vague ideas of the origin of the Druse religion, which has been so thoroughly illustrated by the learned De Sacy in his most invaluable work. The Emir Beshir turning Christian was also a riddle they could not solve.

Another celebrated alim, Sheikh-el-Tunsi, lived near the bridge of the Lion, which is at the south-west angle of Cairo, and forms nearly an oblong square. The bridge is so called from the lions sculptured on it, no doubt the arms of some Syrian hostelry, and a souvenir of the Crusaders, the bridge having been built by Bibars in 1270. The house of the sheikh conveyed no notion of the comfort in which learning ought to live. His selamlic was a damp apartment projecting over the canal, with the plaster peeling off the walls. What makes the Cairo people prefer the canal? I know not, for when the inundation is over, it looks like Fleet ditch.

The sheikh now made his appearance. He was an elderly man, with a green turban, a weak voice, and a mild expression of countenance; but spoke such pure and elegant Arabic that it was a pleasure to hear him. The sheikh had led a wandering life. He was originally a native of Tunis, and of course acquainted with the coast of Barbary; but he had spent no less than eight years in the kingdom of Darfour, where no European traveller since Brown had penetrated up to the close of the last century. Sheikh Omar-el-Tunsi wrote a book giving an account of Darfour, which has been translated into French. "Darfour," said he, "is very good for the blacks, but a white man is half roasted alive." He praised the delightful climate of Cairo, which was the happy medium between the heat of Darfour and the intolerable cold and rain of Syria. He gave me some humorous details of the capital of that sable kingdom; and explained how the dignity of the monarch was shewn by an officer of a certain rank wiping up his expectorations as soon as they descended upon the ground. He also spoke of the luxury of having a cool bed of white ashes during the intense heat, at Darfour relieved by the monsoon rains, which do not extend to Egypt.

There were two parties in the ulema,—the great majority being obstinately opposed to the Frank innovations of the Pasha, but offering only a slight passive resistance, through fear of the government. A certain number, however—some from superior intelligence, some from good nature, and others from interested cupidity—were accommodating. Among the more intelligent was Sheikh Rifaa, one of the leading classical professors (in Arabic) at Cairo. When he spoke of the growing taste of young Egyptians for European literature, I mentioned the "Cours de Literature" of M. Villemain as being the most delightful critical work that I knew of, throwing all the Blairs, Marmontels, and Laharpes into the shade; on which he at once called his secretary, and gave the order for its being got from Paris immediately. A specimen of a good man, opposed to all Frank innovations and of the true old stamp of primitive Moslems, might be mentioned in Sheikh-el-Mawardy. He was considered one of the Ehl-el-Hakika, or people of truth, to whom God makes direct communications. He was a very pious and generous man, gave all he had to the poor, and was much respected. Coffee being a forbidden narcotic, he served to his friends vinegar and water to quench their thirst, and not to heat the blood. He had a habit of speaking straight on, like a preacher in a pulpit: he gave all sorts of good advice to visitors, to avoid the devil and his works; and drew magnificent pictures of heaven at the last day, when God would be surrounded by his ministers, prophets, and welis, Gabriel, Michael, Azraeel, Abraham, Noah, Jesus, and Mohammed, Imam-es-Shafei, Said-el-Bedaweey, and Abd-el-Kader-el-Gilany. He scarcely gave time to ask a question, but kept pouring out such a cataract of angels, archangels, prophets, imams, and welis, that visitors were usually silenced.

The strictest sect in Cairo was certainly that of the Wahabys, whose lives had been spared on the fall of their cause in Arabia, and who were living in exile at Cairo. I have already detailed the great revolt of these covenanted puritans of Islamism. These exiles lived at first on the road to Boulak, and when the great plague of 1835 raged, they got leave to quit Cairo, and go to Aboudalih, where the plague swept away nearly the half of them, notwithstanding the change of residence. I was introduced to the principal of them, a relative of Souhoud; but on his desiring to know my motive for making his acquaintance, and on my answering that it was the vivid interest I had taken in the struggle of this singular people, he seemed puzzled, incredulous, and reserved. Literary curiosity, or a vivid human interest, seemed to be something he could not understand; and we parted without my having succeeded in making him comprehend the why or wherefore of my visit. He was sure that a man wearing the Turkish costume, having a fair complexion, and making now and then perceptible slips in Arabic, was not a Wahaby, and therefore could not be an ally of his: I might be an imprudent friend, and, most likely of all, I might be a spy of Mohammed Ali. Such were the surmises that passed through my mind after an unsuccessful attempt to establish familiar intercourse with this remarkable sect. But as I was treated with polite reserve, without the slightest display of fanaticism, or even discourtesy, I had no reason to complain. The Wahabys, in Cairo, although their political pretensions were at an end, continued their customs. If a dog passed during prayer they began washing and praying. They never ate green vegetables, but rice and flesh, and were particularly fond of that of young camels. After the great plague, they maintained that the ceasing of this scourge was attributable to the appearance of a star called Touyah. Like the people of Nablouse, and of Syria and Bagdad, they are of the sect of Hambaleh, and it is generally remarked that those of this sect are of a more straightforward disposition than those who are of the sect of Shafei. The Shafei are Jesuits; not liars, but men of Jesuitical meanings.

The principal Arabians of Cairo may generally be met with at the house of the Egyptian Agent of the Shereef of Mecca, who receives strangers politely and presents a variety of the coffee berry, which may be relished in Arabia, and is even preferred, but is the most nauseous to the European. There are usually at least fifty Meccakewy in Cairo, and ten or twelve from Medina. In the summer there are from a hundred to two hundred natives of the Hedjas in Constantinople; but they cannot stand the cold, and rarely remain in winter. The wekeel told me that he even felt the cold of Cairo to be bitter and piercing. He spoke with enthusiasm of the delightful groves of Tayf in summer. An earthquake having taken place in Cairo a few days before, I asked him if he was afraid. He opened his eyes in astonishment, and said, "Why afraid, do not I put my trust in God?" So it is in the East: the undoubting, unquestioning, undissecting awe of the Deity, is the keystone of their theory of temporal government. To elude the operation of the physical laws, even when they are noxious or destructive, may occur by instinct, but is systematically reprobated. Man is supposed to be chained helpless in the prison of fate.

Earthquakes occasionally occur in Egypt. Sometimes temples and mosques are thrown down, and there are frequently movements of a slighter description. In all probability the pyramids were constructed for the express purpose of defying not only the ordinary ravages of time, but the extraordinary convulsions of nature. I was one day sitting with my sheikh, when I felt a shaky motion which prevented me from writing. Some people, particularly absent and absorbed men of letters, have a habit of crossing one leg over the other, and shaking their foot. I said, "What makes you shake your foot so vigorously?" "You are mistaken," answered he. The house next mine had been recently pulled down, and we had been frequently troubled with noises of falling stones; so I said, "In pulling down the next house, I hope they will not knock down mine." Scarcely had I said this, when, sitting on the divan, I seemed to be in a carriage, jolting over a rough pavement, and my Sheikh Hanife, rising up, pale as death, said it was an earthquake; and we both rushed out into the street, which was instantaneously filled with men, women, and children, in a state of the greatest alarm, some of whom said, "that the world was changed from one horn of the great bull to the other." However, the only damage done was in the fall of an old minaret, and the circumstance of so many beautiful and slender minarets still subsisting in Cairo, is a proof that severe earthquakes are not frequent in Egypt. They come with extraordinary violence at intervals of some centuries, but, altogether, much less frequently than in southern Italy and Greece.

The principal religious ceremonies have been so fully described by Mr. Lane, that it is not requisite to go over the same ground. The most striking of the superstitions, not being in any way an essential ceremony of Islamism, is the doseh or treading by the sheikh of the Saadeey dervishes, on the festival of the prophet (Moolid-el-Nebby). I may briefly describe it, as witnessed by me on one occasion. Those who bordered the line of procession were made to lie flat down on their faces; and when they were packed closely together, the sheikh—a stout jolly man, with a green kaouk—approached, the horse on which he rode being led by two grooms. It was evident that the horse did not like treading on the backs of the prostrate Moslems, and moved from side to side; and the sheikh was evidently also much embarrassed, and did not keep the animal steady in hand. At last the horse moved rapidly and shouts of pain were heard. Those who were closely wedged in, were raised up by the spectators, either seriously bruised or quite unconscious. Death sometimes ensues from this abominable contravention of the physical laws, as if such delicate machinery as that of shoulder-blades, the spine, ribs, and veins, had been constructed to bear the pressure of the hoofs of a horse, weighted by a stout man and a heavy saddle. That such a superstitious procedure should be pleasing to the Deity who made the laws it violates, must appear to every intelligent man one of the most striking instances of human delusion, paralleled only by the macerations of monkish superstition, the un-Christian horrors of a Scotch sabbath, or the more inconceivable tortures of the Indian peninsula.

The superstition of the people of Cairo shows itself in many other ways, and is quite as absurd as that recorded of the ignorant, in the time of the ancients. To this day shrewd people in Cairo make a living by pretending to drive evil spirits out of harems by spells and incantations,—not only the Evil Eye (Ain-el-wuhsh), but all sorts of evil spirits. Wives in harems are always taking alarms of this sort, and by a trifling gratuity to an impostor, who goes through a *hocus pocus* in which reading verses of the Koran forms an essential part, repose is restored to the harem for some weeks and months at least. If a strange cat enters a house and knocks over a jug or glass, and awakes the servant in a dark night, he may possibly leave on the following day, on the pretext that the house is haunted by afreets. Behind the Moristan, a new house was pointed out to me with an aloe hanging at the gate, placed there to keep away afreets. Sheikh Ahmed-el-Kotoby, who in my presence ridiculed the excessive credulity of his fellow-countrymen, several times insisted that the Bairactar, or "Standard Bearer" of Sultan Selim, had been living since the Turkish conquest of Egypt, in 1517, at Constantinople.

I may mention one or two more instances of this description to which my attention was drawn during my researches in the highways and byeways of this capital. On the line of street from the citadel to Bab Zueileh, is a mosque called Giama-el-Sais, or Mosque of the Groom. At the corner of it is a high Corinthian pillar, evidently an antique. I asked how the lower part of the pillar came to be covered all over with a thick coat of plaster, and received for answer, that this was the celebrated Amood-el-Metuely, which was proclaimed by a Mogrebbin sheikh to have miraculous effects, and that if sterile women licked it with their tongue, they would become mothers. All on a sudden the pillar was so besieged by people wishing to lick it, that the streets were blocked up, and the Pasha, hearing of the delusion, caused a guard to stand, while the masons plastered and built the lower part of it round with bricks.

There is a bridge over the Khalidge called Cantarat-el-Kafir, which was formerly called Cantarat-el-Djedeed. This change of designation arose from the eccentricities of one of those religious fanatics who are tolerated according to Moslem usage. This man was called the Wely Ali-el-Tantawy. He was a native of Fantah, a considerable town in the Delta, whither pilgrims throng to the shrine of the celebrated Said-el-Bedawy. I was informed by Sheikh Ahmed-el-Kotoby, the glass-eating bookseller, who figures in the Preface to Mr. Lane's "Modern Egyptians," that he had made the acquaintance of this Wely at Tantah in a very curious manner. "One day (he said) I was in the mosque of Said-el-Bedawy, at Tantah; and, after the midday prayers, fell asleep till night, on a mat; I then looked up, and found myself awakened by a man who said, 'It is Eshia, arise and pray.' After prayers he opened a bag, which was full of flat cakes and bread. I said, 'What do you do with all those loaves?' He replied, 'They are begged in the course of the day, and I feed the dogs of Tantah with them; that is my sole occupation.'"

When the Wely Ali came to Cairo, he used to stand naked on this bridge, and when Mohammed Ali passed, he said, in allusion to his new Frank reforms, "That man is an infidel!" A multitude of other persons were called infidels by him, whose external appearance indicated a departure from the old Moslem costume. He was quite naked, and when clothes were given him, used to tear them. I saw several such persons in Damascus; but the authorities are gradually getting rid of them.

Bab Arab-el-Ysar is a gate of the suburb of Cairo to the south, not far from the citadel, the literal translation of the expression being "The gate of the Arabs to the left." This quarter of Cairo has altogether a curious aspect; it is close under the chain of hills called Mokattam, which have not a blade of grass upon them. Here is an oratory, which is called Zawiet-el-Wahsh, literally "of the animals," for from its proximity to the mountains, it has been known to be frequented by jackals and other beasts that prowl between the cultivated and desert territory. Not far off, the strangely called mosque of the Messiah has its name derived from two Christians that turned Moslem and built the mosque. Christians often called themselves Messihieheen, or if I may so translate it Messiahites. The women of this quarter are mostly employed in washing wool. I found here a Dakroory—a man from the upper country, almost a black—who sat at an open stall and was consulted on confidential family matters, by women from all parts of Cairo, and was supposed to make a considerable revenue. They would come saying, for instance, "Oh Sheikh! open the book, I am barren and desire a child;" or, "Oh Sheikh! my husband wishes to divorce me; pray consult the book, and turn him from his purpose." He had two books of divining science before him, the one called "Abou Maa'sher," the other, "Hodour." He made me separate beads to the right and left, three times, and consulting his books, said "that I was to start on my journey on a Wednesday, but not to wear stockings on the first day of my journey, and that I should arrive safely in my own country." There appears to have been no hanging or burning for witchcraft in Europe later than the seventeenth century, but in Cairo, an execution took place a few years before the French expedition to Egypt, so as to be remembered by many persons in Mohammed Ali's time, although I regret that I was unable to get the exact year. The name of the so called-wizard was Sheikh Hussein, and he was accused of being able to write powerful talismans, producing hatred between persons that loved each other. For this he was hanged at the Bab-Zawiet-el-Wekeel.

CHAPTER XXV.

State of the Christian Population in the Last Years of Mohammed Ali's Rule.—Laudable Enforcement of Tolerance towards Christians. —Basilios Bey's Death.—The Copts.—The Franks.—Mr. Lane and Clot Bey.—The Syrians and Greeks.—The Caraite Jews.—The Castle of Dogs.—Music and Musicians.—Jugglers.—Nubian Population.—Negroes.

Having given the reader some sketches of the classes which have the Moslem character most distinctly stamped upon them, I may now proceed to say something of the Christians and Jews.

Close to the Ezbekieh, is the Coptic quarter, with passages dark, dismal, gloomy, and noisome. Here are neither arabesques, nor covered mustabahs, nor effendis with pipe-bearers, nor ulema in their white turbans and smooth chins, and the bazaar itself is shabby and out of repair; the inhabitants are the descendants of the former rulers of Egypt, of the constructors of Thebes and the pyramids. It is chiefly since the time of Caliph Hakem, that the Copts have fallen into such a wretched condition. Memorials of the former magnificence of the Copts, their high positions among the earlier Moslems, and their learning, are occasionally discoverable. Mr. Lieder, an intelligent German missionary, informed me that he had seen a magnificent copy of the Gospels, with much of the text and beautiful Arabic poetry, and a Coptic commentary. Five leaves being wanting, he went to the patriarch, expecting to be able to find five analogous leaves in the library of this Pope of Eastern African Christianity, but was astonished at being told that the patriarch had never seen any copy of the Gospels so beautiful, and did not even know of the existence of such a manuscript.

One of the principal characteristics of the rule of Mohammed Ali was religious tolerance; and, so far as the Pasha was concerned, complete indifference. His great object was to get the European powers to think favourably of his rule; and this was most likely to be accomplished by strict protection of Franks and Christians, and such an effective curbing of native fanaticism, as produced the deepest exasperation in the Moslem mind. The Pasha not only made the most use he could of the Copts, who both before and since the Turkish conquest have always shown a singular expertness in arithmetic and book-keeping, but he raised several persons of this race to the dignity of Bey. The most respectable and intelligent was Basilios Bey, the head of his account department, who died in November, 1847, to the great regret both of the Christian and the French population. Equally intelligent, but infamous, was Abderrahman Bey, who had turned Moslem, and proved himself a most cruel exactor of tribute for the Pasha's purse; so that out of decency, and in deference to European opinion, this man was suspended, chiefly in consequence of the evil effect which his exactions had produced by being commented upon in the European newspapers. Mohammed Ali did not care two straws about the exactions of the renegade Copt, but he found it politic publicly to repudiate any connection with the tortures which this heartless man had inflicted on the peasantry. Much praise must be bestowed on the German missionaries, who, chiefly with English funds, have been most active in educating Copts and giving them a smattering of Frank science.

On one occasion I determined on attending Divine

service on Palm Sunday in the Coptic cathedral, where the patriarch was to officiate. Plunging into the Coptic quarter, I passed through a succession of crooked lanes, and at length arrived at the temple of this ancient people, which was undistinguished by any architectural decoration,—a truly remarkable lapse in the external circumstances of a nation, when we think of the colossal magnificence of the Pharaonic and the elegance of the Greek periods of Egyptian architecture. But one circumstance vividly recalled the physical conditions of the region which gave birth to Christianity. The street was crowded with lads selling palm branches, without which no one entered the church. The temple was an oblong square, and lighted from above. A screen of inlaid chips of carpentry, ebony, and mother-of-pearl, disposed in all sorts of arabesque devices, separated the *sanctum sanctorum* from the body of the church, and from the gaze of the congregation: a door in the centre allowing the altar to be visible in the distance. At the other end of the church, which was all railed and trellised off by curiously turned and combined wooden spars, might be seen fair white ruby-ringed hands, corners of silk dresses, cashmere shawls, and a bright diamond sparkling in the obscurity, denoting that behind the fairer portion of the Coptic flock was separated from the males. The body of the church was covered with a thick Turkey carpet: and next the door, were hundreds of pairs of shoes, from the bright new morocco of the ma'alem, to the cobbled and stitched old slipper of the pauper. Five hundred luxuriant branches of palms, held upright by the male part of the congregation, gave to the place an aspect of a greenhouse.

The patriarch and his deacons made their appearance, the former in a dress of purple and gold, beautifully embroidered, and which, being clasped in front with a hood covering the head, reminded the spectator of the mosaic representations of the Lower Empire. The deacons were dressed in simple white robes of linen and gold, just as one sees in the pictures of the old Florentine masters. The patriarch was so infirm, and coughed so often, that when, after the Psalms, he rose to read a passage in the Coptic Gospels, his voice did not rise above a whisper. A grey-bearded priest then came to a desk, and putting on a pair of spectacles—which being without ear-joints, and simply fastened to his nose by elastic compression, gave him a strong nasal twang,—he commenced reading in an Arabic manuscript Bible the account of the entrance of Christ into Jerusalem from St. John. The congregation during the whole service made the sign of the cross, and bowed at the name of Jesus; but there was certainly a want of that reverence and absorption which is visible in our own service. Nothing can exceed the reverence and humility of a Copt in the presence of a Pasha; but here there was much general conversation and whispering, and at one moment a most audible discussion between the deacons as to the forms of the service. And when the Gospels were read in Arabic, there was so much whispering and talking, that a priest cried out, "There is no hearing on account of the noise." The patriarch now retired, and came back in a vestment of red satin, richly embroidered with gold, and then administered the sacrament, the communicants going round the table in turn, and receiving a mouthful of bread, and also a gold spoonful of wine, poured from a goblet held by the left hand of the priest.

There is an old Coptic quarter in the upper part of the town, close to the citadel, but now abandoned to the Moslems in a great measure. I visited its church, which looked very old, shabby, and neglected; but in the shrine is preserved a pretended relic of primitive Christianity—an arm of St. Theodore, or Mar Tadros (Theodorus), as the Copts call him. Certainly, in antiquity, none of the oriental churches can reasonably take precedence of that of the Copts, or of Alexandria, as it is sometimes called; for in Alexandria, then the second city of the Roman empire, the Gospel was preached by Mark, the evangelist, and to this day, Abyssinia receives its patriarchs from the Coptic church of Egypt.

The occupations of the Copts are various, the most important being, as already stated, that of keeping the government accounts, in which they are most expert. In the Siagha, or goldsmiths' and jewellers' bazaar, we find Copts and Jews at work, but no Moslems or Syrian Christians. Nearly all the millers in Cairo were Copts, and most of the water-carriers, and many carpenters. Besides the division by trades, there is also a distinction between Copts, native of Cairo, and those who have come from the Fayoum, or still more remote provinces, to essay their fortunes in the metropolis. Sometimes these latter succeed, get into easy circumstances, and bring their relatives to Cairo. I heard a pleasant story of a Copt of the humblest origin from one of the villages of the Upper Nile, who, after being successful, brought his widowed mother to Cairo, and thought to honour her by offering her a diamond ornament; but she refused it in anger, saying "What! shall I wear glass? No! I will only wear bendekeey" (Venetian sequins).

The Frank quarter of Cairo is so well known to overland travellers as to require very little description. The old Frank inhabitants used to wear the native costume, and the females spoke Arabic as their native language; but the establishment of the overland passage, and the Frank inundation, have given a different character to the Frank society of Cairo. To this we may add, that nearly all government officials of the superior rank, and many also of the inferior rank, speak French; so that, except in Pera and Smyrna, there is no part of the Ottoman empire where the native languages are less requisite for the ordinary necessities of the passing traveller than in Cairo. On the other hand, very little is to be learned from these Europeanized Moslems; and Cairo, in all its peculiarities, remains a sealed book to the man who has not so much of the language as enables him to converse fluently with the natives.

The most interesting Franks residing in Egypt in the time of Mohammed Ali were Mr. Lane and Clot Bey: the one introduced Frank medical science to Egypt, and the other has done more than any other individual to acquaint Europe with the genuine native Egyptian in all his peculiarities. These two men were, therefore, the continuators of the double function with which Bonaparte wished to invest his Institute of Egypt —the one to acquaint the people of Egypt with Frank science, the other to acquaint the people of Europe with the religion and the manners of Egypt. And without detracting from the acknowledged value of the men of the Institute of Egypt, who—including such names as those of Bonaparte, Monge, Berthollet, Fourier, and Larry—were of a higher stamp than their successors, I must say it is in reality the latter who, by much longer residence in the country, and by living in an assured and comparatively pacific state of society, have given a certain impress to the Egypt of more recent times. I place Mr. Lane and Clot Bey in juxta-position, not because their labours were in any way associated, but because the one is the most complete type of the European profound in Arabic lore, and in knowledge of the arcana of Cairo life; and the other, a man of European science who has shown himself active and practical in its application to the wants of Egypt.

Mr. Lane avoided Franks, and seldom quitted the Moslem quarter; but, through the kindness of Her Majesty's Consul, Mr. Walne, I was introduced to him. One Friday, after the afternoon prayer, we mounted our asses, and alighting near the Bab-el-Halk, asked for Mansour Effendi, and were shown into a room fitted up with book-cases. Mr. Lane wore a dark-green Nizam dress, and had allowed his beard to grow. He was then engaged in writing a dictionary of the Arabic language, and was extremely laborious, although not enjoying vigorous health. Some persons supposed that, like Burckhardt, he made a profession of Islamism; but this is a mistake,—he simply conformed to the manners, language, and dress of the Arabs. Endowed with intelligence and perseverance, and with that plasticity of temperament which has enabled him to utilize his opportunities; the result has been a large mass of valuable matter added to the common stock of information on Egypt, in which he has no rival, much less a superior.*

On being introduced to Clot Bey, he gave an amusing account of the way in which he first broke through the prejudices of the Moslems in reference to anatomy. "First of all," said he, "let us get a dog and dissect him—not even a Moslem's dog, but a Jew's dog, or a Christian's dog," and after a little grumbling they con-

* Mr. Lane told me that when he first arrived in Egypt in 1826, there being no steamboats or overland transit, and only a few travellers, great hatred existed towards the Franks; and although the Pasha had begun his reforms, very few French costumes were to be seen in the Mousky, and on several occasions, going to out-of-the-way villages, he was in danger of being killed. Sometimes sitting in cafés, and overhearing conversation, when no one suspected the presence of a Frank, he was more than once disagreeably surprised by finding that the project of massacring all the Franks in Cairo as a lesson to the Pasha not to proceed further with his Frank innovations, was no unusual topic of discussion. On his second visit to Egypt in 1834, there was much more toleration and facility for Franks; but there was still so profound an irritation against the government, that every man who had relations with it, or with Franks, was an object of suspicion to the ulema, although he might be a Moslem. Even a man suspected of frequenting the houses of government people or conversing with them had a difficulty in getting books out of the mosques to read or copy.

sented. Then at a cemetery outside of the town some skeletons and skulls were scattered about. "Really," said he, to his pupils, who were adults, "what harm if we get a few of these skulls and bones for the sake of explanation to you; they may as well lie upon my table, as to lay bleaching in the sun." This point was acceded to, but when he proposed to come to the dissection of bodies, there were some murmurs. "Well!" said he, "we will not take a free white man, but a black slave." Again, at length, the point was given up; and thus, by one step after another, the educated Egyptians have arrived at a knowledge of anatomy. With reference to the translations of European medical and scientific books, he added, that an entirely new technology had been created out of the existing elements of the Arabic language, and combined in strict accordance to its ancient principles, so that Arabic had been amplified without any violation of the fundamental structure of the language.

Close to the Frank quarter is the so-called Derb-el-Djennein, or street of the garden, which is inhabited by a large number of Damascene Christians. Both in the Frank and Syrian quarters there is an intermingling of mosques, tombs, and Moslem houses: for instance there is the Zawiet, or oratory of El-Shooshtery; and, at the annual festival, the old Franks of the quarter used to light up their houses out of compliment. Moslem landlords generally like Frank tenants, because they get a better rent than they get from Moslems in other quarters of the town.

The Khan-el-Hamzawy, is almost exclusively composed of the shops kept by the Damascene Christians, who inhabit the Derb-el-Djennein, and there is only one Moslem shopkeeper in the khan. It is consequently closed on Sunday, and is on that account a curiosity in a Moslem country. One side of it was in ruins, having been burnt down some years before. The best cloth in the native bazaars of Cairo, was to be found here, and came mostly from England, France, and Austria. When a native wishes to get a good suit of clothes, he does not order it from the tailor, but purchases the cloth and consigns it to the tailor. Oriental robes, not fitting close to the body, do not require to be of so fine and thin stuff as the clothes of Europe. I saw much excellent cloth in this bazaar, but all much thicker than the usual cloth of Europe; and both in Yorkshire and Moravia, there are particular sorts destined for the Levantine market. One of the reasons why the cloth is thicker and stronger is that it has often to bear heavy silk embroidery. Some of the favourite colours, such as bright chocolate, with which black silk embroidery harmonises admirably, are not usually worn in Frank countries. The consumption of bright scarlet cloth, which was the staple export of England in the 17th century, has necessarily greatly fallen off, since the change of costume on the part of the government officers; for the Mamelukes used to wear mostly bright scarlet upper robes, as many of the sheikhs of Syria do to this day. The last of the Mameluke beys whom I saw in the halls of Mohammed Ali in 1840, was dressed from top to toe in scarlet.

The wealthier Greeks were considered as Franks, and resided in the Mousky, or Frank quarter. Here also were to be found many Greek artizans, some of them Hellenic subjects, and others from the Archipelago. The proper Greek quarter, for Greeks settled in Egypt from generation to generation, is in the upper and north eastern part of Cairo, in which is a handsome convent in connexion with that of Mount Sinai. After the Greek revolution more than one instance occurred of Greek priests favouring the escape of Mamelukes of Greek origin to the European side of the Mediterranean.

The Caraites are to the Jews, what Protestants are to the Catholics. Their book is the Old Testament and the Old Testament alone. The Talmud and the traditions are rejected as damnable innovations. They reside in the Jews' quarter, with its narrow, unhealthy lanes, but are not exactly mixed with the Israelite Jews. The synagogue of the Caraites appears internally just like a mosque, lamps being hung in broad day on transverse beams, and the arches which separate the roof longitudinally and transversely being carved in stalactites, precisely in the Arab manner. The hakam, or priest, dressed in a plain brown turban, stood at the door, and the synagogue was immediately filled with the community in their holiday clothes. The inner part of the church was railed off and carpeted. In the outer part there was a mat, with a fountain. I was told that prayers were said in the morning and at sunset; that those who were dressed and pure could go into the inner space, but that those who were in their daily costume remained outside.

Taking off our shoes, we entered the inner space, and we were led up to the *sanctum sanctorum*, where a veil was withdrawn, and we were shown the Old Testament in Hebrew manuscript, of a large character on parchment—not bound, but on wooden rollers in the antique manner. In conversation with the assembly, they told me that they were the original Jews, and that the split took place nearly two thousand years ago. They spoke of their co-religionists in the Crimea, where there are supposed to be three thousand; and a young man, who was represented to me to be the wealthiest of the community in Cairo, stated that he had gone to the Crimea to try and get Russian protection, but without effect. The Cairaite community was originally in Arabia, but was obliged to quit at the Moslem conquest, their name Caraite being derived from that of a town near Jambo.

An Abyssinian Caraite presented the contrast of a healthy swarthy mountaineer to a rather sickly looking townsman. He had eyes of fire, a finely chiselled aristocratic nose, and smooth black hair, but he had the complexion of a creole, which showed that his Caucasian blood was largely mingled with that of Ethiopia. But, maugre his dusky tint, the Jewish cast of features was distinctly visible. One of the community asked me to look at a house of his, in course of being built; and looking through the rooms I regretted that a decent house should be erected in so infected a quarter. Going to the roof, the prospect was dismal beyond description: a Khamsin wind darkened the atmosphere, and everything looked brown and yellow. All around were the house-tops, looking half ruinous, and the prospect was without a single palm to relieve its monotony.

The Jews' quarter was formerly that of the Circassians, but is now entirely inhabited by Israelite and Caraite Jews. The latter are much fewer in number, and are mostly hawkers; one or two make cheese. The most fanatical Jews are the Mogrebbins. Many instances have occurred of Egyptian Jews turning Moslem, but very few of Mogrebbins turning Moslem. The Israelites are the much wealthier sect, and are engaged as money-changers and merchants. They have also to this day continued to connect themselves with the process of coining. All the female servants of the Jews are Moslems, and everything is sold dearer in these two Jews' quarters than in the town, because a proportion of the profits goes to the synagogues. Instances have been known of some unprincipled Moslems going to other parts of Turkey, wearing the Jew turban, and gaining money, by pretending to be converted to Islamism.

Jewesses frequent the harems, buying and selling articles of dress, as well as valuing and exchanging dresses. The wife of one of the inhabitants of the Derb-el-Habbaleh, used to receive the visits of a Jewess broker of ornaments. Her husband was a Turk, connected with the government, and the wife, who was remarkably handsome, had brought him a dowry; but he was a man of pleasure and expense. He bought whatever his wife took a fancy to, and being himself fond of company, her dowry was soon dissipated, with her own consent, and they got into difficulties. One day the Jewess broker entered with a splendid diamond ckoors, or head ornament, which took the fancy of the Turk's wife, who pressed her husband to purchase it for her. At length he seemed to agree to the purchase, being in reality without money. The Jewess came when the wife was absent in the bath, and the Turk, pulling out his dagger, murdered her in the courtyard, and took the ornament. He then dashed water on the spot so as to wash away the blood; and, having hacked the body in pieces, hid it in the garden. A knock was heard at the door; and he, at this moment seeing one of the Jewess's articles of dress, which he had forgotten to conceal, ran into the manearah, or reception room, and placed it under the cushion of the divan. His wife asked the cause of the traces of blood, and he said "he had killed a sheep for a neighbour." He then went upstairs and gave his wife the ckoors; but, forgetting the article of dress, and his wife happening to find it, the truth flashed on her. She did not dare to speak; but, on the trial, it came out that she saw her husband pounding diamond ornaments in a mortar so as to separate the diamonds and disfigure the metal, in order to make the articles no longer recognizable. The police had been following up the traces of the woman, and the house being examined, and both husband and wife placed under arrest, the latter related all she knew, and the man was executed.

Besides religious or fanatical Moslems, educated Franks, industrious Christians, and penurious Jews, there is a large slothful, thoughtless, and pleasure-loving population in Cairo, who begin with indulgences and end in the misery of dining on rat ragout. Some quarters are more disorderly than others. One of these was the Kalat-el-Kleb, or Castle of Dogs. This quarter is not far from that of the Franks, which is very high and has good air, having been formerly the locality of the dog-kennel of the Emir Yezbek, or Uzbek, after whom the Ezbekieh is called. Hence its name "Castle of Dogs," (Kalat-el-Kleb); but from its good air, and the jolly manners of its inhabitants, it was sometimes jokingly called Kalat-el-Tiab. Massive walls of a tower were still visible when I was last in Cairo, and close by is the so-called Koom-Sheikh-Selameh, built on a pile of shot rubbish, and mostly inhabited by the families of servants and grooms in Cairo. But to return to the Castle of Dogs, the sheikh of the quarter is generally actively employed in procuring marriages and divorces; and this locality is therefore convenient for rakes, who wish to enjoy a rapid succession of wives. This ought not to surprise the reader. In the Sikket-el-Tableyta lived a man, called Said Mohammed-el-Mawardy, who had married one hundred and fifty wives. When any one of them was obstinate and would not be divorced again, he used to put her into a room with a great number of cats, which usually frightened her into consenting to a divorce. This man was, however, surpassed in uxoriousness by Ahmed Pasha Tahir, one of the wealthiest men in Egypt, and who had a noble palace not very far from this quarter, which Franks may remember from its beautiful portal in white marble, adorned by the tortuous folds of snakes. Ahmed often married a fresh wife after the interval of a week, but his divorces were always effected with handsome compensations to the discarded spouse.*

Musicians are the chief levers of amusement at these jovial marriages of the Castle of Dogs, and I caused one of the most celebrated violin players to be brought to my house by the invaluable Sheikh Ahmed. As they entered, Sheikh Ahmed, to show his zeal, said, "Here is the prince of the fiddlers, whom I have brought hither by the beard for you. Ask! ask! ask!" The violin player was a stout well-dressed man with a white turban and chequered red and brown robe. He said they learned only by ear, but had names for the octave—doka, siky, girky, nua, husseini, oraá, kirden. The octave is mohair, which is called the jewab, or answer to doka. The different musical instruments have been fully described by Mr. Lane, and in the French "Description d'Egypte," is a very able treatise on Arab music. This man told me that the average gain for a party of six musicians was from a hundred and fifty to three hundred piastres per night, or from thirty shillings to three pounds sterling (the pound sterling being then about one hundred Egyptian piastres).

One must be a helluo musical to enjoy Arab music, but the European ear soon gets accustomed to it. The range of musical ideas is very limited, but it is a pleasing dreamy accompaniment to the reveries of the brain, and the enthusiastic musician finds it interesting to trace the relations of those chromatic inflexions to the music of Europe of various schools. As I have elsewhere had occasion to say, the music of Lully, when heard, strikes

* In the great plague of 1835, above fifty persons of his household died from plague, and this was attributed by the Frank physicians, justly or not I cannot say, to his not keeping quarantine.

at once upon the ear as Arabic in character, derived through the Spanish court of Naples from Spain (for the root of all Spanish music is Arabic). It is curious too to watch how music of the Arabic character has been idealized and beautified by the genius of the great European composers, while still preserving the distinct moods of Hispano-Arab melody. The most striking examples of this are in Weber's overture to "Preciosa;" the "Idole de ma vie" in Meyerber's "Robert le Diable;" the Neapolitan dance music in Auber's "La Muette;" several airs in Auber's "L'Enfant Prodigue;" the great work of Felician David, and Conrad in Kreuzer's "Nachtlager." As an instance of failure to produce beauty, and as an illustration of the absence of the Arabic vein, we may adduce the eccentric "Turkish march" of Beethoven, in spite of his indisputably occupying a place in musical invention certainly inferior to none who can be named. The Neapolitans did not derive the Arabic character of their popular music solely through importation from Spain; for we must remember that Sicily was a Moslem and Arabic country for a very long period. It is curious to note how tides of civilization turn. We have been describing the violent efforts of a Turk to fit Egypt with European forms of every description; and a few centuries back, the aspect of Venice was entirely Saracenic; the commercial terms were derived from the Arabic language, and even in music the Arabic form had found general acceptance.

The chief of the jugglers, Sheikh Ali-el-Caudeel, was also brought to me by Sheikh Ahmed. He told me that he was the commander of the Awlad-el-Fen, or men of ingenuity or dexterity. In Syria, Arabia, and the Upper Nile, they are called Skelolo. He informed me that there were three or four persons in Cairo who had the real science of divination according to the secret orthodox rules, but that all the rest were impostors. He styled the fortune-tellers Toraky. All these "sons of dexterity," as they were called, pay ferdeh, or capitation tax, this sheikh aiding in the classification. He took up a clothes brush and asked if it was of hog's hair. I said "Yes," and asked him why he handled it. He said, "It was dry." Conversing on the subject, he told me that a dog's mouth is unclean in the sects of Hawifeh and Maleky, but not its body. In the sect of Shafei, as also in the sect of Hanbale, it is all unclean. There are seven so-called vain arts, fonoun-el-battal:—1st. The jugglers already named, who are sometimes also called Hawi. 2nd. The violin scrapers at cafés, so that music is certainly not noble in the East. 3rd. The reciters. 4th. Medaheen—those who beat instruments and sing rhapsodies at birthday festivals. 6th. Mohabaseen, or jackpuddings. 6th. Ghisawaty (not Ghwazee), a sort of harlequin. 7th. Migalateey, or jokers in words. "Not practical jokers, like the merry-andrews," said Sheikh Ali to me.

Then come active arts (Tuabak-el-Amaly), such as quarter staff, sword and target, and an art called feu-el-elay, wa-el-sera, a species of wrestling or *savate.* As for the redoubtable feu-el-sinnia, or incantation on the grand scale through the agency of afreets, Sheikh Ali declared positively that it was to be classed among the extinct arts, although there was no doubt that this art did exist. According to this luminary, another of the extinct operations of magic was that of changing the sexes.

A large proportion of the domestic servants of the Franks, as well as of a multitude of Moslem families, are Nubians belonging to the Berber or Barabrah race, who stretch from the Red Sea almost to the Atlantic, having been driven southwards from the coasts of the

Mediterranean by the Arabic immigrants into what was once Numidia; and hence the name Barbary coast applied to the ancient seat of this north African race, now squeezed up between the Arab of the sea-board, and the negro of the interior.

The Berbers of Cairo are a copper coloured race, with Caucasian, not negro, features; a dependent and not an independent race, plastic, not indurated by martial vigour and thirst for domination—a conquered, not a conquering race; apt for service, not for mastery; flying from the conquering immigrant, and returning to his feet to sue for service, which may gratify the love of ease and gain. The Berber possesses in an eminent degree the qualities that fit him for domestic employment; he is honest, saving and economical both of his master's goods and of his own purse. He is quite adequate to the various duties of domestic service, and has much observation within a limited sphere, but he has no ideal. He cannot create, or rise by his creations in the arts of peace and war: hence he has no ambition that gives umbrage. He is a machine man, and his nationality is not aggressive, but strictly defensive; for the Berber loves the Berber. They herd together, and although they are Moslems in religion, carry out the principle of fraternity in a manner that might shame Christians. When a young Berber comes fresh from Nubia, one after another entertains him until he gets comfortably settled. It does not signify if he landed at Boulak without a fuddah in his pocket, for he will be supported even if they have to sell their turbans.

They are both honest and despised—rather a curious conjunction, or rather the moral qualities are not sufficient to efface the slight esteem in which the nation is held. Hence a pleasant story of an Egyptian who reproached a Nubian with the lowness of his race: "For," said he, "there is not a bey or alim of your nation in all Cairo." "That may be," said the Nubian, "but you cannot find in all Cairo a Barabrah with his hand cut off" (*i.e.* a convicted thief). There are also some few descendants of Kashefs, who fled from Cairo and took refuge in Nubia on the approach of the French, and who are in dialect and other particulars assimilated to the Nubians. Hence they give themselves the title of "Sons of Kashefs," mispronounced according to the Nubian dialect "Ebn Kafesh." They consider themselves noble, and will not act as domestic servants, but engage themselves as assistant brewers of beer. The Barabrah pronunciation of Arabic is peculiar: the hard aspirates are pronounced soft, and all the k's (Arabic kafs) are pronounced as if they were g's; for instance, kalah (castle) is in the mouth of a Nubian, gaelah. In conclusion, the Nubians have a riwack, or division in the mosque of El Azhar, and are devoted Moslems.

There is a large black slave population in Cairo, in domestic service, who are so well treated that they view with horror leaving the family they serve. There is an Arabic proverb which does not give a very favourable idea of the negro character—at least of those negroes who come to Egypt, for in so vast a continent as that of Africa there must be numerous gradations of character: it is "that the negro, if in misery, sneaks away from his fellow men; if well fed and prosperous, he is cruel,"—

En ja'a harab;	Hungry, he flies;
En shiba a katil.	Satisfied, he kills.

"This is the reverse of the lower animals," said a bagdadli to me; "for if a wolf is full of food, he flies away; if hungry, he kills." There are, comparatively speaking, few eunuchs in Cairo. Belonging only to the rich, and having no passions, no family ties, they are in the familiar confidence of the great. Hence they treat all other servants with great hauteur. The proper Arabic name for eunuch is "toashy," but they would be very angry if called "toashy," and style themselves "aga."

CHAPTER XXVI.

IBRAHIM PASHA'S HEALTH FAILS.—HE SAILS FOR TUSCANY AND FRANCE.—SPLENDID FETES GIVEN HIM BY THE FRENCH.—IS HOSPITABLY RECEIVED IN GREAT BRITAIN.—MOHAMMED ALI VISITS CONSTANTINOPLE.—THE NILE BAR.—DOTAGE OF MOHAMMED ALI.—SHORT GOVERNMENT OF IBRAHIM PASHA, TERMINATED BY HIS DEATH.—DEATH OF MOHAMMED ALI.

IN the course of the summer of 1845 the health of Ibrahim Pasha failed him, from the combined effects of excesses in strong liquors and the severe heat of the climate. In Syria, where the climate is much cooler, and where he had great corporeal activity in the regions of the Taurus and the Orontes (for his head quarters were usually at Antioch), these excesses were not so injurious; but in Egypt, where inaction is in a great measure compulsory during the long summer, the health is undermined, if great abstemiousness be not observed. In the end of August Ibrahim disembarked at Leghorn, and after spending September and October in Italy—principally at the baths of Lucca—he proceeded, in November, his health having been partially restored, to Toulon and Marseilles. At Toulon, fêtes of every description were offered to him by the naval and military authorities; but, amid the decorations and epaulettes of a naval arsenal, he maintained the requisite gravity and decorum of an ex-commander of a large army. At Marseilles, however, he found himself in a congenial element among the relations and correspondents of the leading French houses in Alexandria; and he threw off restraint and surrendered himself like a youngster to the dissipations of the place. Some of the addresses presented to him during this trip were so fulsome that the Pasha could not help laughing heartily in the faces of the deputations; and when the parties who offered their homage asked, in disappointment, what the hilarity meant, the interpreter answered, with the voluble plausibility of this class of men, "that His Highness expressed his satisfaction."

The personal appearance of Ibrahim Pasha was graphically described in many journals. He seemed to the Marseillese to be of middle stature, inclining to stoutness, having the fair complexion of a Turk,—not the bronze brow of an Egyptian. His beard was silver white, his look piercing and intelligent, his smile coming rapidly and going as rapidly; in his general appearance there was an absence of all nobleness and distinction. It is not surprising that, coming from Alexandria and Cairo, where he had mingled with a European community that had accommodated itself to oriental habits, he should ask for cigars, and that, in the midst of a ball at which the élite of Marseilles were present, he should have puffed forth volumes of smoke amid the polite titter and curiosity of the fair sex. Although he knew the theory of European manners, yet he looked upon Marseilles as a sort of European extension of Alexandria. In the beginning of December he went to the baths of Vernet, where he found a triumphal arch inscribed, "To the conqueror of Koniah and of Nezib."

After visiting Bordeaux, Ibrahim Pasha proceeded to Paris, being everywhere fêted by the authorities; and, arriving at length in the metropolis, he lodged in the apartments of the Elysée Bourbon. He was presented to Louis Philippe by the Turkish ambassador, and in the evening dined with the royal party, being seated on the left of the king; the circle, as a matter of course, including Mons. Guizot, the Minister for Foreign Affairs. On the following days he was shown the sights of Paris; and, at the "Invalides," the veterans stood in order to receive him, headed by the Duke of Reggio. Ibrahim said on this occasion, "The honour done me is more than I deserve. I wished simply to visit the old soldiers; I came here not to receive honours, but to pay a compliment to them." Among other sights he was much pleased with Horace Vernet's striking representations of the military scenes of modern France; but when shown the celebrated picture of the Massacre of the Mamelukes, he turned away at the first convenient opportunity from that disagreeable chapter in the history of Mohammed Ali, with the remark "that it bore no resemblance to reality." As a matter of course, large reviews were not omitted in the compliments offered him; and these he attended in full uniform, riding on an Arab charger from the royal stables. After the poignant disappointment and exasperation which the failure of Mons. Thiers' policy had produced in the minds of the French nation, Ibrahim Pasha came in for a full share of the sympathy with which a staunch but luckless ally is usually regarded under such circumstances; and in fact nothing was omitted by the French government which could possibly flatter his vanity.

In England he had equal success as a "lion," to use an expression now incorporated into the language. A sincere wish on the part of the government to forget the irritation that had been produced by the obstinacy of Mohammed Ali during the Egyptian crisis, and at the same time frankly to acknowledge the facilities which the Egyptian government had afforded for the overland transit,—joined to a disposition to put in good humour the supposed future ruler of Egypt, a natural curiosity on the part of the general public, and the recollection which a multitude of eminent individuals in England retained of the hospitalities they had received from the Egyptian government, when in Egypt and Syria,—all conspired to procure for Ibrahim a reception which would have filled with surprise those who lived in the time of the Greek war, when his name was the bugbear of Christian Europe. At a banquet given to him at the Reform Club, at which Viscount Palmerston and Sir Charles Napier were the principal speakers, all political differences were forgotten in the complimentary toasts and speeches of the occasion. A British steam frigate conveyed Ibrahim Pasha, in July, to Lisbon, and thence to Egypt, where he landed with his health apparently restored.

Mohammed Ali was absent from Egypt when Ibrahim Pasha returned, having received an invitation from Constantinople to pay his homage to the Sultan. The Pasha took a large sum with him, arrived at Constantinople on the 19th of July, 1846, and was lodged in Riza Pasha's villa of Ortakioi. On being presented to the Sultan in full Grand Vizier's uniform, he desired to fall down and kiss his master's feet, but he was raised up and seated. After this comedy the interview lasted an hour. He also visited in a spirit of reconciliation his old enemy Khosreff Pasha, after nearly a century of plots and counterplots. The reader would be rather fatigued than amused with the details of such festivals as were offered to the Pasha of Egypt, who had not come empty-handed. He knew the foibles of the metropolis, and took care to make himself a welcome guest. His prodigal expenditure did not confine itself to presents to the imperial family and the great men of the State, but comprised the project of erecting in a prominent position on the Bosphorus an additional palace for the Sultan,—a design which, considering the abundance of imperial lodgings, from the gorgeous seraglio to the fancy kiosk on this glorious strait, was something like adding a fifth wheel to a coach.

On the 17th of August Mohammed Ali sailed to Cavala, his birth-place, in which town are benevolent establishments endowed by his liberality. Alexandria was illuminated on his return; and, overjoyed with his reception in the metropolis, he received the visits and congratulations of his friends, wearing the portrait of the Sultan, adorned with brilliants, on his breast.

For some time back a project had been pressed on the Pasha which appeared to him to be likely to cause a large accession of revenue to Egypt: this was the damming of the Nile, called by the French engineers "Le barrage du Nil." In order to explain this project, we must remind the reader that the volume of the Nile during the dry season is not above the thirty-second part of what it is during the inundation,—when it seems to make lakes in all parts of its course, and when the thirsty land is abundantly saturated with the floods from Abyssinia, holding in solution a large proportion of virgin alluvial soil, the finest of all natural manures. But if such are the facilities for preparing cultivation at one season of the year, there is the opposite period in the spring of the year, when the Nile is at the lowest; and, as rain is exceedingly deficient, except during the winter, and even then rarely extends much inwards, the design of the Nile-bar was to force the limited volume of the river into three arterial canals, so as to create an artificial inundation in all Lower Egypt, and thus utilize the water which would otherwise flow waste into the sea by the Rosetta and Damietta branches of the Nile. The engineer of this work was M. Mongel, a gentleman who has attained a high and merited reputation both in France and Egypt, although his views in reference to the Suez canal have been entirely disapproved by the most eminent practical British engineers.

On the 9th of April, 1847, the foundations of the barrage were laid by Mohammed Ali, in presence of the principal civil and military functionaries of Egypt and the foreign agents. A parchment roll, describing the ceremonies and written on in gold, was sealed by the Pasha, signed by those present, and then deposited, along with specimens of all the coins of the Egyptian mint in Mohammed Ali's time, within the foundation stone. The old man laid the stone, using, as is customary, a silver mallet and golden trowel; and sumptuous repasts and night illuminations on the banks of the Nile took place on the occasion.

The execution, or even the commencement, of the glittering project of the Suez canal does not fall within the period of the life of Mohammed Ali; but in succeeding years commissions of European engineers had every facility for a preliminary survey. It would be presumptuous for a mere political and historical writer to present any opinion on this great question. Suffice it to say, that the sure and practised eye of a Stephenson saw no estimable limit to the sums that might be engulfed in such an undertaking, even supposing it practicable,—the artificial harbour at Pelusium alone requiring an expenditure beyond the French estimate of the cost of constructing the whole canal.

Towards the end of 1847, clear indications showed themselves that the hitherto vigorous physical constitutions of Mohammed Ali and Ibrahim Pasha were giving way. Ibrahim Pasha, although by no means a very old man, not yet having attained his sixtieth year, was attacked by general constitutional decay, and spent the winter in Tuscany. In February, 1848, Mohammed Ali's intestinal functions became deranged, which much affected his mind; and the news of the troubles in Europe, carrying with it the moral of the insecurity of all dynasties, so operated on his spirits as to react on the malady during his residence in Malta from the end of February to the beginning of April, 1848, when he returned to Egypt more weakened in intellect than when he departed. In June, 1848, the dotage had so increased that Ibrahim Pasha became virtual ruler of Egypt, notwithstanding the feeble state of his health.

In August, Ibrahim Pasha proceeded to Constantinople, and in the beginning of September was installed in the Pashalic of Egypt, the Sultan decorating him in person. Public opinion, however, paid no respect to his bodily sufferings, and the new ruler was unpopular. Not only was Ibrahim Pasha more feared, and less liked personally, than Mohammed Ali, whose disposition was generous, and whose manners were conciliatory; but he had not a single sincere friend. In the prime of his career, his influence was sustained by the terror which a knowledge of the severity of his character excited; and during the peace that succeeded the termination of the Syrian war, his large income and prospective succession to the Pashalic caused him to be sought after by schemers, dependants, and flatterers, though often with slender success; his sagacity, avarice, and comparative indifference as to the light in which he stood before Europeans, rendering his system a contrast to that of Mohammed Ali. He had just as few Moslem prejudices as the old Pasha, but he was a cold, hard-hearted man, and had bursts of passion and periods of sullen temper which repelled all sympathy.

The arrears of taxes due by his brother Said and his nephew Abbas, were sharply exacted, to their great displeasure; for the finances of Egypt were again in a wretched condition, owing to profuse expenditure, which

Ibrahim promised to check, and which intention he no doubt would have carried out had he lived. But his web was spun out, and on the 10th of November, 1848, at one in the morning, he departed this life, in his 60th year; his immediate disease being consumption, accompanied by spitting of blood and neuralgic pains which ceased four days before his death, and were succeeded by general prostration of the faculties. Eleven hours after death, he was buried in the family mausoleum at Iman Shafei, on the south of Cairo, under mount Mokattam.

Abbas Pasha was then absent on a pilgrimage to Mecca, not unwilling to get out of the way of his unsympathetic uncle; and, on Ibrahim's death taking place, a council was held at which it was agreed to solicit his immediate return to Egypt. On the 24th of December, Abbas Pasha arrived in Cairo, and was warmly welcomed as a returning pilgrim, as a decided Moslem, untinged by Frank prejudices, and individually popular among the Moslems, both Turk and Arab. Abbas being now the eldest of the family, the investiture of the Porte took place without difficulty.

Like the lamp whose oil and wick are both burnt out, Mohammed Ali, effete in mind and body, at length died at Alexandria on the 2nd of August, 1849. At any other period this would have been an event of importance; but for some time previously he had been morally dead, and, in fact, his real action on the political stage terminated with the year 1840. Other and graver matters now occupied public attention in Europe. The tremendous collapse of the monarchy of July, an event as sudden as it was unexpected; the return of a Bonaparte to the supreme power in France, an event equally unexpected, but not so sudden; and the revolutionary incidents in Italy, Germany, and on the Danube, had conspired to thrust the affairs of Egypt into the background. On the intelligence of the death of Napoleon Bonaparte at St. Helena, some one said to Talleyrand, "That is an event." "No," said the acute ex-minister, "it is not an event: it is merely a piece of news." So it was with the intelligence of the death of Mohammed Ali, which being simultaneous with the conclusion of the Russian campaign in Hungary, passed unnoticed in Europe, more especially as it had been preceded by a second childhood of nearly two years' duration.

On the 3rd of August, as the sun rose behind the barren tawny beach that leads to Aboukir, the consuls-general and leading functionaries of Egypt assembled at the palace of the promontory of Figs. In the midst of the Hall of Audience a cashmere shawl covered the coffin that contained the remains of this remarkable man. His sabre and a Koran lay on the breast, and at the head was deposited the red Tunisian woollen cap worn by the deceased. Censers shed perfumes around the bier, and twenty-two of the ulema, wearing white turbans, read appropriate extracts from the Koran with the accustomed chanting intonation. The scene was unanimously described as having been affecting, and forming a contrast to the frigidity with which Ibrahim Pasha had been consigned to the tomb; for Mohammed Ali, with all his faults, had made devoted friends, and more than one of the Europeans who had known him intimately for forty years shed tears at the sight of the coffin of a man who had surpassed all the Moslems in tolerance, and who was noble and generous to his friends and dependants.

Said Pasha, the son of the deceased, was—to use a European expression—the chief mourner; and, on his arrival, the procession—composed of the functionaries, the ulema, the European community, camels loaded with provisions for the poor, and attendants who sprinkled perfumed water on the people—set out on its way to the place of sepulture, while from the windows of the harem came the loud wails of the women who had formed his family and household.

The body was taken to Cairo by Said Pasha, and Mohammed Ali now reposes in the castle of Saladin, within the walls of the alabaster columned mosque, which he himself constructed in the noblest and most prominent position of the Egyptian metropolis.

CHAPTER XXVII.

Material Aspect of Cairo at the Close of Mohammed Ali's Career.—The Khans, Bazaars, and Thoroughfares.—The Slave Market.—The Hasheesh Shops.—The Corn Market.—The Butchers' Quarter.—Nubian Breweries.—The Suburban Population.—The Peasantry of the Environs.—The Various Markets in Cairo, its Suburbs, and Environs.

It is in the khans and bazaars, scattered all over the metropolis, that we find the middle classes of the true Caireen type; and to this portion of the population, in the later years' of Mohammed Ali's rule, I shall now denote a brief additional chapter.

The Sebá Kaat, is the quarter in which the principal khans of Cairo are situated, and in which wealthy Mogrebbins reside. In the so-called Seven Saloons, are the warehouses of the principal wholesale dealers. The interiors are picturesque, and one sees, piled pell mell, the coffee bags of Mocha, the cotton bales of Manchester, and the carpets of Persia. These khans are generally court-yards, with wooden galleries running round them, and droll looking verandahs to protect the sunny side from the heats of July and August. They are all built with great solidity, and some are of great elegance. The immense portal of the Khan-el-Turcomany is one of the most splendid specimens of Saracenic architecture in Cairo; but being sequestered among narrow out of the way streets, it is not surprising that it should have escaped the attention of tourists and bookmakers. The structures of beautiful and solid masonry in Cairo seem really endless, but the school is extinct, and in the new houses built for the natives (I do not mean the palaces for the higher Turks) one observes a bastard Turco-Greek style, marked by particular baldness and inelegance.

There is a great inequality in the means of the merchants, and it may readily be seen how position modifies manners. Those who possess ample capital, and whose ancestors have held a good position, are distinguished by great courtesy and dignity, and their affairs have nothing of the hurry-scurry and bustle of Frank business. Their transactions more resemble a series of polite morning calls,—coffee, pipes, and complimentary expressions preceding all business. But with all these fair external forms, the amount of business actually done is small, compared with that of the corresponding classes in Europe; and gross frauds, such as would cover a British merchant with indelible disgrace, and in many cases bring him within the pale of the criminal law, are here but little thought of. I once heard a curious expression used in a discussion between two merchants, one of whom seemed to have no faith in the assurance of the other, who answered, "Are you a Frank? I swear to you by our Lord, and you do not believe me."

Near Hosh Bardak, is the Wekelet-el-Furrayn, or furriers' bazaar. One would suppose that in the climate of Egypt furs were not necessary, and in fact they are not; but during the forty cold days in the middle of winter (for of frost there is no question) furs are worn by orientals of sedentary habits without inconvenience. There can be no doubt, however, that this is a Turkish and not an Egyptian custom. In Damascus, where there is frost almost every winter, furs are worn by all the wealthier effendis; but in Egypt the practice seems rather to have been confined to those high official functionaries who in the Ottoman Empire wore furs as a mark of distinction. Sultans, pashas, and ulema wore fur pelisses of great value, and of most picturesque cut and disposition, the collar and ledge being of sable and ermine, which, in combination with the ample folds of the white or cream coloured silk turban, gave great dignity to the appearance. The human body seems to be seen to most advantage, either partially covered—so as to leave the limbs free and the proportions of the frame distinctly pronounced, as in the Greek sculptures; or in those voluminous oriental furred robes, which to a great extent suppress the true outline of the frame and concentrate on the head the attention of the spectator. The modern European dress disguises the real proportions of the frame, but it is certainly convenient in temperate climates, and allows to the body an activity which is impossible in those gorgeous but cumbrous robes, which, however picturesque, are suited only to classes who are sedentary in their occupations and inactive in their habits.

At the gold and silversmiths' bazaar might be seen artificers with their little pots of fire making some artistic object or ornament for women. Here, rose diamonds, and diamonds of small size, bring a higher price than in England or in France; but when diamonds of a very high class come to market in Egypt they do not fetch the European price. In Egypt the ornaments of women are a sort of investment which creditors may not touch and which a family can always fall back upon. There is in this bazaar a great sale for blood-stones to be worn in rings, being supposed to be an antidote to hemorrhoidal complaints. At the silversmith's may be seen articles of oriental family plate: narghileh-heads in the form of flowers, censers for perfumes, salvers and basins for preserves, sprinklers for rose-water, semi-globular drinking cups with inscriptions from the Koran, and small writing cases for reeds, sponge, and ink.

Wekelet Abou Zeit is the bazaar for perfumers' spice and drugs. I asked for some tea, but could find it only at one shop, and the entire stock was contained in a paper-bag. When I asked, "Who purchased tea?" the shopkeeper answered, "Generally Mogrebbins, coming from Mecca, who have exhausted the stock brought with them from Morocco." Khans and wekelets are both places of sale and places for the reception of travellers who bring their own bedding, and who can be supplied with coffee and cooked provisions from the bazaar-shops in the immediate neighbourhood. Each locality has its distinct set of customers. For instance, the people of Tantah in the Delta mostly alight at the Wekelet-el-Rokn, which was formerly the great place for shoemaking, but has ceased to be so. The people of Yemen and Hadramaut usually alight at the Wekelet-zul-Fighar; the people from the Hedjas at the Wekelet Morgian; and Syrians at the Wekelet Djedeed. The Wekelet Saboon, or khan of soap, is much frequented by Syrians, and here may be heard much news from that country.

For retail trade the most animated part of Cairo continued to be the great line of bazaars from the gate of Zueileh to the gates of Succour and Victory. Let us therefore make an imaginary promenade between these two points, noting what may be most worthy of attention. We first come to the bazaar of Moeyed, which is called the Sukareey, from the numerous grocers' shops with pyramids of dates and other dried fruits. Many stolen goods are sold here by the auctioneer brokers whom we may call hawking agents; and, in consequence of the number of travellers, purchasers are quickly found. I have elsewhere described the movement in this remarkable thoroughfare, and the following paragraph from "Melusina" is, with the omission of matters relating to that tale, perfectly applicable to the object of this chapter.

"On the left of the crowded bazaar El Moeyed rise the tall walls of the mosque of that name, which is joined to the Bab Zueileh, the Temple Bar of Cairo's Strand and Fleet-street,—an enormous gateway, flanked by two sturdy towers, such as the luxuriant imagination of a scene-painter would give to the castle of a giant in an Eastern pantomime: while, above the iron-ribbed and iron-bolted gate, twin minarets—"fine by degrees and beautifully less," shoot up into the blue sky. Here is the greatest thoroughfare—here are the best furnished shops—here are many of the noblest architectural monuments—here is seen the oriental and Arab type of Cairo—here is the greatest artery of metropolitan life: it is the quarter neither of the poor, nor of the rich exclusively; nor of the townsman, nor of the stranger, but the quintessence of all. 'Dahrak, mind your back!' Here comes a loaded donkey, pinning the passenger as effectually to the wall in the crowded passage as the 'gare' of the French coachman in the days of Mercier's inimitable picture of Paris. The pipe-cleaner with his implements goes about soliciting employment. The sherbet-man, with tinkling cup, appeals to the thirsty passenger—the Moslem townsman, decently dressed in white or yellow turban, long cloth robe—slow, stately, and sleepy, caring little for wealth, or power, provided he be kept well-dressed, with little to do, and as little in the sun as possible. There, too, may be seen the Coptic clerk, with black turban and inkstand in his girdle; and the fakeer, or pauper, with a single blue shirt and cotton cap, without a turban. And then what a hubbub ahead, while the crowded retinue of a bey clears the way for a great man mounted on a foaming barb in all the splendour of caparison."

The oldest of the bazaars of Cairo is further on—that of the Shouaeen, which means "of provision dealers;" but no provisions are visible, all the shops being those of mercers. Grey domestics and the printed calicos of Manchester and Glasgow are now sold in the same locality where, in the time of the Fatimite Caliphs, the kebab was roasted and lentiles and rice were cooked. At the bazaar of Sultan-el-Ghoury, we seem to enter a magnificent Gothic cathedral, an effect which is produced by a mosque on one side of the street, and a tomb of colossal proportions on the other; while, notwithstanding the breadth which separates them, the street is here roofed in by great rafters which stretch from cornice to cornice. The dimly lighted, pure, and beautiful Saracenic architecture of the beginning of the sixteenth century, with the brilliant colours of the dresses of the throngs within, produce an effect like that of a grand picture of the Venetian school; while a golden ray of sunshine shooting through a crevice in the roof bisects the limpid gloom with its bright and well defined radiance.

Rents of shops are higher here than in any other part of Cairo, owing to the central situation; and further on is the Khan-el-Halily, where street sales by auction of praying carpets, pistols, poniards, silk turbans, and girdles lend their interest to the locality. Halil is the Arabic word for Hebron; and this khan was built by a native of that town, called Abd-el-Ma'aty, rikabdar, or equerry of Saladin. The tombs of the Fatimite Caliphs were here, but owing to the enmity entertained by Saladin's party towards that of the Fouatem, or Fatimites, these tombs were pulled down, and the khan built. Halil was killed at Damascus, and his carcase being left exposed, and not receiving the honours of sepulture, it was said that this was a judgment on him for scattering the bones of the Fatimite Caliphs.

Further on, a gorgeous confusion of towers, minarets, and lofty walls are visible in the contiguous mosques of Kalaon, Mohammed-el-Nasr, and Barkouk. The whole of this portion of the high street of Cairo is called to this day the Bayn-el-Kasrayn, or place "between the two palaces." Makrizi declares this to have been the most populous and delightful quarter of Cairo in his time, being the locality of festivals and the exercises of the troops; and here for many a long day, after the elevation of Saladin to power, was the scene of tilt and tournament, as gay and splendid as that which an Ivanhoe may have seen at Ashby-de-la-Zouch, as far as horse and foot, knight and squire, could make them, but in which no Eastern Rowena could award a palm of victory. These were the days of the pride of the Moslems, when a sliding scale was applied to even the reception of the Byzantine ambassadors; for if the antipathy was stronger than usual, they had to walk uncovered from the gate of victory to one of the palaces. A Nilometer also existed in this busy quarter during the earlier centuries of Cairo's existence. This is well authenticated by several authors, but after a careful search I could find no trace of it. The process of inquiry, however, made me acquainted with the existence of a magnificent old Saracenic house, now tumbling into ruin, and inhabited by poor persons, but which present such remains of its magnificence that, at the period of the Mameluke Sultans, I judge it must have been one of the most luxurious abodes in Cairo. It is called Kasr-el-Bedowee, or palace of the Bedouin, and no doubt was the residence of one of the wealthiest beys or emirs of some bygone century.

The fountain of Abderrahman Kiahia marks the separation of the line of bazaars into two branches, one leading to the gate of Succour, and the other to the gate of Victory. Although this was once the court end of the town, it has now little of the bustle and wealth that it had at the time of the Fatimite Caliphs; but the large poor population and the numerous provision-shops and khans for the sale of rural productions, give an animation of a humble but not uninteresting character to this part of the town. The decadent Place Royale of the days of Henri Quatre, and the halles near the Rue de la Verrerie and the Rue des Lombards flash upon the European traveller who rambles through this part of the town, as a sort of distant resemblance. The palaces of the Fatimites have disappeared as completely as the Palais des Tournelles; but many a house, by the relics of its ornaments—many a Cairo Hotel de Senlis—still exists, to tell an obscure mysterious tale of better days. A strong odour of garlic is wafted from an archway, and, without being informed through the ears, the olfactory nerves at once announce that this is the famed Wekelet-el-Töm, or garlic market; while a fragrant odour from another large khan close by comes from the lemon and orange store.

Close to the gates of Succour and Victory is the slave market for blacks, called Wekelet-el-Jelabah Gelab, meaning literally "a bringer," or slave merchant. A square court was surrounded with black boys and girls, thoughtlessly laughing and singing, and waiting to be sold. They are not used for agricultural labour, but for the domestic service of the wealthier classes. One cannot think without horror of the violent separation of these creatures from their parents. But in reality the condition of those who come to Egypt is better than those who remain amid the sanguinary barbarism of the interior. Darfour is the point whither most of the slave convoys of the interior are made to converge, from which point to Upper Egypt they are brought by the ordinary caravans. I noticed the mats to be of a very different sort from those of Cairo, and one of the "bringers" said that they came from Darfour.

Close to the mosque of Hakem is the hemp-eater's coffee-house, called Kahwet-el-Hashasheen, which is frequented by those who indulge in the abominable narcotic called hasheesh. Of these coffee houses there are five in Cairo and its environs, and two in Boulak. But at least twenty per cent. of the male population eat hasheesh in private, and there were no less than thirty-five retailers of lozenges of hasheesh. It is divided into three kinds, the dawa misk, which produces simple gaiety—the geraweesh, which gives virile power—and the Hindy, or Indian, which throws people into ecstasy.

The Wekelet Kamh, or corn bazaar, near to Bab-Foutouh, is one of the busiest and most characteristic scenes in Cairo. There being little or no rain here, the corn is all piled up in the open air. A crowd of millers, fellaheen, bakers, and other townspeople, thronged the passages so closely, and spoke so loud, that the corn sellers were obliged to announce the quality of their corn by bawling out. On examining the sorts on sale, that of Upper Egypt seemed the best. Each seller comes forward shaking the corn in his hand, each sort having its name. Menoufieh from Menouf, Kelioubieh from Kelioub. "Shereefey! Shereefey!" cried one, to denote that the grain belonged to the Shereef of Mecca, to whom the Pasha of Egypt had presented 1000 feddans of land. This corn, owing to the semi-religious character of the shereef, always gets a good price. The Indian corn in the adjoining market was mostly ground into flour.

Having now terminated our imaginary promenade in the town, and arrived at the northern gates of the city, we find outside the walls a considerable industrious population, occupying the suburbs to the north and north-east. In the so-called Hassaneey reside the butchers of Cairo, who never wear cloth, but cotton and serge, even in winter. They are a race powerful in body, as well as resolute in will; and at the great revolt of Cairo against the French were the most active amongst the insurgents, in consequence of which their quarter suffered severely. To this day, on walking through it, one is struck with the number of ruined edifices dating from that time. A Turkish mosque and convent, that of the Bayoumi, is conspicuous in this quarter, the inmates of which, according to the rules of their order, wear their hair long. Close at hand is the so-called Sook-el-Belah, or date bazaar, in which this fruit, or rather food, is sold wholesale. But there is a superior description, the long red dates of Breem, in Nubia, which are sold wholesale in Boulak in the so-called Wekelet-el-Breemy. There are also some manufactures in the quarter; for instance, in the Derb-el-Soualy, I found a manufacture of the description of cloaks called abays; but all the finer and gold worked abays come from Syria. The original abays are those of the Bedouins, and made of camel hair, or original camlet. Subsequently, as luxury increased, it became a manufacture chiefly carried on in Damascus, a large amount of gold and silver thread being used on the fabric. Further north is the quarter of the Adouy, and the Kantarat-el-Wiz, or "Bridge of the Goose," is directly on the opposite side of that part of Cairo in which is the bridge of the Lion. Hence the expression, "All Cairo from the bridge of the Goose to the bridge of the Lion."

On this side of Cairo, near Bab Sha'eb, is the best beer establishment in Cairo. I allude to the so-called *booza*, or Egyptian malt liquor, which is the favourite drink of the Nubians. A large portion of both the grooms and the house servants of Egypt are of Nubian extraction. Booza is therefore the pest of many a Cairo household. When the Frank finds his servant coming in late, and talking thick, he may be sure that the cause is a beer-symposium of Nubian servants—a *boozing* bout.

Beyond the suburbs, and within the influence of the Nile, are villas and market and pleasure-gardens; and beyond them both up and down the Nile is the true rural population. It is remarked how suddenly the style of language changes as we leave the walls of the town. When a townsman sees a well-shaped woman pass, he says, for instance, "By the life of Our Lord, that girl is graceful!" The gardeners say, "Such and such a girl is a gazelle!" but the rude peasant says, "What a capital cow!"

There are various markets in and around Cairo; the principal one for asses, horses, and camels, was at the large public square between the citadel and Sultan Hassan. The Boulak market was, in the last years of Mohammed Ali on Saturdays, from sunrise to midday, at which cattle, fruit, and provisions were sold. The market at Old Cairo was for the same object on Sunday; but much business was done at the markets for agricultural animals, more particularly ploughing oxen, once a week at Embabeh and Ghizeh, both on the other side of the Nile, where I repeatedly went to mingle and converse with the peasantry.

It is needless to expatiate on the grain-producing capacities of Egypt, for the Banat of Temeswar has not richer humus than that of the Delta of the Nile. But what Egypt wants is population, not only much more numerous, but better skilled in the processes of agriculture. The degraded condition of the fellah is partly the result of the physical condition of Egypt itself. There are no mountainous districts supplying an energetic rural population to the plains, and nourishing ideas, if not of a political independence, at least of individual right. The vigorous races have been Circassians and Turks, who came to Egypt to rule it. The native Egyptian, enervated by an exhausting climate, although in the midst of a large agricultural production, has been, during this century at least, pressing on the limits of subsistence,—a wretched creature, who has taken no share in the revived prosperity of Egypt caused by the overland transit, the improved communications, and the enormously increased export of agricultural produce to Europe. The family of Mohammed Ali, his numerous descendants, and the principal mercantile houses of Alexandria have made their fortunes; but the fellah remains what he was before—*misera contribuens plebs.* Even before Mohammed Ali's time the fellah was degraded and brutified; but not so much so as since, because small landed properties were scattered all over Egypt, and even under the Mameluke beys the cadis and ulema were able to protect the proprietors in the fee-simple. After the Pasha became the one great proprietor, the fellah had the worst landlord in the world, a bureaucracy with habits and traditions the very opposite of the patriarchal relation which ought to subsist between peasant and proprietor. The old proprietors were more or less responsible to local public opinion, and often took a pride in acting handsomely; but the sub-steward of the Pasha knew that his promotion lay in making the largest returns to the treasury without reference to right or justice. Hence the apparition of such monsters as Abderrahman Bey, the renegade Copt, who invented new tortures for the purpose of despoiling the peasantry of their most secret stores. It is only justice to the successors of Mohammed Ali to say that they have, to a certain extent, mitigated those evils in accordance with public opinion in Europe, although every one of all the Egyptian governments I have ever known held the doctrine that the fellah will not work without the stick.

CHAPTER XXVIII.

Management of the Mosques and Charitable Endowments.—Mosque of Touloun.—The College of the Azhar.—The Mosque of Sheikhoun.—Mosque of Hosseyneyn.—Mosque of Hakem.—Mosque of Daher.—The Hospital of Kalaon.—Mosque of Hassán.—Mosque of Moeyed.—Mosque of Sultan-el-Ghoury.—Dervish Convents.—Oratory of the Hindoos.—Various Mosques, Fountains, and Schools.

We described in the beginning of this work the rise of Cairo, and grouped the historical facts around the principal mosques, as they were successively constructed by the eminent men who ruled over Egypt, and perpetuated their memory by the splendour and extent of these religious edifices: we may now therefore examine in detail the condition and management of these institutions in the later years of Mohammed Ali's rule.

The mosques of Amru, at Fostat, and of Touloun, at Kataé, which preceded Cairo Proper, were both in a ruinous condition, and objects of archæological curiosity rather than the magnets of religious worshippers. To the south of Cairo I examined the ruins of Fostat, the embryo of the Egyptian metropolis, and found only mounds of rubbish; the characteristic features of the landscape being the long line of the arches of an aqueduct, a few scattered palm groves, and, in the distance, the barren ribs of mount Mokattam. The house of Amru and the famous Street of Candles have all disappeared; but the mosque itself remains, and when the historic student sees this noble forest of columns, he asks himself how many a temple of the Olympic deities, consecrated for Christian worship, must have been despoiled to adorn the precincts of the new construction. In the enormous quadrangle of the mosque of Touloun, surrounded with the far-famed arcade of pointed arches, I found that many of them were in process of being walled up, to form cells for lunatic asylums. The minaret to which I ascended by a spiral staircase was in a ruinous condition; but I have since learned that efforts have been made, under the successors of Mohammed Ali, to rescue this most singular monument of the acknowledged precedence of the Oriental to the European pointed arch, from further ruin and decay.

The Azhar, which is at the same time the theological university of Egypt, deserves especial attention. The origin of the mosque has been indicated in the introductory book.* I shall therefore confine myself to the Azhar, as it was under Mohammed Ali.

The Azhar had seven gates: 1st. Bab Goharieh, from Gohar-el-kaid, the general of Moezz, the founder of Cairo, who built the first form of the mosque. 2nd. Bab Said Omar Mekram. 3rd. Bab Riwack-es-Saidy, or the gate of the cloister of Upper Egypt, which was built by the celebrated Abderrahman Kiahya. 4th. Bab Riwack-es-Shuam, or gate of the cloister of the Syrians. 5th. Bab Riwack-el-Mogharbeh, or gate of the cloister of the Mogrebbins. 6th. Bab-el-Meidah. 7th. Bab-el-Kubeer, which is also called Bab-el-Mezeien, or Barber's

* The Azhar was begun on Saturday, the 6th last day (or last day but five) of Jemad-el-Ewel, in the year 359 of the Hegira, and was finished on the 9th, last day of Ramadan, 361 A.H., and bore the inscription, "Built by the command of the servant of God, Abou Temim Ma'ad-el-Imam-el-Moezz-Cedin Allah, the Prince of the Faithful, on whom and on whose fathers be the blessing of God by the hands of his servant, Gohar, the secretary, the Sicilian (Gohar-el-Kaid-el-likily)." I have omitted the beginning of the inscription "In the name of the most merciful God," etc., etc. The first Friday that it was prayed in was the 7th Ramadan, 361 A.H. Ten years afterwards it was endowed, and the Fackihs got an allowance out of land which had been bought and entailed for them in the neighbourhood of the mosque itself. These readers were thirty-five in number, and each of them had a new dress at the great Biaran, and a mule. The Caliph Hakem further repaired and endowed the Azhar, and the deed of settlement as given by Makrizi is a curious specimen of Cairo conveyancing in the tenth century. A silver rail which crossed the niche was removed by Saladin, both here and in the mosque of Amru at Fostat, each rail weighing 500 drachms of silver. Four orange trees were attempted to be planted in the court yard, but they died.

gate, from the circumstance of many of this profession waiting for business there. We may also add that each of the gates has three porters.

The Mameluke Sultan, Kaid Bey, greatly extended the Azhar; but the great reconstructor in modern times was Abderrahman Kiahya, who completely transformed its appearance.

The Riwack-el-Shuam, or compartment of the Syrians, is large, and has no less than three hundred pupils; and the Mogrebbin Riwack has about a hundred. There is also a Riwack of the black Dacroorees, and one of a god in India called Goawy; one called Sharkawy, with an endowment of two hundred loaves a day, in the neighbourhood of Damietta, for the people of the eastern part of Egypt. The Riwack of the Upper Shark, or that portion of the country to the east of the Nile, which is nearer to Cairo and more remôte from the sea, is numerously attended, but has little bread. The Riwack of Bahyrieh (western maritime Egypt) is also called that of the Leiptigaweey, but why I cannot tell. The Riwack-el-Tabarseey is for the people of the central part of the Delta. The Riwack of Yemen has few students. The amount of loaves daily consumed is four thousand in all.

The Azhar used never to be shut, day or night, but shortly after the conclusion of the Syrian war of 1840, all the gates were shut except the great one. It has been remarked that professional robbers are ostentatious in attendance at the Azhar, and notwithstanding the supposed sanctity of the place, many thefts occur, and many pockets are picked here. It has now ceased to be an asylum for murderers, which it was in the beginning of the century. That formidable personage the Mohtissab, or examiner of weights and measures, had no power over the immediate neighbourhood of the Azhar, which had separaté officers called Gindy-el-Mudbach, or trooper of the kitchen. These were two in number, one in the house of the sheikh of the Azhar, the other in the house of the sheikh of the sect of Malek; and I may remark that while there are in Cairo sheikhs of the sect of Hanifeh, as followed at Constantinople; of Shafei, as followed in Egypt and Syria; and of Malek, as followed in Morocco,—there is no sheikh of Hambaleh in Cairo, as there are only a few Wahabys of this sect in that city. The bastinado used to take place in the rice-kitchen, for these theologians were sometimes rather unruly. Formerly the shereefs in Cairo were all under the so-called Nackeeb-el-Ashraf, and not directly under the civil power, just as in certain countries of Europe monks were under purely monkish jurisdiction. But this system was abolished by Mohammed Ali, and all the shereefs, or green-turbaned descendants of the Prophet, were placed under the head of the police like other men. The ulema, if they commit a theft or any great transgression, are dealt with by the police; but if their offence has been merely quarrelling or fisty-cuffs, the sheikh of the mosque judges and punishes them.

Another distinction which we may mention, is, that the Azhar and Hosseneyn have each of them a mikaty, or astronomical time calculator, expressly for their own use; and the time as given by the mosques from the observations of these men is the rule for all the other mosques of Cairo. At the house of the mufti I happened to meet a khatib of the Azhar, and asked him "if the Khotbet for the Caliph was prayed for in the old form;" "No; in old times when the Caliphate was contested it was necessary; but since the Sultan of Constantinople was recognized as Caliph, without dispute, he confined himself to *waas*, or preaching."

The reader may see from these statements, that there is an endowment of Spartan fare for the theologians of the

Azhar.* In fact, the revenues of the mosques of Cairo were considerable; but very little remained, after the direct and indirect exactions of the government and the jobbing of the inspectors. The endowment of mosques is often a subject of criticism and even ridicule, and in illustration of this, I may give a legend and an anecdote of the mosque of Sheikhoun, not far from the citadel, and one of the most solid constructions of the second class of these religious edifices.

Every traveller in Catholic countries has heard wonderful accounts of the origin of monasteries and convents,—the appearing of angels, the returning of the shades of the departed, and the indications of treasure, etc., etc. Connected with the mosque of Sheikhoun there is a similar legend. This Sheikhoun had been a poor man, and became an Emir. According to this story, he had a dream of grapes that fell into his mouth, and a voice was heard, saying, "Arise and take your wealth from Egypt, in the place where you used to sleep there." So he left Damascus, where he was residing, dug in the earth at the place told him in the dream, and found a treasure, of jewels. He then built this mosque. A hungry hypocrite entered it when it was finished, and wrote up, in allusion to the absence of any liberal endowment of idleness, such as was associated with several of the principal mosques at Cairo:—

"Giamâ bela eish,
Bunia l'eish."

(Gaudy mosque, and nought to eat,
Is not this a pious cheat?)

* Sultan Barkouk instituted the law, that whatever property the fellows of the College possessed, was, like churchmen's property in Europe, to go to the brethren. As a corrective of the indolence of such institutions, violent reformers occasionally arise. Such was the Emir Sodula, the inspector, a sort of John Knox, who in 818 turned out, together with their boxes and trunks, hundreds of old students, who found themselves in the most miserable condition. Some went back, and even blows were resorted to, to drive them out. The Emir then caused a black covering to be put on the manbar, but this harshness created clamours, and the Sultan being appealed to, the Emir was seized and confined till he died.

The founder of the mosque, or one of his friends, wrote below that:—

"Bunia lil sala,
Ya kaleel el heia."

(Built for prayer and praise,
Pert Mr. Brazenface!)

The mosque of Hosseyneyn, which is considered the most sacred in Cairo, contains the head of Hosseyn, the son of Ali, who was put to death by the partisans of the Damascus Caliphate. This mosque was formerly very small, and for its present form was indebted to the oft-mentioned Abderrahman Kiahya. It has now seven gates,—1st, Bab-el-Meshed; 2nd, Bab-el-Mediah; 3rd, Bab-el-Hanifeey; 4th, Bab Sirr, for women, and the two larger gates. The festival of the birth of Hosseyn is one of the greatest of the religious festivals of Cairo. In the mosque I remarked that the fountain is very large. One of the peculiarities of the mosque is that the curtains of the Beit Allah in Mecca are brought every year and are sewed and repaired there, the place being thronged by people anxious to put in a few stitches. The great festival of this mosque is one of the most remarkable in Cairo. Many mashals, or cressets, are lighted by religious incorporations; and during the preparations one hears the expressions, "Leile azime!" "This will be a magnificent night; Sheikh-el-Gouhary's Zikr is to be performed. Everybody will be at Saidna Hosseyn."

The quarters of El-Azhar and El-Hosseyneyn are the residences of the principal ulema; and at the festival of Hosseyn most of the bazaars in the neighbourhood are lighted up, and the confectioner's shops, more particularly, have a splendid display of lamps. Lads may be seen at various points filling cressets with wood, and lighting them; and the shrill tones of the distant clarinet, and the throbbing drub of the drum, approaching and crossing the angles of the street, announce that the procession of Bayoumi dervishes to the mosque of Hosseyn is about to commence. On the steps of the fountain of Abderrahman Kiahya, stood the naib of the Bayoumi dervishes, who are nearly all bakers. This naib wore a red robe, and was supported on each side by his two so-called caliphs or delegates; and these olive complexioned dark-eyed youths, with fanaticism depicted on every feature, would in turn go forward to kiss his hand. A forest of cressets shed a flickering blaze on the curious twisted pillars inlaid with devices and elaborate stalactites of the fountain of Abderrahman Kiahya, which stood out from the depth of the obscurity of night so as to make a picture with a force of chiaroscuro, that rivetted itself firmly on the memory. The *coup d'œil* of the interior of the mosque is striking; the roof is supported by about fifty columns, between each of which there is a light chandelier. The zikr goes on in the centre, and the mosque is so crowded that there is scarcely standing room, but all speak in a whisper. When the zikr is done, thick wax candles, about a yard long and a couple of inches in diameter, are lighted, and a procession is formed, which passes into the sanctuary beyond, where is the head of Hosseyn Imam, son of Imam. Here the heat is stifling. The walls are covered with various coloured marbles, and a truly regal bronze railing that would have done honour to a Torrigiano, encloses the magnificent tomb around which the procession slowly passes chanting solemn words from the Koran. The magnificent oriental costumes, the impressive bearded and turbaned heads, the oriental architecture, the blaze of illumination, and the associations called forth by the recollection of the striking and affecting incidents of the death of Hosseyn, all conspire to make an impression on the historical and archæological student never to be forgotten.

All the memorials of the Caliph Hakem, who had so much method in his madness, are of interest, but not many traces of the Cairo of his day are still extant. Near the Bab-Zueileh, we still find Derb-el-Ahmar, or the Crimson-street, so called to this day, from the blood shed in the massacre of the inhabitants of Cairo by his Turkish troops. The mosque of Hakem is a vast ruin. The gypsum tracery and the massiveness of the minarets, with outlines resembling the monuments of ancient Egypt, have nothing in common with the later style of Cairo, and carry back the spectator to the period when the architecture of Bagdad, Irak, and Coufa, still influenced that of Egypt.*

The mosque of Daher Bibars is an immense construction forming a square rivalling in extent those of Hakem and Touloun; but, like those once splendid constructions, it is a ruin. From being a mosque of the first order, it became in the time of the French, Fort Sukowski, named after that lively Pole who spoke so many languages.

* The so-called mosque of Hakem was begun by El Aziz Ebn Moezz Abou Hakem, and finished by Hakem, in its first form. It was outside the town, until Bedr extended Bab-el-Nasr and Bab Foutouh outwards, when it came within the town. It was first called Giama-el-Khotbeah, or mosque of the Litany, then Giama Hakem, or the mosque of Hakem, and last, Giama-el-Enwar, or the luminous mosque. It was first prayed in, in the year 380, by Aziz, who wore the teglasan or mitre, and carried a sceptre in his hand, accompanied by his son. In the time of Negm Eddin Salih Eyoub, it was turned into a stable, for the Eyoubites hated the Fatimites. In the great earthquake in the eighth century of the Hegira, it was still further damaged. But what a noble pile it must have been to withstand such a pressure! for in this great convulsion boats were thrown out of the Nile an arrow's distance, while only two of the minarets of Hakem were thrown down. Bibars repaired and endowed it, for the Eyoubites, who hated the Fatimites, and were in turn hated by the Balrirites. It was in its day the Azhar of Cairo, being plentifully supplied with ulema; and these mosques had their separate sets of partizans, public opinion and royal favour inclining sometimes to the one, and sometimes to the other. Hakem himself repaired and made additional endowments for the Azhar; and in his time it was more frequented then the mosque of Hakem, being more in the centre of the town. Up to the completion of the mosque of Hakem, the Azhar had the exclusive privilege of the Litany, but afterwards it was repeated by turns in the Azhar and Hakem. Saladin, however, fixed the Litany in the mosque of Hakem on account of its size, and for a hundred years no Litany was said in El Azhar, until Bibars restored it to the latter mosque.

In the latter years of Mohammed Ali, it was a bakehouse of the government, and eighty ardebs of corn were daily made into round cakes where the tricolor waved when the century began.

I had no difficulty in recognizing the style of architecture,—a sort of transition from the plaster tracery in the Bagdad forms of Touloun and Hakem, to the more recent Cairo styles. On entering, one sees—instead of the long arcade, the spacious basin, the elaborate chair of the preacher, and the bending lines of the congregation in prayer—something like a factory yard; with a couple of palms seeking a scanty existence among mounds of cinders and mean huts frequented by white-coated millers and bakers. Lines of asses, loaded with grain, tread where mosaic pavements once shone. The complete line of fretted windows, each with its inscription in cufic—a character that seems formed for architectural decoration,—was still visible, a striking monument of departed splendour over which ruled the Turkish nazir, sitting motionless on his mat at the gate under the shade of a sycamore, smoking his pipe, while beside him a blear-eyed Coptic clerk, wearing a black turban, registered the entrance of corn and the exit of loaves.

In the earlier part of this history I gave some account of Sultan Kalaon who finally expelled the Franks from Syria, rebuilt the castles, towers, walls, and gates of Damascus, Aleppo, and other cities, and was also the father and grandfather of Mohammed-el-Nasr and Sultan Hassan,—thus shedding the combined lustre of arms and arts on this family.

The principal edifice erected by Kalaon, in Cairo, was the great hospital, called the Maristan, which had been the locality of the house of Sitt-el-Molk, the sister of Caliph Hakem, who had brought about his death. This edifice was built in the year 682 of the Hegira, (A.D.

1283) the cause of Kalaon's building it having been the cure of a disease, effected on him in the Maristan, or hospital of Damascus, which had been built by Noureddin and Saladin; and he swore that, if ever he had the power, he would build a similar establishment.* His work was aided by a casket of jewels, of considerable value, found by labourers while employed in digging for the fountain, and which had doubtless been concealed by some princess of the Fatimite dynasty. The value of these jewels was said to have been nearly as much as the cost of building, for a considerable portion of the palace of Sitt-el-Molk was retained.

I think it highly probable that Frank architects or builders may have been employed in the edifices erected by Kalaon and his son; for a portal on the great line of bazaars is as like Gothic as possible. Most of the materials were taken from the ruins of buildings in the island of Rodah, and everyone passing was obliged to carry a stone, so that the road was deserted. In this matter there seems to have been more of vain-glory on the part of Kalaon than of charity. It does not appear who was in possession of the palace of Sitt-el-Molk at the period in question; but it is certain that it was pounced upon by force, and that the ulema made great obstacles to consecrating the contiguous mosque, as the ground that it had been built on had been taken by force, and the edifice reared by compulsory labour. The argument of the Mamelukes of Kalaon, was, that the prior possession had been obtained by force; and, secondly, that there was no instance of getting people to work in Egypt without compulsion.

* This edifice exists to this day in a dilapidated state in Damascus. The entrance gate is one of the greatest curiosities in Syria; it is of perfectly preserved Roman architecture of the third or fourth century, and above it is a stalactite superstructure of Saracenic architecture; the whole aspect being an odd jumble of a reminiscence of Diocletian and Saladin.

The deed of settlement and endowment states that it is "for the cure and aid of all—of the king and of the slave (malek-we-memlook, literally possessor and possessed), private and commander (or trooper and emir), great men and small men, free and bond, masculine and feminine." Kalaon appointed physicians, servants and attendants, male and female, and laid down beds for the sick, with four wards adapted to the climate—one for ophthalmia, one for dysentery, one for the wounded, and one for fever. Besides these there were, a kitchen, laboratory, and dispensary for out-door patients; while those sick at home and unable to attend the dispensary were assisted from this place. The vastness of the arrangements may be inferred from the fact that the consumption of sugar alone was five hundred pounds daily. The mosque, which was also liberally endowed, is an edifice which the traveller may remember by its fine antique columns, adapted by the architect. It had a complete establishment of inspectors, imams, muezzins, and readers of the Koran, including six librarians. In short, all the accounts concur in representing it as a magnificent establishment. As time rolled on, however, the funds were gradually dissipated by unfaithful trustees; and at last it became one of the lions of Cairo —for the maniacs were kept chained in dens like wild beasts—until, through the exertions of Clot Bey, in our own time, a more suitable asylum was provided for these unhappy persons, with a treatment more in accordance with the humanity of modern notions. The lofty roof of the mosque of Kalaon is supported by superb granite columns, which were, strange to say, painted of a light green colour when I was last in Cairo. At the great entrance stood local physicians and apothecaries, prescribing and making up prescriptions, with their drugs in curious old gallipots, some of considerable size and value.

The most remarkable monument of this family is the mosque of Sultan Hassan, the son of Malek-el-Nasr, and the grandson of Kalaon. It was as much intended to be a collegiate seminary as a mosque, and the buildings for the former purpose range eight stories high. It was the original intention of Sultan Hassan to have had four minarets; but in the great earthquake of 1361 a minaret fell, and then occurred those great slits in the wall and breaks in the cornice which are still visible. Hassan's eunuch, Beshir, completed the mosque, but large endowments by Hassan for this object were withheld by his successors. The mosque is generally in a ruinous condition; for, being opposite to the citadel, it was invariably occupied during the innumerable rebellions and civil wars constantly recurring in Cairo, so that the wonder is that it still stands at all. It was used in this way in the time of Sultan Barkouk, the first of the Circassian sultans, who caused the stairs that led to the roof to be pulled down: they were however built up again. By this long dark staircase I ascended to the roof, and then to the balustrade of the minaret. The panorama of Cairo visible from this height is not so good as that from Touloun, because Hassan itself, the principal object in the prospect of the city, is the point of observation, and is not itself seen. But still it pleased, like a varied version of a tale worth telling. The gates are of bronze, and rivetted with bolts in which zinc and even some gold and silver enter. The mobakharah, or censer of bronze, is not the original one, which was transferred to the mosque of Moeyed. Thus the mosque of Sultan Hassan has had the disadvantage of not only being dilapidated through earthquakes and war, but of having been dismantled to gratify a vanity that failed in its aim; for the mosque of Moeyed has made its reputation on purely architectural grounds.

Those colossal letters carried round the alcoves, in which verses of the Koran are written, are called "Toomar," so denominated from one of the seventy-two characters in Arab caligraphy,—a pedantic conceit, as if the *tokalon* of writing was not that which is easiest of comprehension. But in reality there are not above three or four styles of writing Arabic, as known to the most accomplished persons. It is certainly a characteristic of the Arabs that there is a greater union of written character and architectural ornament with them than with us. As the representation of the human form (that is to say, a larger proportion of the most beautiful and ingenious devices of the later Roman styles, comprising all sorts of ingenious caryatides, consoles, and mouldings, in which male or female heads or bodies appear) was forbidden to the Moslem architects, they were compelled to eke out the baldness of the earliest mosques by an ornament which was not vain and sensuous, but commemorative of the Deity and the leading doctrines of Islamism. The object, in the first instance, was, just as in Christian art, to make it the vehicle of religious sentiment: but afterwards came a reverse somewhat analogous to what is presented by later Christian art, and religious decoration was used solely to display the ingenuity of the architect, and please the artistic taste of the worshipper, often with very little reference to didactic objects. Letters were put together with the symmetrical ingenuity of a Chinese puzzle, for some geometrical design had to be aimed at in the disposition, no matter how difficult it might be to decipher the enigma; and it is amusing sometimes to see the most learned orientalist attempting to spell out the sentence in which the architect thought only of the symmetrical disposition of his lines and pot-hooks, never troubling himself about the likelihood of the words being read. In short they ceased to be sentences of the Koran, and were mere arabesques, with anagrammatic apothegms for their materials.

The Roumelyeh, or large public square of Cairo, so often represented in prints, having the mosque of Sultan Hassan on one side, and the castle on the other, is, like the Durwe-sheey of Damascus, crowded with a motley population. Seeing a number of people going out of and into a dark covered court, with a tank, I entered and saw the Mughtas-el-Sultany, or washing place of the bodies of criminals, which is close to the Giâma-el-Moumeneen, so called because the imam prays over the dead with these words, "Nawaito assala ala min hadar amuat el moumeneen:" "I hold up my hands and pray for the defunct believer." Opposite the mosque of Nezm-Eddin is that of Sultan Barkouk, remarkable for having the largest Korans in Cairo, and, as some of the ulema maintain, the largest extant anywhere. Each page is a large calf-skin, dressed with the greatest care and cut square. Both parchment and character are beautiful, and the illumination, mostly in blue and gold, surpasses anything I have seen in arabesque. Being too large to be moved, the boards, desk, and stand form one piece of furniture. In another mosque near the citadel I found other colossal Korans. The mosque of the Emir Akhor, or master of the horse, is small, but none in Cairo is more beautiful in proportions. The relations of minaret, dome, and elevation to each other are all perfect. I found it internally mouldering and tumbling to pieces, and one of those enormous copies of the Koran on vellum, beautifully illuminated was covered with half an inch of dust and dirt, thus showing that I had been the first person who had opened it for several years.

The mosque of Moeyed is altogether the handsomest

in Cairo, taken in connection with the gate of Zueileh. Unlike the mosque of Sultan-el-Ghoury, the grand entrance of Moeyed is lofty and noble in the extreme: the interior is surrounded by an elegant arcade with horse-shoe arches, and the pillars are all antique, some in porphyry and some in white marble. The Mobakharah is the most magnificent of those taken from Sultan Hassan. The walls in the Moharrem are covered with porphyry and old Damascus porcelain, and a large separate pulpit stands for the reading of the chapter of the Seven Sleepers from the Koran. Several lofty sycamores have been planted around the mayda, or fountain for ablution, which adds much to the noble effect. The masonry of the whole mosque is painted in alternate courses of white and red. The interior of Moeyed may not have the awe-striking lines of the Ewaween of Sultan Hassan; but the two minarets towering loftily over Bab-Zueileh, the extent of the mosque, its excellent distribution, and the picturesque effect of the colour, render it altogether the most pleasing edifice in Cairo.

Although the bazaar of the Ghoury is the most magnificent in Cairo, the mosque itself is not conspicuously separated from it. The tank of water is outside the mosque, and in an out-of-the-way corner, as if it were not intended for the use of the mosque at all. The visitor ascends a staircase where a wooden barrier of about a foot high marks the place where shoes must be taken off. He then steps over the barrier upon a richly coloured mosaic pavement in which the dark red of porphyry is conspicuous; and, going through a dark angular passage, like the entrance to a bath, enters the mosque of El Ghoury (whose reign we have described). The interior is small and dark, but of extreme elegance, the windows being glazed with a profusion of curious symmetrical arabesques. This mosque was not finished in the lifetime of the Sultan. The minaret is exceedingly beautiful, being encased with purple tiles, so as to form one of the most picturesque objects in the city. Here also is the celebrated reliquary of the Prophet Mohammed, consisting of his robe, his box of kohl, or blue dye, a copy of the Koran, and various other articles, as described in the following Arabic verses, beginning:—

> "Mohalaf ataka subhatan wu mishafon,
> Suvakon kissan ibrik wu nalon," etc.;

which may be translated thus:—

> "The relics of the Prophet are beads and a Koran,
> A box of black ointment, and a carpet well worn;
> A stick, a tooth-cleaner, a robe and a handmill;
> Ewer, sandals, and cloak, and a mule called Dil-dil;
> Greaves, mats, and a camel, whose name was Adbad,—
> When with reverence approached, bring good health out of bad."

Considering the extraordinary rapidity with which Islamism spread, even in the lives of those who had seen Mohammed in their youth, and the immediate grasp which the Koran took of the human mind, from its comparatively lofty morality, and the incomparable eloquence of its style, these relics are unquestionably less apocryphal than those of the first Christians. Three centuries had elapsed between the reign of Tiberius and the public recognition of Christianity throughout the Roman Empire: during that time much concealment had been practised, and the public recognition of Christianity was followed, in the middle ages, by centuries of enthusiastic credulity as to the relics of the martyrs; so that if it were really of any interest to possess the bones of a disciple or apostle, the means of identification were almost null. The Koran was written, not only in a far more impressive and striking style than any of the four gospels, but it appeared at a time when the Empire of the West was extinct, and when that of the East wanted the compact military power which characterized the Romans in the time of Tiberius, and long afterwards, in a state of intimate connection with the Olympic mythology. We may therefore assume, from the early and rapid conquest of Islamism, and the absence of a Moslem period of persecution, that there is much greater probability of these being genuine relics of Mohammed, than those of the Roman Church being authentic remains of the first Christian martyrs.

Adjoining the mosque of Moeyed is the Gulshany, or convent of dervishes,—mostly Turks, in the middle of which rises the famous porcelain mosque and tomb, so as to make it one of the most curious monuments of Cairo, but quite concealed from view. Although in the Turkish style of architecture, the elevation is entirely composed of this fine material, the tiles having mostly all been manufactured at Damascus. This pottery was abandoned in the latter part of the last century, and long since nearly everywhere else, which is the more striking when one reflects that the great Italian school of pottery is of Moslem origin, and that the original Majolica came from the then Moslem Majorica and Sicily.

The Tekiet-el-Agem is a convent of dervishes, in which are Turks and Persians: it is an off-shoot of the celebrated institution of Mollah Hunkiar, in Konieh. Such establishments are not very numerous in Egypt and Syria; and the Arabs look upon most Persian and Turkish dervishes as adventurers. In addition to this, although the Turks have established their rule in Egypt, Syria, and the Hedjas, as well as in other Arab countries, yet the real old Egyptian or Syrian alim looks on all Turks having pretensions to religion and learning as still retaining something of the neophite or semi-barbarian: they scarcely except the learned cadis that come from

Constantinople, and who are so superior to themselves in external breeding. They can never forget that Islam is essentially of Arab origin, and that the Caliphates of Damascus, Bagdad, and Cairo were in Arab dynasties. Theirs is something of the feeling with which an Athenian regarded a Roman, even when the eagles were the sign of dominion from the Pillars of Hercules to the frontiers of Persia, and from the Nile to the Frith of Forth. Arabic literature may be said to be dead, and to have been so for three centuries; but the contrast between the voluminous abundance of Arab literature and the scantiness of the Turkish, is a fact which never disappears from the Arab mind. The Arabs are also much less familiar with the charming poets of Persia, than the Turks are. If a Turk has a theological turn, it is to the Arabic doctors that he devotes his attention; but the Turkish dilettante, who wishes to kill time with a little literature, has a constant resource in the twin poets of Persia.

The so-called orthodox Islamism of the Sunnite Turk is acknowledged by the Arab, but he is always looked upon as a stranger, although Egypt has had none but Turks, or Turkish speaking Circassians, as rulers for a period of six centuries.

The Arab is also struck with the superior magnificence and variety of design of Arabic over Turkish architecture; and it must be confessed, that, in the eye of the artist, picturesqueness of situation apart, the architecture of Constantinople can bear no comparison with that of Cairo. Turkish mosques are usually picturesque objects; and the Byzantine dome and the tapering minarets are generally associated with well grown trees which partially conceal the body of the edifice out of which they arise. But there is a great monotony in the constant repetition of the same lines, even although the scale be large. It is not so with Arab architecture, which has far greater variety, both of form and colour, and the instances of which need not be adduced to the reader.

Zawiet-el-Hinood is the oratory of the Moslem Hindus, many of whom are to be found selling cutlery and other articles: they are nearly all pedlars, who have made the pilgrimage to Mecca. I visited the mosque of Indian dervishes, which was small and neat. The principal ornament was a plan of a large mosque hanging from the wall; the sections, elevations, and ornaments bearing a rude resemblance to the working plans of European architects.

On the high line of the bazaars is the mosque of Negm-Eddin-Salih, a curious ruin, the columns evidently belonging to the antique. The Moezzin, making great difficulty, took me into the tomb of Sultan Salih, and, to my surprise, shewed me seven conical vases around the tomb, said to have been sent as a present from a king of the Franks, but filled with powder that they might explode. There were eight of them, one having exploded. But as gunpowder was not invented and in use in the time of this monarch, it is evidently a fable. The saddle of this Sultan is still hung up at his tomb, and it may be well imagined that after five hundred years it looks very shabby; but the tomb itself is a most curious specimen of woodwork. Near here is also the ancient mosque of El Akmar, which carries us back to early Cairo: it was built by the Vizier Mamoun, according to the orders of Ahkam Allah, in 519, and was repaired by Bibars. The well belonged to a Christian convent before Islamism, and Gouhar-el-Caid inclosed it in the original palace of Moezz, on the foundation of Cairo, and its name Bir-el-Taam, or "well of repasts," is a proof that the water was used for the culinary purposes of the palace, or for drinking water at the Caliph's repasts.

It were an endless task to go in detail through the rest of the hundred mosques of Cairo ; for almost every one has its marvellous apocryphical legend—its real history associated with the phases of political history, or some quaint illustration of extinct Arab decorative schools of art. A thick volume might be made out of the undescribed curiosities of Cairo. At the mosque Giama Symadian, built by a native of Tlemecen in Algiers, is shown a running spring which the people of Egypt believe to find its way into the sea subterraneously at Suez; but I dare say it finds its way into the Nile, somewhere between Boulak and Shoubrah. The mosque of Sheikh Hamoudeh, a small one in the upper part of Cairo, was frequented by women desirous of having the afreets driven out; and it was also said that assignations were occasionally made here. The mosque of the Daoudeey is celebrated for the high steps by which it is entered, and which are cemented with lead, from whence it is called Giama-el-M'allak, "the cemented mosque:" it was named after a Sultan Daoud, and the quarter around it was formerly that of the prostitutes, but they were transported by Mohammed Ali to Upper Egypt, and now the quarter is inhabited by a laborious population. Its former history gave rise to an untranslatable distich on the fixedness of the mosque, and the looseness of the female population.

There are mosques which recommend themselves by their artistic beauty in strange out of the way streets. For instance, the mosque of Siganem, between that of Kaisoun and the Derb-el-Ahmar, has a mosaic pavement of plain black and white marble, much admired on account of the excellence of the joining, and the peculiarity of the arabesque pattern, in which great elegance is united with the most curious ingenuity. The mosque of Kaisoun itself is most picturesque in summer, when the sun shines fiercely without; while, within the court-yard, umbrageous foliage spreading over the tank of ablution produces an agreeable coolness, and the chequered rays of an Egyptian sun turn the wall of the mosque, with its partial dilapidation, into a scene which De Hooge would have prized as a subject.

A real and unmistakable gem is also in this part of Cairo; for there is in all Egypt and Syria no more beautiful specimen of inlaid architectural elevation than the fountain of Caid Bey, one of the later Mameluke Sultans. Although marked by the ravages of time, and dimmed in many parts, the effect upon the eye is somewhat like that of a colossal table of Florentine Pietra Commessa turned over from the horizontal to the perpendicular. Such marquetrie in marble, precious stones, and lapis lazuli, is to be seen in no other part of Cairo. Faded though this ornament be for want of cleaning, which would cost but little, one could detect the superior richness and beauty of the style of the Mameluke Sultans over that of the moderns; for certainly no workman could be found in Cairo, at this day, capable of producing this ornament of the so-called "ropemaker's-road."

The great renovator of the mosques and fountains of Cairo, was Abderrahman Kiahya, who lived in the middle of the eighteenth century. He was a very wealthy man, and envious people circulated reports that he had discovered the philosopher's stone, had acquired his gold by alchemy, and that his piety was a sham. But when was good done without detraction? The more probable assumption is that he may have found a treasure: certain it is that his means, large as they were, and the munificence with which he acted, seemed out of proportion to each other. In the oriental style of exaggeration, it was said after his death, "that he had built as many mosques as there were days in the year." This munificent man, in addition to the many mosques which he built and repaired, constructed in Cairo twenty troughs of stone for watering asses and camels, with water-wheels attached to them, so that kindness to animals was included in the schemes of his beneficence. These erections have now mostly fallen into ruin.

The master of Abderrahman Kiahya was Osman Kiahya; —and in the mosque of Osman Kiahya, there are said to be two pillars of glass, but I did not see them. Sheikh Ahmed, the last of the great astrologers and astronomers of Egypt, was connected with this mosque and lived at it. There were still, in Mohammed Ali's time, three or four mikaty, or astronomical time calculators, attached to the great mosques, who preserved the Arabic traditions and instruments, being entire strangers to the astronomical science of Europe. They made their observations nightly in the clear atmosphere of Cairo, keeping the time of the town, so that the hour of prayer might be accurately proclaimed by the muezzins, and they were sadly puzzled by the orthodox tradition of the sun moving round the earth, and the Copernican theory which threatened to subvert the old system. One of my acquaintances had a passion for astronomy, and read all the Arabic mediæval authors on this science, and was quite familiar with all the stellar phenomena that immediately meet the naked eye and with the copious Arabic nomenclature of both constellations and individual bodies; but he was firm in his belief of the falseness of the Copernican theory. I confess, that to me a learned native Egyptian is always more interesting than those natives of the East who are half-educated Franks, for the one has the national stamp, while the other is a mongrel. Thus wars the logic of congruity with abstract reason!

The Sibeel of Abderrahman Kiahya is one of the most characteristic specimens of the semi-scholastic fountains of Cairo. A vast grated window stands at the corner of the street, bordered with the most florid tracery, presenting in miniature something like a Saracenic translation of such ornaments as those that adorn the chapel of Henry VIII.; and beneath it are a couple of brass spouts, supplying water, while on the first floor above are heard noises such as those that proceed from a school or charity endowment—giving food to the mind, and water to the body. This monument is neither Greek, Roman, Moorish, nor Turkish, but its general effect is strikingly picturesque. Upstairs sat from twenty to thirty children on mats, all bowing in turn, and reading aloud extracts from the Koran from wooden boards. A child, called up to give a specimen, kissed the master's hand, and then sitting down, cross-legged and swinging its head, began to read. The system is the same as Jacotot's, although not taken from him. They learn to read without knowing the meaning of the words, the meaning being left to break slowly upon the pupil's mind afterwards. The specimens of writing are beautiful; for the Arab character has more of the lines of beauty than the Roman, but it is inconvenient in practice from its being so involved. The perusal of oriental writing, except it be very clear, is almost as much spelling as reading, and therefore must yield the palm to the perspicuous system of Europe where all the vowels are presented on the same level as the consonants.

INDEX.

B.

J.

K.

L.

M.

N.

O.

P.

THE END.

CPSIA information can be obtained
at www.ICGtesting.com
Printed in the USA
LVHW100519120522
718524LV00004B/149

9 783375 000622